CONTENTS

For Heather

ACKNOWLEDGEMENTS

Rags of Time would not exist in its current form without the help of a number of people.

I thank my family for their continued forbearance and encouragement throughout the book's lengthy gestation. The achievement of its publication is theirs, as much as mine.

Although several characters in *Rags of Time*, such as Henry Jermyn and Nicholas Culpeper, are not fictional, the parts they play within this story are. The main protagonists, Tom Tallant, Elizabeth Seymour and Edmund Dalloway, were all born in my imagination, like their adventures. Any similarity to reality is coincidental and entirely unintended.

Mike Ward
Chorley
June 2019
.

PROLOGUE

21st October 1639
Kensington, London

As he strode across the lower meadow of his country home, Sir Joseph Venell considered his sin, and smiled.

He felt a surge of shameful joy as the late autumn sun bathed the village of Kensington, burnishing the leaves that rained from the tall beech trees surrounding the field. A warm breeze stirred the branches, releasing a further golden shower.

He should not exult in making money, he knew it. Except it would be so much money! And it would fall at his feet like these leaves, each year without fail. A God-fearing man, Sir Joseph rebuked himself, but heard his voice laugh out loud as he calculated his future wealth.

He worked his way down the slope. The grass was lush for the time of year and his stockman had kept the sheep in the upper field. They would be moved to the meadow next week to gorge themselves on the fresh pasture.

Sir Joseph hummed a Gabrieli motet, breaking the tempo to match his bouncing steps as he let the slope take him down the hill. It had been his father's favourite piece of music. What would Papa think if he could see his son now, about to secure his place among London's leading merchants, and through the King's favour no less. Excitement coursed through Sir Joseph. Had life ever been better? The sun was shining, the air was clear and he was off to see his beloved bees. They had remained active during the extended summer but now it was time to make a final inspection of the hives before the cold weather arrived.

The sun cast lengthening shadows, picking out tiny black moths which flew from the grass, disturbed by his steps. This indeed was a heaven on earth, Sir Joseph mused. Even the infernal pigeons had stopped their incessant call: koor, koor, koorrrrr... koor, koor, koorrrrr... koor, koor! Gone! Strange—but most welcome.

The first blow to Sir Joseph's head threw him forward violently. He staggered but remained upright. It came from behind and he had no time to recover before he was hit again, this time from the side.

In shock, he wheeled around to confront his attacker. Behind him, the pasture stretched up to the gate he had entered minutes ago. He could see the path he had made through the grass. There was no one in sight.

He turned quickly back the way he had been heading, breathing hard. Ahead lay his route to the hives. He looked right, up the slope to the tree line. No one there either. As he turned to the left to check the bottom of the field, he was pitched forward by another jarring blow to the back of his head, this time accompanied by a piercing pain in his scalp.

1

Sir Joseph fell to his knees, hands out in front. The grass was cool between his fingers as he stared at the ground, his ears full of his ragged breathing and the beating of his heart. O Sweet Jesu. He is quick, this villain. I cannot see him! I must get help, somehow.

'I have no money on my person,' he shouted into the ground, hearing the rising panic in his voice. 'But I am not an unwealthy man. Let me live and I will be generous.'

As he spoke, a rivulet of blood dripped from his head onto his hand. The smell of the warm blood mingled with the scent of crushed grass beneath his knees.

Sir Joseph's panic changed to rising anger. Who was this bastard toerag to attack him on his own land?

'Yes, I will be generous… with the rope,' he muttered to himself, as he staggered to his feet. He carefully quartered the field, north, south, east and west. It was empty.

His anger was quickly doused by the chill of fear. Where was his attacker? He did not understand what was happening but he must get out of this damned meadow immediately. The quickest way was downhill. He ran towards the hives, and the shelter of the surrounding woods.

Four steps later, Sir Joseph was sprawling on the ground once more, hit by another sickening blow to his right temple. He stumbled to his feet and started running again, now gripped by mortal fear. In a moment, he had realised his fate. This was not a robbery. It was a lesson in humility. He had dared to believe he had created a heaven on earth and now was being taught by the Almighty that such arrogance required swift correction. He had been handed to the demons for punishment.

Pain seared his brain as he was hit again. Sir Joseph shouted to the skies, waving his arms in the air, as his steps became more uncertain. He stumbled up the slope, no longer sure of his direction.

'Oh God, forgive me. I am a mortal sinner.' Another crash as his words went unheeded. 'I dared to be filled with selfish pride. Oh Jesu, forgive me.'

Blood was running freely down his face, filling his eyes and mouth. Blinded, he staggered on, turning this way and that across the meadow, screaming.

'Forgive my greed. I will give my money to the poor. I will do anything if you will only spare ….'

Sir Joseph's pleas were silenced by another lacerating blow. Again he was pitched forward, but this time lay still on the ground. His eyes stared across the empty field as stalks of grass blew against his face. The sun was now lower in the sky and the air had turned cooler. Blood slowly spread across the ground under Sir Joseph's head. The buzz of gathering flies filled the air.

2

The breeze shifted direction and caught the tallest trees at the top of the pasture. More leaves fell and danced through the amber light before landing gently on Sir Joseph's prostrate body.

The sheep called to each other in the top meadow. Evening was approaching.

And from the trees a familiar sound returned: Koor, koor, koorrrrr... koor, koor, koorrrrr—koor, koor.

Chapter 1

The next day
A warehouse on the north bank of the Thames, east of London Bridge

From the top floor of his family's warehouse, Thomas Tallant looked across the Thames. Peering through the open loading bay, he surveyed a forest of masts, so many that he could no longer see the south side of the river.

Leaning forward, a warm breeze touched his face. Morning sunlight swept the river, bathing the houses lined along London Bridge to his right in its pale glow. It would be another fine day for late October. Dear God, it was wonderful to be home.

Tom cautiously looked down at the quay. His dizziness on dry land after months at sea was finally receding. It was three days since he'd docked in London, his ship laden with pepper and mace. Quite long enough to be stumbling like a drunk.

Tom stepped back from the loading bay and straightened his back. Dark brown hair tumbled onto his broad shoulders framing a handsome sun-tanned face and ready smile. He was clean-shaven, with no attempt to hide the evidence of childhood smallpox on his face. He had been lucky. The blemishes were slight and he had been pleased to discover that women found his rugged complexion attractive.

Angry voices rose above the rumble of cartwheels on the stone quay below. Looking along the wharf, Tom saw an official from the nearby Customs House arguing with two men who were both pointing at the dock and shouting. Directly ahead, ships were at anchor row after row. The Pool of London was full.

He turned and faced the tall, distinguished man who had been viewing the river over Tom's shoulder. 'It is even worse today, Father,' Tom sighed.

'Aye, Tom. A fleet of merchantmen has been waiting in the estuary to come upriver. The wind's finally changed so the wharf will be packed tight this morning, everyone fighting for a berth.'

Sir Ralph Tallant moved from the loading door and eased his six-foot frame into a chair. Tom studied his father and saw he'd aged in the two years Tom had been away. Flecks of grey hair, a thicker waistline and the skin around his face a little looser. But those sapphire eyes still flashed like the sea in a summer storm.

'You will find much has changed while you've been in India, Tom. Trade has grown apace and the port is full to bursting. Word is out there's money in London, so half the population of England has moved in. The

4

city has grown, but not quickly enough. There's nowhere for people to live and conditions for many are unspeakable.'

Tom picked up a ledger. 'That's hardly our problem, is it, Father? Trade is good, so the Tallant family benefits. People have to take their chances if they come to London.'

Sir Ralph sighed. 'It's not that simple. After a few weeks back, maybe you'll see that all is not well in this city, and that's not good news for the Tallants or anyone else.' Sir Ralph shifted in his seat and grimaced. 'Lord, the weather is about to change. My bones know it.'

Tom ignored his father. 'We need to sell this pepper. The warehouse is almost full.'

Sir Ralph looked around the family pepper store at the sacks piled neatly from floor to ceiling. 'The price isn't right. A large shipment was placed on the market at the Exchange earlier this week. It's pushed the value down again. We have to be patient.'

'But why are we still importing pepper if we can't sell it? We should stick to mace and cinnamon.'

'Tom. It's harder these days to get a good price for pepper because of over-supply but it still sells in volumes that far exceed any other spice. We make less per sack, but we sell a lot more sacks... if we are patient.'

'But the real money is to be made in the new spices like cinnamon. If we...'

'When will you understand there isn't always a quick profit to be had? You can't simply act on impulse, Tom. We need safe bets as well as more risky options.'

Sir Ralph stood and held his son's gaze.

Tom felt his face colour. 'I wondered how long it would be before I heard that speech again. Home again after two years away, but nothing has changed, has it?'

'Tom. Have a care. You cannot expect all that happened before you left to be simply forgotten. Show willing to learn from it, instead of shouting at me at the first opportunity.'

There was a call from below. Visitors had arrived.

'I must be going anyway,' Sir Ralph added testily. 'I have an appointment at the Customs House. No, don't show me out. See to your guests.'

With practised ease, Sir Ralph ducked his head under the doorway to the main stairway and was gone.

Tom slammed the palm of his hand onto the ledger. Three days back and he was arguing again with his father. He sighed. That much, he knew, was normal; but there was something about Sir Ralph's expression. He looked more worried than angry.

Another shout from below. Tom clattered down the wooden steps to the ground floor, crossed the back office and entered the parlour.

'Edmund! I wondered when you would soil your elegant shoes on the waterfront and visit my humble abode.'

Edmund Dalloway spun away from his conversation with a dark-haired man and walked quickly towards Thomas.

'My dear Thomas. It's so good to see you safely home,' he said, grasping Tom's shoulders and embracing him warmly. Edmund held Tom at arm's length and surveyed him closely.

'My goodness, your face is weather beaten, and are those muscles under your doublet? Turn over your hands. Look! Calloused! Tom, what have you been up to—sailing the seven seas single-handed?'

'We can't all be gentleman merchants, Edmund,' Tom laughed. 'Some of us take our turn hauling in a rope.'

It was a standing joke between them. Both from merchant families, they had grown up and been schooled together. The Dalloways were one of the founding Merchant Adventurer dynasties, making their fortune from the lucrative wool trade. Tom's father had instead diversified into spices early in his career after meeting and marrying Beatrix Simons in Amsterdam and learning about the East Indies trade from her brother Jonas. Tom now oversaw and lived in the Tallant spice warehouse when not at sea, a hectic life that bemused Edmund—'Far too much like hard work, dear boy, when the wool market is so established. And all that travel!'—but Edmund was Tom's oldest friend and he had missed his easy smile and companionship during his time away.

Edmund's pale golden hair was fashionably long and now matched by a blonde beard and moustache in the style of the King. It made him look older but his hazel eyes still held the promise of mischief. It was good to see him again.

Edmund pulled away from Tom and turned towards the tall stranger.

'Tom, please allow me to introduce Mr Robert Petty. Mr Petty works as an investigating agent for the Merchant Adventurers.'

Tom extended his hand and Petty shook it firmly, inclining his head towards him. 'I am your servant, sir. Mr Dalloway has told me much about you.'

'Tom, I am sorry to trouble you when we have not spoken for so long but Mr Petty is on urgent business and I have suggested you might be able to help him. You and I will dine together later this week and you can tell me all about India. But at this moment Mr Petty needs your advice on a matter of the highest importance'—Edmund paused and lowered his voice—'and delicacy to the Adventurers. Is there somewhere private we can talk?'

Tom ushered Edmund and Petty to three chairs around the parlour hearth, where a fire had been lit. Thick grey smoke, streaked with yellow, billowed from the sea coal stacked in the grate and disappeared up the chimney while the base of the fire crackled and glowed.

'We can speak in private here,' said Tom. 'Neither my manservant nor my housekeeper are latch-listeners and, to be honest, gentlemen, if you want my undivided attention, you must allow me a little heat.' He turned his palms towards the smoking fire. 'I am accustomed to a warmer climate.'

They sat down. Tom offered refreshment but both men declined. Robert Petty twisted in his seat and put a hand in his pocket. He spoke quietly.

'Mr Tallant, can you identify these?'

Petty removed a piece of folded cloth and opened it, revealing two feathers which he offered to Tom, who carefully picked them up. Petty regarded Tom intently. His eyes were the deepest brown Tom had ever seen in an Englishman.

Tom held the feathers to the weak light from the parlour window. One was over four inches long. It was grey with regular paler markings down its length. The other was similar, but a little shorter.

'If I am not mistaken they are wing feathers from an adult peregrine falcon,' he told Petty, handing them back. 'But anyone who knows about hawking could have told you that. Why ask me?'

Petty folded the feathers carefully back into the cloth, which he returned to his pocket. 'Mr Tallant. Do you know a merchant called Sir Joseph Venell?'

Still the unwavering eyes, the colour of hard, ancient oak. Tom began to feel a little uncomfortable.

'Most people in the city know of Sir Joseph. He and Sir Hugh Swofford own one of the largest wool merchants in London. I've met him occasionally at the Royal Exchange.'

'Did you know Sir Joseph was killed yesterday?'

Tom wasn't sure what surprised him most. The news of Sir Joseph's death or the simultaneous realisation that Robert Petty was searching his face for any reaction. The sea coal was now well alight and he could feel its heat. With a start, Tom realised he was flushing under Petty's gaze.

An image of Sir Joseph came to him. He and Swofford were unusual partners. Together they were highly successful but they could not have been less alike. Swofford loved his food and drink and enjoyed the trappings of a leading city merchant. In contrast, Venell was an ascetic. Lean in stature, he was more reserved than Swofford and played no part in London's merchant society. He lived alone outside the city in Kensington where, if Tom remembered correctly, he devoted most of his time to a large collection of productive bees. However, Venell and Swofford did share one passion. They loved making money. Lots of it. And they were very good at it.

Tom knew conditions had toughened in the wool and cloth market with increased competition from the continent but it was the smaller merchants who were suffering. Families like the Venells, Swoffords and the

Dalloways had managed to maintain their market share and showed little sign of being squeezed. Indeed, they were prospering if Edmund's new home on London Bridge was anything to judge by. Tom's father had pointed it out to him this morning. It must have cost his friend a small fortune.

'I told Mr Petty you were unlikely to know about Sir Joseph's death, Tom, as I think you were out yesterday when his body was discovered?'

'Yes, I was,' Tom nodded. 'We had finally emptied the spice from the holds. It was my first free time, so I took a wherry along the river to see what had changed on the waterfront in my absence.'

Edmund's expression softened.

'Tom, I am sorry about this. Sir Joseph has died in unpleasant, but also mysterious, circumstances. As you can imagine, this has greatly shocked the other Merchant Adventurers. Mr Petty was instructed to investigate immediately and visited Kensington at first light today to view Sir Joseph's body and survey the scene. As a fellow member of the Adventurers, I was asked to accompany Mr Petty as I am familiar with where Sir Joseph lived. Did you know he kept bees? He gave my father some jars of honey—not to eat, but to treat that dreadful sore on his leg. I happened to mention Father's condition to Sir Joseph one day at the Exchange and he insisted I visit and collect some honey. He said it was a guaranteed cure if applied liberally and regularly in a poultice. Frankly I didn't believe it, but Father was desperate so I collected the honey from Sir Joseph's house about a week later and, do you know, it worked perfectly. Absolutely extraordinary. Father was so grateful. So to see him yesterday…'

Edmund's voice faltered as his face clouded with the memory of Sir Joseph's dead body.

Petty looked at Tom and continued. 'Mr Dalloway kindly accompanied me to Sir Joseph's estate and I found these feathers where his body was discovered. I think they could be material to the cause of death. When you learn more of the circumstances, Mr Tallant, you will know why this matter must be investigated with as little public attention as possible. The Merchant Adventurers wish to establish the facts of Sir Joseph's death, but it will not be in anyone's interest if this knowledge becomes widely known and taken up as title-tattle on the streets and in the penny pamphlets.'

'Tom, we must keep this within the merchant family,' Edmund added, gripping his arm. 'When Mr Petty mentioned the feathers and the need to seek someone with expertise, I thought immediately of you. Someone who understands hawking but whose discretion can be relied upon.'

'But if Sir Joseph has been killed, and if something is amiss', Tom said, 'the magistrate will have to be informed.'

'And he will be,' Petty nodded, 'once we have established the facts—with your help, I hope, Mr Tallant.'

Tom puffed out his cheeks. 'Well I'm not sure what I can do. Yes, I did learn a little about training and hunting with hawks from my uncle Jonas but that was a number of years ago. I do not run any birds. They need regular handling and flying and I am away too often on merchant business.'

Petty nodded. 'I realise that, Mr Tallant, but even basic information may help at this stage. I have little else to go on.'

Tom looked at Edmund, who had a pleading expression like a hungry puppy. He had seen that look before and felt a weary resignation. He didn't have the time to spare as there was a great deal of work still to do from the voyage, booking in the cargo and repairing the ship. But Tom did not take to this Mr Petty, and he did not want to make his friend look foolish to the investigator.

'Edmund. What do you want me to do?'

It was Petty who answered. 'Mr Tallant, I need you to come with me to Kensington at the earliest opportunity to see Sir Joseph's body and the scene of his death. Would this afternoon be convenient?'

Tom was annoyed by Petty's presumption. His offer of help had been to Edmund, as a personal favour. He was being put under pressure by this agent and he did not like it. However, Sir Joseph's body could not be left without burial for long, and he reluctantly nodded his assent. Better to deal with the matter quickly and then return to his business. It wouldn't help to be uncooperative.

Petty and Edmund stood, preparing to leave, but Tom held his old friend back. 'Edmund could I have a word?'

'Mr Tallant, thank you for your assistance and I will see you this afternoon.' Robert Petty bowed slightly and strode from the room.

Edmund looked apologetic. 'Tom, I am sorry to bother you with this but it will only take an hour or so.'

'Will it, Edmund? We'll see, but I need to ask about another matter.'

Tom paused. There was silence. He did not want to pose the question on his mind, for fear of the possible answer.

'Alice Rushworth?' Edmund suggested.

'Yes. Alice. Was she... is she?'

'Poor Alice was struck down by the plague less than two months after you sailed for India. She was dead within a week. So we'll never know if she was... in the condition she claimed just before your departure.'

Sweet Alice. A young beauty who welcomed Tom to her bed in the months before his departure for India. Two days before he sailed they had a furious row. She told Tom she thought she was with child. Tom accused her of making it up to persuade him to stay. His last memory of Alice was her tear-stained face, empty and desolate, as he rode from her house.

In the three days since he'd docked in London, he'd expected Alice to walk into the warehouse at any moment. And if she did, would she be alone?

Tom listened to the port outside. He could smell the endeavour and opportunity. Now Alice would never come. And he realised, God forgive him, that this made him glad.

Chapter 2

The afternoon of 22nd October 1639
Kensington

Cold air hit Tom in the face as he stepped onto the cellar steps. Jesu be praised. The stink will be less.

Robert Petty stood in front of him, raising his lantern to reveal a chamber extending deep under Sir Joseph Venell's house. As his eyes adjusted to the gloom, Tom saw a faint glow ahead from a small room to his left. Dust and damp filled his lungs as he edged carefully down the steps to the cellar floor. A grey-haired servant stepped past him with another lantern. Tom caught his unshaven, haggard expression in the lamplight. Little sleep in the Venell household last night. Too much fear of what the future held.

'The previous owner stored his wine and liquor in this cellar,' the servant's broken voice echoed through the dark chamber. 'Master Joseph did not drink, so we have never used it… until now. When Mr Petty here said we could not bury the master yet, I knew we had better get him out of the heat, being so warm for October. We had the devil's own job getting a table down the stairs, but we wanted the master laid out proper-like but private, for his last day in his home. Not that this place brought him much joy.'

The servant led the way towards a low room lit by four candles in brass stands positioned at each corner of a long rectangular table. Lying on his back, on the tabletop, was Sir Joseph Venell, still fully clothed, his face and head covered by a muslin cloth. The cool cellar delayed decay but also kept the body away from prying eyes. The Merchant Adventurers would approve of such arrangements.

In the chamber there was barely room to shuffle down either side of the table. Petty went down Venell's left and stopped at the top behind the merchant's covered head, facing Tom and the servant. Tom went to stand by Venell's right shoulder. The servant remained near the entrance by his master's feet, holding back slightly. This was official business, not for him.

Petty told the servant to pass the two candles at Sir Joseph's feet to the top of the table. Their flames flickered as they moved, casting shadows onto the wall and ceiling above. Tom took the proffered candles and placed one by Venell's left shoulder and the other by his right. Petty put his lantern on the table, looked straight at Tom then, without saying a word, removed the muslin cloth.

This time Tom was too distracted to notice Petty's eyes. Sir Joseph's face and hands were not marked. There were grass stains on the knees of

11

his breeches and dried blood on his jerkin. But otherwise the 53-year-old Merchant Adventurer appeared untouched. Except, that is, for the crown of his head. Tom bent down to take a closer look and, as he neared Sir Joseph's face, was finally confronted by the unmistakable smell of death.

Sir Joseph had fine hair, cut short for comfort under his formal wig. It was plastered to his scalp, matted with congealed and crusted blood. The scalp itself was ruptured in six or seven places with short, livid, dark red wounds. It looked like he had been beaten with a jousting mace.

Tom fought the nausea rising inside and took a step back, stumbling against the wall. He shut his eyes and gripped the edge of the table as he struggled to maintain his equilibrium.

'Not pretty, is it?' Petty said. 'But that's not what killed him. Look at his right temple.'

Reluctantly Tom opened his eyes and lowered himself onto his haunches in the narrow space between the table and the wall, his eyes level with Sir Joseph's defiled head. Petty passed the lantern to Tom who held it close to Sir Joseph's face.

'Turn his head away from you,' said Petty.

Tom was used to handling the dead, having buried too many shipmates at sea, but was shocked by the dead merchant's wounds. His single desire now was to escape the small dark chamber in this cold and lonely house as soon as possible. Holding the lantern in his left hand above the victim, Tom used his right to ease Sir Joseph's head to the left and then pushed it more firmly. He bent over again.

'There's a dark purple bruise covering his right temple and part of the skull above,' Tom commented. 'And I can feel a soft swelling at the centre of the bruise. You think this was the fatal blow?'

Petty nodded. 'Cracked open Sir Joseph's skull, I suspect, and caused bleeding from the brain.'

Tom gently probed the swelling with his fingers. It was not large and there was a small, dry wound at its centre, indicating a steady leakage of blood before death. Poor Sir Joseph had met his end slowly.

Tom scanned the rest of the body. There was something odd about Sir Joseph's clothes—of course, he was in beekeeping attire. Tom surveyed the neat jerkin and breeches. They looked new, the jerkin resplendent with a large bee embroidered on the left breast, underneath a motto in English: "We profit through industry." Clearly Venell had taken his pastime seriously.

Tom had seen enough and needed air. He motioned to Petty that they should leave the chamber. Minutes later they were outside, standing in silence, savouring the fresh breeze. Tom studied the stone house in front of him. Despite his wealth, Venell's two-storey home, fronted by simple mullioned windows, was not impressive. A modest stable block stood to

the right but there were no outhouses, towers or turrets. It looked like a local squire's residence, not home to one of the richest men in the city.

Inside, the house had been drab. There was a single chair and table in the main room and another high-backed seat by the cold, empty fireplace. Cheap wall hangings depicted scenes from the Bible but otherwise Tom had not seen any sign of ornament.

'I know what you are thinking,' Petty said. 'What did he spend his money on? By all accounts, precious little. Sir Joseph Venell was one of those singular people who loved to acquire wealth but not to spend it. For him, the possession of money was everything.'

'It is a sad, solitary place,' Tom reflected. 'But you did not bring me to Kensington to view the property.'

'Indeed. I would value your opinion on Sir Joseph's wounds, Mr Tallant. But first, shall we inspect the place where he was discovered as it may shed more light on the cause of his death? It is not far from here.'

Tom welcomed the prospect of a brief walk to dispel the chill damp of the cellar and smell of decay. The weather was changing but, even though cloud was coming in from the west, it was still pleasant for the time of year. Petty led them along Sir Joseph's tree-lined driveway, away from the house. After 200 yards, he stepped off the drive and turned to his right, through a gap in the trees, and walked towards a gate in the low wall that ran alongside the driveway. Through the gateway Tom could see the ground sloped down into pasture land below.

'From here on, Mr Tallant, please can you follow my footsteps closely, and be careful to only tread where I do.'

Tom nodded as Petty opened the gate and stepped through. The two men worked their way down the slope, through a copse, to the edge of a large meadow. Trees lined either side as it descended to a low hedge at the bottom, with a stream beyond the hedge and a smaller field beyond.

The meadow was empty and its grass lush for the time of year. Tom noticed a series of branches, used as stakes in the ground across the field to their right and down the slope from where they were standing.

Petty bent down and looked carefully along the top of the meadow grasses. 'Unfortunately, it is as I suspected,' he murmured to himself.

'What is, Mr Petty?' Tom asked.

Petty looked up. 'Forgive me, Mr Tallant, allow me to explain. When I arrived here at first light today, the dew was heavy on the ground and you could see clearly where the grass had been disturbed and, in a number of places, trodden by feet.'

'So this is where Sir Joseph was found?'

'Yes, yes... over there,' he said, pointing to the largest stake impaled in the field. 'But the dew has lifted and the breeze has been blowing on the grass. The pathway is now much less clearly defined.'

'Which is why you—'

'Yes, I placed the markers this morning to identify the different patterns and destinations of the footprints. As you can see, they appear to be random.'

Tom looked at Petty anew. Clearly he had done this sort of work before.

They worked their way slowly down the meadow, Tom stumbling on rocks hidden in the long grass. They reached the spot where the thickest branch was rammed into the firm soil. The surrounding grass was still flattened.

Petty stopped and pointed. 'This is where Sir Joseph's stockman found his master, lying on his front. He was still alive, just, murmuring something about being a sinner, his punishment and—' Petty paused and fixed Tom with his steady gaze. '—and the wings of demons. The stockman is sure of it.'

Petty's eyes remained fixed on Tom. 'He didn't know what to do for the best, so stayed with his master, attempting to reassure him. Eventually, after Sir Joseph had been still for some time, the man hauled him onto his shoulders and carried him back to the house. You can see his footsteps going up the slope to another gate at the top of the field, there on our left. He had entered the meadow through the same gate and I questioned him carefully about the state of the grass in that area of pasture where he had entered and left. He said there were no footsteps other than his. He was sure no one had been that way.'

Tom examined the spot where Sir Joseph Venell had fallen. A large stone was streaked with dry blood at the lowest point of the flattened grass.

'I think that is what did for him,' Petty explained. 'As you can see, this field is littered with rocks, hidden among the long grass. I suspect Sir Joseph has fallen full length and cracked the side of his head on that one,' pointing to the stone by Tom's feet. 'His head was at that end, where you are standing, with his body sloping up the hill, when he was discovered. Would you stay there for a moment please, Mr Tallant?'

Petty turned and walked back the way they had come. He stopped ten yards away and turned to face Tom. Behind Petty, Tom could see the faint impression of a line of disturbed grass leading up to the gate where they had entered the meadow. In front of Petty lay a confusion of flattened areas, with lines of trodden ground in between.

'It looks to me that Sir Joseph entered the meadow through the top gate where we came in and walked down to this point, where I am standing. If you were to continue the line he was taking it would end over there, on the other side of the field, where Sir Joseph kept his bees.'

Petty was pointing and Tom, looking over his shoulder, could see small boxes in the distance near the tree line, which he took to be hives.

'After reaching here, it is not possible to be certain but there were signs this morning that Sir Joseph then stumbled in a number of different

directions, falling here, here and here.' Petty pointed to the branches impaled in the ground around him. 'Before staggering further down the slope to his final resting place, where you stand.'

Tom noticed for the first time that the tops of two stakes were tied with twine. He pointed at them.

'What do these signify, Mr Petty?'

Petty paused and rubbed the twine between his forefinger and thumb.

'They indicate where I found the falcon feathers,' he replied.

Tom said nothing. It was his turn to hold the agent in his gaze. He could see what Petty was suggesting and the ridiculous idea irritated him. Wings of demons and falcon feathers. He had no more time to waste on this nonsense.

'It's not possible, you know.'

'What is not possible, Mr Tallant?'

'Hunting falcons could not have killed Venell.'

'I know that, Mr Tallant. He was killed by the blow to his head when he fell on the rock.'

'Well, he wouldn't have been attacked by falcons either, for two good reasons.'

Petty looked at him with steady eyes.

'First, I have never heard of hunting falcons attacking a person, certainly not in the sustained manner that would have caused those injuries. They hunt to eat, Mr Petty, and to the best of my knowledge they do not have the taste for human flesh. However, let us assume for one moment that, for some unexplained reason, a peregrine, or more likely a pair—for that is how they often hunt—decided to repeatedly attack a man's head. If that had happened, Mr Petty, you would have found more than a man's body and a few feathers on the field. You would have found the broken remains of two hunting birds.'

Robert Petty walked back to Tom and stood close to him, listening intently.

'Have you ever seen a peregrine falcon execute a hunting stoop, Mr Petty? They climb to a great height and dive on to their intended target at a prodigious speed. Faster than an archer's arrow, I wager. They are particularly partial to wood pigeons, which are not small birds. If you retrieve a falcon's prey, such as a pigeon, you notice the falcon has not attacked the pigeon's head or body. No, it goes for the wing, smashing through the bone near the shoulder. This immediately halts the pigeon's flight and half kills it through fright. The falcon avoids the solid body of a fully grown pigeon because the shock of hitting it, full on, and at that speed, would cause the falcon fatal damage. The weight of a female adult peregrine—for the females are usually larger—can be up to three pounds. Dropping to earth at stooping speed, carrying that weight, a glancing blow will be sufficient. It does not want to meet a solid object, like a pigeon's

body... or a man's head. Also, a man's head is six feet at most from the ground. Falcons look for prey in the air to give them recovery time to arrest their dive after they have taken their quarry.'

Petty turned away and looked around the field. 'So you say they hunt in pairs?'

'Yes, but listen, Petty. As well as being impossible, falcons would have no reason to attack a man in a field. Why should they? Isn't it more likely that Sir Joseph's attacker followed his path carefully down the field, as we did, attacked him from behind, and once the deed was done, left the field the same way he came? As for the falcon feathers, I think if you searched this meadow you would find another dozen. This is good hunting country for peregrines. They'll make bird kills here every day.'

Tom stopped and realised he was breathing hard. He heard his last word echo across the field.

Petty smiled. 'You are right, Mr Tallant. A foolish theory of mine, even though I didn't even have to share it with you. You saw it right away.'

Inside, Tom felt a growing anger. Petty had deliberately let him talk at will. Irritated that his time was being wasted on this wild theory, Tom had shown his annoyance, his voice strident and forceful. Hell and damnation. He had sounded like he wanted to persuade Petty to dismiss the falcon theory. What impression would that give?

His father's admonishment returned to vex him and he boiled with frustration. When would he learn not to jump in with both feet? He had come to Kensington as a favour to Edmund, to offer expert advice. What did it matter to him if Petty was on the wrong track completely? Yet the agent had turned the situation inside out and Tom realised that he now cared—no, more than that—he was concerned, about what the agent thought of him.

What game was Robert Petty playing?

Chapter 3

Early November 1639
The Tallant warehouse

Tom examined the lane from his warehouse up to Thames Street and frowned. Days of rain had turned the track into a bog and the streets would be like this throughout London. After weeks on land, his body was soft and his breeches tight. The Tallant family were dining together for the first time in two years and he had planned a vigorous walk to his parents' home, Bolton Hall, north of Clerkenwell. But not now. He would have to ride.

Andrew Lamkin led Meg from her stall by the warehouse. The horse saw her master and whinnied softly, shaking her pale mane. Tom studied his approaching groom closely.

'Let me look, Andrew.'

He turned the boy's face upwards and inspected his swollen nose and purple bruising under both eyes.

'Those bastard Apprentice Boys. They need taking down a peg or two.'

It was Isaac Ufford, Tom's warehouse manager, coming around the side of the building. He ruffled Andrew's hair.

'Tell Master Thomas what they said to you.'

The boy looked down and squeezed Meg's reins in his hands. Isaac gave Andrew a nudge and haltingly the boy spoke, still staring at the floor.

'They were hanging around the Black Dog, looking for trouble. Next thing, a group started following me, shouting "King or Parliament? King or Parliament?" They caught me at Dob Alley. Pinned me to a wall and kept asking "King or Parliament?"' Andrew turned his battered face to Tom. 'So I gave them the answer I've heard you say, Master Thomas, and one of them gave me this,' he said, gently feeling his broken nose.

'You said "I am loyal to both", and he hit you?'

'Yes. With his head. Jesus it hurt. He said everyone had to choose a side. Even better to support the King than sit in the middle like a Hackney whore, trying to please everyone.'

Isaac and Tom looked at each other.

'Andrew, the Apprentice Boys constantly look for trouble,' Tom said. 'Today it's King or Parliament, next week it will be the price of ale. Any excuse to fight. I think it's time you learned how to look after yourself. You need some instruction. Isaac will arrange it. Now give me Meg and think no more about it.'

Andrew handed over the reins and dipped his head in thanks, before returning to the stable.

Isaac took Tom to one side. He was a tall, stooping man with a curious gait, his right shoulder lower than his left and bent forward, the result of an accident on the wharf ten years ago. The shoulder had been trapped by falling cargo and crushed under the weight. The constant pain Isaac carried with him since that day was etched into the folds of grey skin on his long, lugubrious face.

'Master, do you really think this attack was the usual Apprentice Boy bullying?'

'Of course. Why should it not be?' Tom replied, distractedly.

He was late starting his journey and the Apprentices had a reputation across the city for boisterous, bad behaviour, especially after a session in the ale house.

'Trouble on the streets got a sight worse while you were in India. It's not only the Apprentice lads. People are angry. They don't like the changes the Archbishop is bringing to the churches. Some say it's a Papist plot to bring back the Catholic faith. People speak shamefully about King Charles in public. I blame Queen Henrietta and that interfering mother of hers. Do you know they both go to Catholic mass in the Queen's private chapel? What poison is she dripping into His Majesty's ear?'

Isaac Ufford was a loyal and reliable manager but a terrible gossip. He heard all the rumours and believed too many. Tom leaned closer and lowered his voice.

'Isaac, from time to time all kings are unpopular. The difference between, say, old Henry Tudor and King Charles is that no one dared whisper a word against Henry, in case he chopped off their head. I think we have moved on from that, would you not agree?'

Isaac nodded but looked unconvinced. Tom decided to say no more on the subject. The King clearly had an unshakeable belief in his divine right to rule. His Royal Highness would not be worrying about tittle-tattle on the streets or the views of drunken Apprentice Boys, and neither should Isaac.

Tom took his leave and led Meg carefully through the deep mud to a passageway through the houses on to the south side of Thames Street. Wide enough for a two-horse cart, the short tunnel took cargo from the Tallant warehouse to the streets of London. It was cold and damp and, as he entered, the choking stink of piss made him cough. Meg's hooves clattered on the cobblestones, echoing along the arched ceiling. Gradually, movement and light appeared ahead and then, in a moment, they cleared the ginnel and entered the heart of old London town.

The noise was overwhelming. Traders lined the length of Thames Street selling their wares as far as Tom could see, shouting to be heard above the hammering of coopers in the nearby barrel works. Opposite, a cutler sharpened knives on a whetstone, pausing to spit on each blade before continuing the rasp of Norwegian ragstone on steel. The harsh sound

competed with a tentative violin refrain repeated continuously from a window above, as young hands struggled to master a difficult passage. And, rising above it all, the continuous creaking of dozens of shop signs lining the street, swinging in the breeze.

Tom inhaled the street aroma: roast meat and rotting fish, warm brewer's malt, and the pungent reek of urine from the tannery. The sulphurous tang of soot caught the back of his throat. London had exhausted its supplies of wood fuel while he was away and now relied on sea coal shipped from Newcastle, its dense fumes slowly choking the life out of the city.

He heard a familiar voice above the racket and looked to his right.

'Tom... Tom, it's me, Peter!'

Tom looked more closely and saw his brother emerge on horseback from behind two other riders. Peter's horse edged slowly through a herd of geese hissing and snapping at the mare's feet. Tom turned Meg towards his brother, leant across his saddle and embraced Peter warmly.

'Forgive me brother... the noise, everywhere... I did not hear you clearly.'

The driver of a cart was screaming oaths at a ragged boy and girl who had jumped off to herd the geese without success. The man lunged backwards and punched the boy on the head. The boy reeled and slipped on the muddy cobbles. He staggered to his feet and tried again to gather the geese.

Peter's eyes hardened. 'That boy will learn nothing from such brutality.'

'Except how to keep his distance,' Tom countered. 'I suspect he has felt his father's fist before and was foolish to get so close. Peter, what are you doing here?'

'I had business in the city and decided to drop by to see if we could ride together to Bolton Hall.'

Peter had not long returned from the Americas and Tom was pleased to share time with his elder brother. They had been too much apart in recent years.

They moved westwards through the crowds along Thames Street. A bull bellowed in a side alley and Peter's horse shied violently to the left. He brought it under control and looked with appreciation at Meg, who had not stirred.

'Your horse is steady, Tom, just what you need in London.'

'Aye, Meg is well used to the comings and goings and she knows every hole in the road. There is only one thing that will spook her.'

'What is that?'

'Pigs. For some reason she does not like pigs at all. Gets skittish if they come anywhere near—and there's far too many pigs on the streets of London for my liking.'

Peter laughed and they continued to work their way west, turning right into Fish Street Hill. Here the road was wider and a little less crowded, and Tom was able to ride alongside his brother.

'I have still not become accustomed to how much the city has grown while I was in India, Peter. But can you believe that some people blame me and other merchants for this overcrowding? Never mind that trade is booming, bringing a fortune into the city. Of course that also brings a flood of people, determined to get their share. Good luck to them.'

Peter frowned. 'I know. They think nothing could be worse than starving in the country until they get here and discover there is nowhere to live in the city, no clean water, overflowing human excrement and pestilence everywhere. The only reason we are not swamped by this invading army is because it's easier to die in London than anywhere in England. It keeps the numbers in check, just.'

Tom shrugged and patted Meg's neck. 'If people want to better themselves and take their chances, who are we to stop them?'

'I must remember this when times are hard in America and I long for London,' Peter continued. 'Winter is the worst. Cold you cannot imagine and barely enough food to keep us alive. But we have a roof over our head, fresh water in the river and land as far as you can see.

'You see a future over there?' Tom asked.

'The future, an opportunity for God's children to make a new world, with freedom to worship the Lord and do his bidding without interference.'

Tom's mind turned to America as they rode into Great Eastcheap. He sensed the New World's vast potential for business, but their Indies trade took up all his time and was so profitable. Demand for spice was strong and steady, which was welcome news. As was the disappearance of Mr Robert Petty. Tom had heard no more from the agent since their visit to Kensington. Edmund had been out of town at his family's estates, so Tom had no idea if Petty's investigation was complete and, frankly, he didn't care.

There was a shout and the sound of breaking glass. People were running to the entrance of St Clement's Lane. Tom stopped at the edge of a gathering crowd as three brawny figures emerged from St Clement church carrying a long piece of wood. The crowd erupted into cheers as the men waved the wood in the air before throwing it to the ground. Tom looked to Peter and saw his jaw clenched tight, his face flushed. Minutes later the men emerged again from the church with a second length of timber, to more cheering and whistling. Peter was shouting something but Tom could not make it out. Soon the excitement was over and the crowd dispersed as quickly as it had formed.

What on earth was that about, Tom thought, and turned to his brother to find him twenty yards along the road, heading for Clerkenwell. Quite

right. His mother was preparing her famous game pie. On no account could they be late for that. The road ahead had cleared and Tom set Meg to a brisk trot to catch up.

An hour later Thomas Tallant was sitting with his parents at their dining table, together with Peter and his younger sister Ellen. When had they last been together? Well over two years ago. Now the family was reunited, Tom hoped it would be for some time.

He thought of the two who should be with them—brother Matthias, drowned in an accident at the age of two and sister Mary, lost to the pox at eight months. He said a silent prayer for both.

Tom's mother looked up from her plate and frowned. 'Ralph, Peter… please, no arguments today. Our time together is too precious.'

Peter wasn't listening. 'Father, surely you agree. Archbishop Laud is not a true Protestant. He is an Arminian.'

Peter was leaning towards his father, his face red and both fists on the table, clenched tight.

'What's an Arminian, Peter?' It was Ellen who had spoken, looking carefully at her brother, concern etched on her face.

Peter ignored her question. 'The Archbishop is determined to change the church, and for the worse. He is building rails around the communion table like a fence, to keep the people away and allow only the priests near the altar, even though the people are the church!'

Peter hit the table with a fist, sending his plate and food into the air. Lady Beatrix looked up sharply. Peter lowered his gaze and voice.

'The people will not have it. They are reclaiming their churches and ripping out these altar rails. We saw it happening this morning, didn't we Tom?'

All eyes turned to Tom whose face was buried in his plate. He had only been half listening. He lifted his eyes and looked around the table, bemused.

'Did we not observe the people of St Clement Eastcheap this morning, reclaiming their church?' Peter repeated, in exasperation.

Recognition dawned on Tom's face.

'You mean the crowd cheering as those men threw pieces of wood out of the front door? Looked like a rowdy mob to me, especially when we heard glass breaking.'

Sir Ralph spoke quietly.

'That will be the stained glass windows they took exception to. Did they bring any statues out?'

Tom shook his head, his mouth full of the last of his mother's game pie.

'The verger will have locked them away if he had any sense,' Sir Ralph continued. 'Otherwise the Puritans would have smashed those as well.'

He glanced at his son Peter who now looked around the table at the faces of his family who watched him with concern. Sir Ralph knew Peter

loved them all but, increasingly, he felt his son saw his destiny lay elsewhere, on a different path. It started when the Tallants were introduced to the teachings of John Calvin by Dutch relatives. Peter was struck forcefully by Calvin's doctrine that only a select number were predestined to enter the Kingdom of Heaven. By his twenty-fourth birthday, two years ago, Peter Tallant's interest had hardened into the unshakeable belief that he was one of the chosen. His eventual place in Heaven was assured. His mission now was to form communities of others to live as God commanded.

'Why does the King allow the Archbishop of Canterbury to take us back to Popish ways,' Peter said. 'As Tom saw today, the people are not happy. However, if the King is behind Archbishop Laud, I fear such street protests will be futile. No, we must remove ourselves from Laud's influence and establish our own kingdom on earth in the Americas, away from royal interference.'

'Do you plan to return there soon?' Tom asked.

Peter nodded vigorously.

'We are seeking investors for a fresh expedition in the new year. We have identified parcels of land suitable for development. Among God's children there are many who wish to join our venture.'

Sir Ralph shrugged. 'It's risky, Peter. Highly speculative and fraught with problems.'

Beatrix gave Ralph a hard look, trying to catch his eye. She glanced at young Ellen who was listening to her father with a look of anguish. Beatrix knew her daughter had been worried about Peter on his first trip to America.

Ralph did not notice his wife's look. 'Remember what happened at Jamestown. The colonists built it on a swamp, came close to starvation and then were routed by the natives.'

'It's come a long way since the first settlements, Father,' Peter explained patiently.

His previous anger had evaporated, replaced by the gleam in his eye that all who had grown up with him recognised instantly and loved. People always warmed to Peter Tallant's driving enthusiasm.

'Ships arrive from different countries every month, bringing new settlers. And no one has any idea how much land there is. It stretches as far as the eye can see, north, south and west. And the natural resources are endless. Timber, fish, land to grow food. Who knows what minerals are waiting to be mined.'

Sir Ralph grunted. 'So the merchant spirit is not yet extinguished in my Puritan son. Good! You'll need every last drop if your colony is to make enough money through trade to survive the crop failures and other calamities you'll face in the early years.'

The meal over, Lady Beatrix announced she would like everyone to see her new indulgence—a glass house for her plants. Beatrix Tallant had created a garden renowned throughout London for its grace, elegance and innovation. The many hours Tom spent there fostered in him a love of plants and nature. His one regret about living in the warehouse was that he could not have his own garden. His collection of potted plants had survived Isaac's care while he was in India but, with winter approaching, he had noticed many had been moved to his mother's new glass house and he was eager to see them.

The family left the table, still in conversation. Beatrix linked arms with Peter and Ellen. Tom followed with his father, who gently pulled him back.

'Your mother will be more than happy to do a repeat tour for you, Tom.' Sir Ralph smiled. 'Anyway, there's not room in there for the whole family. Let's you and me have a chat.'

Tom bristled. What will it be this time? He was wary of his father's 'little chats'. Why couldn't he be left in peace to run the warehouse and make the Tallants lots of money? Isn't that what his father wanted?

They sat by the open fire at the rear of the hall where they had dined. Wood, not the sulphurous sea coal, was burning in the grate. He appreciated the gentle warmth and comforting smell.

'Did you get a good price for your cargo from India, Tom?'

'Yes, Father. I am sure you will know that from your contacts at the Exchange. What's really on your mind?'

Sir Ralph paused and gave his son a searching look. He spoke again, in measured tones. 'Have you heard any more about the Merchant Adventurers' inquiry into the death of Joseph Venell?'

'Oh, that. No, it seems to have blown over.'

'What makes you think that?' Sir Ralph replied evenly, holding Tom's gaze.

'I met their agent a few weeks ago, as you know,' Tom replied. 'He wanted my advice on a damn fool theory about Sir Joseph being killed by falcons! I told him it was impossible and haven't heard any more about it. Didn't take to the agent. Unpleasant fellow.'

'That would be Robert Petty?' Sir Ralph asked.

Tom was surprised. 'Why, yes, but how did you know that?'

'An educated guess, Tom. And if I may make another, you had best assume that until Sir Joseph's death has been explained, Robert Petty and members of the merchant community will not feel it has "blown over". The death of a senior member of the Merchant Adventurers, who was also an Alderman of the City of London, is not an everyday occurrence, and when it occurs in such unusual circumstances there is talk of little else, and that continues to this day. Have you not heard it in the Exchange?'

Tom realised few people had spoken to him about Sir Joseph on his frequent visits to the Royal Exchange, which now struck him as odd.

'No, you haven't, have you?' his father said. 'I feared as much. Why might that be? Why would people not wish to be seen discussing the death of Sir Joseph Venell with Thomas Tallant?'

Sir Ralph's tone had become strident, betraying his concern. He lowered his voice.

'Tom, I know your intention was to help the investigation but city gossips rarely let the truth obstruct a good rumour. Any involvement with the inquiry associates you with Sir Joseph's death. That alone is enough to get idle tongues wagging. He was a wool trader. You are one of the new breed—the spice merchants. Rivalry exists between both. We are all battling for berths along the Thames. You know the competition for prime space. Maybe, the gossips whisper, rivalry has gone too far? Many wool merchants are hurting in the current trading market and they'll look for anyone to blame for their ills. Who better than an upstart spice trader, so full of himself and his easy profits? Let's see one of them get their comeuppance, particularly when they… ' and here Sir Ralph reduced his voice to a whisper '… are not truly English.'

Tom's mouth was open but no words came out. Sir Ralph leant forward and patted his knee.

'Tom, you need to learn more about the English and the Dutch—how we get along, and how, sometimes, we don't. Wool merchants have good reason not to like the Dutch. Twenty years ago the English traders needed fresh markets and started exporting more dyed cloths. The Dutch banned their import into the United Provinces and many blamed that for the collapse of the plan shortly afterwards. A few years later the Dutch and English were competing for trade in the Moluccas and an English colony was overrun by the Dutch. There were stories of death and torture and the merchants did not let the Dutch forget. The East Indies Company displays a painting of the incident in their building to this day. And Dutch merchants are among the biggest moneylenders in the city, never a popular occupation. A number have even been brought before the Privy Council, accused of taking bullion out of the country and undermining our finances.'

Tom's anger flared and he lowered his gaze to the giant stone flags on the hall floor. Sir Ralph leaned still closer. His tone softened.

'Tom, you must tread carefully and keep your wits about you, particularly in the City. Your mother has lived unmolested in this country for over twenty-five years. She feels at home in England. But the City can be a snake pit. It's a world of its own, with its own rules. You must never forget that. People far cleverer than you and I have been chewed up and spat out, broken. Do you understand?'

Tom took a deep breath, then nodded. They stood and embraced, holding each other for some time. Sir Ralph finally moved away.

'Oh, and Tom, I saw that look in your eye when Peter was talking about America. The trading possibilities are interesting, are they not? We must discuss how to work together and exploit them if Peter starts a colony there.'

Tom smiled.

'Good.' Sir Ralph clapped him on the shoulder. 'But first, how would you like to become a Member of Parliament?'

Chapter 4

March 1640
The Tallant warehouse

Thomas Tallant's wish was granted. The family was together for much of the bleak winter of 1640. Trade was disrupted while the weather worsened, and Peter discovered that finding backing for a new colony in America was taking longer than anticipated.

One morning, following another bitterly cold night late in March, Tom stood by his front door and surveyed the lane up to Thames Street. The ground was stone hard with all colour drained from the trees and bushes. London looked tired and listless, save for a dusting of sparkling frost. Tom's breath steamed as the icy air scorched his lungs.

Tom had lately been considering his father's invitation to become a Member of Parliament. He had thought little about Sir Ralph's offer at the time because King Charles had ruled without a Parliament for over ten years. However now it was to be recalled. Apparently, the King was completely out of funds, and for taxes he needed Parliament's assent.

Elections were imminent and Sir Ralph wanted Tom to take over his old seat. The Commons would be useful for contacts and business, and Parliamentary duties were not onerous. Tom was starting to like the idea of being the next Tallant on the Members' benches.

Meanwhile, despite his father's concern four months earlier, Tom had heard no more about the Venell investigation. It appeared, after all, that the matter had blown over. The old man was starting to fuss too much in his old age!

He noticed a sound like sobbing coming from inside the house and turned to see Isaac approaching.

'It's the kitchen maid, Master Thomas. Another couple of stiffs found on the wharf this morning. One was a young good-for-nothing who often came a-knocking after scraps. The maid, being soft-hearted, used to give the whoreson a crust or two. Looks like him and some old lag had a good day's thieving yesterday because the two of them, by all accounts, had a skinful last night. Came down to the warehouses for a warm but were locked out. Silly buggers curled up on the wharf under some sacking. Coldest place in the city. No wonder they copped it.'

Tom recalled lying warm in his bed during the night. Less than a hundred yards away, two men were freezing to death. They wouldn't have knocked on his door for shelter because he wouldn't have answered. Everyone knew the rules. London was a city driven by fear. Fear of disease, robbery and deprivation. You didn't offer a helping hand to a

brother or sister in need in case you were pulled down into the clawing, heaving mob yourself.

He left Isaac to comfort the maid and entered the ground floor office where the groom Andrew Lamkin was listening intently as apprentice Samuel Barnes read from a pamphlet. Samuel was the second son of a yeoman farmer, a tenant on the Berkshire estates of Tom's Uncle John. He received the best education his village could provide before moving to London to begin his apprenticeship in the Tallant warehouse over two years ago. Samuel Barnes could read and write better than any of the warehouse crew and was diligent, able and a quick learner. He soon earned Isaac's trust and became the first person other than Tom allowed access to the manager's warehouse ledgers. It wasn't long before Isaac was relying on Sam's neat bookkeeping and facility with numbers.

'What news, Sam?' Tom called out as he entered the room.

Andrew looked over. 'Sam's got hold of a coranto, Master Thomas. He's been reading it to me.'

'What does it say, Sam? Let me see.' The news sheet would only have foreign news as the King banned reports of domestic events. Sometimes they contained information about the never-ending war between the Dutch and the Spanish.

'Where did you pick this up, Sam? By the north door at St. Paul's?' The cathedral's churchyard was a popular place to buy news books and pamphlets.

'No, Master Thomas. I couldn't afford such a thing. The stationer, Master Sheffard, had copies in his print shop. This one hadn't come off the press clean. Look, you can see the ink is missing on part of the second page. So when I saw it had a story about the Dutch, Master Thomas, I asked him if I could keep it.'

Sam Barnes was built like a yeoman farmer: broad shoulders, large hands and sinewy forearms covered in ginger freckles matching the shock of red hair that refused to lie flat on his head. He was the image of his father whom Tom had met when Sam came to London. He pictured the farmer now and felt uncomfortable.

The Barnes family had sacrificed a great deal to send Sam to London. His elder brother would inherit the farm one day and now worked many more hours to make up for Sam's absence. The cost of the apprenticeship, including food and lodging, was another strain on the family resources. The first son was the family's best hope of a secure future but Samuel was their back-up plan. An apprenticeship to a city merchant—what a wonderful opportunity!

But Tom could see Sam's head had been turned. While Tom was in India, young Samuel Barnes's heart had been stolen. He still trained to be a warehouseman, but his ardent wish was to become a stationer. Tom assumed the spark had come from his love of reading and the opportunity

27

to work with words. He volunteered his help at Sheffard's as often as they could take him, even after a hard day in the warehouse. Sheffard was one of many London stationers now producing corantos and the printer was eager for Sam's help when he discovered how well Sam could read.

Tom checked on his work in the warehouse and was forced to admit that Sam continued to be a model apprentice. So what he did in his spare time was his own affair, certainly better than getting into fights with the other apprentices in the Black Dog every night. But Tom could not help feeling a stab of guilt each time he looked at Sam's trusting face and saw his father smiling back at him.

Tom scanned the coranto and handed it back to Sam. He climbed the stairs to the first floor store. The weather had eased and a shipment was due to leave for Amsterdam in the morning. It was not a large consignment, mainly ground cinnamon bark. Its price had risen steeply in Amsterdam because of the war in Europe—God bless the King's continuing neutrality—and Tom was supplying Uncle Jonas with additional stock.

He counted the sacks Sam had gathered for dispatch to the waiting ship. Tom reached the end of the row and stopped. There were eight more sacks propped against the cinnamon, slightly smaller and heavier. Puzzled, he checked the cargo manifest recorded in Sam's neat hand and sighed, as he recognised one of his great ideas coming back to haunt him.

While in Goa, Tom had found a new spice with a distinctive colour and aroma. The Indian merchant assured him it was highly popular in Goan dishes. Tom had a little space left in the hold and, excited by his find, bought eight sacks. This spice could be the next to sweep London, all the rage at the tables of the rich and famous. His fortune would be made, as the trader promised him monopoly supply on very favourable terms.

However, that was now unlikely as the city had shown no interest in the wonders of turmeric, despite months of hard selling by Tom in the Royal Exchange. He finally stopped when he saw that 'Tom's Folly' was becoming a joke among rival traders.

Tom knew his desire for instant riches had once again betrayed him but his pride would not let him dump the unwanted spice in the Thames, despite it taking valuable warehouse space. As a final throw of the dice, his father suggested offering it on the European market. And so here were the eight sacks of Tom's Folly lying forlornly at his feet, ready for shipment to Amsterdam. Tom aimed a kick at the final sack in the row, then heard voices and footsteps coming up the stairs. His frustration lifted as he recognised his sister's laughter among the chatter.

Ellen was three years Tom's junior. As the youngest surviving child, and the only girl, she grew up in the wake of her boisterous older brothers. Tom felt a little guilty about Ellen's exclusion from the games and play of their childhood years. She must have been lonely at times. However, it

never clouded her sunny disposition and she clearly loved him and Peter unreservedly. As a result, Tom was hugely protective and proud of his sister. Her entrance into any room brought a smile to his face.

'So here you are hiding, Tom,' Ellen cried, as she skipped around the cinnamon sacks to embrace him.

She has mother's dancing feet, Tom observed, as he gave her a hug.

'We were sitting at home, bored, and so decided to visit my brother Tom, to marvel at the wonders he brings to our shores from around the world.'

Ellen grinned at her brother and swept her arm around the dusty warehouse with a flourish fit for a treasure trove from the Orient.

'Ellen, ask Tom if he has any unicorn horn.'

It was Marjorie, one of Ellen's friends whose parents lived near the Tallant's house. Marjorie's question set her and another girl Tom did not know into a fit of laughter.

'Or maybe one of those pin apples?' Marjorie added, almost incoherent with giggling. Ellen gave Tom an apologetic look.

'I think you mean "pineapple",' Tom replied, 'and, no, we do not have any. Actually I have never seen one. My father offered a sack of pepper to the first of his captains to bring one to our table, but unfortunately I was away travelling when it arrived. Ellen can tell you what it was like.'

'An interesting fruit, the pineapple. I hear it has the roughest skin but, inside, the sweetest flesh. Is that true, Ellen?'

The voice came from the back of the room. Tom had not noticed a fourth person enter from the stairs. She was standing behind the others, her face hidden by the hood of a large, dark blue, fur lined cape. She lifted her pale hands and lowered the hood and, for Tom, the rest of the room disappeared.

'Yes, Elizabeth,' Ellen replied, 'the fruit under the skin is quite delicious.'

Ellen saw Tom was staring at her friend. 'Brother, forgive me. I forgot you have not met Elizabeth before. Tom, may I introduce Elizabeth Seymour. Her family moved into the manor house in Clerkenwell not long after you left for India. We have become good friends, haven't we, Elizabeth?'

Tom had to force himself to concentrate as Ellen and Marjorie asked him endless questions about what was in each sack in the room. There were more squeals as they approached the open loading door and Marjorie pretended to push the other girl. But his gaze constantly returned to Elizabeth Seymour as she slowly walked around the store selecting samples of spices, smelling and examining each closely.

Even under the cape Tom could see she was little more than five feet tall with a slim waist which he had the most absurd urge to put his arms around. As the room became warmer, Elizabeth undid all but the top clasp

of her cape. Tom tried not to stare but stole a glance and saw a pale blue silk dress underneath, gathered at the waist. It didn't follow the current fashion for whale boning up the front of the bodice, and Tom caught a glimpse of Elizabeth's natural shape and the fullness of her breasts. His mouth went dry.

Her dark brown hair was pinned, flowing down the back of her slender neck, disappearing under the cape in natural curls. Her cheeks had a slight blush but it was Elizabeth Seymour's eyes that transfixed Tom. They were the rich colour of the earth itself with flecks of emerald green, full of vital life but also an essential truth. He had never seen anything like them.

Elizabeth was holding a piece of nutmeg. 'Is it true that most of the world's nutmeg comes from one small island out in the East Indies?'

Her voice again. It was clear and soft, but with a husky undertone. Now he was completely undone.

'Err, yes. That is true. The island of Row in the Moluccas,' he stumbled.

'It must be full of nutmeg trees then, so no room for people. I wonder who looks after the harvest?'

Tom was about to reply that nutmeg actually grew from the mace tree but he was interrupted by the flustered face of the maid at the top of the stairs. She curtseyed hurriedly to Ellen and the others.

'Begging your pardon, Master Thomas, but there are two gentlemen who have come to call and they are most insistent they see you at once. A matter of the greatest importance, they said.'

Tom stared at the maid in a daze, then hesitantly excused himself and walked slowly down the stairs, ill prepared for what confronted him in the parlour.

Standing near the fireplace was the investigator Robert Petty with a smaller, weasel-faced man.

'Mr Tallant. Forgive us for calling without invitation, but we needed to speak to you as a matter of urgency. Please allow me to introduce Mr Nathaniel Franklin. Mr Franklin is a magistrate. He has been appointed by the City's Aldermanic Court to investigate the death of Sir Joseph Venell. I have been asked by the Merchant Adventurers to provide him with every assistance.'

Even in his distracted state, Tom sensed a tension in Petty's voice.

Nathaniel Franklin stepped forward. 'The Merchant Adventurers are, of course, entitled to investigate the murder of one of their members, but first and foremost Sir Joseph was an Alderman of the City of London. I have been called in because the Court is concerned the investigation is making little progress after so much time. It is essential the culprit is caught and made an example of.'

The scorn in Franklin's voice made it clear he had little time for Petty's methods.

'There is still no proof this was an act of murder,' Petty replied. 'I think it more likely that—'

'Proof? What more proof do we need?' Franklin exploded. 'One of the most venerable figures in the city is attacked in daylight on his own estate, grievously and fatally assaulted. You've seen the wounds, Petty. Do you think Sir Joseph did that to himself?'

Tom was in shock. Two minutes ago he had been sinking into the depths of Elizabeth Seymour's eyes. Now he was confronted by a snarling reptile. And what was he saying about murder? He needed to recover his wits.

Franklin turned to Tom. 'Petty told me his cock and bull theory about killer falcons, I considered it complete nonsense. Too clever by half. But then I saw that perhaps birds could have been used to distract Sir Joseph, to allow his killer to approach secretly and bludgeon him… particularly as Petty has finally done something useful and found a person linked to a bird attack.'

'You have? Who is that?'

'Why, you of course, Mr Tallant,' Franklin grinned, his cold eyes glinting.

It felt to Tom as if the floor had collapsed beneath him. He looked at Petty open-mouthed. Petty's face showed no expression but, as ever, his eyes were fixed on Tom as he spoke.

'As Mr Franklin said, it has been several months since you and I visited the scene of Sir Joseph's death but I have not been idle. Despite your reservations about a falcon attack, Mr Tallant, I believed it was the most likely cause given the evidence I was presented with. I accepted your view that falcons were unlikely to launch an assault of their own volition. But what if they could be trained to do so? I began to investigate who might have the skills to undertake such training and after many weeks, I made an interesting discovery.'

Petty paused. His gaze did not waver.

'Have you heard of a place called Valkenswaard, Mr Tallant?'

Tom knew at once what was coming, and that he had been a bloody, stupid fool. Petty did not give him the opportunity to reply.

'Valkenswaard is a town in the Duchy of Brabant in the United Provinces. More importantly, it lies on a route taken by peregrine falcons flying south through the continent. The people of Valkenswaard have become adept at capturing these birds—and training them. As a result, Valkenswaard falcons have become famous across the courts of Europe for their skill and responsiveness to instruction.'

Petty paused again. The silence filled the room. Franklin opened his mouth to speak but stopped when Petty levelled his unblinking, hard oak eyes on him. He turned back to Tom.

31

'I decided to journey to Valkenswaard to see for myself. It was a very fruitful visit. I spoke to the falcon trainers and learned two important things. First, falcons can be trained to take prey while not in full diving stoop, making a ground level attack possible. And second, they know all about you in Valkenswaard, Mr Tallant. They remember you well from visits with your Uncle Jonas when you were learning your hawk craft.'

Franklin could contain himself no longer. 'So you see, Tallant. Being half Dutch,' he sneered, 'you had the connections. You could have hired someone with a pair of birds to do your dirty work.'

Tom's mind returned to his father's warning at Clerkenwell.

'Let's see one of those spice merchants get their comeuppance, especially one who is not truly English.'

How had Father described the City? A snake pit? He looked again at Franklin's triumphant face and, for the first time, understood the trouble he was in. He had to fight back.

'How in God's name could I have hired anyone?' he snapped. 'My ship only berthed in London two days before Sir Joseph was attacked.'

'Yes, I wondered about that as well,' Petty replied calmly. 'But did you land with your ship?'

Tom stared at Petty blankly. 'What do you mean?'

'Mr Tallant, is it not true that, on your way back to England, your vessel had to dock at Porto for extensive repairs after you were hit by a storm south of the Bay of Biscay?'

Tom recalled the mountainous seas and the sound all sailors dread, the rending crack of his ship's main mast splitting under the strain of a tumultuous wind. It had been a miracle the holds had not been swamped and the cargo lost.

'Er, yes, gentlemen. We were berthed in the shipyards of Porto for almost three weeks while they replaced the main mast. But what has this to do with me?'

Robert Petty's speech was slow and methodical.

'One thing is clear about the attack on Sir Joseph. It took a great deal of planning. The perpetrator would have prepared everything thoroughly, particularly their escape from detection. No one would consider you responsible if you'd just returned from India. And in a crime like this, such a convenient excuse simply draws my attention, rather than deflects it.'

'So you see, Tallant,' Franklin jumped in, 'you could have hopped on another vessel from Porto and arrived in London weeks earlier to plan the deed while your ship was being repaired.'

'But people would have seen me here,' Tom shouted in exasperation. 'Ask anyone. I arrived on my ship when we berthed from India.'

'Do you take me for a fool, Tallant?' Franklin spat back. 'You landed from Porto in secret, organised the attack and then rejoined your ship as

she stood in the queue in the Thames estuary, waiting to enter the Pool of London. And if that meant your family was in on it, that would not surprise me!'

Once again there was silence in the room. Tom felt desperate. Petty clearly would not rest until he believed he'd found the truth and Franklin would feed on any discovery along the way to prove Tom's guilt. Robert Petty was the first to speak again.

'Mr Tallant, it is my job to consider all possibilities when investigating a crime. It is one thing to discover that something is possible, quite another to prove that it did happen, and I will not move against someone without proof.'

Franklin opened his mouth to speak but again stopped when Petty stared at him before returning to look at Tom.

'But when my investigations unearth connections, like Valkenswaard, that you have kept from us, it arouses my suspicions.'

Tom knew he should have volunteered the information about the Dutch connection to Petty when they first met. But he hadn't thought it important. That was the problem, he hadn't thought.

He tried to keep his voice steady.

'Gentleman. Of course I know Valkenswaard and I did visit there with my uncle Jonas. I apologise for overlooking this information but many other Englishmen have also been there, I suspect, and that does not make them guilty of anything. And where is my motive? I seek good terms with all fellow merchants and had no dispute with Sir Joseph. Indeed, I hardly knew him. So, Mr Franklin, until you can provide firm evidence linking me with his death, which you will not as I had nothing to do with it, I suggest you take your wild accusations elsewhere.'

Franklin coloured and sprang to his feet. Petty kept Tom in his steady gaze, but was that a faint nod of approval? If Tom didn't know better, Petty appeared to be signalling some support for his stinging rebuke of Franklin and his methods. Tom was now in a complete daze, not knowing what to believe.

Franklin launched one final splenetic attack as he headed for the door. 'We will keep checking, Tallant, have no doubt. And when we find someone in Porto or Valkenswaard who will point the finger at you, we will be back with a warrant for your arrest.'

Franklin marched out of the house followed by an expressionless Petty. Had Tom imagined the nod? He carefully watched Petty for another sign of support as he left, but the Merchants' agent simply turned his back and followed Franklin out.

Tom slumped back in his chair breathing deeply, staring at the ceiling. He noticed Isaac had quietly entered the room and was standing discreetly in the background.

'Yes, Isaac?' Tom said wearily.

'Sorry to disturb you, Master Thomas. Miss Ellen and her party have left but she asked me to leave these with you.'

Isaac handed over two sheets of paper, each carefully handwritten and folded in two. Tom broke the seal of the one carrying his name. It was an invitation to a post-party entertainment in Piccadilly at the end of the week, to mark the occasion of one of the Royal masque performances.

'Miss Ellen said one is for you and the other for Master Dalloway. She also told me to specially mention that Miss Seymour will be attending.'

Tom looked up smartly and searched for a smirk on Isaac's face, but it was impassive.

'Thank you, Isaac. Please take Master Edmund's invitation to his house.'

Isaac nodded and paused.

'Yes, Isaac. Is there anything else?'

Tom was completely spent. He needed time to himself, to take in the day's events.

'Forgive me asking, Master Thomas, but is everything all right? Try as I might I could not avoid hearing that wretch of a magistrate railing at you in your own home.'

Isaac moved his weight from one foot to the other as a flicker of pain crossed his grey features.

'I wouldn't be too worried about that runty little weasel, Master Thomas. I have met his type before. All piss and wind. But the big fellow with him? I don't like the look of him one bit. I'd watch my step with him, if I was you, Master Thomas. He's a hard bastard, and no mistake.'

Chapter 5

Four days later
London Bridge

Tom twisted his neck to look up.

'This is why I love London,' he murmured to himself, entranced by the building that rose above him, a house four storeys high, covered from top to bottom in decorated panels. Square towers stood proud at each corner, crowned with onion domes and gilded weather vanes. They sparkled in the afternoon sunlight which, as he watched, transformed the leaded window glass into a myriad of glittering diamonds. Best of all, this glorious confection had been created not in a country park or a smart city street, but on London Bridge.

Tom loved everything about the building. He loved its name, Nonsuch House, and the effrontery of its ambition, taking its title from King Henry's royal palace in Surrey. He loved the swagger of its design and that all who entered London from the south had to pass through an archway running through its middle. For Tom, Nonsuch House gave each visitor a clear message: Welcome to the city of wonder.

But most of all, he loved Nonsuch because it was Dutch. According to his mother, the wooden structure was designed and built in the United Provinces, then taken apart and reassembled on its current site. He knew his mother secretly loathed the house's extravagant design but whenever she entertained visitors to London, Lady Beatrix insisted they visited Nonsuch to marvel at the Dutch workmanship. She never tired of telling people, 'There is not a single nail in the building. It is all held together with dowelled joints.' Ellen would get a terrible fit of the giggles whenever her father mouthed these exact words silently behind Lady Beatrix, as she was holding forth to her visitors. Tom had never dared ask his mother if she knew what a dowelled joint was. He rather suspected she did.

In truth, Tom was also proud of the house's Dutch origins. But what he liked more was that Nonsuch House had been imported and shipped to the city. To him, this represented what London had become—the merchant centre of the world.

He looked again at its south wall and read the motto on a sundial: "Time and tide stay for no man".

'True enough. I am going to be late,' Tom muttered and, pausing to pat the wall affectionately, he strode along the bridge, looking for Edmund Dalloway's new home.

Dozens of houses had been built on London Bridge at prices well beyond Tom's pocket. This was clearly not an obstacle for Edmund who

purchased a two-storey home above a silversmith shop several months ago. Alterations had been made to suit Edmund's tastes but he was now finally in residence.

As he walked along the narrow road, Tom considered recent events. He had decided to accept Sir Ralph's offer of his seat in Parliament and would soon visit the constituency for his election. He had been jolted by the visit of Petty and the magistrate. He might need all the influence he could muster in the coming months and being in Parliament could be advantageous. However, tonight he hoped to forget his troubles in the company of Elizabeth Seymour.

Buildings lined the road on either side of the bridge and the ground floors of many had been made into shops. In places, grand houses like Nonsuch straddled the entire width of the bridge, with a passageway in the middle for the road to pass through. Occasionally buildings were missing due to fire or collapse. Here the vast majesty of the Thames suddenly appeared, and with it the prevailing weather, be it glorious sun or stinging rain, before the houses returned and the outside world was lost once more. At times it was almost possible to forget you were above water, if not for the constant rumble of the tidal river as it roared past the bridge supports beneath.

Edmund had told Tom to look for the silversmith's sign and there it was, jostling with others for attention. Tom approached the shop and viewed the position of Edmund's new home above, on the first and second floor. It was on the left as Tom travelled south across the river, so its main windows would face east towards the Pool of London and Tom's warehouse. Edmund could enjoy majestic sun rises and the long, dramatic shadows thrown by the bridge onto the Thames on summer evenings. It was a spectacular location and Tom experienced an unwelcome twinge of envy.

The silversmith was closing his business for the day as Tom approached. Looking through the leaded and barred windows at the front of the shop, Tom watched the owner carefully removing the display items. Even through the thick glass and poor light, Tom could see they were fine pieces of work made for the well-to-do local clientele. He admired a silver clasp engraved with flowers, picturing it on Elizabeth Seymour's dark blue cloak, next to her slim neck. It had been hard not to think of Elizabeth as the day of the party arrived. Their brief meeting had left him hungry for more of her presence, to look into her eyes and hear that soft yet husky voice. He had never anticipated seeing someone so keenly. It would not be long now.

The front door to Edmund's house was on the street side, to the left of the silversmith's shop. Tom smiled as he noticed the Dalloway coat of arms above the house entrance. Trust Edmund. He pictured his old friend saying 'Mind your manners' to all who entered—Edmund's loose

translation of the family crest. He knocked and the door was opened by Edmund's manservant, Beesley.

Tom followed Beesley down a passageway and up a flight of stairs, everywhere the smell of fresh timber and beeswax. They walked down a corridor and stopped at the second door. The servant cleared his throat, knocked, then opened the door, ushering Tom through as he announced his arrival. Edmund leapt from a long padded chair overlooking the river. 'Tom. At last, I didn't think you were ever coming.'

Tom caught his breath. He had never seen such windows before. They took up the length of the room's eastern wall, providing an unmatched view of the Pool of London, full of anchored ships and, beyond, the menacing grandeur of the Tower. Tom peered through their swaying masts. Was that the pepper store he could see, at the top of his warehouse? It was strange to think Isaac or Andrew could now be in that room. A ragged cormorant flew past the window, yards from the glass.

'Oh Edmund. This is prime,' Tom exclaimed.

'Yes, it is rather fine, isn't it?' Edmund flashed a grin. 'It's taken the devil's own time to build the windows, but I think it was worth the wait, don't you? I have had the master builder back twice because they leaked when the wind blew the rain upriver. They finally have them about right, so I moved in. Do forgive the mess, Tom, we still have unpacking to do, haven't we Beesley?'

Edmund's manservant nodded with a weary expression. Tom smiled at the 'we'. The notion of Edmund Dalloway undertaking any manual labour was comic.

'Tom, I would love to show you around but your delayed arrival has left us with little time if we are not to be horribly late for the ball, and there is nothing more boring than arriving at a social event when the fun has finished. Come, we must leave… but on our way out, allow me to reveal one small surprise.'

Edmund swept past Tom into the corridor. Instead of turning right for the stairs to the ground floor, he walked left towards another staircase, which led to the second floor. He stopped on the first step and pointed upwards.

'These are the stairs to the top floor, bedrooms and such, but also to a mystery I have discovered. I will show you at another time but guess what I have found behind a panel at the far end of the corridor above? A secret door!'

His old friend's excited face reminded Tom of their school days together when Edmund would be forever full of secrets and fantasies. Tom supposed it was their opposites that attracted: Tom, practical and rather earnest in his youth; Edmund, full of imagination and fanciful at times. They filled a need in each other which made them stronger together than apart. They were the unlikeliest, but the closest, of friends.

'Tom, you can imagine how I excited I was when I forced the door yesterday. It led on to an enclosed staircase, with another narrow passageway at the top of the stairs that runs through the roof space of my neighbour's house on the left. I could see another enclosed staircase descending at the end of the passageway in the roof, but I haven't explored any further yet. I could hear people talking below me and was fearful my neighbours would detect me walking in their roof. Not the best way to make an introduction.'

Typical of Edmund to buy a house with a secret passage. In some ways Edmund, his face lit with a beaming smile, was still a boy. Tom's heart filled with affection for his old friend and, on impulse, threw his arms around him.

'Tom, be careful! You will crush my new lace shirt. What an extraordinary fellow you are. Come, we cannot wait a minute longer. We must go.'

It was clear the fun had not finished when they arrived at the post masque entertainment at Lincoln's Inn Fields. The area, adjacent to the Lincoln Inn of Court, was one of a number licensed by the King for development and a number of grand residences had been built. Music and laughter spilt into the night air from one of the mansion houses. Tom's pulse quickened at the thought of Elizabeth Seymour waiting inside and he strained for a glimpse of her through the glittering windows as he approached the front door.

They knocked and entered a fairytale. Men and women strode the hall in gold, silver, reds and blues, verdant green and yellow. Gathers, pleats and swags—slashing, pinking, stamping—collars, cuffs and exquisitely embroidered buttons. It was a feast of the dressmaker's art. The cast from the earlier masque performance was still in costume, some in masks or exotic headdresses sparkling in the light of a thousand candles. Liveried servants, silent among the hubbub of the room's chatter, moved among the guests with trays of food and wine. Tom had stumbled upon the cream of London society, out on the town and determined to enjoy itself. Even Edmund was impressed.

'How on earth did you get an invitation to an evening such as this, young Thomas?' Edmund shouted in Tom's ear.

Before Tom could answer, Edmund had snatched a glass of wine from a tray and, with a wink, dived into the crowd in front of him. Edmund was in his element. That will be the last I see of him until the night is over and all the wine drunk.

How did I end up at an evening such as this? Tom thought, as he surveyed the room for Elizabeth, or any familiar face. He noticed his sister Ellen standing in a corner talking to a man he did not recognise.

Tom went to join them as a servant approached with a tray of drinks. Tom did a quick sum in his head and calculated the Venetian goblets on

the tray were worth about twice Isaac's annual wages. He chose a glass of red wine. Bordeaux; probably the best he had ever tasted. The owner of this house was accustomed to excellence, and extravagance.

'Tom. There you are. I was beginning to wonder if you would ever arrive. Please allow me to introduce you to my new friend, Mr Henry Clark. Mr Clark is one of the King's Players who have been performing today's masque at Whitehall. Mr Clark, this is my brother, Thomas Tallant.'

Even such a distant link to royalty as Henry Clark made Ellen's eyes sparkle. Ellen Tallant did not usually move in such vaunted circles, but she had friends who knew those who did. The royal court was an exotic foreign country, one she longed to visit.

Tom exchanged brief bows with Clark. He was of similar height to Tom, about ten years older with dark shoulder-length hair, greying at the temples. The brow above his dark eyes carried deep, permanent furrows, giving him a countenance of constant worry.

'I hope the masque was a success, Mr Clark?' he asked.

'It is hard to know, Mr Tallant. It is not like the playhouse where you soon discover if your performance is to the audience's taste. The masque is such a formal entertainment, and the audience is so refined, especially at court, that we have learned to trust in our own abilities rather than feed off any appreciation. In the final act, the audience become the players when they join in the dance, so it can be a little confusing for those of us more accustomed to treading the playhouse boards.'

'It sounds like the masque is not much to your liking.'

'No, no, please do not let me give you that impression, Mr Tallant.' The furrows on Henry Clark's face deepened.

'Do not mind my brother and his direct manner,' Ellen replied soothingly. She glared at Tom with mock annoyance.

'Forgive me, Mr Tallant. A player's life is a precarious one and we have come to rely increasingly on commissions from the court for our livelihood. In the past I was a member of the honoured company of Queen Henrietta's Men and was grateful for it. I was a young actor building my repertoire, first female parts and then the men's roles. But four years ago the plague shut our theatre and most of the others in the city for a year and a half. The company fell apart, and there I was, back where I started. So, no, we are honoured and pleased to perform this masque, particularly as their Royal Highnesses both took part.'

This news was too much for Ellen, who was hanging on Clark's every word. King Charles and Queen Henrietta Maria? She could hardly contain herself.

'They joined you in the masque today?'

Clark was beginning to enjoy his rapt audience. 'Oh yes. Her Royal Highness has taken part in several productions at court. She enjoys it very

much. But this is the first occasion I have seen His Majesty play a role. I believe this is the second time they have performed Salmacida Spolia as the first occasion at the beginning of the year was such a success.' Here Clark lowered his voice. 'However, I understand the reception was slightly less enthusiastic today.'

Ellen looked aghast. 'Not because of their Majesties' performances?'

Again the exaggerated concern from Clarke. 'Oh no dear lady. Not at all. They were both... majestic, as you would expect. No, it was more because of... of the theme of the masque. Sir William D'Avenant wrote an elegant play, and the splendid costumes and settings were from Mr Inigo Jones who also, by the way, designed this magnificent building we are standing in—a most gifted gentleman. Personally I considered Sir William's theme to be particularly generous. It was approved by His Majesty and conceived, I understand, to set an emollient tone for the forthcoming Parliament. His Majesty played the part of the King Philogenes—the lover of the people. Philogenes is beset with disorder in his kingdom yet through his generosity and wisdom is able to restore harmony by the end.'

'Well, who could take exception to that?' Ellen asked.

'Indeed, you may ask, but there was much muttering and murmuring after the performance. Some of the assembled crowd took exception to Sir William's conclusion that disorder was caused by the willfulness and disrespect of the common people and only calmed by the King's magnanimous kindness and patience. Indeed, when I spoke the line "the people's giddy fury", I heard muted hisses and a cry of "No!" from the back of the room.'

Ellen turned. 'Tom, what is happening? First, that trouble in the church, and now this—dissent shown to their Royal Highnesses in their very presence!'

Tom told Ellen not to worry. Privately he recalled Isaac's warning about the changing mood in the city and the beating given to Andrew by the Apprentice toughs: King or Parliament? King or Parliament? It's time to choose. Kings were accustomed to people venting their discontent on the streets but this unrest was taking root more widely. More worrying was Charles's belief that it was the people's fault, and the best way to respond was through the allegory of a court masque. For the first time Tom realised the King was dangerously out of touch with the public mood.

As he pondered, he scanned the room, looking for Elizabeth. The tension rose in his chest. She must be here, but he didn't want to ask Ellen and reveal his interest.

'But there I go again, speaking out of turn,' Clark continued. 'It really will not do, particularly in this house.'

He looked around the room with theatrical furtiveness.

'Why, what is the significance of this building?' Ellen asked in an innocent tone.

'You do not know who lives here? This is the home of the gentleman who generously provided the extensive funds for today's performance. If you had seen Mr Jones's ingenious sets, the clouds, the chariot descending from the heavens and the light, my Lord, the light—I have seen nothing so brilliant—you will appreciate the masque incurred considerable expense to stage. To finance this was generous indeed but to offer also this marvellous refreshment to the players at the masque's conclusion is truly bountiful.'

Tom was becoming irritated by Henry Clark's obsequiousness and concerned by Elizabeth's absence. The evening was not turning out as he had hoped. His voice betrayed his increasingly sour mood.

'So who is this paragon of patronage, Mr Clark?'

Clark did not notice Tom's tone, or chose to ignore it. 'Why, Sir Hugh Swofford, of course. You know of him?'

The hairs on the back of Tom's neck rose. Was this the hand of fate, or persecution? He makes a rare excursion into London society to forget his worries only to visit the business partner of the man he is accused of murdering! Tom desperately dredged his memory for the face of Sir Hugh. He must avoid meeting him at all costs. Tom would tour the other rooms and, if there was no sign of Elizabeth, make his excuses and leave. He was about to move into the salon when a group of men approached, at their head an imposing figure—tall with broad shoulders, a confident face framed by thick, auburn hair with a goatee beard and moustache.

'Oh my word, we are honoured,' Clark said. 'Henry Jermyn is approaching.'

'Henry Jermyn, the Queen's Master of the Horse?'

'Yes, and the Queen's privado,' Clark whispered. 'Jermyn's star is very much in the ascendancy. They say that if you want the ear of His Majesty you must speak to the Queen, and if you want the ear of Queen Henrietta you must speak to Jermyn. It is said Jermyn and Her Majesty are inseparable, and he is master of more than her stables, if you get my meaning.'

Clark's gossip died in his throat as he noticed Jermyn heading straight for him. A look of fear flashed across Clark's face as Jermyn stopped in front of them. He was beautifully clothed in dark blue velvet and lace but Tom hardly noticed as he was trying hard not to stare at the man standing next to Jermyn. Tom had seen the effects of syphilis on too many of his crew to mistake the signs. The man had lost the bridge of his nose to the pox and the attempts to cure it, leaving him with a snout like a dog, which did little to enhance his long chin and protruding eyes.

Jermyn spoke. 'You, sir,' pointing his silver tipped cane at Henry Clark, 'you were one of the players at today's entertainment, am I right?'

Clark scraped the floor with a bow. 'Yes, my lord, I had that good fortune.'

'Sir William D'Avenant,' and here Jermyn nodded to the ruined face next to him, 'has been told the most damnable thing—that members of the audience were hissing at his excellent libretto, in particular when he expressed our mutual gratitude for the wisdom and generosity of their Majesties... which, if I may say, Sir William, you phrased most elegantly.'

Sir William acknowledged Henry Jermyn with a slight bow.

'Of course, this cannot be true, and I told Sir William so. However, rather than hear it from me, why not talk to those in the heat of the action, so to speak, the players. I saw you across the room. So here we are.'

There was a pause. This could be tricky for Clark. Does he lie to the Queen's privado?

'Well, speak up man,' Jermyn prompted brusquely.

The thespian in Clark came to his rescue.

'Sire, forgive me. I was momentarily rendered speechless by the absurdity of such a claim. I can assure both you and Sir William'—prompting another ostentatious bow towards the librettist—'that I heard little during the performance as I was so entranced by the whole effect of the masque and the honour of playing my small part in it. But what I did hear from the assembled crowd was universal expressions of praise and wonder.'

Remind me never to trust an actor, Tom thought, as he marvelled at Clark's ability to deliver this instantaneous fiction without missing a beat.

'Hah, there, told you so, William,' Jermyn beamed. 'Just as I said, the people love your masques almost as much as they love their Majesties.'

Sir William nodded in acknowledgement, but looked unconvinced.

Jermyn swivelled to his right to look at Tom.

'And you, sir, what did you think of the entertainment?'

'I very much regret I did not have the pleasure of seeing it. I am here by invitation. Allow me to introduce myself: Thomas Tallant, member of the East India Merchant Company of the City of London.'

Sir William's disfigured face became animated and he spoke for the first time.

'East India Company, you say. You are a spice trader?'

'I am indeed, Sir William, working for my father, Sir Ralph Tallant.'

'You must have visited Madagascar. That most blessed isle, the land of milk and honey.'

Tom was puzzled. He had sailed along the east coast of the island on his way to Goa but could not recognise it from Sir William's colourful description. He saw Jermyn too was beaming at Sir William's description.

'I have sailed past it, Sir William, on a number of occasions.'

Jermyn cut in. 'You have actually seen the land that inspired Sir William's greatest poetic work? But you say you sailed past it. Why in God's name did you not land there? Such a land of strong magic. I have seen many wonders from Madagascar such as dragon's blood and stones made of iron. Did you see the rukhs flying? Huge birds strong enough to carry off an elephant.'

Tom was familiar with fanciful accounts of foreign lands but was surprised to hear them from educated men.

'Gentlemen, unfortunately I am ignorant of such wonders but I do know that both the Portuguese and the Dutch tried to settle the island. Both came to grief at the hands of the local tribe, the Sakalava.'

'Where is your resolve, the English sea-dog courage that destroyed the Armada?' Jermyn retorted. 'Surely that is more than a match for a tribe of savages?'

For the second time that evening Tom sensed his irritation rising, but his voice remained calm.

'East India ships are equipped to trade and, to a limited extent, protect ourselves. We do not have the means to mount a war, even against savages. The charter given to the company by Her Majesty Queen Elizabeth made it clear there is no requirement or expectation on the company to conquer other peoples on behalf of England. We are simply to trade with them for our country's economic benefit.'

Jermyn frowned and glanced at Sir William who had started a new conversation with Ellen. Tom felt the pressure of Jermyn's hand in the small of his back as the large man guided him away from the group towards a quiet corner of the room.

Jermyn leaned down and spoke into Tom's ear.

'I understand your position, Tallant, but I never lose an opportunity to press the case for a landing on Madagascar. Sir William is obsessed with the island and, as he is Poet Laureate... you didn't know that? Oh yes, appointed last year to succeed Jonson... so, as he is Poet Laureate, I try to keep him happy. At times I think it is my job to keep everyone at court happy. So, let us forget Madagascar. However, there is a service you could perform for your King and Queen and, if you were to oblige, I would make it my business to ensure they knew of your loyalty.'

Tom's pulse quickened. The prospect of royal favour was flattering but he had a sense of foreboding about this large and powerful man.

'I assume you trade with Europe as well as the Indies?'

Tom nodded.

'Excellent, so you will have ships regularly travelling between Europe and London?'

Tom nodded again.

'So if I needed cargo or passengers to be transported confidentially, on his Majesty's business, you could oblige?'

Tom looked at Jermyn closely. He's talking about spies and coded information, Tom thought. For a second he was tempted by the thought of having an influential figure like Jermyn to help him in his current troubles. But Tom knew his father would find out and be furious and, looking into Henry Jermyn's eyes, he was not convinced the Queen's privado would put himself out to help him, no matter what services he performed. Tom would be only one of a network of couriers for his spying activities.

'Sir, I thank you for feeling I am worthy of your trust in such matters but I regret I cannot provide such a service.'

Jermyn's body stiffened and he straightened, moving away from Tom.

'It is my responsibility, both to my father and the East India Company, to be accountable for all cargo and passengers aboard our ships, which I could not be if I was carrying either in confidence for you.'

Jermyn gave Tom a withering look.

'You bloody little upstart, Tallant. Who do you think you are, declaring your pathetic statements of honour to me, a member of the royal household. You should think it your duty to perform such a service, and be bloody glad of it. Do not think I will forget this slight in a hurry.'

Jermyn turned on his heel and strode away, summoning Sir William D'Avenant to follow. Within seconds he was smiling and talking to other guests as if nothing had happened. Tom was beginning to loathe the artifice of the whole event.

Ellen had not noticed anything amiss. She was too excited by her proximity to royalty and was still deep in conversation with Henry Clark. Tom resumed his search for Elizabeth in the large salon at the rear of the house. Here, if anything, the crush was greater and its tall decorated ceiling reverberated with the tumult of people meeting, greeting, gossiping, wooing and, occasionally, arguing.

He saw her, merely a glimpse through the crowd. She had her back to Tom and was engaged in animated conversation with two men, both much taller than her. He saw her put her hands to the back of her neck and then she was gone again, lost in a sea of faces. Tom edged forward, but by the time he reached the spot, Elizabeth had once again disappeared.

'Damnation,' he whispered under his breath. Tom was increasingly uncomfortable under Sir Hugh Swofford's roof but, now he knew Elizabeth was there, he could not leave until he had spoken to her. He searched the room again but there was no sign of her. He entered the final chamber which was half full and quickly saw Elizabeth was not there either. Had he missed her leaving the salon? Perhaps she was departing the party.

He re-entered the salon, squeezing and pushing his way past guests, leaving a trail of protest in his wake. He emerged, red-faced and flustered into the reception room at the front of the house, and ran into Elizabeth talking to Ellen.

'Hello Tom. Goodness you look a little red-faced. Is it too warm in the salon?'

Ellen's sisterly concern was well meant but was not what Tom had in mind as an opening conversational gambit with Elizabeth.

'No, I am fine, dear sister.'

Tom turned to Elizabeth but she had already moved away towards a tray of drinks. She chose a glass of white Rhenish and gazed vacantly around the room. Tom and Ellen looked at each other. Ellen gave Tom a little shrug.

'How are...' Tom stopped to clear his throat. 'Err, how are you Miss Seymour? I trust I find you well?'

Elizabeth continued to stare around the room. There was a long pause.

'You did not answer my question about the nutmeg trees,' Elizabeth said, still looking away. Her voice was slurred.

Tom was nonplussed. 'Nutmeg trees?'

Wine was dripping from the tilted glass in her left hand while she tapped the side of her leg with a closed fan in her right.

'Oh, no matter. Ellen, are you bored? I am bored.'

Tom was struggling. Was this the same Elizabeth Seymour he had met in the warehouse, captivating and exceptional, the woman who had rarely left his thoughts since?

Ellen pointed to Elizabeth's neck.

'Oh Elizabeth, you have come out undressed! You have no decoration aroound your neck. Weren't you going to wear that lovely sapphire necklace?'

Elizabeth's face flushed and her small body became ramrod straight.

'Ellen Tallant. You are such a bloody fool,' she shouted, loud enough for all nearby to hear above the noise.

Elizabeth threw the fan on the floor and stormed out of the room. Tom was too shocked to move as Ellen dissolved into tears. Marjorie Burgoyne was standing nearby and, for once in her life, acted wisely.

'Ellen, come with me to the powder room where you can compose yourself.'

Tom mouthed his thanks to Marjorie as she led Ellen away. The silence dissolved into the hubbub of renewed conversation but Tom could see people were looking and pointing. What on earth had happened to Elizabeth?

'I see you look a little shaken, sir.'

Tom looked around to see a squat man wearing a thick white wig standing next to him.

'I hope the lady is not too upset?'

'Who? Ellen?' Tom replied, still dazed by Elizabeth's explosive outburst. 'No, my sister has a strong constitution, sir. She will soon recover from the shock. But I thank you for your concern.'

'If I may venture a little advice, sir. I would steer well clear of Elizabeth Seymour. She's a dangerous sort and could be a very bad influence on your sister. Only this evening she was confronted by men seeking payment of a large gambling debt. They would not leave her until she settled the matter. I hear previous promises of payment had not been honoured. She had no choice but to surrender her sapphire necklace, there and then, in front of other guests. The shame of it. Her father, James Seymour, works in the Privy Council office. He would have been mortified to witness this tonight. Mind you, she can expect no better if she chooses to swim in such deep waters with members of Henry Jermyn's set.'

Tom could not keep the incredulity from his voice. 'Elizabeth Seymour plays cards for money with Henry Jermyn?'

'I doubt it. She is of insufficient influence for Jermyn to waste his time on. No, I hear she lost her money to a group of his camp followers. Not the first time either. Such a beauty will always be welcome at their table, particularly if she is also a reckless gambler and profligate loser.'

So that's what Elizabeth was doing when I saw her in the salon. Paying off her gambling debts. No wonder she was upset when Ellen drew attention to her missing necklace. Oh dear, poor Ellen.

'Why is Henry Jermyn here tonight?'

'He wanted to pay public tribute to Sir Hugh's generosity, on behalf of their Majesties. He also gave a small speech of thanks to the players, Sir William D'avenant and Mr Inigo Jones. Sir Hugh looked well satisfied.'

'So this party, all this expense, is so Sir Hugh can receive royal approval in public?'

'Partly, but also because Sir Hugh, a plain man of… of commerce'— here the man could not hide his distaste —'wants to become popular among the playwrights and actors. He finds their world exciting.'

Tom smiled at the description of one of the richest merchants in the City as a 'plain man of commerce'. He would welcome such a description but Sir Hugh would be apoplectic to be so called.

At this moment Ellen reappeared, her former composure restored. Tom excused himself from the conversation with the bewigged man and strode towards her.

'Are you all right, sister? I do not—'

'Sir! Yes you, sir! How dare you enter my house uninvited.' The voice rang through the room, stilling all conversation.

Tom turned slowly to be confronted by a stocky, red-faced man with a black wig slightly askew, pointing a trembling finger at his face.

'I have heard about your doings, your involvement in Sir Joseph's death. And you have the effrontery to walk into my home, bold as brass, and stand there quaffing my wine and laughing up your sleeve.'

There was an embarrassed titter around the room. It was clear Sir Hugh Swofford had been drinking large quantities of his own wine.

'I have a good mind to summon the magistrate Franklin and have you dragged to Newgate.'

'Oh Tom, what is this man talking about?'

Ellen looked like she couldn't stand another fright and might faint at any moment.

Sir Hugh leveled his bleary gaze on her face.

'We all heard that little flibbertigibbet Seymour calling you out,' pointing at a terrified Ellen. "Ellen Tallant" she said, which, I am told, sir, makes you her brother Thomas. I have my informants!'

Sir Hugh swept his arm triumphantly around the room and almost lost his balance.

'I won't have any Tallants under this roof, not while the killer of my business partner roams free.'

Tom watched this nightmare unfold before his eyes, rooted to the spot and unable to say a word. First, his encounter with Henry Jermyn. Now this. He looked around for help and saw Edmund moving towards him.

Edmund approached Sir Hugh. He spoke with a firm, but quiet voice.

'Sire, I beg you. Thomas Tallant is a man whose honour I would defend before all others. You have no reason to berate and accuse him so.'

Sir Hugh stood swaying, breathing heavily like an angry bull. He pointed at Edmund and cleared his throat to speak.

'Enough, sir,' Edmund cut in. 'We will listen to this no more. Thomas and Ellen—come, let us take our leave.'

Edmund took Ellen's arm and guided her to the front door. Tom followed and they didn't stop until they reached the road. Tom stopped and breathed deep lungfuls of the cold evening air. He could feel his face burning red with anger and shame for his sister.

'Tom. What on earth happened?' Edmund asked. 'I was in the back room and heard Sir Hugh bellowing. Not unknown when he is in his cups, but then I heard the name Tallant.'

He turned to Ellen. Her shoulders were heaving as tears ran down her face.

'Oh my dear Ellen, has that stupid old goat upset you? It really is unforgivable. Here, take my cloak.'

And he has upset me, Tom thought, a quiet fury welling up inside. This has gone far enough.

Chapter 6

A week later
On the road to Clerkenwell

Night was approaching as Meg picked her way carefully through the ruts in the broken road. That part of a safe passage could be left to her. Tom's job was to be on the alert for any trouble. As he rode through the gathering gloom, Tom knew he was carrying an open invitation to robbery on his saddle: a wooden box tied to the pommel and swaying gently on Meg's left flank. It had attracted unwelcome attention as he left London, figures emerging from the shadows to take a closer look then retreating at the glint of steel from his sword.

A thin, ragged fox loped silently across the road in front of Meg who did not break stride. Not for the first time Tom thanked his old horse for her steadfast nature. The sky above would soon be black but Meg knew this road from her frequent journeys to his parents' house, north of Clerkenwell.

Tom recognised the entrance to the village emerging through the semi-darkness. A noise made him freeze. Meg sensed his tension and stopped. Tom raised himself in the saddle and peered down the road. Two shapes approached. He quietly moved Meg into the deep shadow of an overhanging roof and placed his right hand on the hilt of his sword. Slowly the shapes turned into two burly men, one carrying a long knife. Tom swallowed hard. It had been a stupid idea to come out this late in the evening carrying a package. Inch by inch he silently drew his sword, his heart pounding as he calculated the odds in the impending fight. On horseback he had the advantage of height and speed of escape over the two men. But this would be lost if one of them grabbed Meg's reins while the other went for him, or the box. He didn't like the look of that knife. It could do terrible damage to him or Meg.

He could hear the men talking. By a miracle they must not have seen him yet. Best lie low and hope they pass. Patting Meg's neck, he slowly moved her still deeper into the shadow and bent forward in the saddle.

'All right, Meg, nice and quiet now,' he whispered in her ear. Tom remained completely still as the men approached. They were less than fifteen yards away. His right hand was tensing as he gripped the sword's hilt, the sweat gathering on his palm. Long seconds elapsed and then the men passed within ten feet. In the weak moonlight, Tom could see the smaller man with the knife more clearly. He had enormous shoulders and walked with a bow-legged gait.

The men were arguing. Thank you, Jesus. Keep talking to each other and ignore me. Meg moved her feet; Tom held his breath. The men headed

down the road, back towards the city. Meg started to fidget. Not now, Meg, not now. The taller of the two men looked over in Tom's direction and stopped talking. Come on, you two, there's nothing over here. Both men paused. Tom could feel Meg's body tense and he struggled to control 900 pounds of straining horseflesh.

Meg snorted, whinnied and stamped her feet on the ground. The smaller man wheeled around, knife aloft. Oh hell, there's nothing else for it, and he tried to charge Meg out of the shadows. He raised his sword and shouted, 'Stand back you two. Don't move.'

But it was Tom who did not move. He had rehearsed the next ten seconds while waiting for the men. However, when the moment arrived, it did not go to plan. Meg did not charge out of the shadows. Instead she pranced up and down, whinnying and pawing the ground, then reared up, throwing Tom back in the saddle.

The men did move, fast. Both fell to the ground.

The taller man shouted: 'Sire, please. We mean no harm. We will go back and move what we left, but please don't arrest us. We are simple tradesmen struggling to make an honest living.'

The smaller man hissed at his friend to be quiet while Tom struggled to bring Meg to order. What is wrong with her? She's only like this when near to… pigs. In that moment he saw that the man carried a butcher's knife, and everything fell into place. Tom laughed with relief but soon checked himself. These men could still be dangerous and he must maintain the upper hand.

As the panic subsided, his senses returned and he noticed both men smelt strongly of offal—pig's offal he would wager. His legs were starting to shake but he spoke with as much authority as he could muster.

'Get up. Stop grovelling on the floor. Why are you two abroad at this time of night? Dumping your butcher's waste, I'll be bound.'

The two men stood. Both were wearing blood-caked aprons. The taller one looked at the other who shrugged his massive shoulders. Tom carefully watched the long knife in his right hand, its blade covered in gore.

The taller man spoke.

'Sir. What can we do? We run an honest butchers in Smithfield but have nowhere to dispose our waste. Had a nice spot in the local churchyard until the preacher threatened to get the magistrate on us as he was overrun with rats.'

Tom knew the problem well enough. The demand for fresh meat in London was never-ending, with slaughterhouses opening in side streets and backyards across the city. It was profitable work but there was nowhere to dump the waste. Isaac was constantly on the lookout for butchers loitering outside the warehouse and kept an old halberd in the kitchen to discourage persistent offenders.

'You are two lazy whoresons,' Tom said sharply, 'who are fortunate I am on important business, otherwise you'd now be on your way to the constable. Go and remove your filth. I will check on my return tomorrow and, if you have not, I will have the Smithfield authorities on to you.'

Before the men could protest, Tom turned Meg and trotted away. He waited breathlessly for the sound of a butcher's knife flying through the air. Instead the men began arguing again, this time with greater vehemence. He heaved a sigh and set his sights for Elizabeth Seymour's house.

As Meg clip-clopped through Clerkenwell, Tom relaxed and pondered the events of the past week. He didn't know which bothered him more— Sir Hugh's accusations or Elizabeth's rebuff. His mother had been furious when Ellen described Sir Hugh's outburst at the ball. Sir Ralph had listened in stony-faced silence and simply asked Ellen if she felt recovered. Ellen was stoic as ever and made light of what had happened, but Tom could see she had been badly shaken.

Ellen had forgiven Elizabeth's outburst as soon as Tom explained the gambling debts, her anger turning to shock and worry. Tom said he might be able to help her with her gambling and Ellen readily agreed to arrange a meeting between her brother and her friend. But now that time had arrived, Tom's doubts returned. Could he really do anything? What had made him think he could? Which of the Elizabeths would he see tonight? And why had she requested they meet after dark?

When Tom eventually reached Bolton Hall, he continued northwards on the road. As he passed, he could see lights in his parents' house and heard voices. They were entertaining tonight and it was strange not to turn into the drive. Meg also faltered, her mind on food and water in the Tallant's stable block. She was unfamiliar with the track ahead, so he dismounted and led her on foot the rest of the way.

The Seymour manor house was a welcome sight when it finally came into view. A servant showed him into the great hall where a wood fire was crackling in the grate. Tom was surprised to see Ellen sitting by the fire. He put the box on the floor and embraced his sister. There was no sign of Elizabeth.

'Brother, Elizabeth asked me to be here to receive you as she is not in the house.'

Tom's face fell.

'No, no… she is here, but not in the house.'

Tom frowned. Was anything about Elizabeth Seymour straightforward?

'Her parents are in the city overnight, and so I assumed Elizabeth wished me to accompany her when she met you, but apparently not.'

Ellen sniffed. She clearly was not comfortable with this arrangement.

'Tom, I know you to be entirely honourable but Elizabeth must protect her virtue and reputation. I told her this but she laughed and waved me away.'

'Her parents are at their wits' end. They say Elizabeth's reckless gambling will ruin them. It's the only reason I agreed to help with such an unsuitable rendezvous. Do you think you can do anything for her?'

'I will try. But where is she?'

'In the garden, in the dark, of course,' Ellen said without a trace of a smile. 'It is most unseemly, but you had better go. She is expecting you.'

Tom picked up the wooden box and, feeling slightly ridiculous, followed a servant who had appeared with a lantern. They left the house and, after twenty paces down a side path, reached a door set in a high wall. The servant handed his lantern to Tom and pointed to the door.

'You will find Miss Elizabeth in there, sir.'

Before Tom could answer, the servant bowed, turned towards the house and disappeared into the dark.

Tom didn't move, his thoughts racing. What would he find beyond the door? Was she locked into the garden for her own safety—or everyone else's? Clearly not, as he had not been given a key. Had something happened to her? Why did she only want to be seen in the dark? Perhaps she'd had an accident? The lantern cast its pale light on the trees and bushes. A bat swooped in front of Tom's face, making him start. Perhaps Elizabeth Seymour was a phantasm that captured men's hearts with one look. She had certainly mesmerised him.

What had he been thinking? She would laugh at the gift he had brought. He wasn't even sure he liked her after her outburst at Swofford's. But he knew he must see her again.

Transferring the lantern to his left hand, with the box jammed under his left arm, he carefully lifted the iron latch and stepped into the gloom beyond the door. To his right, he could see the outline of a formal knot garden in the light from the house; to his left, an expanse of grass, leading to a tall hedge with a dark structure on its left. The garden was silent except for the occasional screech of a distant owl. The sky was blue-black with more stars appearing with each passing minute.

He set off left towards the hedge, the wooden box clutched tight against his chest. As he approached, the structure on the left became a six-sided platform with trellis on four sides, each panel three feet high and covered in rose plants. He raised his lantern for a better view and saw movement in the pale lamplight. It was smoke, he was sure of it, coming from behind the rose panel in front of him. He moved carefully to his right and peered around the trellis onto the platform.

Elizabeth was sitting on a low bench, pipe stem clenched between her teeth, studying a large shape by the light of a small lamp. The bowl of her pipe glowed in the dark as she drew in the tobacco smoke before releasing

it gently into the night sky. She was humming softly. For a reason he could not explain, Tom pulled his head out of sight and hid behind the panel. He stood silently in the dark, unable to take a step forward. He had the strangest—and strongest—feeling that if he walked onto the platform his life would change forever. He considered fleeing, finding Meg in her stable and galloping back to the familiarity of the warehouse. But he knew he would arrive home and wish immediately he was here in this garden with Elizabeth.

Before he knew what he was doing, Tom moved from behind the panel and gently called her name. Elizabeth looked over and took the pipe from her mouth. Tom caught the smile on her face in the light from her lantern and experienced a jolt of intense happiness.

'Thomas Tallant. You came to see me.'

That soft voice with a husky undertone.

'I wondered if you would, after the other night. Come, sit here next to me.'

Her hand touched the bench on her left. Tom moved forward, careful not to trip over the shape in front of Elizabeth. It was some sort of apparatus. He sat down and placed the wooden box next to his feet. Now closer to her, the air was filled with a heady mix of jasmine and sweet tobacco. Elizabeth was wearing her cloak bareheaded.

'Do you look at heaven, Thomas? I do, most nights when that infernal coal fog is not clouding my view.'

Tom looked up. It was turning into a clear, star-studded night.

'I do not understand why more people do not,' she continued. 'Is there anything else to consider, day or night, that can match this?'

Her pale hand emerged from within her cloak and pointed to the stars.

'Is there anything else to make us wonder more than this? I have studied the night sky for as long as I can remember. Then I discovered Galileo, or rather his Sidereus Nuncius. Have you read it? I have, about two hundred times, and I still learn from it. Galileo is my hero. I would love to meet him but, of course, that will never happen.'

Elizabeth returned the pipe to her mouth but it had gone out. She gently tapped the bowl against the wooden bench to dislodge the charred remains of tobacco.

'I weep to think of such a brilliant mind locked away simply because he speaks the truth. Copernicus was right. Of course the earth moves around the sun. The Inquisition would not accept that. They could not imprison Copernicus. He'd long gone. So they accused Galileo of heresy instead and placed him under house arrest in Florence. It makes my blood boil.'

Tom heard the scorn and anger in Elizabeth's voice and his eyes turned towards the dull shape in front of him. Of course, it was a telescope, the

largest he had ever seen. It was not pointing upwards, hence his confusion. Elizabeth caught Tom's gaze.

'Do you like it? It is a Kepler. I hate to admit it gives a clearer image than my old Galileo. I am still getting accustomed to it and was making adjustments when you popped out of the undergrowth like a woodland troll.'

Elizabeth flashed Tom a beaming grin that stunned him.

'Kepler was a genius. He was another to calculate planetary motions and how they move around the sun. Do you know they accused his mother of witchcraft? Why are people of science so persecuted? Am I boring you?'

Tom looked at Elizabeth and shook his head. He did not understand a great deal of what she was saying but he could not think of anyone he would rather listen to.

'No, I am, aren't I? I often talk too much when I am nervous.'

Tom was surprised. 'Nervous? You?'

'Well, I did not behave terribly well at the masque ball and no doubt you have heard of my weakness. It is not something I am proud of.'

Tom felt the box by his feet. Was this the right moment to mention it? He didn't get the chance.

'So, you see, I much prefer to come into the garden on my own to search the skies and enjoy a pipe. Do you smoke, Mr Tallant? I could not endure life without tobacco. It soothes the senses and helps me concentrate. Turning my teeth rather yellow, though.'

Tom had not noticed and he was not sure he would much mind if he did. He was completely captivated by this extraordinary woman.

'Here I am talking again. Let me ask you a question. Why are you here?'

Tom could not answer. The well considered phrases he had prepared crumbled like ashes in his mouth. Once again he was totally disarmed by Elizabeth Seymour's presence. He wanted to say he had thought of little else but her since they met in the warehouse. Instead he managed something less elegant.

'I think I can help you with your gambling problem.'

Tom sensed Elizabeth stiffen and marvelled at his own insensitivity.

'Well thank you for coming straight to the point, Mr Tallant. And what makes you believe a virtual stranger could stop my… problem? Do you not think I have received advice from many who know me better? Do you even know why I play the tables, Mr Tallant?'

Thomas fell silent and looked at his feet, stung by Elizabeth's scorn.

'I will tell you,' she continued. 'When you understand what is out there, in the heavens, you realise you are nothing. A speck of dust in a moment of time. What does it matter what you do or say? You really are not important in the natural order of life.'

You have become absurdly important to me, Tom thought.

MICHAEL WARD

'At least while I gamble I get a brief sense of excitement, a feeling that something does matter, because frankly I cannot afford to lose. But usually I do. I am aware of my family's concern and the hurt I am causing. Do you think I would not stop if I could? So, Mr Tallant, you presume much to think you can make a difference, particularly when you are so heavily outnumbered.' She pointed to the stars once more. 'Each one of my friends above provides me with ample reason to ignore you.'

For the first time there was silence between them. The distant owl screeched again. Tom did not trust his tongue, so instead he reached down, gathered the box and silently offered it to Elizabeth. She looked at Tom, then at the rough wooden container. She reached forward, took it and placed it in her lap.

'Well, Thomas Tallant. You have my attention again. I think I would like to know what is inside.'

Elizabeth looked at Tom searchingly with her enormous brown eyes and then started to unfasten the leather clasp on the box. Tom raised his lantern above the container and Elizabeth removed its top. She reached down into the box with both hands and gently lifted out a plant in a terracotta pot. It was upright, nine inches tall with three broad leaves growing from its base around a single graceful stem, which was topped with a small flower bud. Elizabeth gave Tom a quizzical look.

'Plants and flowers have always been my passion. But this one is special,' he explained.

'What is it?

'It is a secret,' Tom said, 'or rather it holds within it a secret I have not shared with anyone. A secret I keep close to my heart. But I will share it with you, if you do one thing in return.'

'Name it.' Elizabeth's eyes flashed at the prospect of a mystery.

'I will share my secret with you but you must promise not to play the tables from this day until the plant flowers.'

Elizabeth looked at the plant then back at Tom. She sighed deeply and then grinned.

'Perhaps you see that as another gamble? However, I do not. I can return to my cards after the flower has bloomed, can I not?'

Tom nodded.

'In that case I accept your wager. You have piqued my interest, Thomas Tallant, the surest way to my heart.'

She looked again into his eyes. His pulse was pounding. There was another long pause.

'Now, shall we look for Jupiter and her four moons?' and Elizabeth reached forward to pull the telescope upwards.

There was a shout from the direction of the house. It was Ellen.

'Tom, Elizabeth, where are you?'

Tom heard the alarm in his sister's voice.

54

'Over here, Ellen, by the hedge. What's the matter?'

Ellen walked quickly across the lawn guided by a servant with a large lantern. She was breathless and shaking in the cool evening air. Tom put his arm around his sister.

'What is it, Ellen, and why have you come out without a coat? You will get a chill.'

'It's Ma and Pa, Tom. Something terrible has happened at home.'

'They are not hurt, are they?'

'No, no. They are all right but… but—'

She burst into tears in Tom's arms. Elizabeth spoke for the first time, her voice gentle but firm.

'Ellen. Try to calm yourself. What has happened?'

'Oh Elizabeth, It's awful. They had guests for dinner and one of them… one of them has died.'

'What, did he become ill?' Tom asked.

'No, it was terrible. He fell down the stairs. Father says his neck is broken.'

'Oh, poor Ellen, what a terrible shock for you. Accidents can happen—'

'No, Tom, you don't understand. The man who has died… it's Sir Hugh Swofford.'

Chapter 7

The same night
Bolton Hall

By the time Tom and Ellen returned to their parents' house, the guests had left. Tom found his mother sitting by the remains of the hall fire, her eyes closed. She opened them as Tom approached and smiled weakly. He had never seen her look older.

'Oh Mama,' Tom said, as they embraced. 'What has happened? Where is father? Why was Swofford here?'

Lady Beatrix's body slumped in the face of Tom's questions.

'Your father is with the servants. They are moving Sir Hugh's body to the garden outhouse.'

She turned her gaze to the fire as a burning log collapsed in the grate with a shower of sparks. Lady Beatrix was one of the strongest people Tom knew, but now she looked close to breaking. For the first time he noticed lines and age marks on her hands. Ellen moved forward and silently sat at her mother's feet. She placed her head in Beatrix's lap who started to stroke Ellen's hair absentmindedly. In a quiet voice, she broke into an old Dutch lullaby. She stopped, still staring at the fire's glowing embers.

'I told your father not to invite Swofford, but he insisted.' She turned her empty gaze towards Tom. 'Now look at the trouble we have.'

There was a noise at the back of the room and Sir Ralph entered, dusting dirt off his hands. He walked towards the fire to catch its warmth. Tom approached him.

'Father, what were you thinking of, inviting Sir Hugh Swofford to our house after he humiliated Ellen? He as much as accused me of causing Venell's death and said he would not have a Tallant under his roof, and yet you entertain him here a week later? I am surprised he accepted the invitation.'

Sir Ralph's lip tightened and his face flushed.

'Thomas, I would have a word with you, in the parlour. Now.'

Tom's father spat out the final word under his breath, before turning on his heel and leaving the room. When Tom entered the rear parlour his father was pacing the stone floor, hands behind his back. Eventually he turned to his son.

'I invited Sir Hugh to offer him a trading partnership in the New World, initially with Peter's colony when it is founded.'

Tom was speechless. Could he be hearing this correctly? Sir Ralph had suggested the same to him less than two weeks ago. His father knew Tom wanted to open a route to the Americas but instead he was offering it to

the man who had treated two of his children so abominably? Tom sat down.

'Father, how could you? That was promised to me!'

'Tom, it was not promised to anyone. I merely said we should discuss the opportunity, and I intended to do that, before your current gift for making enemies in the city reached a new level.'

'What do you mean, make enemies? If you mean that drunken oaf Swofford, I am sorry father, I know his body is not yet cold in our outhouse but his behaviour to me and Ellen, was unpardonable. There was nothing I could do about it.'

Sir Ralph looked at his son with a cold expression Tom had not seen before.

'Do you have any idea how much trouble you are in, Tom? After the events at Sir Hugh's house, you had three people on your trail for Joseph's Venell's death: not only Petty and the magistrate Franklin, but also Sir Hugh. You may not wish to believe it but I can assure you the talk of the Exchange last week was open speculation about your guilt and when you will be arrested—yes, even within my earshot!'

Sir Ralph was pacing up and down again.

'I warned you about your position but you have done nothing but make the situation worse. You treated Petty's inquiries too casually. Why were you not open about your visits to Valkenswaard? You must not give the investigators any reason at all to suspect you. Venell and Swofford were members of the merchant nobility. These people look after their own and both Petty and Franklin will be under enormous pressure to solve this case, one way or another. Franklin for certain will not worry too much about who hangs, as long as someone does. You are becoming dangerously isolated, Tom. Why are you the only person who does not see that? Edmund tells me he is worried for you. He understands how the City works and has tried to reassure those in his circles that the gossip is completely unfounded, but he senses they are not listening. Remember, Tom, what I have told you. To some in the merchant community, families like the Tallants are brash interlopers, in need of taking down a peg or two.'

Sir Ralph's voice was getting louder.

'I have seen this rumour frenzy before. Reputations ruined—and worse. I needed to act immediately to build bridges because you clearly were not inclined, or capable, of doing so. Edmund told me Sir Hugh was furious with you but had regretted including Ellen in his tirade. I saw my opportunity to open a discussion with Swofford, so I visited him at his home.'

'What, so you could apologise on my behalf? For what?'

Sir Ralph shook his head vehemently. Tom had rarely seen him so angry.

'Sir Hugh would have no interest in apologies, I can assure you. You cannot simply apologise for being involved in the death of someone's partner, as he appeared to think you were. No, I had to offer something that would turn his attention from revenge to profit. I knew, whatever his views about the Tallants, Swofford would find the prospect of a profitable venture irresistible. So I dangled the New World opportunity in front of him. He grumbled and grunted a little at first, but eventually accepted my invitation to dinner, as I knew he would.'

The room fell silent. Sir Ralph sat down, breathing heavily.

'It was not a pleasant experience, I can assure you. Clearly Swofford had been drinking before he got here and carried on after his arrival. He was loud and boorish with the other guests, interrupting their conversations to demand more wine and offer his disgusting snuff. I had heard stories of Swofford's love of the stuff but rarely have I seen a man consume such quantities. After we had eaten, I needed to talk to him on his own, so I suggested we view a new picture on the landing upstairs, an old Martin Schongauer print. Your uncle Jonas bought it for your mother in Amsterdam as a birthday gift. I told Sir Hugh it would be a good investment in years to come and that caught his interest. He was puffing and blowing as he climbed the stairs but managed to reach the landing. I thought he wouldn't pay it that much attention, but he became transfixed by the print and then began sweating profusely. He gave out a low moan and shifted from foot to foot, turning his head left and right.'

Sir Ralph's voice lowered. He spoke slowly and deliberately, reliving the scene.

'Then, without warning, he began to rant and claw at the air around him with both hands. I put an arm on his shoulder but he twisted away and staggered backwards towards the top of the stairs. He started shouting "No" and "Leave me be", crouching down and swatting at the air above. Again, I tried to hold him but Sir Hugh was a large, strong man. He said "No sir, you will not trap me here, for them to get me" and he spun around, out of my grasp. By now the other guests were gathering at the foot of the stairs. Sir Hugh stumbled forward, still writhing and twisting, swatting the air around him. I could see what was about to happen, but, the Lord forgive me, I could do nothing to stop it.'

He lent back in his chair, uttered a deep sigh and closed his eyes.

'His left foot landed on the edge of the top step. It was carrying all his weight and he was off balance. His left leg slid beneath him on the polished wood, fouling his right foot as he tried to place it on the next step down.'

Sir Ralph swallowed hard.

'His arms were flailing like a windmill sail as he fought for balance. But his weight was carrying him forward. He screamed, the guests moved back in a panic…and he fell full length down the stairs, landing on the

hall floor. I knew he was dead. I have seen too many falls on board ship, and I knew. I looked down and saw everyone looking up at me, with the body of Sir Hugh at their feet.'

'Father, they cannot think you pushed—'

'I do not know what they think. Fortunately most of the guests were family friends. They saw Swofford was drunk and will vouch for my good reputation. One or two told me so. But, Tom, will you never understand? It is not what they think that will matter. It is what Petty and Franklin think... and what the City rumour mill will make of it, particularly after so many witnessed his accusations against you at his house.'

Sir Ralph stopped, his previous anger eclipsed by utter weariness.

Tom spoke hesitantly. 'Father. I am truly sorry you have become involved in this pernicious business. Please forgive me for my anger over the American trade, I was—'

Sir Ralph waved a dismissive hand and sighed.

'There's nothing more to be done tonight. We must get what rest we can. Tomorrow will be a trying day as the world hears the news about Swofford.'

He gazed at his son, before turning to walk stiffly out of the room, his shoulders bowed. Tom was in despair. Was this truly his destiny? To be ensnared in a fate not of his making and to drag his family down with him? Was his life—family, good name, the business—built on such shifting sand? At that moment he longed for the comfortable certainties of old, to how he felt the moment he saw London Bridge on his return from India. For the first time Tom realised he was truly afraid.

He left the parlour to examine the staircase. It was oak, wide and straight, running up the left side of the hall. Pausing to look at the spot where Sir Hugh's body landed, he climbed the broad steps to the top, where his father had stood with Swofford. His tired legs ached as the oak steps creaked and groaned under his weight. He stopped in front of the Schongauer print. In the candlelight Tom could not make out every detail, but he saw enough. The Temptation of St Anthony pictured the saint in mid-air, surrounded and tormented by flying demons. One of them was about to club him on his exposed head.

The room began to sway. The image of Sir Joseph's lacerated scalp in Kensington flashed into Tom's mind. What had Petty said... 'Venell had spoken of the "wings of demons".' He grasped the top of the stair rail to keep his balance. His breath was coming in short, sharp bursts as he sank onto the top step of the Tallant's fine oak staircase and huddled against its curved bannisters.

Elizabeth was studying the stars through her telescope. From a distance Tom watched her silently for a time, then another figure approached in the gloom. He recognised the muscular features of Robert Petty. What

was he doing here? Elizabeth moved her head away from the telescope to talk to Petty. Tom couldn't hear them but she was laughing. Petty moved closer. Was he whispering something in her ear or was that an embrace? Damn this gloom, I cannot see clearly. Petty turned away from Elizabeth's upturned face and, his smile disappearing, stared at Tom. His eyes hardened as he lifted his arm and pointed. Elizabeth slowly swivelled the lens towards him. She bent down to look through the eyepiece as Petty continued to stare, pointing silently in his direction...

His body began to shake.

'Tom... Tom.' Someone was calling his name.

'Tom, can you hear me?'

With a start, Tom opened his eyes and saw Edmund Dalloway's concerned face, his hand shaking Tom's shoulder.

'Tom, are you, all right? I have had the devil of a job waking you.'

Tom blinked and took in the familiar surroundings of his old bedroom at Bolton Hall. Was he dreaming? Had he returned to his childhood? No. Edmund was looking very adult, so why was he here, why was...? The memory of the night before crashed into his consciousness and filled him with sickly fear. The reality of Swofford's death and the implications for his father invaded his mind. He closed his eyes tight.

'No, you don't. You cannot go back to sleep, Tom. That investigator Petty is downstairs.'

Tom sat bolt upright. The memory of Elizabeth and Petty returned from his vivid dream. So did I dream meeting her and giving her the box? No, no, that was real. He cursed the tired, hot confusion in his head. His eyes ached with fatigue. He had crawled to bed last night but could not sleep, his final memory hearing the birdsong at daybreak. He must have finally drifted off less than an hour before Edmund woke him.

Tom swung his legs out of bed and sat slumped forward, desperately needing to clear his head.

'Edmund. What are you doing here?'

'I heard about Swofford as soon as I awoke this morning. Beesley told me. Usually a bad sign when he feels the need to share news before I break my fast. I left as soon as I could and... well, I'm afraid the Exchange is full of it. Tom, the City is scandalised. They can scarcely believe Sir Joseph Vennel's partner is also dead.

It's a bloody outrage what's being said by some of the traders. I boxed the ears of one gossip who was connecting you with Sir Joseph and Sir Hugh's death. It was really too much. I mean, it's simply a coincidence that Sir Hugh has died here in the Tallant house, and I told them so.'

Tom remembered his father's warning from the previous evening. It's not what happens that matters, it's what the City believes has happened that is important. Thank God Edmund's mind was not poisoned by this sea of innuendo, and he grasped his friend's arm in gratitude.

'As soon as I sensed the mood in the City, I rode out to warn your father,' Edmund continued, 'but I never expected to find you here as well. That makes everything much more complicated… and Petty has arrived. What will he make of this? Your father says you were not here when Sir Hugh died, so your presence should not interest Petty. But it is the most damnable luck, Tom, given the current rumours. You could have done with being tucked up in bed at the warehouse last night. Perhaps you should stay in your bedroom until Petty has gone. I will find out if your father or mother has mentioned your presence to him yet.'

Reluctantly, Tom found himself agreeing with Edmund. He could not cope with Petty's piercing eyes and forensic questions at the moment. His brain throbbed with exhaustion. He could not get the image of Petty and Elizabeth out of his head. In addition, his own presence at Bolton Hall could put his father at greater risk, suggesting Sir Ralph's involvement in some form of conspiracy. If only he had not been nearby at Elizabeth's house.

But that is what families do at times of crisis; they come together. Tom's fear turned to anger. Damn this poisonous atmosphere of intrigue and suspicion, where a son's natural instinct can be twisted into proof of a foul conspiracy. Everywhere Tom sensed suspicion and unrest. On the street. In the churches. Even among the merchant community.

What was happening to his beloved England?

Chapter 8

A week later
The Tallant warehouse

Jonah Dibdin was the most foul-mouthed, chiseling, mean-spirited individual Tom had ever met, but no one could handle a pair of sculls better.

He was the third generation of Dibdins to row the Thames and had an unrivalled knowledge of its tides and dangerous currents. Hundreds of watermen worked the river, taking passengers up, down and across the busy waterway in their clinker-built wherries. Jonah's boat would dart across its surface like quicksilver and Tom hailed him whenever possible, his impressive speed compensating for the lack of cultured discourse.

Tom preferred the river wherries to the broken roads of the city. For any journey east of London Bridge, he would look for Old Jonah at the wharf steps. For his part, Jonah would keep a keen eye on the landing by the Tallant warehouse. Tom was a valuable customer, a lightweight often travelling alone, and a generous tipper. Mind you, that didn't mean Jonah had to be civil, and today was no exception.

It was six in the morning and the river was coming to life.　　ands swarmed up and down the ratlines on anchored merchantmeɪ　　ɔwds formed around the Customs House. Cries of 'Oars' and 'Sculls' echoed across the glassy water as the watermen took to the Thames seeking business.

'Oh, it's you,' Jonah grunted, as he pulled up to the wharf steps. 'Abroad early aren't you? Not been to bed, or to sleep, more like?'

Tom ignored the implication of the question and stepped carefully into the wooden boat. He settled himself in the stern seat, facing Jonah. He had the perfect build for a waterman. Smaller than average, not too heavy but with strong, powerful shoulders and a wide chest. Jonah's breathing at full tilt on a long run remained slow, deep and even. He made a difficult job look effortless. His muscular arms stretched his red jerkin with its gleaming waterman's badge.

'Where to, then?'

Jonah's grizzled face was covered in grey stubble and his lank brown hair tied back. He looked like he was recovering from a heavy night in the tavern.

'I am happy to sit here and take your money at my leisure,' he continued. 'But life is not so sweet. You'll be wanting me to haul you somewhere?'

'Yes I do, Jonah, somewhere quiet.'

'Ah, something on your mind, eh? No, don't look so surprised, I've had every kind of fare over the years. Can usually tell pretty quick why they're on the river. Usually one of three reasons: business, a lovers' meeting or for thinking time.'

Jonah kept his grip on the mooring post while he appraised Tom.

'If it's quiet you want, why don't we sidle down to the Executioner's Dock in Wapping? Don't think the fellow tied to the wharf there will be too chatty. He's had the rough of the hemp tight round his neck, then been strung to a post two tides past. One more ducking and they'll cut the poor bugger down. Strong price for thieving from a coal barge, if you ask me. Does that take your fancy?' Jonah asked with a sly grin. 'No? Well maybe we could park up and watch some fool try to shoot the bridge. That's usually good sport.'

The Thames had a strong tide which, when in flood, could produce a six-foot drop in height from one side of London Bridge to the other, caused by the surging water pushing through the bridge arches. Over the years many had perished attempting to ride these rapids and shoot the bridge. A number had survived, prompting others to try, but experienced oarsmen like Jonah knew you didn't row under London Bridge unless you had to, and then it had to be at the right time on the tide.

'Have you ever shot the bridge on the flood, Jonah?'

Tom expected a swift denial and a curse for such a stupid question. Instead there was silence. Eventually Jonah spoke.

'Maybe I have and maybe I haven't,' he grunted. 'Not something to boast about—or talk about.'

Tom was intrigued by Jonah's answer but let the matter drop.

'Jonah, take me along the middle please, as far away from dry land as possible.'

Jonah pushed away from the wharf grumbling under his breath about the hard work ahead, maintaining his position in the strong currents at the centre of the river. Tom ignored his complaints. Jonah would have moaned if he had suggested they rowed to the nearest tavern and broke their fast at Tom's expense. It was just his way and, sure enough, as the wherry picked up speed and skimmed across the water, the waterman's grumbles tailed off, replaced by his deep, rhythmic breathing.

Tom eased back, closed his eyes and tried to fill his mind with the calming sensation of surging through water. He enjoyed the pause at the end of each stroke before the blades bit into the river and the wherry pushed on once more, pinning Tom gently back in his seat. Soon the familiar sounds of splashing water, oars creaking and Jonah's rhythmic breathing had the desired effect. Tom felt his fevered thinking start to subside. Since Sir Hugh's death, he had not slept for more than two hours at a time. His days were full, either at the Exchange or in the warehouse.

He would arrive home exhausted but, once in bed, questions would invade his thoughts.

Who killed Vennel and Swofford, and why? What was the force seeking to entangle the Tallants in this deathly business? Staring at the timbered ceiling of his bedroom this morning, as the sky outside lightened, Tom decided he needed water beneath him to calm his spirits. Sitting now in the wherry, his anguish was easing but still the faces of Robert Petty, Franklin and Sir Hugh Swofford returned. As his thoughts drifted, the memory of Joseph Venell's lacerated skull transformed into the pained face of Isaac Ufford warning Tom about Petty.

Opening his eyes, Tom dipped his hand in the river and splashed his face with the cold Thames water. He must concentrate. He was under suspicion for two deaths he had nothing to do with. Yet there were connections. The two victims were merchants and business partners. Both their deaths were unusual and, most startling of all, when they died, both appeared to believe they were under attack from a demonic force. Was it all coincidence? Venell may have been hit by a rogue falcon and Swofford, given his drinking, could have fallen down stairs in a hundred London houses. Tom dismissed this instantly. If Venell had been struck by falcons, it must have been a hunting pair, given his injuries. One rogue falcon was rare, but two? And Swofford had been clawing at the air around his head before he fell. It wasn't simply a drunken stumble. He clearly believed he was under attack.

Tom's desperate mind travelled back and forth through recent events, desperately seeking an explanation. Maybe it was witchcraft. Had the Tallants unwittingly angered a business client who now sought revenge through the dark arts? Or perhaps it was another spice merchant who would benefit from their downfall? No better way to create trouble than stir up existing tensions between wool traders like Venell and Swofford and the new breed of spice merchants. A distant memory returned of a Russian merchant Tom met in a Danzig tavern who said he had been cursed by a shaman, a Mongol healer from a remote part of north Asia called Siberia. Ever since, he'd been haunted by dreams of demons. At the time, Tom noted how much ale he had drunk and was not convinced. But perhaps he had been wrong. Could a merchant have hired a shaman to curse Venell, Swofford and the Tallants? Thames Street was bursting with sailors of every nationality. Surely it was possible to find someone with spirit powers in the Port of London.

Jonah paused and they began drifting downriver with the tide. He was staring at something behind Tom and, without shifting his gaze, he slowly rowed with the tide, picking up speed away from London Bridge.

Tom returned to his thoughts, which now embarrassed him. How could he really believe someone was dabbling in the spirit world? Imagine what Elizabeth would make of it, with her scientific methods? But why were

Venell, Swofford and the Tallants being targeted? What was the connection between his family and the other two? Tom sighed. He reflected on the turmoil in his head and how it matched the world around him. Tom's mind wandered again… Andrew Lamkin's bruised face, Isaac's alarm at the talk of popery and the cold fury in Henry Jermyn's eyes as his wishes were thwarted. A storm was approaching.

Old Jonah had stopped again. They were now nearer the river's northern bank, between the Customs House and the Tower of London.

'Hmm, thought as much,' Jonah muttered. 'Well, there's one way to be sure.'

Without warning he pivoted the boat in a half circle and heaved on the oars, rowing hard towards London Bridge.

Tom was pitched backwards by the thrust of Jonah's sweeping strokes. Within seconds they were skimming across the water, travelling faster than Tom imagined possible in a two-oar wherry.

'Jonah. What are you doing?' he shouted.

'Keep your eyes to the front,' Jonah snapped between lungfuls of air. 'See a wherry straight ahead of us?'

Tom raised himself gingerly in his seat and peered over Jonah's bobbing head and hunched shoulders as he maintained a cripplingly fast stroke. Even he could not keep this going for long. Tom saw a wherry closer to the shore that was also building speed, heading for a landing near the Customs House.

'I see it, Jonah!' he shouted above the creaking oars, rushing water and Jonah, grunting with the effort of maintaining his speed. 'They're heading for the Customs House.'

Jonah glanced over his shoulder, adjusted his stroke and the wherry turned. Tom marvelled at how the waterman steered his craft while maintaining uncanny speed. Even so, he had lost precious seconds. Jonah was a picture of concentration, his eyes unseeing, his face turning the colour of his waterman's jacket as the muscles on his neck bulged, straining with the effort.

It was clear Jonah was determined to catch the other boat but Tom had no idea why. Perhaps he'd spotted someone who'd skipped a fare. They were gaining on the other wherry but gradually Jonah's breathing became more ragged. His oars still flashed in and out of the water—in-pull-out, in-pull-out—but the stroke was now less measured and the forward surge was weakening. Slowly, inch by inch, Tom could see the other boat making headway and would reach the landing before them.

'You're gaining on him, Jonah,' Tom said, willing the boatman on.

Jonah glanced over his shoulder as the other wherry approached the Custom House steps and eased up.

'I will not kill myself on your account, good fare or not,' Jonah gasped. He stilled his oars and hunched over them, breathing deeply but steadily.

'On my account?' Tom cried. 'What do you mean? I didn't ask you to chase that wherry. I assumed you had unfinished business with the boatman or his passenger.'

Tom watched a small, stocky man with a beard leap out of the boat and up the steps. Within seconds he was lost among the crowd on the dockside. Jonah straightened, turned his head to one side and spat into the river.

'He's been following us since you took to the water. I don't owe anyone money and my lady wife makes sure I don't stray, so it stands to reason the bearded cove in the other wherry was interested in you. Means nothing to me but I don't like being followed, especially on the river. This is my patch. I tried to get between him and the shore, but he wasn't having it and changed position. In the end I got bored and took a run at him even though I was too far away. Still. Got close.'

Jonah chuckled before launching into a racking cough.

Tom studied the other wherry moving away from the quayside and again the crowd milling around the Customs House. The head of the bearded man appeared briefly before vanishing among the crush of people, cargo and handcarts on the quay.

'Jonah, why don't you speak to the waterman who was transporting him? He's still nearby.'

Jonah smiled, enjoying Tom's discomfort.

'Watermen treat their fares as private. Like I told you, there can be all sorts of reasons a man takes to the river. If a waterman got known as a blab-mouth, he wouldn't stay working long, would he? How would you like me telling my next fare what your business was?'

Tom frowned and Old Jonah grinned mischievously.

'Anyway, what could he tell me that we don't know? That a bearded gent got in his barky and told him to follow us, but not get too close?' Jonah's smile faded. 'Mind you, he wanted to keep out of your clutches pretty bad. He'll have put good money down to get that much speed out of his wherry. Watermen as a rule don't like to break sweat.'

'But what about you Jonah? You were going full speed!'

'That's different. A man has a position to maintain. I am not having people trailing my boat. Anyway, you don't know what my full speed is.'

Jonah was about to looking offended, but instead turned on his sweetest smile.

'What next? Another meander down the river?'

Tom had had enough of getting away from it all. He shook his head and slumped back in his seat. Grinning broadly, Jonah headed back to the Tallant warehouse. Once again the boat hit its quiet rhythm: Old Jonah's steady breathing, his head bobbing back and forwards—in-pull-out, in-pull-out—the water gurgling past the prow.

Tom's mind was anything but steady. He had come to the river to clear his head and make sense of his tangled life. Instead he now faced another unanswered question. Who was this bearded man? He had never seen him before, he was sure of it.

Chapter 9

13th April 1640
Bolton Hall

Tom could feel the pressure of a steel point against his throat.

'Do not move, Thomas Tallant, or there will be blood shed.'

There was a sharp tug and a snap.

His mother stood back, needle and broken thread in hand, and scrutinised Tom.

'That's better. We can't have you meeting the King improperly dressed. I really despair at the quality of tailoring these days. I order you a new shirt and it arrives with a loose button. It's too bad.'

His father approached, smiling.

'Never mind your mother's fussing, Tom,' he said quietly as Lady Beatrix took her sewing box out of the room. 'She's needed something to take her mind off Swofford's death. The King could not have recalled Parliament at a better time. It will also provide an opportunity to try my new carriage.'

He winked conspiratorially. Tom was relieved to see his father more like his old self. As a rule, Sir Ralph was not conspicuous in his wealth. However, he had one weakness: his love of horse-drawn vehicles. He had been among the first in London to own a sprung carriage and his new coach had been designed in Paris. This would be its first outing but, before they could leave, Lady Beatrix returned to the room and demanded a final inspection.

Tom bowed to his mother and turned full circle. She beamed her approval, took her son by the shoulders and reached up to kiss him lightly on the cheek.

'What has become of my little Thomas,' she sighed. 'A Member of Parliament, no less.' She leaned forward and whispered in his ear. 'I am so proud of you, Tom. You have no idea.'

Lady Beatrix moved back, her eyes full.

'Away with you both. I don't know, Ralph, look at you, eager to go and play with your new toy.'

She brushed a speck of imaginary dirt from his shoulder and shooed them both towards the door. Ellen was visiting friends in the city, so Lady Beatrix stood alone in the doorway as her husband and son walked towards the carriage. Tom looked back to see his mother bend down and pluck a weed from the ground. She stood and shaded her eyes from the early morning sun. The air was still and it promised to be unseasonably warm. Tom waved and climbed into the gleaming carriage, which dipped alarmingly on its springs as he hauled himself in and sat next to his father.

'What do you think of her, Tom? Isn't she a beauty?' Sir Ralph chuckled as he tapped his cane on the carriage roof and the coach moved forward. 'Did you notice the extended suspension arms and the balance of the wheels, smaller at the front and large at the back? The central positioning of the carriage and the greater distance to both front and back wheels makes for a smoother journey, as you will discover.'

Tom smiled at his father's eagerness and saw the young boy within. He experienced a surge of affection for his parents. In his turbulent world, he held these feelings close.

Soon they were clattering towards Clerkenwell village and joined St John Street, passing the playhouse on their right with its flag of a snorting red bull hanging limply in the heat. The street was busy with travellers entering London from the north. They rode past the court houses in Hicks Hall and headed towards Smithfield. As the carriage swayed, Tom reflected on his election as the Member for Dunwich the previous week. He had travelled to Suffolk with his father to find most of the buildings in the ancient coastal town under water. Sir Ralph held the seat in the previous Parliament eleven years earlier and often joked it was surely right that a merchant represented a town half in the sea and half out. Centuries earlier, Dunwich had been a major port in Suffolk and capital of the ancient kingdom of the East Angles. But floods and coastal erosion had since swallowed buildings and silted the river. Sir Ralph had remarked that the village had shrunk even further since his last visit.

So it was a depleted group of worthies who had met Sir Ralph and Tom outside the remaining tavern in Dunwich to cheer their new Member of Parliament and confirm his election. Less than an hour later, Tom and his father were on the road back to London. Tom was taken aback by the perfunctory nature of his accession. Sir Ralph had grunted, pointing out that his son had at least visited his constituency, more than some Members of the new parliament would ever do.

Outside the carriage, the noise and smell of livestock grew as they approached the vast animal pens of Smithfield. Sir Ralph gazed out of the window as the coach moved past London's meat market towards Holborn.

'I wonder how the King will handle this new Parliament?' he mused.

'What do you mean, Father?'

Sir Ralph turned. 'Tom, there are two things that matter in this great city of ours—religion and money. The King needs the second but does not seem to understand the first. He requires money for an army to fight the Scots. Why does the King have to fight the Scots? Because they take exception to his attempts to reform their church.

Whose support will he need to raise this money? Why, Parliament, of course. But they will also take exception to the King's reforms of the English church. Remember the altar rails, Tom? That's simply a part of it. Unrest is growing.'

Sir Ralph paused as the carriage lurched to the right into Fleet Street.

'London is in ferment but the King does not see it. The English may lock horns over which Protestant faith they prefer, but they agree on one thing: their hatred of Papists. They believe the King's church reforms smack of popery, meanwhile he permits the Queen to practice her Catholic faith openly! Half of London thinks the King is in the pocket of the Catholic Queen and her mother Maria de Medici, who apparently has moved in with the King and Queen, and with no intention of leaving. It seems the King is no longer master in his own household. The King, I ask you!'

The carriage slowed as they reached Temple Bar.

'His Majesty's latest master stroke is to give that bully Thomas Wentworth the job of sorting out the Scots in return for the title he craves. Diplomacy is not one of Wentworth's strong suits so he—our new Earl of Strafford—has decided to bolster the army with troops from Ireland… Catholic Ireland Tom… to fight Scottish Protestants? It's a nonsense, and it cannot happen. Which means His Royal Highness is back where he started—needing Parliament's support to raise funds to equip this completely unnecessary force.'

Tom was taken aback by his father's outburst.

'Father, be careful what you say. The coachman might hear,' Tom hissed in Sir Ralph's ear. 'You cannot speak of the King so. It is treasonable.'

Sir Ralph paused and lowered his voice as they gathered speed along the Strand.

'All our household think the same, Tom. But you are right, it is not something to be said in public. But let's see if your fellow Members of Parliament will feel so constrained.'

Crowds were forming on the approach to Westminster forcing the coach to slow down.

'I wanted you to ride in style to the opening of your first Parliament, Tom,' Sir Ralph sighed. 'Unfortunately, it seems everyone had the same idea.'

They came to a complete halt. Coaches and carts blocked their way and, ahead, the old spire of the Eleanor Cross stood above a sea of confusion. The carriage lurched as the coachman climbed down to investigate.

'Have you heard any more from Petty, father?'

Tom had been wanting to ask throughout the journey, once they were away from his mother.

'No. As you know, he came to the house the morning after Sir Hugh's death. He examined the body extremely thoroughly, even looked like he was smelling it at one point. Anyway, he also checked the stairs for any loose treads, peered at the Schongauer, asked me a few questions and left. It's a cat and mouse game, Tom. He clearly suspects you. But he knows

he will need firmer evidence if he is to take me on. In a way, I have done you a favour by becoming entangled in your mess,' his father said with a tired smile. 'Neither Petty nor Franklin can now prove a Tallant conspiracy against Venell and Swofford without accusing me also… and that, with no disrespect to you, Tom, is a completely different proposition for them. The Tallants may not be part of the merchant aristocracy but I have my friends and influence. However, we must watch them closely. Petty in particular is both determined and clever. Remember how he unearthed your Valkenswaard connection. The real question is who, if anyone, is responsible for these deaths? Who or what attacked Venell? Swofford's death was an accident, as I saw. But it is such a coincidence, Tom. You had never mentioned Venell's last words about flying demons—and why should you? It was so fanciful. But if I had known, I would not have shown Swofford the Schongauer. Whose hand is at work here, to bring these two events together under my roof?'

Tom considered his encounter with the bearded man on the river. He had not told his father who had enough to worry about, and anyway, what more could Tom say? He hadn't seen the man before or since.

The coachman returned with bad news. A coal cart had broken its axle at the Charing Cross blocking the route to Westminster Abbey. Sir Ralph swore quietly. He was to be denied his moment, riding to the Abbey entrance in his new carriage.

'I fear this is journey's end for me, Tom. You will have to walk the rest of the way, unless you can get a chair, but I'll wager they have all been taken.'

Tom leaned over and embraced his father.

Sir Ralph spoke softly. 'We will see this through, Thomas, have no fear. You will not be denied the promise of a shining future if I have anything to do with it. What the future holds for the country is a different matter. Keep your ear to the ground in Parliament.'

Tom left his father sitting in his coach, penned in front and back. He set off on foot and with each step the press of people became greater. The sun was higher in the sky and Tom could feel its heat penetrate the protection of his hat. He reached the broken cart and, mindful of his new suit, pushed and pummelled his way to one side and finally beyond it. The crush eased as the road widened but the numbers on King Street were increasing by the minute as men, women and children joined the throng from side roads and alleys along its length.

King Charles would process from Whitehall along this route and crowds were now lining the street with soldiers stationed at regular points. Tom saw faces in the windows of every house he passed. All vantage points would be for hire today. He noticed men wearing heavy cloaks despite the warmth, walking the street, talking quietly to passers-by. Occasionally a pamphlet appeared from inside a cloak to be exchanged

quickly for a coin. Tom guessed the pamphlets were not the permitted foreign news corantos, more likely a polemic about the people's expectations of this new Parliament. Thousands were gathering to witness the first sitting of the Lords and the Commons in eleven years and the pamphleteers would not miss such an opportunity to spread their message.

At this rate he would not reach Westminster Abbey in time for the service. He checked his new doublet for signs of damage from cut-purses. All remained intact. A small gap appeared and Tom broke into a trot, his anxiety rising. He must not be late. He was sweating, his new shirt tight around his neck anchored by his mother's sturdy needlework. If he could maintain this pace, he might make it to the Abbey before the crowds became impassable.

'Stop there, Thomas Tallant. Stop immediately or I will summon a constable'.

Tom turned towards the harsh voice to see the sneering face of magistrate Nathaniel Franklin, running to catch up. Tom slowed down.

'Mr Franklin. Under any other circumstances I would be happy to stop and talk but I am late and perilously close to missing my seat in Westminster Abbey for the opening of the new Parliament.'

Tom resumed his brisk walk. With shorter, hurried steps, Franklin struggled to keep pace.

'Yes, I heard your father had given you his old seat. That is why I am here. I must speak to you on a most urgent and pressing matter. I knew you would be attending the service and have waited for you. Mind you, I expected a more dignified arrival, Tallant, not shoving your way through the crowds. I should have known better.'

Tom considered explaining about the broken cart but decided not to bother. He did not have the time.

'I am sorry, Mr Franklin, but nothing at present can be more urgent and pressing than my imminent appointment at Westminster Abbey.'

'Oh is that so, Tallant? Nothing more important, you say? Not even the devil's work?'

Tom stopped amid the rush of people. He could hear the royal procession approaching and some of the waiting soldiers looked over at Franklin's mention of the devil. If he did not untangle himself from the magistrate within the next minute, all hope of attending the service would be lost. Not an auspicious start to his parliamentary career. Franklin sensed Tom's dilemma and pressed home his advantage, raising his voice.

'The devil got your tongue has he, Mr Tallant?' he shouted. 'You are not usually short of something to say.'

Tom saw a couple of Apprentices talking to a soldier and pointing in his direction. Franklin pulled Tom towards him and hissed in his face.

'Ah, that's got your attention, hasn't it, Tallant? The crowd is in a febrile mood. Mentioning devilry with the King so near has attracted some

interest. Now what would they do if I was to…' Franklin pulled Tom even closer, the spittle on this stubbly chin brushing Tom's new doublet '... let's see, if I was to shout "Papist!"'

He spat out the word in a hoarse whisper, his bloodshot eyes bulging with the effort of keeping Tom close.

'I could not venture to guess how they would react, Mr Tallant, but I do not think there would be much left of you when it was all over.'

They stood, silent, face to face. A cheer from behind signalled the procession's imminent arrival. Tom finally nodded and Franklin slowly let go of his lapel. Tom was disgusted by the magistrate's willingness to incite mob fury against him. He had now surrendered all hope of getting to the Abbey. Let this maniac say his piece and be rid of him. He could then walk to the House of Commons in St Stephen's Chapel to join the other Members when the service in the Abbey concluded.

'That's better, Mr Tallant. I suggest we move away from the caterwauling pie-sellers and find somewhere quieter to have our conversation.'

They turned right at the next side street, still working against the tide of people heading for Westminster. Franklin led Tom into the first alley on the left which led to a small walled yard. Its floor was covered with rotting food scraps and human excrement. The decaying carcass of a cat was attracting swarms of flies. Tom tried to find a clean place to stand in his new shoes. The sun blazed over the tops of the surrounding houses.

'Say what you need, Franklin, so I can get out of this midden. You may be at home here, stirring the shit, but I am not.'

Franklin jerked his head up and snarled. 'How dare you speak to me in such a manner. I am a city magistrate. You insult the office I represent. You can be sure I will report your foul, disrespectful words to the Aldermanic Court.'

Tom instantly regretted his outburst as it prolonged his time in the yard. The noxious smell, made worse by the intense heat from the sun, was overwhelming and he put a handkerchief to his mouth to staunch the worst effects. Nearby, the cheering reached a crescendo. The King's carriage must be passing.

Franklin raised his voice. 'Despite the efforts of the Tallant family to hide the fact, it is now common knowledge in the City that Sir Hugh Swofford feared he was being attacked when he plunged to his death down your father's staircase. Attacked not by man… but a group of demons! It has also been widely known for some time that his business partner Sir Joseph Venell suffered the same fate when he met his untimely death in a meadow near his Kensington home.'

Tom could not retain his silence. 'Franklin. You are a magistrate. A rational man. You cannot believe Venell and Swofford were killed by flying demons, surely? This is completely absurd.'

'You miss the point, Tallant. The talk in the taverns, even heard in the Exchange, is that the deaths are a sign. The Almighty has forsaken these merchants because of their greed. God has abandoned them to the devil to do his worst and Lucifer's merry games have resulted in their unpleasant but deserved deaths. As you can imagine, in the current climate of unrest, both the Merchant Adventurers and Aldermen are extremely nervous that such thinking could cause a religious backlash against the merchant community and the City as a whole, particularly from those of a Puritan persuasion who hold seats in the new Parliament.'

Sitting in Jonah Dibdin's wherry, Tom had dismissed the notion of witchcraft and sorcery as cause of the deaths. It was a ridiculous idea. But now he could hear the echoes of his father's earlier warnings. What Tom thought was of no account. Even the truth was of no account. What really mattered was what people believed.

A black rat scuttled into the yard, stopped in surprise on its hind legs at the sight of the two men, sniffed the air and ran out. Franklin ignored it. Indeed, to Tom, the magistrate was oblivious to the wild cheering, burning sun and fearsome stench, or anything else that would distract him from his frenzied accusations.

'So you see, Tallant, we take your family's dabbling in devilry seriously. Why would your father show Sir Hugh a picture of demons attacking Saint Anthony if not to send him a message? Indeed, why have such a depraved image in his house?'

Tom was struggling to respond to Franklin's assault. It was pointless to explain that Martin Schongauer was a respected artist whose engraving depicted a Biblical scene.

'It's simple, Tallant. My job is to stop the rot and settle this problem for the City. Make it go away before Parliament sits and the Puritan members start taking an interest, and things get out of hand. I tagged along with Petty while he dithered around, trying to establish your connection. I did believe he was on to something when he found you were known in that Valkenswaard place but no one would come forward to connect you with the attack on Venell. Complete waste of time. Now Swofford is dead and there's talk of devil's work. Don't you see? Belief is becoming more powerful than proof and that suits my purpose. Satan can be summoned by an evil, tainted mind, so why not yours, eh? If I can get enough people to believe that, your goose will be well and truly cooked, young sir.'

Franklin spat on the ground and strode off, leaving Tom in a daze. He took a minute to regain his composure then left the yard and its putrid stink. Walking back to King Street, his worst fears were realised. The crowd ahead of him had thinned, so the procession must have entered the Abbey. He could not go in after the monarch. He would have to miss the service.

Cursing his luck, Tom skirted left across Old Palace Yard and walked towards the Commons in St Stephen's Chapel. The ancient edifice of Westminster Hall reared up on his left as he approached the entrance to the chapel. He would wait here for the service to end. Away from the Abbey it was quieter with small knots of people gathered in conversation and clerks scurrying back and forth, manuscripts and ledgers in hand. He looked for shade and found a low wall to the right of the chapel entrance. He sat down and closed his eyes to block out the image of Franklin's revolting mouth and broken yellow teeth, flecked with spittle. Slowly he relaxed and allowed his mind to drift.

'My dear fellow, are you well?'

Tom opened his eyes to see a stranger's face, quizzical but full of concern, examining him closely. How long had he been sitting there?

'I watched you sitting against the wall, taking your rest, and said to myself I wager this gentleman is a fellow traveller arrived to claim his seat in the new Parliament after a long, weary journey. I will see if I can be of assistance. Allow me to introduce myself: Sir Bartholomew Hopkins from the county of Oxfordshire, at your service.

The stranger was shorter than Tom and a good deal broader around the girth. His bright eyes danced with humour. Tom rose and bowed.

'My name is Thomas Tallant, and I am indeed a new Member of the Commons, but no stranger to London. However, I am a complete stranger to these proceedings. I did not anticipate such a press of onlookers and have been unable to take my seat for the service in the Abbey. Instead I was knocked over and dazed in the crush.'

Tom had no wish to mention his meeting with the magistrate.

'God's wounds, sir, not set upon by a footpad, I trust?'

'No sir, only pushed around by an unruly mass of enthusiastic Londoners, impatient to see the King and the new Parliament.'

'Yes, I too was caught out by the crowds. Ah well. I suggest we get you registered with the sheriffs while you're here. Would you like to look inside the chamber? It will be strange to return to the old place again after so many years. What, you say? Surely I am too young to have been a Member of the previous Commons? An understandable mistake my dear Tallant, given my youthful vigour, but I was underage at the start of the last Parliament… and I was not the only one, I can tell you.'

Tom looked carefully at his new acquaintance with his hefty stomach and caught a twinkle in his eye. Is he mocking himself? Yes, I rather think he is. Tom was warming to Bartholomew Hopkins.

They entered the lobby of St Stephen's and waited to be signed in as Members of the Commons before stepping into the chapel itself. Sir Bartholomew looked around with an air of satisfaction.

'It is good to be back. I wondered if I would ever see the inside of St Stephen's again, but his Majesty has need of us once more and I, for one, am honoured to serve. Come, let me show you the commons chamber.'

He led the way further into the building. Tom appreciated the cool temperature after the heat outside. Their footsteps echoed on the stone floor below the vaulted roof high above. Sunlight streamed through tall windows, picking out dust swirling softly through the air. Tom took a deep breath. So this was it! The House of Commons. It still looked and felt like a church, particularly in the silence that surrounded them.

'We appear to have arrived after the preparations have been made but before the guests arrive,' Sir Bartholomew said. 'That brief moment of solitude. Or rather the... umm... calm before the storm? Let me explain how it works, Thomas. May I call you Thomas? Please call me Barty, everybody does. As you can see, there are two sets of choir stalls lining the chapel on both sides, facing each other. This is where the Members sit. A word of warning, there are never enough seats when the chamber is full; many have to stand. But on quieter days you can usually take the weight off your feet. When you address the House, you stand in your seat to talk.'

Barty pointed to the other end of the chapel. 'There, where the choir stalls end, you can see a raised area. That was the church altar but now it's where the Speaker's chair resides. Look, you can see it in the middle.'

Barty looked around the room.

'I see the last of the wall paintings are boarded over and most of the stained glass removed, otherwise it feels like I have hardly been away. Let us sit for a while and enjoy the peace, while it lasts!'

Barty and Tom climbed into one of the choir stalls and sat quietly for some time, listening to the footsteps and quiet voices echo around the stone walls. Tom tried to imagine it packed with Members in full debate. His thoughts were interrupted by a young man's voice.

'The service in the Abbey will shortly be concluding. The King and his retinue will then process with members to the House of Lords. Please clear the chamber.'

'Ah, time for us to go, Thomas,' Barty announced, standing up and ushering him towards the door.

Tom was reluctant to leave the calm of St Stephen's. Old Palace Yard was now bustling with activity as crowds lined the route to the House of Lords, waiting for the short procession from the Abbey to get underway.

'This is something, is it not Thomas? The King, all his lords and leading commoners, once again gathered together! The fascinating thing is you cannot tell, by looking at them, who has the power. Some of the lords, in all their finery, are complete boobies. But other plainly dressed fellows like the small man who walked past us as we left St Stephen's, did you see him?'

Tom nodded.

'Well, appearances can be deceptive. Did not look much, did he. But my money is on John Pym becoming powerful in this new Parliament. And if you were not so new to this game, I would suggest a small wager and offer you odds you could not refuse—and I would win.'

Barty ended the sentence with a wheezy laugh and a knowing wink.

'I just want to see the King,' Tom declared, like a small boy peering through the crowd.

'Oh, I'm afraid that is unlikely, Thomas. As we have missed the service, you will have to wait here behind the crowds until the procession has entered the Lords and then wait to slip in at the back. You will see very little, and afterwards the Commons will be busy with registration and setting up committees. The real business will start tomorrow. And I must go, to secure my lodgings. It has been a great pleasure to meet you, Thomas. I look forward to us working together in the House.'

With a small bow Sir Bartholomew Hopkins disappeared into the throng of people milling around Old Palace Yard.

Tom sighed. His disappointment was complete. He looked down at his new clothes, his polished shoes now scuffed and muddy. What a waste of time this had been. He could have been in the Exchange instead, trading and making some money. If this was the life of a Member of Parliament, he was not impressed.

A movement to his right caught his eye—the distinctive auburn hair and broad shoulders of Henry Jermyn, the Queen's favourite. To Tom's surprise, a man talking to Jermyn was pointing in Tom's direction. Jermyn moved his head to the left and fixed Tom with a cold look before turning on his heel and stalking off towards the entrance to the Lords.

Jermyn's abrupt departure revealed a small bearded man who immediately ducked his head and turned away from the crowd, before heading towards King Street.

Chapter 10

Two days later
The Manor House, Clerkenwell

Tom knocked on the front door of Elizabeth Seymour's house, his heart beating heavily in his chest. That afternoon a letter had arrived at the Tallant warehouse. Elizabeth had some good news to share. Could he visit at his earliest convenience?

Tom was shown into the long dining room. It was thick with swirling tobacco smoke, the dying sunlight struggling to penetrate the rich, sweet fug. Outside, the garden was alive with early evening birdsong. At the end of the room two figures sat by a fire reduced to glowing embers, looking out of the window.

'Elizabeth?' Tom called hesitantly.

Both figures turned towards him.

'Thomas Tallant, is that you?' Tom heard the soft voice, with a trace of huskiness, and his heart swelled. He didn't know why, but he found Elizabeth's habit of using his full name deeply attractive.

'Yes, Elizabeth. I received a message you wanted to see me.'

'And so I do.' Elizabeth stood and turned to the figure next to her. 'Come, Nicholas. The spell is broken. Let me call for lamps and you can meet my friend Mr Tallant.'

Tom was taken aback. What did she mean, 'The spell is broken'? Who was this man?

'Thomas, allow me to introduce Master Nicholas Culpeper. Nicholas, this is Thomas Tallant, a city merchant and curer of addictions.'

The man stood and approached Tom.

'I vouch he will not cure my particular love, which friends tell me is an addiction,' Culpeper replied. In the gloom his voice sparkled with life.

Elizabeth laughed. 'You two get to know each other while I get one of the servants to provide some light and restock the fire.'

'She is extraordinary, is she not?' Culpeper said, when Elizabeth left the room. 'I never believed I would find another person with my passion for the best tobacco. And now I have, by God, it is a woman!'

Tom said nothing as Culpeper drew on his pipe, one of the largest Tom had ever seen, a red glow illuminating his face in the fading light. He felt threatened by Culpeper's familiarity with Elizabeth.

'That is how we met. I purchased a consignment of prime, rich Virginian, fresh from America. Elizabeth came into my shop in Threadneedle Street. She had been scouring London to find it.'

A servant entered the room with two lit church candles, placed them on the table and left for more. There was no sign of Elizabeth. Tom could

now see Nicholas Culpeper's face more clearly. His brown hair was fashionably long, falling in light curls onto his collar, framing his young face with a luxurious moustache and mischievous, twinkling eyes.

'You have a shop?'

'Yes, an apothecary shop. Well, it's not exactly mine. I share it with my partner, Samuel Leadbetter; it's somewhere to make up my medicines and administer treatments.'

'You are a trained apothecary?'

'Samuel is, but I abandoned my apprenticeship. In five years I had three separate masters and I doubt I learned much from any of them, and I was certainly not a farthing richer. Faced with two more years, I decided to find my own way.'

'Is that not both dangerous and illegal, dispensing cures without full training?'

'The world of medicine is changing, Mr Tallant. My dear Mama died last year. The licensed doctor who attended her used methods handed down over hundreds of years, since Galen's time, but his treatment didn't help her a jot. We need new thinking—in medicine, in our government, in faith… in life itself.'

Tom considered Nicholas Culpeper, his eyes burning bright with conviction. Elizabeth re-entered the room but Culpeper seemed not to notice.

'London is alive with a hunger for change,' he continued. 'Everywhere you look. Have you been to Coleman Street, Mr Tallant, in the north of the city? No? You should seek it out. A most singular neighbourhood. Not the safest, I grant you, but it is… it contains an alchemy of new thinking.'

Elizabeth laughed and clapped her hands with delight.

Tom bridled. 'What type of new thinking?

Culpeper grinned at Elizabeth and continued. 'Well, take matters of religion. Archbishop Laud commands people should kneel at the altar rail to receive the sacrament. But our local minister, John Goodwin, prefers to take it to the congregation in their seats. The Anabaptists and Millenarians have set up nearby. Even Thomas Lamb, the soap boiler, has opened his own church in Ben Alley!

'But surely you can't allow just anyone to set up a church?' Tom exclaimed.

'Why not?' Culpeper countered. 'People walk off the street and preach about a New World. Not surprisingly the King's men are in Coleman Street from morning until night, sniffing around for sedition and blasphemy. I find it a most stimulating place to visit.'

Again Culpeper grinned and winked at Elizabeth.

'Nicholas will treat anyone who needs help,' Elizabeth said, her eyes sharing his excitement. 'He makes remedies in his shop and offers them to all, even those without money.'

Tom relaxed. He was unsettled by Culpeper's sway over Elizabeth but clearly the man was a dreamer. He would be destitute within three months giving away expensive remedies. He began to smile indulgently at the young philanthropist when he noticed Culpeper looking at him searchingly.

'A New World... a New World.' Culpeper mused aloud. 'By God, I have it', he exclaimed and slapped the table. 'Tallant, you say. You have a relative called Peter?'

The smile froze on Tom's face. 'Why yes, he's my brother.'

'Well I must say there is a family resemblance now we can see each other across the room!' Culpeper laughed.

'How do you know Peter?'

'Through his work with the Coleman Street Puritans. They have strong links with the Massachusetts Bay Company which is establishing colonies in New England. Two expeditions have sailed to New Haven to found churches beyond Laud's interference. Your brother Peter is leading the effort in London. Surely you knew?'

Tom looked at Nicholas then Elizabeth, lost for words. Nicholas Culpeper paused then turned to Elizabeth.

'Anyway, I must be gone. I have a list of remedies to put together for tomorrow. There will be a queue waiting when we open for business. A great pleasure to see you again, Elizabeth.' He turned to Tom. 'Mr Tallant, I am frequently in the Exchange, sampling and buying tobacco, spices and other ingredients. I hope to meet you there sometime.'

Before Tom could reply, Culpeper bowed and swept out of the room, followed by Elizabeth.

The servant returned with more candles. What was Peter doing mixing with the radicals? Was he being watched by the archbishop's men? Perhaps they were spying on the rest of the family. He thought of the bearded man on the Thames.

Elizabeth returned, laughing to herself. Tom had never seen her so happy and a pang of jealousy rose in his chest.

'Is Nicholas not wonderful?' she exclaimed.

'He certainly thinks you are,' Tom retorted.

Elizabeth stopped and gave him a querying look.

'What do you mean?'

'All that grinning and winking, it was as clear as day... even in this smoke-filled cave!'

Tom's attempt to turn his complaint into a jest sounded even more contrived than it was. The previous atmosphere of companionship vanished, and was replaced by hollow awkwardness. He looked at Elizabeth's expressionless face and regretted his words immediately. This was not going the way he had planned.

'And what is it to you if he does think I am wonderful?'

He squirmed inside. What was it to him? How could he tell her? He was talking like a jealous husband when in reality he and Elizabeth barely knew each other. He remembered her cold fury at the masque ball and braced himself for a withering dismissal. He looked at the floor and sensed her approach. Holding his breath, he felt time stop to witness his humiliation, and then Elizabeth Seymour's slim arm slipped inside his.

She guided him out of the room, her gown rustling as it brushed against his side. He smelt her fragrance of roses and saw her chest rise and fall with each breath. Finally she spoke as they entered the hall. Her tone was soft.

'Nicholas Culpeper is a new friend. I like having friends who value what I hold dear and share my love of discovery. Nicholas studied at Cambridge and has offered to improve my Latin. I struggle with the books essential for my learning. Anyway, he is recently married and is greatly attached to his new wife Alice.'

Thomas heard Elizabeth's voice from afar. He was dizzy from this first experience of touching her. It shocked him to be so affected. She paused and looked up at him.

'Thomas, I would like you to be a friend. I am anxious to finally hear your secret of the box, the reason why you came today. Is that not what friends do, share their secrets?'

They had arrived at a heavy oak door.

'Do you want to know one of mine, Thomas?'

Elizabeth stepped ahead of him and, using an iron key on her belt, opened the door into a chamber lit by a single candle. She picked it up and carefully lit another candle, and another, until the entire room shimmered with light. She turned to face him.

'Welcome to my sanctuary.'

She stood among the sea of small flames dancing in the light and smiled. Tom was transfixed.

'Despite my flirtations with gambling, my real indulgence is candlelight. The best beeswax. No tallow. It costs my father a small fortune, but he kindly provides. Strange when, outdoors, I crave total darkness to view the stars.'

Tom looked around the room. A leaded window in the opposite wall looked onto the garden. Beneath, glass vessels and stands covered a bench next to a table where a row of small knives were carefully laid out. Elizabeth's telescope stood in the corner by the bench, next to a fireplace stocked with wood. He turned to his right to see the plant he had given her, standing on another table surrounded by books, their leather covers creased with age. A jug and two mugs were placed next to the plant. Behind the books, Tom spotted a rack of clay pipes of different sizes. More books lined the wall above. Tom's attention returned to his plant. It

had grown a further four inches and was crowned with a single extravagant bloom, each petal a crimson red splashed with white.

'Isn't it magnificent?' Elizabeth smiled. 'I have tended it each day and watched it produce this solitary flower. But, Thomas, what a flower! I have never seen such colour.'

They were face to face, close enough for Tom to realise he was five or six inches taller than her. She suddenly looked serious and placed her right hand across her breast. Tom's gaze followed her movement, his pulse pounding as he saw her hand gently rise and fall with her breathing.

'Tom, I swear I have not played the tables once since we made our pact. If you wish to check with my parents, you can. I have been here most evenings, studying and watching my crimson beauty grow. So I have honoured my side of the agreement, and now you must tell me your secret. I have to know!'

The little girl within Elizabeth Seymour was brimming with curiosity. She poured Tom a mug of beer and sat down, waiting eagerly for his story to begin.

He took a deep breath. He was still reeling from the discovery that Peter was running with Puritan radicals and now Elizabeth was asking him to reveal his deep secret. He had her complete and rapt attention, a powerful realisation, so he motioned for her to move her seat nearer the table and drew up another chair for himself.

'This is a special tulip, a Semper Augustus, and its story is entwined with mine. Three years ago, I was living in Amsterdam, working for Uncle Jonas, my mother's brother, in the trading and finance houses. It was part of my apprenticeship, my preparation for the day I would take over the Tallant merchant business from my father. But, in truth, I found the work tedious. I preferred to be out and about, not studying figures and attending meetings.'

Elizabeth was settled back in her chair, listening intently.

'I was a young man in a hurry, confident I could make money without spending the time to learn how. Then one day I met Hems and Gijs.'

Tom paused. He realised it would be more difficult to share his secret than he had imagined. He lowered his eyes to the floor until Elizabeth leaned over and gently touched his hand. Tom took a deep breath and continued.

'We first met in a tavern popular with Amsterdam merchants. They were both a little older than me, part of a group of traders. By the end of the evening I had drunk a great deal and was talking too much about making money.'

'Hems and Gijs asked if I had heard about windhandel, the wind trade. It could make my fortune, they said. They could show me windhandel later that week, if I wished. I was intrigued and, two days later, we met at a different tavern. As soon as I entered, I sensed excitement and could

hear someone shouting. We entered a low ceilinged back room, full of tobacco smoke and loud talk. Men sat huddled in groups while others ran from table to table carrying documents. Serving girls weaved past with flagons and platters of food. In one corner, two harassed clerks scribbled furiously at a desk, only pausing to soften red wax in the flame of a large candle. From time to time someone would stand and shout out a price, to no one in particular, and the chatter would increase. Hems and Gijs found a table and ordered food. They allowed me to study the room, watching my face. It was unlike any tavern I had seen yet there was something familiar about it.'

Elizabeth stood up.

'Thomas, it is no good. The tension is too much. I must have a pipe. Do you mind?'

Before Tom could answer, Elizabeth reached over the books, selected a pipe and plunged its bowl into a small satin pouch on the waist of her dress. Within seconds she had worked the tobacco into the bowl with one hand while lighting a taper with the other.

'Pray, continue', she said, as she returned to her seat, plumes of smoke rising as the bowl glowed red. Elizabeth sat back, a picture of contented yet concerned concentration.

'It took me a while to realise what was familiar. The tavern reminded me of the Royal Exchange, here in London.'

'The Exchange where you trade your merchant goods? But that is enormous,' Elizabeth said.

'Yes, yes, but what was taking place was essentially the same. People moving from group to group, dealing trades—'

Elizabeth sat up and pointed the stem of her pipe at Tom '— and the clerks in the corner were recording the trades?… writing the contracts?'

'— and sealing them with wax.' Tom nodded. 'It was the atmosphere. The excitement and anticipation, it was unmistakable. But there weren't any goods. The Exchange is full of samples of what is being traded but, in this tavern, there was nothing to see. I asked Hems why; I will never forget his reply. He turned to me, his pale eyes alight with excitement, and said, "Because we trade in promises".'

Again Tom paused. Elizabeth's pipe was finished but she didn't seem to notice. Her gaze was fixed on Tom. 'The promise of what?'

He bent forward and picked up the tulip from the table. The single crimson and white flower gently nodded on the end of its slender stem as he moved it carefully onto his lap. He slowly turned the pot, studying the bloom closely.

'I will answer that but, first, let me tell you about the tulip. It was brought to the United Provinces from the land of the Ottomans over fifty years ago. In recent years the richest merchants in Amsterdam started competing to build the finest houses and grandest gardens, and the flower

they sought above any other was the tulip, particularly when they had markings such as these.'

He gently stroked the outer petals of the Semper Augustus.

'Are they not all like this?' Elizabeth asked softly.

Her expression had changed as she watched Thomas examine the tulip with care.

'No. Most have a single colour, usually red, yellow or white. But some varieties produce these wonderful splashes.'

He traced the white lines gently with the tip of his little finger.

'They became the most prized and most expensive because they are the rarest. Producing these white markings weakens the plant and growing new plants from the original bulb can take as long as three years.'

Tom gently placed the plant back on the table and turned to Elizabeth.

'The merchants began fighting over the two-colour varieties to adorn their new estates—the clearest symbol of wealth and success. However, only a limited number of bulbs were available and the traders who held propagation contracts for the next season's stock realised they had a very valuable asset. Soon, a market was established, not in tulips, but in contracts to supply them in the following season.'

'And that is what you walked into, in that Amsterdam tavern?' Elizabeth asked.

'Yes.' Tom threw his head back and looked at the ceiling. He could do with a strong drink at this moment.

'It seems hard to believe today, the fervour I witnessed that night. I did nothing during my first visit, but Gijs bought a contract for a small consignment of Violletten. They have white streaks like yours, but on a purple flower.'

Tom paused and looked Elizabeth in the eye. 'He paid 800 florins for each bulb.'

Elizabeth looked blank. 'Is that a lot?'

'Enough to employ a master carpenter in Amsterdam for a year.'

'800 for a single flower bulb? How many did he buy?'

'His contract was for the supply of twenty bulbs. Enough to employ two master carpenters for a year.'

Elizabeth's mouth opened but she said nothing.

'But what was even more remarkable,' Tom continued, 'was that Gijs didn't have the money to pay for it.'

Elizabeth discarded her finished pipe and reached quickly for another, filling it with the same fluid motion. For a minute there was silence, punctuated by the crackle of burning tobacco as she drew on the smoke.

'This was against everything I had been taught by my father, to pay for goods you had not seen, to purchase at such an inflated price, and to sign and seal a deal knowing you lacked the funds to honour it. At the Exchange, a dealer's word is his bond. If you ever defaulted on payment,

your reputation would be destroyed. Yet there, in that tavern, it did not appear to matter. I decided I wanted nothing to do with this windhandel. It was dangerous and dishonourable. But Gijs and Hems said I had only seen half of the story and begged me to return with them in two days' time to witness the conclusion. I did not sleep much that night. How could a market operate with no goods and such inflated prices? And how would Gijs pay for his contract? I wanted to cut my ties with Hems and Gijs yet my curiosity would not allow it. I met them again in the tavern later that week. All was the same: the excitement, shouting and frantic scribbling at the clerks' desks. Hems and Gijs followed proceedings very closely. Men were standing, offering selling prices chalked on pieces of slate. Gijs suddenly rose and strode rapidly to a table with a buying price written on his slate. Negotiations ensued with different prices written down and then rubbed off before Gijs rose again and walked to the clerk's table with one of the sellers. Ten minutes later he returned to us, grinning broadly. I could not believe it. How could he buy more bulbs without any money? As Gijs approached, Hems gave him a questioning look. "870" Gijs replied, and Hems shook his hand vigorously and slapped him on the back.'

'They were gambling,' Elizabeth said flatly. 'Gambling on the priceless beauty of a plant.'

'Yes. Gijs had not bought bulbs. He had sold them. He bought the original contract knowing demand was increasing but supply could not. He waited several days before returning to the trading floor in the tavern. He assumed the price would rise and it did. Once he heard an offer that gave him a clear profit, he sold the contract to another trader, making seventy florins profit on each bulb.'

'Seven hundred in total,' Elizabeth added, her voice empty.

'Soon the picture became clear,' Tom continued, nodding. 'Contracts were bought and sold so frequently it was not practical to demand payment at the time of each deal, particularly when sought-after bulbs, like this Semper Augustus, changed hands on a daily basis, sometimes being bought back by a trader as he saw the price rising again. So settlement was made at the end of each week.'

'As long as you bought and sold within a week, you would simply clear the profit, without needing the funds to buy the contract in the first place,' Elizabeth said, her brow starting to furrow.

'Exactly. When Hems and Gijs told me how much they had banked in profit from an initial investment of nothing, I understood where the opportunity lay.'

'Oh, Thomas. You didn't? You started trading?'

'Not to begin with. I was still cautious. The trading was unauthorised, not part of the Amsterdam Exchange. Uncle Jonas would not approve. But the weeks went by and the price continued to rise. I watched Hems and Gjis make thousands of florins as they dipped in and out of the market.

They kept telling me I was missing out. Finally I cracked when I discovered that windhandel trading floors had opened in other cities in the Provinces. It seemed I was the only merchant not trading. I will never forget the day I made my first trade. It was the middle of January and I awoke determined to bid for a bulb contract that night. I was to accompany Uncle Jonas on a visit to his bankers that day and it was snowing heavily, blocking some roads. Would the bulb trading be called off? The meeting at the bank lasted forever but eventually I was able to leave. I ran to the tavern, slipping and falling in the drifting snow. I found Hems and Gijs at their regular table. They were delighted with my intention to trade and promised to help with my first transaction.'

'That night I bought a contract for ten Rosen—white markings on a pale red background—and fifty Colouren. These were the single colour bulbs, much less expensive but also rising in price. My heart was beating like a hammer as I walked back to the table with my first contract in my hand. Hems and Gijs slapped me on the back, ordered wine and welcomed me to the windhandel club. And so it began. I traded the Rosen contract near the end of the week and made fifty florins profit on each bulb. Hems said I should have held out for a higher price but I was terrified of reaching settlement day still owning the contract. However, by the end of the month I had made four further trades and was beginning to accumulate a significant profit. Prices were increasing across the United Provinces as news spread. Then, early in February, prices soared again. Foreign money had entered the market, from France where tulips were also becoming increasingly fashionable. Soon tulips were all I could think of, when I was working for Uncle Jonas, eating at his table, or attempting to get some sleep in my room. The strain was getting to me, particularly when Jonas would rail against the disgraceful windhandel over dinner and I had to nod in agreement knowing that, directly above us, the trunk in my bedroom contained enough bulb contracts to buy his house.'

Tom paused. His mouth was dry at the memory of the fear he felt in Amsterdam. He picked up his mug and took a long draught of beer.

'As the prices continued to surge, Hems visited me one morning in a state of great excitement. Several Amsterdam tulip merchants intended to take their profits and leave the market. They would make their final trades that night, and they would only be selling. Hems told them it was madness to leave but the merchants had made up their mind. They had accumulated enough money to charter another voyage to the spice islands and now they needed the funds. For that night, at least, prices would be held in check as these contracts came on the market and the number of buyers decreased. This temporary lull was a golden opportunity to acquire bulbs of the finest quality before French interest pushed up values again. One trader would be selling the rights to a consignment of Semper Augustus, the most prized bulb of all. If I was willing to offer a small percentage over the

market value that night, I would acquire a number of the finest bulbs in the Provinces at an excellent price, as the French would be queuing at my table to trade by the end of the week. So that night I made the trade. I bought twenty Semper Augustus at… at 4,200 florins each.'

'Oh my goodness, Thomas. How much is that in English coinage?'

'Over £300 sterling. Yes, I know, for a single tulip bulb.'

'More than £6,000 in total,' Elizabeth whispered.

'I went home but did not sleep for a moment. The next morning I was desperate to visit the tavern. I lied to Uncle Jonas, saying I needed to meet a potential spice trading connection. I can still feel the shame as he clapped me on the shoulder and said I had my father's instinct for business. It was too soon to sell my bulbs but I was desperate to see how the market was trading. I went to the tavern in the middle of the day. Business was underway and prices were starting to push up. With huge relief, I returned to Uncle Jonas's warehouse. I would leave it one more day at the most, then sell. The following morning we were checking stock in the warehouse so I could not visit the tavern. I was following one of the warehousemen down the stairs late in the afternoon when I looked past his shoulder and stopped. Uncle Jonas was talking to Hems at the warehouse entrance. I had been careful to keep these two parts of my Amsterdam life apart, so what was Hems doing there? Feeling numb, I moved forward in a daze and, as I reached the bottom step, both men turned to me. Hems was in shock. Uncle Jonas had a face of stone. I knew, in that moment, that my life had changed, forever.

'Hems said the market had fallen heavily and I must sell right away. We both ran to the tavern but it was half-empty. Those in the room only wanted to sell. No-one was buying. People were cutting their prices but still there were no buyers. You could smell the panic. A dazed trader said the problem had started in Haarlem. Their trading floor had been as busy as Amsterdam but only a handful of traders turned up the previous day, all of them prospective sellers. By mid-afternoon they began to fear the worst. Later we discovered an outbreak of plague in Haarlem had kept many out-of-town buyers away, but no one knew this at the time.'

Elizabeth shook her head slowly but said nothing, her face pale and tense.

'The Haarlem traders became desperate. Settlement was due within days, so several did the worst thing possible. They rode at first light the next morning to Amsterdam. They hoped they would find buyers in our tavern but instead succeeded in spreading the panic. When they heard the news from Haarlem, potential buyers left the trading floor in droves, relieved both to have taken profits at the right time and eager not to mingle with visitors from a plague town. Only sellers were left, scrabbling around for deals. I spent three days trying to sell my Semper Augustus contract before settlement was due. The few traders who refused to believe in a

total market collapse saw an opportunity to buy cheaply, but they could name their price. I was fortunate in one respect—my contract was for the best quality bulbs, so I was able to attract one such buyer and sell, but at a hefty loss.'

'How much did you sell for?' Elizabeth whispered.

'I received 300 florins a bulb, and was lucky to get that. A week later the price was below 100 and then all trading was suspended.'

'But that's still a loss of almost 4,000 florins per bulb, 80,000 florins in total. Tom, given your figures earlier, that makes your remaining debt… over £5,800!'

The last words died in Elizabeth's mouth as she realised the enormity of what she was saying.

'What on earth did you do?'

'When settlement day came, I had to pay, or rather my family did. There was no time to summon my father, so Uncle Jonas made the decision. He knew my father would not countenance a Tallant defaulting on a debt. His sister Beatrix was a Tallant, so neither would he. He went to his bankers and was able to raise a loan to cover the full amount. He had to provide one of his incoming ships and its spice cargo as security. I was consumed with shame. I had been a guest in his house and had completely abused his trust. A week later my father arrived. He immediately held a series of meetings with Jonas and his bankers and within days had transferred the debt to his account. To this day I do not know what he used to secure the loan. I left the next day for England. My father did not speak to me throughout the journey home. Four days and not a word. Two days after we returned he told me I was to work for him until every shilling of debt from my "tulip folly" had been repaid. The preparation for my eventual inheritance of the Tallant business was on hold until the debt had been settled. There was no discussion. It was not an offer I could refuse. That is why I currently run the warehouse, nothing more, nothing less. All profits from the trades I make pay off the debt.'

There was silence. Tom felt completely spent. Elizabeth looked at the tulip plant on the table.

'But if you sold your contract, where did you get this plant?'

'The morning I left Amsterdam, Hems visited me. He and Gijs had lost money in the price collapse but were not as exposed as I. They were deeply troubled by my loss and gave me a gift—a single Semper Augustus bulb from Hems' personal collection. It was a fine gesture as the plant was still sought-after and would have raised a tidy sum when the market improved. Back in London, I gave the bulb to my mother and tried to forget about it. Despite the bad memories it held, she could not contain her curiosity and planted it while I was in India. It produced two buds and seed. She propagated the buds and this plant is from one of them. She gave me the seed but I know that will not produce any dual-coloured plants.

They only come from buds, for some reason. Even so, until today, I could not be sure the crimson and white strain would run true to this plant. Seeing it here, I don't know what to feel.'

'And neither do I,' Elizabeth said. 'That you should give this plant to me, when you could have sold it to pay off part of your debt? Whatever bargain we struck to share our secrets, Thomas, you have repaid it tenfold. My trifling gambling is meaningless when placed next to your financial ruin, and you did not need to lay yourself bare before me this way.'

'You are the first person, other than my mother, father and Uncle Jonas, to know of this. Not even my brother and sister have been told.'

'But why me?', she asked.

'It was the look on your face when you were forced to surrender your necklace to Jermyn's men. Anger, but fear also. Seeing you, I was transported to that warehouse in Amsterdam, to my reaction when I saw Hems talking to Uncle Jonas, and what followed. I did not want you to go through what I have, and so it seemed a perfect use for the plant, to distract you from your gambling habit.'

The wind was gathering outside. A branch rattled against the outer wall.

'There was also another reason. My mother always taught me to value the beauty of nature. I remember us spending endless summer days on our hands and knees, studying plants in her garden, she explaining each flower in loving detail. I learned to appreciate the simple perfection of each bloom. I do not know what hurt her more when I returned from Amsterdam, the way I had treated her brother Jonas or that I had debased the beauty of these magnificent plants by using them as gambling tokens. She stood in her garden, fists screwed tight, shouting "Have you learned nothing about true value in life? Have you learned nothing from me about what matters?" So that's what I have tried to do… reach back into my childhood to rediscover what really matters and, with the help of this flower, share that wisdom with someone in a way that might also help them.'

Elizabeth sat quite still, her eyes wet with tears.

'But what made you think I would understand? That your stratagem would work on me?'

'I am not sure. It was instinct, I think. I needed to place this knowledge—this knowledge of me—in the hands of someone I believed I could trust who would appreciate it.'

'But we barely know each other,' she whispered.

'I know. It is strange, is it not?'

Chapter 11

11th May 1640
Edmund Dalloway's house, London Bridge

'What the devil is all that noise?' Edmund Dalloway exclaimed, rising from his chair.

Tom looked at his friend quizzically. It was a strange question, sitting in Edmund's home on London Bridge with its constant rumble of rushing water and the sound of people crossing to and fro beneath. Then he heard it, a rhythmic chanting and drum beat.

Edmund walked to his wide window and peered to his left and right.

'This room affords me the best view of the river in all London,' he sighed, 'but I cannot see a thing on the bridge.' The banging and chanting was getting louder, coming from the north end. 'Come, Tom, let us stretch our legs and investigate.'

Tom grimaced. He had visited Edmund for a few hours respite and was settled in a comfortable chair with a glass of excellent Rhenish. He yawned and stretched. The last month had been exhausting with too many hours spent in Parliament and the Royal Exchange. Little progress had been made resolving the differences between King and Commons. The King had been frustrated by Parliament's refusal to give him funds for his war against the Scots. In turn members of the Commons insisted there could be no money supply until their grievances had been addressed. Increasingly, Archbishop Laud's church reforms became the focus of their discontent. Tom had arrived at the Royal Exchange three days ago to see "Bishop's Devils" scrawled on the outer walls. He could feel the tension rising on the streets. It had been almost a relief when the King's patience finally snapped a week ago and he dissolved the Parliament, less than a month after it had been called into session.

Edmund had gone, wine glass in hand, his footsteps ringing along the corridor towards the stairs. With a groan, Tom heaved himself out of the chair, descended the staircase and walked towards Edmund's open front door. On the street, the air was thick with menace and threat. A tide of angry, young toughs approached from the left, many of them drunk, cursing and chanting 'Bishop's traitors, Bishop's devils'. The Apprentice Boys were on the march. He spotted Edmund bending over a man lying on the ground. The sound of a banging drum was receding to the south bank to his right. The drumming stopped, followed by a distant shout in unison and loud cheering.

Tom ran towards Edmund. A clutch of Apprentices were standing nearby pissing against the bridge wall. They jeered and pointed at him.

'Look at him run, like the Archbishop, William the fox. But we'll flush Will out of his lair and hunt him down.'

One of them aimed a drunken kick at Tom. He reached Edmund's side. His friend was propping up a grey-haired man bleeding heavily from his nose, offering him his wine.

'Young swine,' Edmund shouted among the clamour. 'They've attacked this innocent gentleman.'

The victim looked confused. 'I do not understand. I am of the Protestant faith and for Parliament. I told them so.' He took a gulp from Edmund's glass and nodded his thanks. 'I beseeched them to desist from this ungodly behaviour, but I saw the devil in the eyes of one, who struck me most cruelly with his head.'

'So the King's enemies are fighting among themselves,' Edmund murmured.

As the man swallowed another mouthful of Rhenish, Tom was hit in the back and pitched forward on top of Edmund.

'Clear the way for the Apprentice Boys,' a young man sneered.

A fiddle broke into a marching tune and the swarm of Apprentices cheered and whistled.

'Sir, we must move you before you come to more harm,' Tom shouted.

Tom and Edmund lifted the man from the main walkway to a space between two market stalls where he managed to stand, dabbing at his bloody nose with a handkerchief. He clutched Edmund's sleeve.

'I am told they are joining others massing on St George's Fields at Southwark. They mean to march on Lambeth Palace and burn it down, with Archbishop Laud in it!', the man shouted in alarm. 'They say the King's mind has been poisoned by Papist advisors like Laud and that's why his Majesty closed Parliament before their just grievances could be heard.'

'By God, this is sedition,' Edmund cried. 'London has finally gone mad. We must defend Lambeth Palace and save the Archbishop!'

Tom confirmed the stranger could make his own way before moving Edmund away.

'Hear that chant, "Bishop's Devils", Edmund? Remember the message scrawled on the Royal Exchange last week? It was known there could be unrest once the King dissolved Parliament. Lambeth Palace is the last place they will find Archbishop Laud. He has more sense. I heard so many grievances aired in the Commons which had festered for eleven years without a Parliament. Now it has been dissolved after three weeks with little achieved, provoking a rage which must be released. When these Apprentices find the Archbishop is not at home, they will bang their drums, shout, shake their fists and then go home as the drink wears off and their headaches start.'

Edmund frowned and shook his head.

91

'Each day and week we suffer treasonable talk on the street, attacks on our churches, seditious street-preachers, scandalous pamphlets on every corner and finally this... mutinous gangs of Apprentice Boys! How dare they challenge the divine right of his Majesty to rule and govern his country as he sees fit? We must teach them a lesson they will not forget.'

Edmund ran across the bridge into his house. He reappeared with his sword buckled to his waist and Tom blocked his path, gripping his arm tightly.

'Edmund, are you mad? If you step out with your sword on display, and in your current mood, I wager you will not reach the end of the bridge. If you challenge the mob, they will tear you to pieces. If you must carry your sword, for heaven's sake wrap it in your cloak.'

His friend was shaking with anger but eventually his body relaxed and Tom loosened his grip. Edmund's eyes still blazed with fury.

'Edmund, if you are determined to travel to Lambeth, it seems I must accompany you to keep you out of trouble. But promise you will not attempt to take on the Apprentices on your own. I would hate to disown all knowledge of you in your hour of need.'

Tom grinned and punched his friend on the arm.

Edmund remained stony-faced and pushed into the crowd with his sword hidden. Tom struggled to keep pace. They positioned themselves between two large moving groups of Apprentices and soon reached the south end of the bridge.

'Edmund, we should try for a wherry to Lambeth. It will be quicker.'

They edged their way through the crowd and slipped down a side street to the river, stepping round an Apprentice on his hands and knees vomiting. Two youths walked up the lane towards them.

One of them shouted, 'Looking for a boatman? You'll be lucky. The bastards aren't taking fares.'

Edmund faltered but Tom continued walking past the two men.

'Keep going, Edmund. We'll have better fortune if you loosen your purse.'

They reached a landing and hailed a wherry. The nearest watermen ignored them but another was persuaded they were not drunk and would pay well to be taken upriver. The early evening sun, low on the river, reflected in the eddies and currents on the water's surface as they were rowed towards the Archbishop's residence. Peering into the strong light, they could see its outline.

'Tom, we are too late!' Edmund cried, pointing at smoke billowing into the sky.

Tom had not expected this. Surely the Apprentices have not sacked Lambeth Palace? If so, the King will have them run down in the streets. Maybe Edmund was right and London had gone mad. The light was fading as they scrambled off the boat and up the landing steps. They could

hear the crowd on the other side of the palace, roaring and beating the ground like an angry, taunted beast. They worked their way upriver along the side of the palace fronting on to the Thames. Tom had no idea what they could achieve when they reached the mob.

'Tom. We must get to the palace entrance.'

They moved forward to the edge of the building's west side and carefully peered around the corner. It was both better and worse than Tom expected. The palace had not been taken. The smoke was from two large bonfires lit by the Apprentices in the palace gardens. They had ripped up fencing and wooden sheds for fuel. There was no sign of Apprentices in the palace building. But the crowd was growing each minute as a stream of men arrived from London Bridge. He had seen the Apprentices massing before, looking for trouble, but this was something very different. Not simply brooding and angry, this was organised revolt.

Everyone was looking towards the palace entrance, so Tom waved Edmund forward. They stood at the back of a growing throng as the Apprentices assembled.

'Where are the soldiers? God's wounds, where are the soldiers?' Edmund seethed.

Tom considered the situation. The crowd was a potential threat to the palace but, with luck, their anger would blow itself out like a spring storm. However, if a platoon of soldiers waded into them? Tom shuddered at the prospect.

Another fire broke out by the garden wall of the palace. More cheers and chanting. Apprentices marched around the fire, shouting at the top of their voices. It was clear who they wanted: William Laud, the Archbishop of Canterbury. Tom was reminded of a story told to him by an English trader from the New World, who had witnessed American Indians dancing around a campfire. Who were the savages now? The warm May day had given way to a crisp, cold evening as the crowd quietened and a single voice emerged above the crackling of the fires. Tom strained his ears but could not hear the words.

'Come, Edmund, let us get closer. But keep that bloody sword hidden.'

The two friends worked their way towards the palace gates. Slowly they edged forward into the middle of a hushed crowd of protestors listening intently to the speaker. He was standing on a low stone wall in front of the largest fire with his back to Tom and Edmund. He turned his face right and left as he addressed the crowd, his outstretched arms and shaking fists caught in profile by the red flames behind. Tom looked past the man into a sea of faces, lit by the bonfire's glow. One looked familiar.

'Nicholas Culpeper? Is that Nicholas Culpeper?' Tom whispered to himself.

Tom recalled his meeting with the apothecary and his account of the Coleman Street radicals. Were they behind this? Had they organised the

Apprentices? Tom looked again but Culpeper's face was now obscured by smoke. Tom felt panic rising. If the Coleman Street radicals are here, Peter could be also. His brother's reputation, and the family's, would be in tatters if Edmund spotted him.

The man addressing the crowd turned towards the palace. He paused and pointed at the building. Tom could feel the heat from the spitting, crackling bonfire on his face. The man waved for silence.

'Archbishop Laud… Your Grace… can you hear us… can you here us, Your Grace?'

Each mention of 'Your Grace' prompted a chorus of jeers and whistles. Tom continued to search the crowd for Peter. The speaker signalled for silence again.

'If you can hear us, Your Grace, we have but one question.'

Tom was now sure Peter was not in the group by the nearest fire. He switched his attention to the next blaze. He could only see the faces illuminated by the flames but they were all that mattered. It was imperative Edmund did not spot his brother.

'One question,' the man paused again for effect, holding a finger in the air.

The orator was good. He's done this before. Peter, if you are here, keep yourself hidden.

'We want to know…'

Tom checked everyone he could see and started to feel a sense of relief.

'…no, we demand to know...'

Tom started as he spotted another familiar face. But not who he expected.

'We demand to know…'

It was Bartholomew Hopkins. Why on earth was Barty here?

'…who was responsible… for closing our Parliament.'

The man screamed the last four words at the top of his voice. The crowd erupted in cheers and Barty turned to his right to speak into the ear of someone.

The man next to Barty took off his hat to bend closer. Tom's mouth opened but no words came out. He was staring at the rugged features of Robert Petty.

Chapter 12

14th May 1640
Clerkenwell

The carriage rocked gently as it manoeuvred its passage through the busy streets.

Tom gently held Elizabeth's arm and touched her neck with his other hand. The coach pitched forward and his body slid towards her.

'You may hold my wrist a little tighter, Thomas Tallant. I will not break.'

He did as he was told and felt the warmth of her skin. Elizabeth was facing him, across the carriage. She looked deeply into his eyes.

'What do you feel, Tom?'

He did not answer. Tom was finding it hard to stop his fingertips wandering.

'I... I am not sure.'

In truth, he had never been more certain.

'Keep pressing gently, on my wrist, where your fingers are. Keep pressing.'

And there it was, under his fingers. A gentle pulsing.

'I have it, yes, definitely.'

'Good. Now, with your right hand, press there... no, not there, further over, against the side of my neck.'

The coach lurched to the right and Tom was thrown to one side. He steadied his position and gently picked up Elizabeth's wrist again. He touched her neck with his other hand, concentrated hard and, again, could feel a gentle pulsing.

'I have it again, the same as your wrist but also now in your neck.

'You see. William Harvey is right. Du Mutu Cordis.'

'Du Mutu...?'

'Du Mutu Cordis... Harvey's work on the heart and how it works. The pulse you feel is my blood being pumped around my body.' She gave Tom a knowing smile. 'You will have to take my word for it Thomas Tallant, but if you were to place your hand on my heart, you would feel the beating that drives the pulse. I acquired Harvey's book last year but needed Nicholas's help with the Latin to understand it fully. For hundreds of years physicians have continued to believe that blood forms in the liver and the heart and travels to the organs where it is consumed. If so, where are the organs after my wrist? At the ends of my fingers? Harvey has a new explanation. He says blood is pumped around the body by the heart, and he is right.'

'So the same blood I can feel entering your fingers through your wrist will eventually pass through your neck to your head?'

'Yes!'

'But where does it go then?'

'Back to the heart to be pumped around again!'

Elizabeth sat back in her seat and Tom reluctantly released his hold.

'Most of the treatments used today are over a thousand years old. Why have we learned nothing new? There is so much to discover, Tom, about our bodies, the world we live in and the stars above. And it is all connected! William Harvey is a physician, but do you know he studied in Padua where it's said he met Galileo!'

Elizabeth fell silent and looked out of the carriage window. They were returning from a trip to the theatre. Tom reflected that he'd never known anyone with such a hunger for life and all its mysteries. Elizabeth was as happy immersed in her books as sitting in the audience at the Red Bull Playhouse. Tom smiled as he pictured her crying with laughter tonight, tears of glee running down her face as the jigging clown Andrew Cane mercilessly satirised the country's leaders. Tom had winced at Cane's barbed jibes. The Privy Council wouldn't stand for it, but he was very funny. We could have done with him in Parliament.

Tom had raised an eyebrow when Elizabeth suggested the Red Bull. Built around the courtyard of a Clerkenwell tavern, it had a reputation for rowdiness, petty thievery and trouble. Although on the fringes of the city, it was one of London's largest playhouses. On a busy afternoon a thousand or more would crowd into the yard and surrounding galleries.

She had assured him the audience was better behaved these days and he must not miss one of the final performances by the Prince Charles Players before they moved to the Fortune Theatre in nearby Whitecross Street. And so they had pushed through the crush in the arched entrance on St John Street, past the audience standing in the courtyard, to take their seats in a gallery overlooking the right side of the stage. There were a few other women in the audience, some wearing masks, but Elizabeth was clearly at home and well known. Men doffed their hats, and made way for Miss Elizabeth.

He had enjoyed the play, knockabout stuff with a simple plot designed, as far as Tom could see, to present frequent opportunities for dramatic stage effects. Fireworks exploded, smoke appeared and members of the cast disappeared through trapdoors in the stage floor. A golden sun rose and set through an ingenious system of ropes and pulleys on a tower at the back of the stage, and each new spectacle drew raucous cheers from the rowdy audience.

Sitting in the carriage, Tom realised he had not thought once about his troubles throughout the afternoon's performance—a rare occurrence. His face clouded as the many unanswered questions returned, and he felt

emptied by a depth of despair that surprised then overwhelmed him. He bowed his head.

'What is it, Tom? Did you not enjoy the entertainment?' Elizabeth asked. 'Not the wittiest, I grant you, but there's usually fire and fun at the Red Bull!'

Tom gave her a tired smile, but said nothing. He had been caught off-guard and could feel tears coming to his eyes.

Elizabeth leaned across and touched his arm. 'Tom, is there something the matter?'

He was about to put on his brave face and change the subject but he no longer had it in him. Elizabeth's presence had disarmed him and he felt an overwhelming need to rest his head in her lap and wish the world away.

'I do not... do not know how to explain. My mind has been much troubled for weeks. My afternoon with you is the first respite I have known from the questions raging in my head. However, our day is over and I feel the shadows return. I am not sure if I have the strength to take them on again.'

His weary mind drifted towards the even clip-clop of the carriage horse as it drew them along the country lane towards Elizabeth's house. She squeezed his arm.

'Tom, if it will help to share your troubles with me, I would like to hear them.'

Tom did not wish to involve Elizabeth but was too exhausted to resist her gentle urging. And so he told his story, of the deaths of Joseph Vennel and Hugh Swofford, the way he and his father had been implicated in both, the accusation of 'flying demons', the dogged investigation by Robert Petty and persecution by magistrate Franklin, the mystery man with the beard and the newly discovered link between his friend in Parliament, Bartholomew Hopkins, and Petty.

'The worst of it all is I bring much of this on myself,' he continued. 'My father says I'm headstrong, and I am. Act first, think later. And I never seem to learn. Since my return from India he thinks I've become worse—cocksure and selfish, and maybe he's right. I've ignored his warnings about Petty and the investigation. And look where that's got me.'

Tom heard the self-pity in his voice, and felt disgusted. Being with Elizabeth made him examine himself, how he thought and behaved. It wasn't comfortable, but he couldn't ignore or stop it. He needed to be with her too much. They sat silently until the coach passed the turn to his parents' house. They would soon be at Elizabeth's home. Eventually she spoke.

'Thomas Tallant, you may be headstrong but you are not selfish. Look how you reached out to help me. You care about people and it's a good thing to have the mettle to plunge in where others fear to tread. As for

these events, you have set me a puzzle. There will be a common thread linking them and we must find it. However, one thing I do know.'

Elizabeth moved forward in her seat, took hold of Tom's hand and held his gaze. Tom felt his heart would burst.

'These things you have described are vexing but no more than the intrigues of mere mortals. The moon will wax and wane until the day arrives when all this will be forgotten, and you will be left with the eternal truths of life... and love.' She squeezed his hand again.

Tom looked into Elizabeth's eyes, and whispered, 'Love, all alike, no season knows, nor clime, Nor hours, days, months, which are...'

Elizabeth broke into a beaming smile and finished the verse '... which are the rags of time. Thomas Tallant, you know John Donne?'

'He is my constant companion at sea. Donne knows the words I cannot find, yet we think and feel as brothers.'

The carriage drew up outside Elizabeth's house and they sat in silence. Elizabeth reached over and kissed Tom softly on the mouth.

She breathed in his ear: 'Look, and to-morrow late, tell me, whether both th' Indias of spice and mine be where thou left'st them... or lie here with me?'

Then she was gone. Out of the carriage and running to the front door, which was being opened by a servant.

He sat in the empty carriage, his senses overwhelmed. Her voice, the touch of her yielding mouth, her warmth, her breath in his ear, her very being was there, still with him. And every fibre of his body felt elation.

Tom returned to Bolton Hall in a daze, to be greeted by a familiar face as he entered the dining room.

'Tom. Is it really you? Ralph, he has grown so! Come nearer the candlelight and let me take a better look.'

It was Uncle John, his father's elder brother. Tall, strong, bluff, a smile never far from his face. Tom liked him very much.

Sir John Tallant was visiting London from his estate in Berkshire. He had married well, into a long-established county family, and settled down contentedly with his wife Mary. Six years ago he purchased a knighthood from the King and was now a pillar of the county establishment and a staunch supporter of the royal family.

Tom had not seen his uncle since he sailed for India. Uncle John's face and body looked a little heavier and his hair was starting to grey at the temples, but his voice and grip were as strong as ever. As they embraced, Tom caught the familiar fragrance of Castile soap, his uncle's favourite.

'Aye, he has grown sure enough,' his father replied. 'But he still has a little more growing to do, I fancy.'

Tom nodded and gave his father a rueful smile. He was not sure how much John knew about his Dutch folly, so he let his father's comment pass. They took supper in the dining room.

'Tom, your uncle and I were discussing the current unrest in London. He would value your view, both as a Member in Parliament and a witness to the disturbances outside Lambeth Palace.'

Tom straightened his back and looked at his father and uncle, reassuring figures throughout his life now sitting gravely and attentively, waiting for his opinion on the state of the nation. He tried to focus, his thoughts still with Elizabeth and her soft kiss.

Tom recounted what he had seen at Lambeth: the marching apprentices arriving from Southwark until well after midnight, the organisation required and the clear purpose of the demonstration, to put pressure on Archbishop Laud and blame him for the closure of Parliament.

'You see, John,' Tom's father turned to his brother, 'organisation and purpose, not what you'd expect from the Apprentices.'

His uncle looked grave.

'This is Pym's work, I am sure of it. He means to have Parliament recalled and is using the mob to make his case.'

Tom recalled his first sighting of John Pym, the small, unremarkable man pointed out by Barty on his initial visit to the Commons. Could he really be controlling the Apprentices?

His father leaned forward. 'Pym is clever and highly industrious. He is like the hub of a cartwheel, holding together the different spokes of dissent. He leaves no stone unturned. Tom, did you hear his speech in the chamber?'

Tom nodded. He could hardly forget it. Pym had spoken for over two hours, hunched over his notes, delivering a detailed list of Parliamentary grievances and demands. He was not the most gifted orator and Tom struggled to concentrate but, with each issue raised, Tom's attention strengthened. Pym was building a compelling argument against the King for redress of grievances.

'Pym presented a case for every group that might support Parliament and oppose the King,' Ralph Tallant continued, 'even the merchants. He salted his demands for religious freedom and Parliamentary independence with requests for reduced duties on tobacco from the colonies. Very clever.'

Uncle John pushed his chair back. 'Ralph, surely the merchants are not turning against their monarch?'

'The East India Company will tell you the merchants are happy, but they are not. Petitions of grievance have been suppressed by the board of directors, desperate not to rock the royal boat. And remember, the two merchants chosen by the City to be our Members of Parliament are both involved in the Massachusetts Bay Company, which has strong Puritan backing. Neither are friends to the crown.'

The Massachusetts Bay Company... where had Tom heard that? Nicholas Culpeper. Peter's involvement came flooding back. Tom had not felt able to tell his father or mother yet.

'The King does not help himself,' his father continued. 'There is little finesse in his approach. He recently required the City of London's aldermen to provide lists of the richest men in their wards, presumably so he could press them for money. But seven refused, and they have gone unpunished!'

John gave a low whistle. 'Is the King losing his grip?'

'He has too many people offering different advice and the Privy Council is in disarray. Some say "parley with the Scots"; others "stiffen our northern defences". The Earl of Strafford counsels war, of course, money or no money. And if the King cannot find funds, Strafford says he'll raise an Irish army, God help us.'

Tom's father leaned forward and lowered his voice. 'I have even heard talk of an approach to the Spanish!'

Uncle John looked aghast. 'But that would be madness, inviting a Catholic army to invade Protestant Scotland! Surely the King would not countenance it.'

Sir Ralph looked at his brother and shrugged. Tom was also surprised, both by the news and his father's knowledge. He may no longer be in Parliament, but clearly his intelligence networks remained active.

Ralph stood to stoke the fire. He sighed and looked at his brother, a log in his hand.

'This could get serious, John. Mark my words, there will be more riots, and they could spread from London.'

Sir Ralph threw the log into the burning grate, sending sparks and smoke across the room. The image was not lost on any present and there was a lengthy silence.

Sir Ralph turned to his brother. 'I know your sympathies lie with the King and I respect your view, but I would counsel caution. There is growing support for Parliament across the country. What is the state of affairs in Winterbourne?'

'Oh, the estate and village are loyal. Do not worry about Mary and I. We live among upright, sensible folk. They will not turn on their King.'

'That may be so, John, but please be—'

Tom's father was interrupted by his wife whose head had appeared around the door.

'Ralph, you must come to the parlour. Isaac is there. He is in a terrible state.'

The three men followed Lady Beatrix as she hurried out of the room. They entered the parlour to see Isaac sitting at a table, drinking a pitcher of beer, rocking slightly, his face grey and covered with beads of sweat.

'Beatrix, does he have the ague… or worse?' Ralph asked. 'If so, he should not be here.'

Isaac tried to stand. He spoke in a hoarse whisper, his voice cracking as pain lanced through his damaged shoulder.

'Begging your pardon, Sir Ralph. I am not sick. I have just ridden from Thames Street. It has taken me most of the last three hours.'

Sir Ralph reached out to support Isaac's weight. 'Sit down, man. You're not fit to ride for two minutes, never mind three hours. Beatrix, get something stronger for Isaac. There's brandy in the dining room.'

Nobody spoke until Lady Beatrix returned and Isaac took a large draught of brandy. His shoulders relaxed but his hands continued to tremble. He turned to Sir Ralph.

'The city is in uproar, sire. The Apprentices have broken into White Lion prison, to free those arrested for the march on Lambeth Palace. I came across roads blocked with burning carts, barrels, tables and chairs, and was forced to use the side alleys to avoid attention. An honest man is not safe in his own city.'

'Lord God save us all,' Lady Beatrix whispered.

'Word is they plan to cross the river again,' Isaac continued, 'and attack another of the Archbishop's palaces, this time in Croydon… and—'

Sir Ralph poured Isaac another measure of brandy. 'Here, drink this, you are safe here. But why venture out if there is trouble on the streets?'

Isaac shifted his weight on the seat and gave an involuntary sob of pain.

'It's my sister's boy, master. Young Arthur. Been arrested for taking part in the march to Lambeth Palace. He was one of them banging a drum. They arrested a few of them. Said the drum-beaters were the ringleaders, calling the others to arms. But to Arthur, it was a bit of a lark. He's only seventeen.'

Tom sat down, facing Isaac. 'I am sure it will not come to anything, Isaac. He may be released by the Apprentices tonight.'

'You do not understand, Master Tom. He is not in the White Lion. They put him in Newgate.'

Tom saw his father and uncle exchange glances. His father looked down and frowned. Tom understood Isaac's anguish. If Arthur was in Newgate, the authorities must have special treatment in mind. If they believed he was a ringleader, they will get the names of others from him by any means.

'They will rack him, I know it.' Isaac cried in anguish. 'The bastards will rack him. And then what will he be good for? A cripple like his uncle with nothing to look forward to but a life of pain?'

Isaac's head dropped; tears flowed down his cheeks. Lady Beatrix moved towards Isaac who lifted his hand in apology for his cursing. She squeezed his hand and gently mopped Isaac's brow. His lean frame began to convulse in silent, shuddering sobs.

Tom spoke up. 'Isaac, leave this with me. There is someone I can speak to on Arthur's behalf. It may make a difference. I will see what I can do.'

Sir Ralph pulled his son to one side.

'Tom. What are you thinking? I understand and share your feelings for Isaac but it will not help to give him false hope. If they have locked up young Arthur in Newgate, there is nothing you or I can do to reach him. And it may not go well for you if you try.'

Tom said nothing. To Isaac, Arthur was the son he'd never had. Tom understood better than most just how much Isaac had suffered over the years. If the same thing now happened to Arthur, it would finish Isaac. He had to help, and knew he could. But it was a solution that filled him with misgivings.

Chapter 13

16th May 1640
King Street, Whitehall

Tom looked down King Street for a third time. It was still empty. He was early for his meeting. It had not been easy to place himself in the hands of Barty Hopkins after seeing him at Lambeth Palace and, as he stood shivering on this cold May morning in Whitehall, the first seeds of doubt were taking root. The soldier on guard duty nearby was paying Tom more attention with each passing minute.

Tom sensed his vulnerability. If the guard felt inclined, he could pluck Tom off the street in seconds. Whitehall was the King's official residence and reputedly the largest royal palace in Europe, a sprawling labyrinth of power. A soul could be swallowed in a moment and never seen again.

Tom concentrated on what lay ahead. He'd felt uneasy about approaching Barty. His connection to Robert Petty was worrying. Why had they been together at Lambeth? Barty supported the King and mixed with Royalist Members of both Houses. Perhaps Petty was really an agent for the Crown, not the Merchant Adventurers? Were he and Barty spying on the protest, gathering intelligence? If so, was Robert Petty investigating the deaths of the merchants Venell and Swofford on behalf of the Crown as well? If so, why?

Tom could draw only one conclusion from this tangle. However he looked at it, it made Robert Petty even more dangerous as an adversary. Tom recalled Isaac's dark assessment of Petty—a hard bastard not to be trusted—and shuddered in the keen wind.

A figure appeared in King Street. Bartholomew Hopkins's bustling stride was unmistakable, his cloak billowing around his short body. Tom raised his hand in salute and Barty waved back before clutching at his hat as the wind gusted along the street.

'Young Thomas. How good to see you on this, erm, fresh and bracing morning.'

'Thank you for arranging my audience at such short notice,' Tom replied. 'I was not sure you would still be in London following the dissolution, so I was glad to find you at your lodgings.'

'Oh yes, I will be here for a little while longer. Plenty to do, yes, plenty to do.'

Yes, plenty of Government business to do, no doubt. He was suspicious of Barty but try as he might, he could not dislike him. He was, as ever, kind and solicitous and had acted quickly to arrange the interview Tom sought. Barty clearly was well-connected in royal circles, and that was another cause for concern.

'Let us proceed. We must not be late.'

Barty ushered Tom across King Street towards the guard. He withdrew a small document from his cloak. Tom saw a red seal attached and seconds later the unsmiling sentry let them through to a small side street.

'Have you been in Whitehall before, Tom? No? It will seem more like a village than a single palace. There are buildings everywhere. The royal chambers are sumptuous, of course, but many of the other constructions are modest'— he smiled and made a small bow—'built for the humble servants of the Crown.'

They reached the end of the lane and turned onto a larger road which was also deserted. Tom lengthened his stride to keep pace with Barty's small bustling steps.

'You can find every kind of building here, all to serve the pleasure and needs of their Royal Highnesses. We have palaces, banqueting halls, chapels, bakers, butchers'—he turned towards a low building on their right with a small oak door—'even tennis courts, and if I am not mistaken, Henry Jermyn is about to finish his game.'

He pushed the door open, leant back and whispered, 'And no doubt triumphant again. Jermyn is very good, I am told. On no account ever play him for money.'

They entered a small, dark room. Barty nodded to a man sitting at a table and crossed to a door opposite. Tom could hear raised voices on the other side. Barty opened the door carefully and they stepped into a long, high-ceilinged chamber. Light spilled through a series of windows high up along one wall. Below, two men were running backwards and forwards, calling out to each other, their voices echoing across the room.

Tom had never seen a tennis court before. Henry Jermyn had his back to them, facing a man Tom did not recognise. A net was slung low across the width of the court separating the two players. To the left a low viewing gallery ran the length of the court, continuing part way along the rear wall. Each man held a small racquet in his hand. Jermyn's opponent appeared to be doing most of the running. Beyond that, Tom could not fathom what was going on.

'This is your final chance to get out of hazard, Rollo,' Jermyn shouted at the man who had stopped and was crouching, gulping lungfuls of air. 'You are no match this morning. Too much wine last night, I wager.'

Jermyn laughed, releasing a ball in his hand which he effortlessly struck hard and high past the other man. It bounced off the wall behind Rollo, who twisted backwards in time to lob the moving ball high over the net to the left of Jermyn where it bounced weakly off the sloping gallery roof. Jermyn had anticipated its trajectory and waited for it to land at his feet. The ball gave a low bounce and Jermyn imperiously swept it over the net with a stroke across his body. Rollo flung himself to his left in time to see

the ball whistle past his racquet into the corner of his court, where it skidded across the floor and came to a halt against the back wall.

Jermyn walked around the net and offered his hand.

'My match, I think, Rollo. Dinner is on you tonight.'

Rollo groaned, seized Jermyn's hand and levered himself to his feet, leaning on his racquet. 'Henry, you are too good for me.'

'I know,' Jermyn replied flashing Rollo a grin that died on his face when he turned and saw Tom and Barty at the end of the court. 'Pray excuse me, Rollo. Business.'

Jermyn walked off the court and passed Barty and Tom without saying a word. They followed him into the small entrance room where, placing his racquet on the table, he took a tankard of beer from his servant and threw himself into a chair. He drank the beer greedily, then held the tankard out for a refill as he dabbed the sweat off his face with a fine cloth. Tom noticed damp patches forming where Jermyn's light wool chemise touched his broad shoulders. He breathed evenly and appraised Tom with a bored expression. He finally spoke.

'Barty here tells me you want to see me. You require a favour. I must say, Tallant, you have a nerve after your previous impertinence. I gave you the opportunity to serve your King and, as I recall, you refused. Below you, was it ?'

Barty gave Tom a searching look. This would be as uncomfortable as Tom had feared.

'When Barty explained you had connections with the rabble that threatened His Grace the Archbishop of Canterbury's property in Lambeth, I cannot say I was surprised. Not perhaps as high and mighty as you make out, are you? But come, I am a civil fellow. Unlike you, I will listen to a request without sneering. It's called manners, Tallant. All a matter of breeding. Barty, will you leave us, please, so Mr Tallant and I can discuss his business.'

Barty bobbed a bow and, nodding at Tom, opened the studded door and went to the street outside, followed by Jermyn's servant. The door closed leaving Jermyn and Tom alone. The courtier made no move to offer Tom a seat or refreshment. This was not a meeting of equals.

'If you have any sense, you will be wondering why I have even troubled myself to see you,' Jermyn said.

Tom bridled. 'As Barty will have told you, I have changed my mind about your request to use my ships. In return I need you to arrange the release of Arthur Wetherall from prison.'

Jermyn gave a hollow laugh. 'Do you think I am dependent on your little craft to relay important intelligence for the King? The evening we met, I made alternative arrangements within the hour. You overestimate your value to me, Tallant. I have a network of ships and loyal captains across the south coast to call on when I need.'

Tom's heart sank. He suspected Jermyn was telling the truth. Offering to transport Jermyn's spies and coded messages was his one card to get Arthur free. Jermyn had trumped it easily.

Jermyn ran his finger around the lip of his empty tankard.

'No, you are of no particular value to me as a courier, Tallant. But I am not a man to bear grudges, and there is another service you can perform for your King. However, I must warn you, Tallant, not to try my patience.' He leaned forward and held Tom in his unblinking gaze. He spoke slowly. 'I will think particularly ill of another rejection.'

Tom swallowed hard. Jermyn's trap was set. If he accepted, Lord knows what skullduggery he would be embroiled in. If he declined, not only would Arthur be helpless, but Tom would have made a mortal enemy in Henry Jermyn, not a pleasant prospect. He took a deep breath. Once again, he was regretting his impulsive decision. Had he truly meant anything he had said to Elizabeth about realising his faults? Tom did care about Isaac but there was more. He felt something stronger, a growing anger that people like Jermyn could terrorise the Uffords, who served the Tallants loyally and deserved his protection. Protection? Hah, Tom Tallant against Henry Jermyn. How would that end? What a presumption to think he could ever bargain with this man. He was completely out of his depth, with no options.

'What is it you would have me do?'

Jermyn smiled. 'I know you are a merchant, Tallant, but I understand from Barty you have particular connections with the United Provinces.'

Tom bristled. Was he about to experience the anti-Dutch sentiment his father had warned him about? Jermyn sensed Tom's discomfort and held up a placatory hand.

'I have no truck with those, particularly among your fellow merchants, who denigrate the Dutch. In my business, Tallant, you learn to value every nation. Who knows when they will be your allies? Mind you, at the moment I might make an exception of the Scots, who are being particularly tiresome. And it is about the Scots I wish to speak to you.'

Tom had no idea where this conversation was leading.

'As you know, his Majesty has been sorely troubled by his misguided subjects in Scotland and their objections to his enlightened attempts to unify the church in our land. They have denigrated the Archbishop's sensible reforms, in particular the introduction of a common prayer book, in a most offensive manner. More in sorrow than anger, the King has concluded these dissenters must be rooted out and, as you know, is raising funds to equip an army to march to Scotland and reimpose his authority.'

This was common knowledge. What had it to do with him and his Dutch connection?

Jermyn paced the room. 'Both you and I, Tallant, have witnessed in the Commons the scandalous stratagems of Pym and others to thwart his

Majesty's legal right to raise funds from Parliament. But did you know Pym and his gang are not working alone? We have growing evidence they are acting in consort with the Scottish dissenters, to subvert his Majesty's position!'

Tom could not believe what he was hearing. Could this be true or was Jermyn bluffing?

'You have established a direct link between John Pym and the Scottish dissenters?'

'Not yet, but it will come. We already know that Puritan radicals here in London are assisting the Scots. And you would be a fool not to see the link between those Puritan radicals and the more outspoken Members in Parliament who are against our King, such as Pym.'

'But what evidence do you have of this radical support for the Scots, and what has any of this to do with me?'

Jermyn walked over to his cloak lying on top of an oak chest and took out a bundle of paper. He handed it to Tom. It was a pamphlet, similar to dozens being sold on the streets of London every day. Tom walked to the room's small window for better light and read out loud the pamphlet's title, depicted in large type: '"An INFORMATION from the States of the Kingdome of Scotland, to the Kingdome of England."'

Tom scanned the content. Its message was simple and powerful. The Scots were not the enemies. The enemies were the bishops and popish advisors who had poisoned the King's mind and made him turn against his own people north of the border. Tom put the pamphlet down. He could see why the King wanted this stopped.

'This was bought on the streets by St Paul's this very week,' said Jermyn. 'The Stationers' Company suspect a radical called Richard Overton is responsible. They have not yet caught him in the act, but they have discovered one thing.'

Jermyn picked up the pamphlet and pointed to the title page.

'My learned friends at the Company study every pamphlet, coranto and news sheet sold in this country and are experts in type and other printing symbols. They say each printer has his own style and layout, as distinctive as his handwriting and signature. See here,'— he jabbed at an ornate letter T at the head of the text—'and this'— pointing to a lion and unicorn crest at the top of the page.

'These symbols looked familiar but they could not trace them, despite studying every radical pamphlet produced in this country. Then one of their number, a Josiah Wilmot, had the bright notion of checking the overseas corantos as well. And there it was. The same type and symbols— on a legal news sheet produced in Amsterdam.'

Jermyn paused to let his words sink in.

'So you think these pamphlets are being printed in Amsterdam and shipped here clandestinely?'

'Absolutely. We have watched the ports closely but you know how much trade is passing through London from the United Provinces. Someone with determination and the right contacts could smuggle them in. No, this menace will not be stopped through chance discovery. It will be stopped through acquiring the right intelligence... and that is your job, Tallant. Why do you think I have taken you into my confidence on a matter of such importance to the King? Do you think I would normally share such information with the mere son of a spice merchant? I do it because I need your connections in London and Amsterdam to get to the bottom of this. People will talk to you. We need to know who is shipping the news sheets and then, through them, we can get Overton... unless of course, Tallant, you are the one responsible?'

Tom did not react. He was learning that having a conversation with Henry Jermyn was like playing cards for money. A stony expression was essential. Jermyn let his suggestion hang in the air before giving Tom a bored smile.

'No, I suspect even you have more sense than to get mixed up in this business. These news sheets are dangerous, Tallant. The Scots dissenters are using them to present their case directly to the people of London. Their argument is clever and effective. They claim to be the innocent party, simply wishing to be left alone to worship as they see fit. People are reading this and starting to be swayed. It is causing the King discomfort, and whenever that happens, it is my job to sort it out. On this occasion, I think there is a real problem. Frankly, this subversive pamphlet campaign is undermining the King's position just as he prepares to take on the Scots. And it must be stopped. Now!'

Jermyn slapped the table on his final word, making his empty tankard jump. Tom frowned. To help Arthur he would have to spy on fellow merchants including friends he had known for most of his life. And if he found anything, he would have to inform on them. Perhaps if he played along he could make Jermyn believe he was cooperating and this would at least buy Arthur time.

'And if I do as you wish, you will release the boy?'

'My dear Tallant. Your man is accused of leading a seditious riot against Lambeth Palace, not stealing apples from a market stall. These are very serious charges. However, I am not without influence. If you agree to investigate this matter, the boy will continue to be held in Newgate but he will not be interrogated, you have my word on that. What happens to him after that? Well, that will depend on what you come up with, Tallant, will it not?' Jermyn stood to leave. The audience was over.

He picked up his cloak and walked to the door. As he held the latch, he turned to Tom with eyes of stone: 'Oh, and Tallant, one word of this business to another soul and I will make it my personal business to ruin

you, your family and that drunken doxy who appears to have captured your heart.'

Chapter 14

18th August 1640
The Tallant warehouse

A coin tumbled through the air, capturing the rays of afternoon sun. Tom caught it cleanly and opened his palm. A new gold crown. He fingered its image of King Charles.

'Take a good look at it, Tom. It might be one of the last you ever see, if the King gets his way.'

His father picked another crown out of his purse and studied it carefully. 'What a bloody mess we are in... a terrible, bloody mess.'

Tom had rarely seen his father so despondent. They faced each other, sitting in the warehouse pepper store in front of the open hatch. Three months had passed since Tom's meeting with Henry Jermyn—a hot, stinking summer with the threat of plague heavy in the air. This week the weather had broken and now a cooling breeze was blowing off the river, ruffling his father's hair.

'To the current religious and political troubles, you can now add financial turmoil. A pox on this war with the Scots. They are massing on the border, the King is spoiling for a fight but he still has no money! Parliament would not fund him, so he closed it down and now His Majesty is closeted with the Earl of Strafford and his cronies, dreaming up madcap schemes to pay for his army.'

Sir Ralph jumped to his feet and paced the warehouse floor, too agitated to sit, the floorboards creaking under his heavy step.

'First, the King seizes the bullion in the Royal Mint even though it belongs to his creditors, merchants like me who provided him with funds in the first place. Eventually he graciously agrees to only keep a third of it! When will we see that again? Then he discovers the Mint is also holding gold and silver for the King of Spain. So His Royal Highness decides he will also have that. Has he gone mad? Can you imagine the repercussions? Any English ship in Spanish waters would be fair game. I am told officers of the Mint begged Charles to reconsider, closely followed by a deputation of Merchant Adventurers. So the odious Strafford said the Government would drop the idea if the merchants "lend" the King £40,000. And they have!'

Sir Ralph was in full flood, striding up and down, a cloud of dust stirred by his feet, his words tumbling out in a torrent, getting louder with each step. Tom knew not to interrupt. Muffled voices elsewhere in the warehouse had stopped. The whole building awaited the explosion. Sir Ralph did not lose his temper very often, but when he did, it was spectacular.

110

'Have you been to the Exchange today, Tom? The pepper market has collapsed. Why? Because the Chancellor of the Exchequer obtained a large amount of surplus stock from the East India Company on credit. He dumped it all on the market at a rock bottom price. It's raised £70,000 for the army fund but destroyed the pepper trade. No merchants can get true value for their stock because London is now knee-deep in dirt-cheap pepper! What is the Chancellor doing trading pepper, pray tell me? Maybe I should run the country's finances. Thank God our family does not rely on pepper as we once did, but there are many who do. It will be hard on them. Not that this concerns Strafford.'

Sir Ralph paused and took a deep breath. Here it comes, thought Tom.

'And then, when I believe no greater damage can be done—' another breath, Sir Ralph was struggling to keep his composure '— comes the final insult. The King desires to debase our currency, Tom, our commercial lifeblood. He is to instruct the Mint to produce shillings which will contain both silver and brass, worth three pence in total.'

Sir Ralph was now speaking with great deliberation through clenched teeth.

'Trade is slack because of unrest in the country. He has destroyed one of our prime spice markets, taken our bullion from under our noses, placed the whole merchant fleet at risk to Spanish attack... and now wants to degrade our currency... our reputation... the respect and trust we have earned as merchants... by creating tens of thousands of mean little BRASS LIES, each one STAMPED WITH HIS FACE!'

The final words erupted in a thunderous roar. His eyes and neck bulging, his face flushed crimson, Sir Ralph leapt towards the open hatch and flung the gold crown across the wharf into the river, then slumped back in his seat.

'No doubt this brass money will be used as another threat, to make the City advance him a further loan but, by God, it is making us a laughing stock.'

Tom had a pitcher of beer in the loft and he offered a mug to his father. They sat in silence as the muffled conversations below resumed. The storm had passed.

Finally his father spoke again, staring through the hatch at the sun's rays glittering on the Thames.

'You see, Tom, I have weathered heavy seas and can live with religious intolerance and political unrest. But without commercial stability we have no compass and are truly at the mercy of the elements. I daresay we will find ways to survive, the Tallants usually do, but we are sailing in dangerous, uncharted waters.'

Sir Ralph emptied his tankard and turned to his son.

'However, that is not why I visited, Tom. I am anxious to know how go your affairs. What news of Isaac's nephew? It was dangerous to put yourself in Henry Jermyn's debt.'

Tom thought about his undertaking to Jermyn back in May. He had searched all summer for information on the Dutch pamphlets, but to no avail.

'I felt the same after I met him, Father. It is hard to describe, but Jermyn has the… the smell of power about him.'

'The stench, you mean,' Sir Ralph snorted. 'It's a murky world he inhabits. You would do well to keep out of his clutches. The man is not to be trusted. I know you care for Isaac, as do we all. But I tell you, your search for the source of the Dutch news sheets has not gone down well with many Dutch and English merchants. They don't like you digging around for information about secret shipments, particularly if you're asking on behalf of the King. Once again I've been fence-mending. Tom, I must tell you your stock in the City is near rock bottom.'

Tom shrugged. He knew his father was right but, since his return from India ten months ago, it felt like anything he did caused offence to someone.

'It seems to have come to nothing anyway, Father. I asked my London contacts but no one knew anything. I even questioned Sam, our warehouse apprentice, who works for Sheffard's but he could not help. So I sailed to Amsterdam to investigate. I did trace the original owners of the type but they had lent it several years ago to another printer. Apparently it was then sold to a private individual and the trail went cold. I dreaded returning to Jermyn empty-handed and was shaking while I waited two hours to see his secretary at Whitehall. I am not sure which felt stronger, the relief or the anger, when I was finally told Jermyn had left London for the summer and was currently accompanying Her Majesty the Queen during her confinement at Oatlands Palace.'

'And let me guess, Jermyn had not left a message for you?'

'His secretary had never heard of me and said I was fortunate to see him when they were so busy with the King's business. I then tried my last few contacts before abandoning the search. Hopefully Jermyn is not interested in the pamphlets anymore and, as far as I know, Arthur is still alive in Newgate, unlike the two others they arrested at Lambeth. They went to the gibbet. At least I have saved him from that.'

'I thought you might say that, which is why I'm here.' Sir Ralph reached into his cloak pocket and pulled out a crumpled news sheet. 'The pamphlets are still being published, Tom. I acquired this in Thames Street yesterday.'

Tom took the pamphlet and smoothed out the creases. He read the title: "The Intentions of the Armie of the Kingdome of Scotland: Declared to their Bretheren of England by the Commisioners of the Late Parliament,

and by the Generall, Noblement, Barrons, and Other Officers of the Armie."

The news sheet spelt out the peaceful intentions of the Scottish army which was massing at the border. The boldness of the message and the open link with Parliament astonished him. Jermyn was right. This was an organised campaign to win the hearts of the people of London, here on the streets of the city.

'Her Majesty has safely been delivered of her son and the threat of plague is receding, so she and Jermyn will be back soon,' Sir Ralph continued. 'On his return to London Jermyn will be asked by Charles why he hasn't stopped those damned Scottish newsletters. At that point, Jermyn will be after you like the hounds of hell. The only difference is that three months will have elapsed and nothing achieved, which will not improve his temper.'

Tom shuddered. In his heart he had known this but had convinced himself that events had moved on. He had also been put off digging deeper by a furious row with his brother Peter, the like of which he had never experienced before.

Peter had visited him at the warehouse a month after his meeting with Jermyn. It was not a social call. He said the riverfront was alive with talk of Thomas Tallant's search for an illegal press. Peter wanted to know why his brother was helping Henry Jermyn to suppress the truth about the King's Scottish campaign.

Tom endured a ten minute sermon on the criminal acts of Archbishop Laud, imposing the English Book of Prayer on the Scots and making them observe the same popish ceremonies in their churches that he had inflicted on the English. Tom explained Arthur's predicament but Peter said he was a fool to expect Jermyn to lift a finger to help the boy. He accused Tom of doing Laud and Jermyn's dirty work before storming out of the warehouse, leaving Tom shaken to the core.

Tom told all this to Sir Ralph while they sat in the warehouse, and then also disclosed Peter's involvement with the Coleman Street radicals, which he didn't feel he could keep a secret any longer. Not for the first time, his father surprised him.

'Yes, I am aware of this. He has been active in Coleman Street since he approached the Massachusetts Bay Company to found colonies in America.' Sir Ralph held up his hand. 'I know, I know, there are hotheads there but every man must follow his course in life, and I trust Peter's judgement. But do not tell your mother. She worries too much.'

And you worry more than you are letting on, Tom thought. I can see it in your face.

Sir Ralph stood up wearily. 'So I am not sure what you will say to Henry Jermyn, but I suggest you have something prepared for when he comes calling, as he will. Best to admit defeat and let the boy Arthur take his

chances. You have done all you can, Tom. Everyone, including Isaac, recognises that.'

Sir Ralph headed towards the steps.

'By the way, I was at Sheffard's last week, to arrange their next ink shipment from Antwerp. I remembered Sam worked there in his spare time and asked how he was getting on. They looked a little puzzled as he had not been with them for over two months. They assumed he was too busy at the warehouse. I don't think they were best pleased, Tom, as he did not give them notice he was leaving. You might want to have a word with that young man about his manners.'

Chapter 15

20th August 1640
Thames Street

Tom pressed his back against a wall and held his breath. Rivulets of water seeped through his cloak collar and down his back. He shuddered and looked skywards. London was blanketed in unseasonal grey cloud and the rain had been relentless since first light. Tom was glad. Everyone was hiding beneath their cloaks and hats, looking for a safe footing as summer dust turned to thick mud. No one was paying attention to others, which suited Tom because he was in secret pursuit of Samuel Barnes.

Isaac had confirmed Sam still worked for Sheffard's, often arriving at the warehouse in the morning with fresh ink stains on his hands.

'But I think he's getting tired, Master. Twice last week I spotted mistakes in the stock ledger,' said Isaac. 'Sam apologised but I can see his mind has not been on the job. I will give it another few days and have a word, if it's still a problem.'

So Tom was now following his apprentice, keeping out of sight. If Sam was still printing, but not for Sheffard, then for whom? And ' as he keeping it secret? If they were printing illegally, Sam might be ' find out from them who was distributing the Scottish pamphlets. He had watched his young apprentice leave work at six that evening and walk up the path to Thames Street. He paused and turned left, disappearing from view. So far, so good, Tom thought, as he put on his thickest cloak and walked briskly into the rain. Sheffard's was located near Lombard Street. Sam was heading in the right direction.

Tom followed Sam down Thames Street and right onto Fish Street Hill, the main road north from London Bridge. It was easy to remain hidden among the crowds on the Hill and, as he carried on to Grace Church Street, Tom began to relax. Sam was heading for Sheffard's, and when his young apprentice turned left into Lombard Street Tom's relief turned to shame for doubting him.

As soon as he moves into Pope's Head Alley, Tom thought, I will return home with my tail between my legs, and no closer to tracing the source of these pamphlets. He felt despair seeping into his bones as the rain soaked through his clothes. What would he tell Jermyn?

Lost in his thoughts, Tom noticed with a start that he had passed Pope's Head Alley on his right. He went back and looked down the dark lane but could not see Sam. Damnation! After walking miles in the pouring rain, he had missed the moment of proof he was seeking. His boots were soaked and he could feel the cold water numbing his toes.

With a weary sigh he peered ahead, along Lombard Street. There was Sam striding through the rain, head still bowed. What are you up to, Tom thought, and, with all subterfuge abandoned, he started running up Lombard Street. Tom slid and slipped in the deepening mud as he entered Poultry in time to see Sam cut down Old Jewry on his right. Tom began to panic. If he gets too far ahead of me, I will lose him in the alleys.

Tom ran to the entrance of Old Jewry and turned into the lane. Through a curtain of rain a dark figure wearing a blue cloak loomed into view. Tom tried to stop but slid at full speed into the man's back. He bounced off the stranger and landed in the mud of the street.

'I must apologise, sir,' Tom spluttered, as he struggled to gain his footing. 'I was running—' The words died in Tom's throat. The man was striding off down old Jewry without a backward glance. There, only yards ahead, Sam Barnes was stooping down, squeezing water out of his cloak ends. Tom scrambled to his feet and quickly stepped back into Poultry, rubbing his arm. The stranger's body had been as hard as iron. If he had not collided with the man, he could have run straight into Sam. How would he have explained that?

Tom pushed the question to one side. He must not lose sight of Sam. He waited another five seconds before carefully peering into Old Jewry in time to see his apprentice disappear around a corner. Here we go again. Minutes later Sam was on Coleman Street heading for the city wall at Moorgate. The rain appeared to be relenting as he passed through the wall and started walking up Little Moor Fields. Tom peered into the gloom. Sam had disappeared but Tom could see a sign for "Gunn Alley" with a painted cannon, swinging at the end of an entry on his left. He stopped and looked around the corner. Sam was standing at the end of the alley. He looked around before disappearing through a doorway. Tom hurried down the alley, saw the sign depicting three barrels above the doorway and his heart sank. He'd heard of The Three Tuns tavern. Had he half-drowned to witness Sam getting drunk with friends? Should he wait outside for Sam? But then Tom would not see who Sam was meeting. He shivered with cold as a stream of water poured off the tavern roof and formed a lake around his feet. The thought of spending another minute in the downpour made the decision easy.

The air in the Three Tuns was thick with the steam of drying clothes, the smell of cooked meat and a clamour of conversation. Tom stood near the entrance and surveyed the single-roomed tavern. It did not take long to spot Sam, sitting at a table with his back to the entrance. Tom counted four other men at the same table and knew in an instant they were not apprentices. Too old and, by the look of them, too worldly-wise.

Tom took off his cloak, hung it by the fire and found a table near Sam, sitting back to back to his apprentice. He could hear the toasts and cheers

as more ale arrived at Sam's table. Tom ordered food, tried to get sensation back in his feet and fingers, and listened carefully.

An hour later, Tom had heard enough. Sam's party was celebrating the publication of a pamphlet but he couldn't see any on their table. Sam had said little but enough to convince Tom his tongue had been loosened by the ale. It was time to act. He took a deep breath and, swivelling on his bench seat, tapped Sam on the shoulder. Sam did not notice but the others did. The conversation stopped as Tom tapped Sam's shoulder again. His apprentice turned and the grin on his face froze.

'Master Tom? What are you doing here?'

'Sheltering from the rain and supping an ale like you, Sam. Will you not introduce me to your friends?'

The mood changed. Sam stuttered and tried to say something. A large man in a red jerkin spoke.

'Who do you be, brother, if you are acquainted with our friend Samuel?'

Sam looked at the rushes on the tavern floor, unable to speak.

'I am Thomas Tallant, the merchant, and Sam is my apprentice.'

Tom did not expect what happened next. To a man, they leapt to their feet and cheered at the top of their voices. Tom was slapped on the back, offered a place on the bench next to Sam and had his hand shaken vigorously by each man in turn. Red Jerkin spoke again.

'I propose a toast. To Master Thomas Tallant and the "Perfumed Press".'

The four men roared with laughter and banged the table with their tankards. Red Jerkin winked at Tom and sat down again.

Tom's mind was racing. What was going on? All the colour had drained from Sam's face.

'So, another pamphlet successfully printed, gentlemen?' Tom said.

The men nodded and smiled at each other.

'But not here? I was hoping to see a copy.'

The table fell silent and Red Jerkin grabbed Tom's arm. He pulled him close and whispered hoarsely, 'Steady there, friend. Keep your voice down. You know we cannot show it here. The Stationer's Company has spies everywhere.'

'I need to piss.' It was Sam, stumbling from his seat and heading unsteadily for the door.

Tom wanted to follow but that would arouse suspicion. What had Sam said to make him so popular? For some reason, he was seen as a benefactor by this group. When their senses cleared, these men would wonder why he was in the tavern. He had to uncover the truth before that happened. He ordered more ale. The mood lifted and the men broke into individual conversations around the table. Sam returned and sat silently next to Tom, who turned and whispered in his ear. 'Sam, I will soon order another ale for everyone and then you and I are going to leave.

117

Understood?' Sam nodded glumly. 'And keep smiling, for goodness sake. We do not want to raise any suspicions, do we?'

Tom chose his moment ten minutes later. He ordered food and more ale and, as the trays of meat arrived, he stood.

'Gentlemen. Sam and I must leave you. We are expecting a cargo from Antwerp on the morning tide so we will be at work by daybreak.' Groans and shaking of heads around the table. 'Yes. Pity poor us! But you have reason to celebrate and I'— here Tom lowered his voice— 'I thank you for the important work you are doing.'

There was a growl of appreciation around the table. Red Jerkin rose to his feet unsteadily and held Tom in a long and heavy embrace.

Tom shook his hand and hauled Sam to his feet, hissing in his ear, 'Get your cloak and let's be out of here before they realise I do not have a clue what I am talking about. You have some explaining to do, young man.'

Outside, the rain had finally ceased. Tom and Sam silently picked their way through the mud and the darkness of Gunn Alley, retracing their steps to Moorgate. Tom did not pause until they were back inside the city wall. He had intended to question Sam in the warmth of his warehouse but his anger would not allow him to wait. As they approached the end of Coleman Street Tom grabbed Sam's collar and hauled him down King's Arms Yard into the shadows. Sam squeaked in protest.

'Not a word, Sam, or I will not answer for my actions.'

Tom spat his words into Sam's terrified face. Near the end of the yard, Tom spotted a recessed doorway and pushed his apprentice into it. The moon slipped from behind a cloud, revealing Sam's sullen form in the doorway. He said nothing. Tom tried to speak with a measured voice but his fury was near the surface.

'Sam. You must tell me this minute what is going on. Who are those men? What is the Perfumed Press? And why do they cheer me like a hero?'

Tom tried to maintain his composure. Sam mumbled something.

'What was that?'

Sam raised his head, his tear-stained face shining in the moonlight.

'I said you have no right. You have no right to drag me into a side alley and question me like this. I am your apprentice. There are rules about how a master should treat his app—'

Tom grabbed Sam by the throat and threw him against the doorway, the back of his head hitting the door. Sam slumped forward and Tom grabbed his cloak with his left hand. His right fist arced and buried itself in the apprentice's stomach. The young man groaned as his legs collapsed beneath him. Tom released his grip and Sam slid to the floor, gasping for breath.

Tom threw himself back against the wall and stood panting, looking up at the stars. Months of anxiety and frustration had erupted in twenty

seconds of violence. Sam was soon on his hands and knees, puking like a dog. Eventually he stopped retching and crawled to the doorway where he sat, breathing heavily. Tom slid down the wall to sit next to him.

'Sam, I have been forced to beat sense into you because you do not appear to realise the trouble you could be in. You must tell me all you know about the men you were with tonight. They are not from Sheffard's, are they? They are printing illegal pamphlets. Am I right?'

Sam nodded his head faintly. Tom softened his tone.

'Sam, I understand it takes precious little to get on the wrong side of the Stationer's Company. What are your friends agitating for? Parliament to be opened again?' Tom lent towards Sam and lowered his voice. 'To be honest, Sam. I see the truth in some of what they write. However, it is still illegal. You should have no part of it and you certainly should not have involved me. What did you tell them? That I approve of what they are doing?'

Sam nodded again. Tom relaxed a little. The apprentice had put him in a difficult position but maybe he could turn it to his advantage.

'You must cease working for this group. But first I need you to find something out for me. Will you do that?'

Again a nod from the young man.

'Sam, I want you to talk to your friends and see if they know anything about the smuggling of seditious pamphlets into London from Amsterdam. They are causing a stir across the city and I am sure they will have seen them. Perhaps they know the people behind them. Have they spoken about a man called Richard Overton?'

Sam did not move.

'The pamphlets are supporting the Scottish cause against the King. The latest is on the streets this week.'

Tom felt Sam's body stiffen. Good. He does know something. Tom scrambled onto his haunches and faced the young apprentice. He put his hand on his shoulder. The boy flinched.

'Come, Sam. I will not hurt you again but I think you know about this. For your own safety, you must tell me.'

Sam's head fell forward as he sobbed once more.

'I did not mean to, Master Thomas. I first met them in a tavern while working at Sheffard's. We got to meeting regular. They got me drunk a few times and they started telling me about what they were printing. How the people had the right to have a voice. I... I think they are right, Master Thomas.'

Tom nodded. He was making progress but every minute he expected one of the local whores to stumble into the yard with a customer. His time was limited.

119

'I understand, Sam. But these men, do they know the printers of the Scottish pamphlets? Pray, tell me if they do and we can get home and into dry clothes.'

Another long pause.

'It's them,' Sam mumbled.

'Who's them?' Tom replied impatiently.

'The men in the Three Tuns. They are printing the Scottish papers.'

Tom's tired mind ached with confusion. 'But Sam, that cannot be. They were celebrating finishing a print here in London tonight. I heard them. The Scottish papers are being smuggled in from Amsterdam.'

'They are not.'

'What do you mean? I have it on the highest authority that they—'

'Don't know what you know, Master, but it can't beat the authority of seeing the newsletters rolling off the press, like I have.'

Tom sat back. He was struggling to take it all in. 'But the type and printer's blocks are Dutch.'

'I know,' Sam replied, shifting his position on the ground.

Tom could feel his irritation rise again. He did not have time for this guessing game. Sam must tell him everything he knew. There was a noise at the entrance of the yard. Tom could see the shape of someone walking towards them. Not now, when I am finally getting to the truth.

The figure stopped and paused, followed by the unmistakable sound of a man urinating against a wall. His noisy pissing went on forever, but eventually he moved back from the wall, sighed, stretched and stumbled back into Coleman Street.

'Sam. We do not have long. Tell me everything. If the papers are being smuggled—'

'I told you, they are not. The men explained it to me. It was too dangerous to bring the pamphlets in from Amsterdam each time they printed a new edition. Much better to smuggle once than twenty times over, they said. Less risk.'

The truth hit Tom and his heart leapt. It was not the pamphlets that had been smuggled into London. It was the type. Of course, and the type would be easier to hide than a bulky cargo of news sheets. Once they had it, they could set up in a cellar outside the city wall, close to the Three Tuns, and print the pamphlets right under the noses of the Stationer's Company. Using the Dutch type led the trail away from their door and overseas, back to Amsterdam. Simple but brilliant.

Tom could not believe his luck. He could now present Henry Jermyn with information to stop both the distribution and production of the Scottish pamphlets here in London.

'Sam, you do not understand, but you have done me a great service. All will be well but you must immediately disassociate yourself from these people because very soon they will be arrested by the authorities. I

understand your sympathies but the words they are printing are not only illegal, they are seditious, possibly treasonable. I must stop them.'

'But you cannot report them, Master Thomas.'

Tom studied Sam's face. The young apprentice clearly believed in his friends' campaign for a free voice and Tom admired that. But he had Arthur to think of and, anyway, these men were swimming in very deep waters. Too deep for him and Sam.

'I must, Sam.'

'No, you cannot Master. You cannot.'

An uneasy feeling formed in the pit of Tom's stomach. His memory flashed back to the Three Tuns and the reception he had been given by Sam's friends.

'Master, the type... it was... it was me who smuggled it in for them... on one of your boats.'

Shock gripped Tom's gut. His breathing became ragged.

'I think that was why they got friendly with me,' Sam continued, 'when they found out I worked at a merchant warehouse. They said it would do no one harm if I could get the type into the country. It would fool the Stationers' and keep them off their back. It would be my contribution to the cause. And, as I said, Master, I agreed with what they believed in. They said if I told them the name of the ship and when it would be in Amsterdam, their contacts over there would smuggle it on board. My job was to suggest a safe place to store it in the barky and retrieve it when tshe docked back in London.'

Sam's voice—that stupid, dull, country voice—was, word by word, dismantling Tom's world.

'But how could I get their men onto our ship while it was docked in Amsterdam? And then it occurred to me. I didn't have to. They could hide the type and blocks in the cargo on the quayside and watch it being loaded for them into the hold. But I needed a cargo they could find and that I would reach first when it landed here at the warehouse. Then I remembered your experiment, Master, what was it... the turmeric? It had not sold in Amsterdam, as we feared, and was due to be loaded onto the next boat returning to London. I could not believe my luck. I knew it had never left the warehouse in Amsterdam because, begging your pardon, Master, no one knew what to do with it. So I told the printers exactly where to find it. Their mates broke in one night, planted the type in the sacks of turmeric, carefully resealed them, and took a bag of pepper to cover their tracks. Two weeks later, the boat arrived back in London. No one here wanted to tell you all the turmeric had been returned, so I offered to store it in the warehouse, out of the way.'

Tom surveyed the calamity. Jermyn had been joking when he asked if Tom was responsible for smuggling the pamphlets in. What would he do if he knew the truth? How could Tom now uncover this plot and save

Arthur? Perhaps he could reveal the scheme but deny any involvement by his company. After all, it would be his word against Red Jerkin and his gang. Sam would keep his mouth shut, he'd see to that. It would be risky but he could probably pull it off.

The next words from his apprentice killed that hope at birth.

'Then I discovered most of the sacks had been fouled by sea water. It had been a bad crossing, heavy seas, and some of the hatch covers had blown open. The sacks had been sitting in sea water for days. I opened them carefully. All the contents, the turmeric, the type and the blocks, were soaking wet. And everything—'

'Stank of turmeric,' Tom said flatly.

'Yes, Master. But worse. The metal type cleaned up well enough but the wooden blocks of big fancy letters and page headings had turned bright yellow. I scrubbed and washed them but it wouldn't come off. I met the men in the White Bull the next night and handed it over, the type, the blocks, everything. I was glad to get it off my hands. Three or four days later, I went as usual to help with printing the next pamphlet and could smell the spice as I walked into the print shop. The men thought it was a right joke.'

'The Perfumed Press?'

'Yes, Master. And I am sorry to say I told them you had known about the shipment and been glad to help, but you'd do it once only. I was terrified they would ask me to smuggle something else and did not know what to say.'

Tom was numb. So that was why he had been greeted like a hero in the tavern. Christ alive. He was in deep trouble. He was known throughout the port of London for his turmeric shipment— Tom's Folly. It was like placing his personal signature on the seditious Dutch press.

They both sat in silence for five minutes as Tom shook uncontrollably. He was cold, wet and in despair. Without looking at Sam, he hauled himself to his feet and tramped down the alley towards Coleman Street before turning left for the river, the young apprentice trailing in his wake.

A figure stepped out of a doorway in King's Head Alley and slowly walked to where Tom and Sam had been sitting. He idly poked the pool of Sam's vomit with the toe of his boot, then turned his bearded face to the moonlight, sniffed the air and, gathering in his dripping blue cloak, strolled away.

Chapter 16

25th August 1640
Grub Street, North London

'Tom. This is wonderful. Just like the old days.'

Edmund Dalloway grinned in the gloom and punched Tom playfully on the arm.

'Sssh, Edmund. We must be careful… and quiet.'

Tom, Edmund and Sam Barnes were standing near the entrance to Grub Street, not far from the Three Tuns. Daylight was fading. Edmund was in high spirits and had not ceased talking since leaving the warehouse. Sam looked miserable, bemused by Edmund's chatter.

It had been a risk asking for Edmund's assistance but Tom realised he had little choice. He must retrieve the type and blocks from Red Jerkin and his friends. For that, he needed help, both to carry the heavy mix of metal and wooden type, and in case things cut up rough. Sam would simply lead them to the printing works before making himself scarce.

Tom knew Edmund would be eager to thwart the printers. The King had finally marched north that very week to confront the Scots and Edmund was anxious to support his monarch however possible. Anyway, Tom did not know who else to trust. He and Edmund had been through many scrapes in their youth and they worked well as a team.

'Brandy, Tom?' He turned to see Edmund producing a bottle from a cloak pocket. 'No? Sam, how about you?'

The young man flushed and shook his head vehemently. It would be a while before he touched drink again. They set off.

'Sam, you must lead the way from here,' Tom said. 'Remember. You take us to the front door but no further. Then you must return immediately to the warehouse.'

Sam nodded. Tom could see he simply wanted this nightmare to end. He had told Tom the men only used their first names but he'd heard the leader being referred to as 'Brother Richard'. Tom was sure he now had Overton in his sights.

They could see lights within the timber framed houses and shops as they moved along Grub Street. Ahead, a door opened and a man was hurled into the street. His hat followed.

A voice shouted, 'Take a nap outside if you cannot pay for your ale,' followed by drunken laughter.

The man groaned as the three men stepped over his body and continued their journey.

'Good evening, my prime young bucks. Come in out of the cold, won't you, and share some refreshment with my ladies. We'll make a merry party.'

A diminutive female figure moved out of the shadows and approached Edmund. Her body was the size of a growing girl but she had a lined and tired face, crusted with white powder. Lips crudely painted scarlet, her hair was piled high on her head, also thick with powder and fixed with pins, feathers and ribbons.

The madame stood in front of Edmund and slowly pushed his chin down with the end of her fan until he was looking directly down the plunging neckline of her red satin dress.

'So, what's your fancy, my handsome? I've got young Nancy upstairs. Not long arrived from the country. Fresh as a daisy. Or perhaps you'd like someone with a little more experience?'

She pushed her breasts up with both hands until one spilled out of her dress. She leaned forward to Edmund.

'A little taste of what's on offer, young man, and all clean as a whistle, I promise you that.'

The woman stepped back and smiled, revealing a mouth of gaps and yellow stumps.

'My dear lady,' Edmund gave a short bow. 'I can assure you nothing would give me greater pleasure but my friends and I are on urgent business and we cannot tarry. Another time perhaps?'

Before the woman could answer he propelled a gawping Sam forward and up the street.

The woman shouted back. 'Please yourself, but if it's a shaking of the sheets you're after, you won't find a better house north of the city wall.'

If we carry on like this, Tom thought, we will have the attention of all Grub Street by the time we reach the secret press. At least Edmund declined the invitation. The street was growing darker as the upper floors of the buildings—the jetties—leaned forward steeply on either side, almost touching. Tom jumped to one side as a woman emptied a pail from a second floor window. Sam pulled at his arm.

'It's not far, Master Thomas. You will see an alley on our left in about twenty paces. The door to the press is halfway down, on the right.'

'Is that the only way in and out of the building?'

'As far as I know. The printing press is in the cellar, to hide the noise. They use the other rooms for storing paper, ink, spare parts and finished pamphlets. There's also a room with a couple of truckle beds and a pantry. The privy's in the backyard.'

This end of Grub Street was empty, so they ran to the alley's entrance. Tom looked down its length. No one in sight. Led by Sam, they entered the narrow backstreet with its houses on both sides fronting onto the alley.

They reached a building on their right with a studded oak door which looked new.

'They changed the door after moving in, to keep the press secure,' Sam whispered. Tom gently pushed. It was locked and well built. Breaking through was not an option. Tom stepped back and surveyed the front of the building, two stories high with three windows, two on the first floor and one to the right on the ground floor, next to the oak door. The house was in darkness.

'And you say someone will be in?' Tom whispered. 'I see no lamps.'

'They will be working in the cellar. Likely two or three of them. They do that in the evening. They show no lights to keep attention away.'

'Right, Sam. Your job is done. Off with you.'

'There's one more thing, Master Thomas. They use a special knock as a signal. Two knocks together, a pause, then three more knocks together.'

'Two knocks, then three. Understood. Now go, before someone finds you here.'

Tom slapped Sam on the shoulder and the apprentice hesitated, before turning on his heel and walking rapidly back up the alley. Tom turned to Edmund.

'What do you think?'

Edmund examined the ground floor window. He tutted.

'I think tis a pity someone is in the building now. We would not get past the door in a week, but I wager I could be through this window in two minutes. As it is, we will have to brazen it out... rely on the Dalloway charm.'

Edmund gave Tom an encouraging grin. Tom swallowed hard and took out his sword. He knocked on the heavy oak door with its hilt. Rap Rap. Pause. Rap Rap Rap. The harsh sound echoed down the alley. A dog barked nearby. Rap Rap. Pause. Rap Rap Rap. More barking from the dog and a man's voice shouting. The dog continued, followed by a loud yelp and silence. Edmund shrugged. Maybe their knocking could not be heard over the sound of the press? Tom put his ear to the door but could detect nothing. Perhaps they would have to break in through the window after all. He lifted the hilt of his blade to knock a final time but stopped as he heard a bolt being drawn. He quickly sheathed his sword and stood back. Another heavy bolt was drawn and the door eased open. A thickset man stepped forward, holding a lantern. Tom cursed his luck. He had hoped one of the carousers from the Three Tuns would be on door duty and recognise him as a friend. But this man was a stranger, and suspicious. He held up his lantern and peered at Tom and Edmund.

'Who are you and what's your business at this time of night?' he grunted.

'I have come about the Perfumed Press. My name is Tallant and I met your friends at the Three Tuns. I am the merchant who helped you with your... your special cargo.'

The man looked Tom up and down then turned to Edmund.

'And him?' He waved the lantern in Edmund's direction.

'He is my brother. Also a merchant. It was his ship that carried your cargo.'

Tom had not rehearsed this ruse with Edmund and, for once, his friend said nothing.

'We have urgent news for Mr Overton. It is of the greatest importance.'

The man leaned forward and hissed at Tom. 'Keep your damned voice down, you booby.'

'Well perhaps you should let us in, so we can discuss our business in private.'

The man sniffed and stepped back. 'Wait here,' he muttered, and closed the door.

One of the bolts slid shut. Edmund leant forward.

'So far, so good... brother.'

Tom gave Edmund a tight smile. He fingered the cord of his cloak bag. His heart beat like a cooper's hammer as they waited in silence until the door opened again. The same man appeared and waved them in.

It was pitch dark inside save the light of the lantern. Tom could dimly see they had entered directly into the front room. Two truckle beds were pushed against the right-hand wall. They must keep the printing supplies upstairs, out of sight. There was a doorway in the rear wall leading, Tom assumed, to the pantry and the stairs. They came to another door on the left. The man pulled it open towards him, and light streamed into the room. Tom caught a glimpse of Edmund's stony expression. The time for jesting was over.

The man waved the lantern at Tom. 'Down there,' he said. 'You two first.'

Tom entered the doorway and saw a set of wooden cellar steps to his left. He ducked his head and descended carefully down the creaking treads followed by Edmund. The room below was small and airless with a familiar smell. It did not have the pungency he remembered from India but it was unmistakable—turmeric, mixed with printer's ink.

The cellar was well lit and, with each step down, revealed itself to Tom. He saw the legs of two people facing him. Were there three men in the house? He had hoped for only two. Next, a large wooden machine, barrels and a table became visible. As he reached the bottom step, the faces of the two men came into view, bringing good news and bad.

The good news was one of the men was Red Jerkin. The bad was the expression on the other man's face. It was as hard as stone. Tom smelt danger.

'It is him, right enough,' Red Jerkin told Stone Face as Tom stepped onto the cellar floor. 'Don't know the other cove, though.'

The man with the lantern stopped on the stairs behind them, blocking any escape from the cellar.

Stone Face paced towards Tom and looked him up and down. Tom's chest tightened as he noticed his eyes, as black as Newcastle coal.

'My friend here says you were buying everyone drinks at the Tuns the other night. Why should that be?'

'Perhaps you do not know, but I am young Sam Barnes's employer… the merchant who arranged for your type to be shipped from Amsterdam.'

'Oh, I know that right enough. Sam told me you approved of his little enterprise.'

Tom smiled.

'Slightly more than that. It was my idea and my brother's boat.' Tom nodded at Edmund. 'So Sam told you it was all his work? I am afraid he has a tendency to exaggerate. No doubt he wanted to impress. Well meaning, but a little irritating at times.'

With any luck that will reduce their interest in Sam, Tom hoped. Stone Face said nothing. Red Jerkin had moved behind him. Stone Face was clearly in charge. Tom pressed on. He did not want to stay in this cellar a minute longer than necessary.

'And why did I help you? I will tell you why. The King is a fool. His attempts to raise money to fight the Scots is ruining the city's trade. The sooner the people persuade him the Scottish campaign is a lost cause, the better. Your pamphlets are doing much to turn sentiment against him and sap his support. I congratulate you.'

'So you believe in the struggle, against Laud's reforms of the Scottish church and the other Papist conspiracies consuming the King?'

Tom had carefully considered how he would approach this conversation. Having seen his brother Peter in full godly flow, he knew he could not imitate that convincingly. Better to stick to what he knew.

'I am a man of commerce—a Protestant merchant. I am not fond of the Arminian reforms and my family fought the Catholics at the Armada. However, I would not assume to be one of the chosen. I am a merchant first and the Scottish campaign is damnable for our trade.'

Stone Face held Tom's gaze. His expression softened slightly and he stepped forward.

'Very well. They tell me you want to speak to a Richard Overton? There is no one here of that name so you will have to state your business to me.'

'Are you in charge of the press?'

'That is none of your concern. If you wish to state your business, you must tell me.'

Tom studied Stone Face. Is this Richard Overton? I fancy it is, but he will never admit it. No matter, it is the printing blocks I need and, while

we are here, as much metal type as we can carry. I will tell Jermyn the press has been put out of action. He looked around the room. The press was in the corner behind Red Jerkin. On the table Tom could see type in a frame and a stack of wooden blocks of different sizes.

'As a merchant, I need to keep my ear to the ground, both in the city and Whitehall. Today I heard alarming news the Stationer's Company was close to tracing the Scottish pamphlets.'

'We hear such rumours each day,' Stone Face sneered. 'They wish to scare us into lying low, but the rumours are simply that. They never come to anything.'

'I thought so too,' Tom retorted, 'but, to be certain, I made a discreet check and was informed that Josiah Wilmot from the Stationers' is leading a search of the Moorfields area this very night.'

Stone Face said nothing.

'That's a hundred yards from the Three Tuns and less than half a mile from here. I sat next to your men in the Tuns the other night. If they talk like that every week, I suspect half of Gunn Alley will know your business. I am afraid the game's up here in Grub Street. I am here to warn you to pack up and leave, while you still have the opportunity.'

Stone Face glanced at Red Jerkin, who looked abashed. It was enough to plant a seed of doubt. He turned to the man on the stairs.

'Ezekiel, go and get the others. We may have packing to do.'

Edmund looked at Tom with his eyebrow raised. Tom had not bargained for this.

'There is no need for that,' Tom said. 'My brother and I have come for the blocks marked with the yellow spice. They could lead the Stationers' to us as the source. But we can also assist you in packing your other machinery. Time is of the essence.'

Tom felt the situation slipping from his control. His voice sounded shrill. He had spoken too urgently. He knew they might have to take the type by force. Should they act immediately, with odds of three to two? Or let the man Ezekiel go? That would even the odds briefly but how long before the others arrived? Where were they? In the Three Tuns, or even closer? As he dithered, events overtook him. Stone Face nodded to Ezekiel who put the lantern down and ran up the stairs. They heard his footsteps in the room above, bolts sliding and the door opening. A moment later it slammed shut, followed by silence.

Stone Face turned to Tom. 'Here's a different idea. How's about we keep the type and blocks as we still need them for the pamphlets. We empty the house, lock you two down here and watch for that bastard Wilmot to arrive. If he does, you will have some explaining to do to him… and if he doesn't, well then, you will have some explaining to do to me.'

Tom's plan was now in tatters. He could feel panic rising inside.

'You could keep everything, as far as I am concerned, if it was not for that damnable spice. We must have the printer's blocks which are stained. If they are taken at any point in the future, they will be traced back to me. Then I will be of no further use to you, whereas I could be of service again. My ships travel routes to Europe and beyond. I can smuggle whatever you want in and out of London.'

Tom's mind flashed back to his indignant refusal of Jermyn's request. So much of his life was now inside out.

'Aye, you could,' Stone Face nodded, 'and I dare say you will in the future. As long as we keep hold of these blocks, you'll have to do what we tell you—'

'Oh for goodness sake.' Edmund stepped forward. 'Forgive me, Tom, but we do not have all night, given the imminent arrival of our friend's companions. It is time, I think, for the Dalloway charm.'

Edmund pulled from his cloak a large pistol and aimed it at Stone Face's chest. The effect was immediate. The man stepped back and Red Jerkin ducked behind him. Edmund threw his cloak bag at Tom.

'Brother!' A tight smile from Edmund. 'Get what you need and be quick. I doubt I can stand another minute in this malodorous dungeon.'

Tom looked at the cloak bag at his feet and back at Edmund, the pistol rock steady in his hand.

'Move, Tom,' Edmund shouted. Tom sprang into action.

Red Jerkin spoke up.

'He ain't got no fuse for that pistol. He cannot fire it. Let's rush him.'

'It's a flintlock, you halfwit,' Stone Face retorted. 'It don't need a fuse. Blow your brains out at this range. Go ahead, if you want to try your luck. Nice piece.'

'Thank you,' Edmund replied. 'It is rather fine, I agree. French, I am told. Now, gentlemen, please would you be so kind as to move into this corner, away from the press, so I can keep an eye on you while my dear brother retrieves his items.'

Tom feverishly worked his way through the contents of the table. He took every wooden block and as much metal type as they could carry. Within minutes he had filled two large cloak bags.

'Tom, we must take our leave before the others return. Gentlemen. Please remain where you are and do not attempt to pursue us. Oh, and perhaps I should make my position clear. Unlike my brother, I am a man of firm convictions about the current unrest within our country. I will defend His Majesty the King unto death. I regard your scandal sheets as seditious poison and I would not hesitate, indeed it would give me the greatest pleasure, to plant a musket ball between your eyes and watch you bleed out at my feet. Have I made myself clear? Yes? Good! Tom, please lead the way up the stairs with your bags. I suggest you take the lantern as well.'

Edmund stepped to one side but kept his eyes on the two men. Tom pulled the bags with one hand, held the lantern in the other and walked up the steps, which groaned and creaked under the weight.

Edmund waited a few seconds and then shouted.

'When you reach the room above, drag the two beds over to the door.'

Edmund followed Tom up the stairs, walking backwards carefully. Stone Face moved towards him. Edmund immediately raised his arm and sighted Stone Face's head down the barrel.

'You were admiring the pistol,' Edmund said amiably. 'It is a fine piece of work. Intricately carved, with a trigger as soft as a maiden's kiss. Do not distract me as I climb the stairs. I would hate to stumble and there to be an accident. Always better to live to fight another day, don't you think?'

Stone Face stepped back. Tom dragged the beds across the floor as Edmund backed up the steps. As he reached halfway, he bent down to keep the two men in view. By the time he reached the top he was crawling crab-like, keeping his pistol aimed at the cellar below.

'Tom. Have the door open and the beds ready. Make sure the bags are by the front door. Let me know when all is prepared.'

Edmund perched on the top step, watching the two printers as Tom pulled the beds closer.

When Tom was finished he tapped Edmund on the shoulder.

'Ready,' he whispered.

Edmund leaned forward.

'Gentlemen, I bid you adieu.'

Edmund dived from the top step through the open doorway and tumbled into the room.

'Shut it, Tom, shut it!'

Tom slammed the door closed as he heard the men on the steps. Edmund put his pistol on the first bed and rammed the bed head against the door.

'Tom, stand back. Get the other bed.'

Edmund picked up the pistol as the printers reached the top step and shoved on the door. The bed began to slide backwards. Edmund cocked the pistol, aimed at the door and fired. There was an explosion and bright flash, followed by the splintering of wood and a howl of pain from behind the door. The pistol recoil threw Edmund back across the room.

'Good God, that was loud. How satisfactory.'

'Have you not fired it before?'

'Not in anger. As a matter of fact I only purchased it last week. Seems to work though, does it not?'

Tom shook his head through the gun smoke .

Edmund ran across the room.

'Quick, Tom, the other bed. Jam it against the first!'

They pushed it into position with enough room to wedge both beds end to end between the stair door and the opposite wall.

The hammering resumed on the door, between shouts of pain and cursing.

'As I said, like the old days, hey Tom?' Edmund leapt for the cloak bags. 'My goodness, this bag is heavy. Time to go, brother Tom, that shot will have woken half the street.'

They stepped outside the house and closed the front door quietly. A figure was standing at the end of the alley where it joined Grub Street but they could not wait until the path was clear. With a cloak bag each, they set off. With each step, Tom expected Ezekiel and his friends to appear around the corner they were approaching. But only the single figure remained, standing by a shop lantern, with his back to them. Another twenty yards and they would be in Grub Street with more options for escape. Tom could still hear a faint hammering behind them. One or two lights appeared at windows, but no one came out to investigate. He desperately wanted to break into a run but that would attract attention. Their best chance was to keep walking.

Ten yards later, the man ahead suddenly turned left and disappeared from view along Grub Street. Tom halted. The light from the street lantern was poor but there was something familiar about the figure. Edmund tugged at Tom's cloak.

'Tom, we are ten yards from possible redemption. This is not the time to stop and take the night air.'

'That man ahead, did you see him?' The alley entrance was now empty.

'Which man? Tom, we do not have time for this. They could have broken through the cellar door by now. We must get out of sight.'

Tom reached Grub Street and looked in the direction the man had taken. The empty street stretched away to the left. He paused, straining his ears. Voices were approaching from the left.

'Edmund, turn to the right.'

They moved quickly into Grub Street and, passing the tavern on their right, slipped into a side alley on the opposite side of the road. The heavy cloak bags pulled at their hands and banged against their legs. Twenty yards in they saw a dark passage, again on their right.

'This will be Moor Lane,' Tom said. 'It runs alongside Grub Street to its east. It should bring us out on Fore Street, by the city wall. It's a short walk from there to Moorgate.'

Relief flooded through Tom. It looked like, somehow, they might have rescued the printing type and his reputation. He could not thank Edmund enough. They'd reached the end of Moor Lane and were about to step into Fore Street, when Edmund's arm shot across Tom's chest bringing him to a sudden halt. Edmund dragged Tom back into the dark alley.

'Look,' he hissed.

To their right, Stone Face and three men were standing in the middle of Fore Street. A crescent moon shone in a cloudless sky, a perfect night for stargazing. Tom thought of Elizabeth in her garden and prayed for the coal fog she cursed so roundly to make an appearance.

'They must have run the length of Grub Street at double speed. Obviously eager to have a word with us,' Edmund whispered.

Tom considered their options: to their right, Stone Face and his men; to their left, three hundred yards down Fore Street, the entrance to Moorgate in the city wall, and safety in the alleys and back runs beyond.

'If we break cover and run for it, weighed down with these bags, they will catch us before we reach Moorgate,' Tom said. 'If we stay here, they will find us eventually. That's why they are stationed there. They know we cannot approach Moorgate without being seen.'

Tom sat on his bag, relief turning to anguish. Edmund stirred.

'Wait here, Tom. Do not move. I will be away for ten minutes. Here, look after this,' and he handed Tom his cloak bag. He disappeared back up Moor Lane.

Tom sat shivering on the bags of type. He watched the men in Fore Street who showed no signs of moving. Eventually he heard someone walking down Moor Lane towards him. To his relief, the familiar form of Edmund appeared through the dark.

'What have you been up to Edmund?'

'Calling in a few reinforcements. Wait and see.'

They both hunkered down on the bags in silence. The late August air was chill. Eventually Tom heard a familiar voice. A female voice. It was the diminutive madame with three of her girls in tow walking down the street towards the group of men. Stone Face turned his back on them but some of the others approached the girls. Tom turned to Edmund with a raised eyebrow.

'I dropped by madame's establishment again. She assumed I had changed my mind on her earlier offer but I told her some friends were visiting the area and I wanted to make sure they got a friendly Grub Street welcome. A golden guinea did the rest. They are under instructions not to leave the men until each has, erm, been fully satisfied.'

Tom looked back up the street. One of the men was disappearing down a side alley with a girl while Stone Face shouted at the tiny figure of the madame, threatening her with his fist.

'I think he may have met his match. Edmund you are brilliant! Let us move quietly to Moorgate, while he is distracted.'

They picked up the bags and slipped out of the shadows.

'Keep to the edge and do not look back,' Tom whispered.

They inched along the street and were over halfway to Moorgate when they heard a shout behind them. It was Stone Face in hot pursuit, one of his men running behind, buttoning his breeches.

'Come, Edmund. Full tilt for freedom!' said Tom, as they broke into a sprint.

It was dangerous going. The road was rutted and the heavy bags bounced awkwardly against their legs as they gathered speed. Tom tripped, scraping his shins on a stone. Cursing, he held on to the bag and got to his feet. Edmund did not break his stride and moved ahead. Stone Face had already gained twenty yards and was closing fast. Tom put his head down and pumped his legs hard. Now it was do or die. With each stride the bulky bags became harder to carry. Ahead, Edmund rounded the corner into Moorgate.

Tom's legs started to tremble. His lungs were burning and he felt like he was treading water. If only he could drop the damned bag weighing him down. He slid around the corner into Moorgate and saw the postern gate twenty yards ahead. Edmund was already there. He felt something touch his back and took one hand off the cloak bag to lash behind with his fist. There was a grunt and a curse and, as he glanced again, saw Stone Face scrambling to his feet.

Edmund was at Moorgate beckoning him frantically. His chest screaming with pain, Tom made a final lunge and threw himself inside the gatehouse. Edmund dragged him away as a tall guard stepped forward and blocked the entrance, halberd in hand.

Stone Face stumbled to a halt five yards in front of the guard and bent forward, hands on knees, gasping lungfuls of air. Looking past the guard's shoulder, Tom saw his pursuer slowly stand and spit on the floor.

He glared at Tom.

'You will live to regret this. That I swear on my solemn oath.'

Stone Face turned and walked back into the dark without a backward glance.

Edmund led Tom out of the gatehouse and through the city wall. They sat on a stone bench inside the wall. Tom was still struggling for breath.

'How... how... how did you arrange that... the guard.'

Edmund held up his purse and shook it.

'It has been an expensive evening, Tom.'

They embraced and shook with laughter.

Chapter 17

10th September 1640
The Tallant warehouse

'God's blood! I am glad Father is not alive to see this day.'

Sir Ralph paced up and down the wharf. His anger was becoming a habit. It was a glorious late summer morning. White gulls arced across a sapphire sky as the warm breeze stirred the pennants on shipping moored along the quay.

'He fought the Spanish tooth and nail to keep England free. But now we are invaded in our sleep... by the bloody Scots!'

Sir Ralph swivelled on his heel and stalked down the wharf away for Tom. Twenty paces later, he swivelled again and walked back to Tom.

'The Scots have marched into Newcastle, have you heard? They are sitting on London's supply of coal! I tell you, Tom, if they're still there when winter comes and there's no fuel for London, there will be merry hell to pay on the streets!'

Swivel. Tom looked at the receding figure. A pattern was emerging. Twenty paces away from Tom to fill his spleen and twenty paces back before venting it. Best let him have his say. Swivel.

'Strafford squeezes money out of us to raise an army. They march north to find the Scots already in Northumberland. Both armies come eye to eye over the Tyne and the English start counting. Over twenty thousand Scots against less than four thousand English! Only one possible outcome. What kind of a force is that to send to Scotland? And what in the name of God has our money been spent on? If the Privy Council was a merchant house it would have gone out of business twenty years ago.'

Swivel. Tom blew out his cheeks and stared across the river, bracing himself for the next tirade. Nothing. Tom looked back up the quayside. Sir Ralph had reached the end of his twenty paces and stopped. He was staring at the Customs House, shading his eyes from the early morning sun. Finally he turned and walked briskly to Tom.

'Tom, if I am not mistaken, Robert Petty is walking along the wharf towards us.'

The quayside was bustling with porters handling cargo. Tom could not see Petty but did not doubt his father for one second. Ralph Tallant was always first to spot a sail on board ship. The accuracy of his long vision was legendary among the London merchants and it had not weakened with age.

'When will he be here?'

'At his current speed, I would say in less than a minute. You have a decision to make, assuming he has not yet spotted you.'

Tom considered avoiding Petty. He had nothing to hide, but his father held Petty's investigating skills in high regard.

'If you do not move in the next five seconds you will have the worst of both worlds Tom. He will see you are here and see you go.'

'In that case I shall stay, Father. I am not guilty of anything and, even if he has heard about my latest predicament with the Scottish pamphlets, there is no proof of my involvement.'

'You disposed of the printing type, I hope.'

'Yes, the same night. Edmund and I tied the bags securely and threw them off London Bridge. They went straight to the bottom. They will not be seen again.'

Tom looked over Sir Ralph's shoulder. He could just make out Robert Petty in the distance striding along the wharf towards them. He marvelled at his father's eyesight.

'Edmund did you proud that night, Tom, by all accounts.'

'Yes. He stuck by me when many would not. I am in his debt.'

'What about Arthur, is there news of his release?'

'No. The Stationers' went to Grub Street the next day. The birds had flown, of course, but in their haste they left printing machinery, supplies… everything. That loss, together with the missing type, should disrupt their activities for a time. Jermyn is happy. He sent me a note of thanks.'

'But no release of the boy.' Sir Ralph gave his son a knowing look.

'Not yet!' Tom replied, as he slapped his father on the shoulder and moved towards the advancing figure of the Merchant Adventurer's agent.

'Mr Petty. What a pleasant surprise. Out for a morning stroll along the river? Is not the weather prime?'

Tom's offered hand was ignored. Petty was grim-faced and bowed stiffly.

'Good morning, Mr Tallant. Good morning, Sir Ralph.'

There was an awkward silence.

'If you would excuse us, Sir Ralph, I have official business to discuss with your son.'

Sir Ralph and Tom looked at each other.

'Well, I will wait in the warehouse office for your mother, Tom. She is coming to the city to visit the draper's store and wants my company, God help me.'

He turned and gave the agent a curt nod. 'Mr Petty, I am obliged,' he said, before striding to the warehouse entrance.

'What I have to say will not take long, Mr Tallant. Perhaps we can speak in private, by the water's edge?'

'If you wish, Mr Petty. I am at your disposal.'

They walked to the end of the jetty, out of earshot of the warehouse.

Petty's voice was low and hard. 'I must congratulate you, Tallant. You clearly have friends with influence.'

'I do not know what you are talking about, Mr Petty.'

'Really? Yesterday I was instructed by the Merchant Adventurers to desist from further investigation of your possible involvement in the deaths of Sir Joseph Venell and Sir Hugh Swofford. I was told it would "not be in the best interests" of my employers. Whenever I hear that, Tallant, it usually means one thing. The Palace has intervened and the Adventurers dare not displease his majesty.'

Tom said nothing. This must be Henry Jermyn's work. Was this his way of showing his gratitude? How did he know about the investigation? A foolish question. Jermyn made it his business to know everything.

Petty leaned closer. 'Unfortunately, for you the Palace's timing could not be worse. I have been investigating you assiduously, Tallant, for many months. Although I am no nearer to solving both murders, I had reached one conclusion. I felt certain you did not, and could not, have executed those crimes. If your friend in Whitehall had waited another week, I would have submitted my report to the Adventurers saying so. The case would have remained on the file but all active investigation of you by my employers would have ceased. Instead, they have given me every reason to redouble my efforts. Why warn me off the case if you have nothing to hide?'

Petty was now inches from Tom's face, his eyes unblinking.

'As far as my employers are concerned, Tallant, I am no longer checking on you. But as far as I am concerned, I will be after you, morning, noon and night. No one will know, except me… and you.'

Petty moved back and took a deep breath, his dark oak eyes not leaving Tom's face for a second.

'I regret that my employers bend so easily to pressure from the Palace but the Merchant Adventurers will never bite the hand that feeds them. The King's power to grant trading monopolies sees to that. Not so the City Aldermen. I believe a number in the Aldermanic Court are inclined against the King which means my fellow investigator Nathaniel Franklin, City Magistrate, will not be lent upon as much as I, and we know how zealous he can be. You know, Tallant, over these past months I have exercised a restraining influence on Franklin's wilder accusations against you. No longer. Let them flow, say I. You will soon see the damage your friends at court have done to you. I bid you good day.'

Petty strode away. Tom sat on a wooden mooring post and gathered his wits. An angry Robert Petty was an unsettling experience. He considered what he'd said. Petty's threat to ignore orders and continue the investigation was based on pique, not new evidence. In addition, Tom had not asked anyone to warn Petty off, so the investigator's reasoning that Tom had something to hide was false. Tom stood and stretched his arms. He looked at the gulls, still wheeling and arcing. This time he had the

measure of Mr Robert Petty and his games. He also had one card left to play, should he need it: his sighting of Petty with Barty.

Tom reflected on Henry Jermyn's role in this matter. He felt sure he was behind the pressure on the Adventurers. Jermyn may not have released the boy Arthur, but he had acted to show his gratitude. Tom felt a flush of flattery and a sense of reassurance. What was it Petty had said? 'Friends with influence.' Tom smiled.

'There you are, Tom.' It was his mother stepping through the warehouse door on to the wharf. 'Let me look at you. Too thin. Much too thin. Come over on Sunday. We will have game pie.' His mother embraced him. 'I have a surprise for you, Tom. Come inside.'

He followed her out of the sun into the warehouse office. His father was out at the front, talking to Isaac, but Sam Barnes and the groom Andrew had found an excuse to be in the office. Elizabeth was holding court.

'Elizabeth came to the house with urgent news for you, Tom. When she heard I was coming to the warehouse she requested a ride in the carriage. We had a most interesting journey. She told me about her friend Mr Culpeper and his knowledge of plants. I have asked her to invite him to the house and I will show him the garden. She is a lovely girl, Tom. Such spirit! I do hope you are getting on well?'

His mother looked at Tom inquiringly but he simply smiled and squeezed her arm. He walked over to Elizabeth. What on earth was she doing with the lads?

'Sam, you are the biggest are you not? So you are the sun, you stand here.' Elizabeth pulled the burly apprentice to one side of the room. 'Face me, that's right, and put your arms out like this and shake your hands to show the light coming off the sun. Shake them more.' Elizabeth turned to Beatrix. 'Lady Tallant? Excellent timing. I need another person for my demonstration. Would you be so good as to be our world, the Earth. You must stand over here on the other side and face Sam. Good.'

'My goodness. How exciting!' exclaimed Tom's mother, her eyes alight.

Elizabeth continued. 'Andrew. You will be Venus. Stand here next to me. We must make you smaller than the sun, so can you crouch down a little? That's it. Now I want you to walk past Sam slowly, but still crouching, yes, crouch down. That's perfect!'

Tom scratched his head in disbelief. Sam standing with his arms stuck out, wiggling his fingers, and Andrew trying to walk, curled in a ball. No smirks or jokes, Elizabeth had them eating out of her hand. His mother was also engrossed, if slightly puzzled. Elizabeth grinned at Tom before returning to her lesson.

'Now, as you can see, when Andrew, that is Venus, walks between the earth and the sun, Lady Tallant on Earth can see him in front of the Sun and she can also see how quickly he is moving and how far he is away

from the Sun. Do you know an Englishman has also been able to see all that, but with the real Earth and Sun and Venus, using his telescope? I have just found out. It is so exciting. He has been able to see Venus cross in front of the sun, measure its speed and calculate its distance from the sun.'

Sam dropped his arms. Andrew straightened up.

'Yes, an Englishman, and do you know the most wonderful thing? He is only twenty-two years old.'

'That's only three years more than me,' Sam blurted out.

'An Englishman. Makes you feel proud,' Andrew said.

'And so it should.' It was the voice of Isaac who had been watching from the front door. 'I will be proud of you too if you get that barky unloaded that's docking at the back, begging your pardon Miss Elizabeth.'

Elizabeth smiled and held her hand up in apology.

Tom peered through the rear door. The ship was inching towards the wharf.

'Andrew and Sam, stand by to take the mooring ropes. Isaac, please take over.'

Isaac nodded and walked through the rear door of the warehouse followed by Sam and Andrew.

'Come, Beatrix, we will be late for your appointment,' Sir Ralph called to his wife as he ushered her through the front door. 'Elizabeth. Thank you for the astronomy lesson. Most instructive.' He bowed slightly, smiling at her warmly as he left the warehouse.

They were alone in the room. She looked radiant.

'Tom. This is the most wonderful news. This young man, his name is Jeremiah Horrocks. Apparently he sits at home with his telescope like me, reads Kepler like me, makes his calculations like me and achieves this!'

She clapped her hands with excitement.

'He knew when to look, don't you see? He worked out when Venus would pass in front of the Sun and he was right! And he worked out a way to observe and measure the event. He has already proved the previous calculated distance between Venus and Earth is completely wrong! All from his own observations!'

Tom understood Elizabeth's excitement. This Jeremiah Horrocks had plucked the science of stars from the distant world of Galileo and Kepler, and placed it in her lap. What he could do, she could do.

'Where is this Master Horrocks? We must go and meet him. Why not today?'

Elizabeth laughed and hugged him.

'Tom. There is a world outside London, you know. Jeremiah Horrock's lives in the north of the country, in the county of Lancashire.'

'So how did you hear about his discovery?'

Elizabeth stepped away. She looked through the warehouse door at the blue sky.

'Tom, it is a perfect day to enjoy a pipe on the river. Let us hail a wherry and continue our conversation afloat.'

Ten minutes later they were travelling down the Thames, gliding past the mass of shipping anchored in the Pool. Jonah had not answered his hail so a younger boatman was hauling the oars, occasionally glancing at Elizabeth drawing deeply on the pipe gripped between her teeth.

'Is this not prime?' she said, leaning back and staring at the cloudless sky. 'You asked me how I knew of the transit of Venus? A group of us correspond on matters of natural science and discovery and meet when we can. There is so much to share. I heard a rumour about the transit and wrote to Master John Greaves. He is an acquaintance of William Harvey—'

'Du Mutu Cordis?'

'The very same. You see, Tom, they are all connected. Natural philosophers and scientists with a common goal—discovery.'

Elizabeth examined the bowl of her pipe and knocked it against the wherry's side. The stem snapped in her hand.

'Damnation,' she muttered, and threw the broken pipe over the side. She retrieved another from the folds of her cloak.

Tom reflected on this group of scientists. To accept a young woman into their midst, as a fellow explorer, said a great deal about them and the quality of Elizabeth's intellect. It could never happen in the merchant community.

'I received Greaves's reply yesterday. He had seen an early draft of Venus in sole visa, Horrocks's paper on the transit. Who knows what the young man will discover next.'

Elizabeth filled the pipe's bowl and returned the tobacco pouch to her cloak pocket. She pulled out another small bag and topped the bowl to overflowing.

Tom frowned. 'Why have you refilled your pipe? We have no fire or taper.'

Elizabeth grinned and fished in her cloak pocket. She withdrew a small piece of glass set in a brass ring.

'A girl should never be without her telescope, Tom, or at least part of it.'

She looked towards the sun, held the pipe in her right hand and the glass in her left. She placed the glass above the bowl and moved it slowly up and down, tilting it in her fingers. A white circle of light appeared on the tobacco. She studied the bowl intently for about a minute and smiled when a wisp of smoke came from the pipe.

Tom felt the wherry slow. The boatman had paused, oars in midair, staring at Elizabeth gently drawing on the pipe while carefully

maintaining the distance between the glass and the top of the bowl. She breathed in and the wisp of smoke became a cloud. Elizabeth frowned as she breathed in the smoke and lowered the glass as the bowl glowed red. She lent back with a contented expression and winked at Tom.

'Well, I'll be damned.' It was the boatman, slowly lowering his oars into the water to take up the stroke. 'Believed I'd seen everything on this barky but that tops the lot!'

'I have used my glass in the garden before, but never afloat!' She returned it to her pocket. 'The eyepiece of a telescope makes a perfect magnifying glass. The sun's rays do the rest. I use old tobacco to top the bowl. It is dry enough to take the flame. The first mouthful is not pleasant.'

Tom thanked God for bringing Elizabeth into his life. He no longer felt overwhelmed by her presence, but blessed. She was the only person who could lift the burden of his troubles. She was his salvation, he knew it.

'So the transit was your urgent news, that you mentioned to Mother.'

'Partly, Tom, but I have also been thinking about our conversation after the theatre.'

She glanced at the waterman and lowered her voice.

'About the misfortunes that have befallen you. I am seeking a pattern and I need you to tell me again everything you observed at your parents' house when Swofford died. I want to be sure of something.'

'Of course I will, Elizabeth, when we get back, if you think it will help, but thankfully my fortunes have improved since we spoke. I now have a person of influence on my side to protect my interests.'

He turned and whispered in her ear, 'Henry Jermyn.'

He felt her body stiffen and she pulled her head away.

'No, Tom, you cannot mean it. Not that man.'

'Elizabeth, I know you suffered misfortune at the hands of Jermyn and his associates playing at the tables. However, that is over and he has been of great assistance to me, only this morning.'

Elizabeth lowered her voice. 'Tom, you must listen to me. You have no idea about the extent of my dealings with that man. You do not understand who you are up against.'

There was a long pause. Elizabeth turned away and looked out across the river. The boatman continued his steady rhythm, humming to himself.

She turned back and whispered, 'My father is employed by the Privy Council. Jermyn once threatened to damage his career if I did not cooperate with him.'

'What did he want you to do?'

'Jermyn found out mathematics is among my interests. I use it for planetary calculations and father agreed to my tuition.'

Elizabeth moved closer and Tom could feel her warm breath on his cheek.

'Jermyn invited me to Whitehall. I was taken to a room deep inside the palace containing a large oak chest. He unlocked it and placed several pieces of paper on a table in front of me. They were covered in numbers. Jermyn said they were messages that had been intercepted. It was vital to the King's interests they were decoded but the task had defeated his cipher experts. If I did not discover what the numbers meant, my father's position would become... difficult.'

Elizabeth held on to Tom's coat and whispered urgently.

'He said I could not leave that room until I had broken the code! If I had not achieved it within an hour, he would call me back again and again until I had. I could not remove the papers from the room, nor tell anyone what I was doing or it would go badly with the whole Seymour family.'

Tom had never seen Elizabeth look frightened. He slipped his arm around her shoulder.

'My poor Elizabeth. What did you do?'

'Once I had gathered my senses, I looked at the sheets. I knew within the hour the code was loosely based on number theory developed by Pierre de Fermat in France. If you knew Fermat's work, you could decipher the code in minutes. If you did not, you might not solve it in a lifetime.'

'What did the messages say?'

'That was the last thing I wanted to know. I asked for a quill and paper, wrote down the decoding sequence for each letter of the alphabet and left. Jermyn looked pleased when I told him about the French link, but I said he should never ask me to do such a thing again. And he never has.'

'Why not, once he had you within his power?'

Elizabeth moved away. A mischievous grin lit her features.

'I told him I had been afflicted since childhood by a tendency to walk and talk in my sleep! His secrets were not safe with me.'

'He believed you?'

'Well, he has never asked me again. But Tom, if he has rendered you a service I can guarantee it will only be to put you in his debt. Give me your word you will have nothing more to do with him. You must.'

Tom slowly nodded. He could not ignore the look of alarm on her face but he knew that, should he need Jermyn's help in the future, he might have to reconsider his promise.

A carriage arrived ten minutes later to take Elizabeth to meet her father in Whitehall. Tom waved to her as she left then turned to see Isaac waiting for him in the parlour. Something was amiss.

'I did not want to mention it in front of Miss Elizabeth, Master Thomas, but we have had an intruder.'

'Another petty thief, Isaac? When?'

'While you were out on the river with Miss Elizabeth. We were busy unloading the barky so the office was empty. I came out of the kitchen and heard a noise above. I picked up a loading hook, crept upstairs and

found some toerag, bold as brass, in the first floor store, bag of spice in his hand. One look at the hook and he dropped the bag and made a run for it. But I stopped him with a single punch. Didn't put up a fight. Kept saying he wasn't going to take nothing, and him caught red-handed! They don't usually try it in broad daylight, though. This one was either stupid or desperate.'

'Where is he?'

'I called the constable who's taken him to the magistrate. The City's red hot on pilfering from the docks. Says it's damaging the port's reputation. They'll throw the book at him, at least that's what the constable said.'

Isaac paused. Tom could sense his misgiving.

'Isaac, are you having second thoughts? You usually do not have any time for thieving.'

'You are right, Master, I do not. We work hard enough to make an honest living without these little bastards stealing the coats off our back. But he was different, somehow. I didn't notice to begin with but, after he was taken away, it got me thinking.'

Isaac could be frustratingly vague but Tom trusted his judgement.

'What do you mean exactly, Isaac?'

'Well, he seemed resigned to being caught. Didn't put up much of a struggle, as I say, just sat waiting for the constable. If I had walked out the room and come back five minutes later, likely he wouldn't have moved, as if he wanted to be arrested. Mind you, he looked afeared when the constable mentioned Tyburn Hill. He started babbling on again about not stealing anything.'

'Tyburn? Will they hang him? For a bag of spice?'

'Oh yes, could happen, Master. As I say, the courts are sending a message to all thieves in the city. Keep off the docks. That don't mean he will hang though. After all, he might know his neck verse.'

'His what?'

'His neck verse. Taking the clergy. You must have heard of that, Master Thomas?'

Tom shook his head and drew up a couple of chairs.

'Something I must have missed while on my travels, Isaac. Take the weight off your feet and tell me about it.'

Isaac sat down carefully and mopped his face with a cloth.

'Well, in Queen Bess's time you only had to sneeze in the wrong direction to end up on the scaffold. Soon everyone knew someone who'd shook hands with the executioner. People said there were too many and it wasn't right. Then someone remembered that clergy could not be tried in an ordinary court. So the judges were told that if a man came before them charged with, say, petty thieving, they should allow him to "take the clergy", if he could.'

'What does that mean, Isaac?'

'Well the clergy are learned gentlemen, as you know, and they can all read and write. So if someone in the dock could prove they could read a verse from the Bible, that was good enough for the judge in cases of petty crime. Mind you, they would not get off scot-free. Anyone granted the clergy is branded on the thumb so they cannot claim it again. But they'll take a brand before a rope, won't they, so they all try for it.'

'Even if they cannot read? What is the point?'

'Because the chosen reading is usually the same, Master: the first verse of Psalm fifty-one.'

Light dawned on Tom.

'So if they can learn the verse and pretend to read it from the Bible in court, they escape the gallows?'

'That's about the size of it, Master Thomas, as long as the crime is not too serious. Mind you, stealing a bag of spice is not the same as taking a loaf of bread and the court may take a dim view. Judges can choose another verse to make sure the defendant can really read, if they're so inclined. I even heard of one who told the clerk to use a Latin Bible because he was not convinced. It's not as easy as it sounds.'

Tom wondered how much it would take to make the boy's theft serious.

'Isaac, what was in the bag?'

'Cinnamon, Master. Five pounds of it.'

At today's market price, Tom calculated that would be worth forty shillings. If the court discovered this, the young boy could be in serious trouble.

'Let us sleep on the matter, Isaac. Nothing more will happen today and we have a load of cargo to store.'

MICHAEL WARD

Chapter 18

11th September 1640
Clerkenwell

Meg faltered as Tom guided her to the left. 'Did that confuse you, old girl? No, we are not visiting the family. Somewhere much less pleasant, I fear.'

They were in Clerkenwell. It was the next day and Tom was about to meet his cinnamon thief. He led Meg off St John Street into the path to the village green. He rode past the rear alley to the Red Bull theatre before turning right, down the side of St James churchyard. He pulled Meg to a halt in front of New Prison. The name was misleading. The iron bars across the windows were pocked with rust, its wooden front door chipped and scratched. An air of decay hung over the building, a low, unremarkable stone construction. Still, it could not be worse than Newgate.

Tom thought the boy would have been put in the city's main lock-up, but Newgate was full. Given its reputation for overcrowding, if Newgate was considered full the conditions inside would be unspeakable. He tethered Meg to a wall and entered. Ten minutes later, and several coins lighter, Tom was led down a dark stone corridor to a bolted w   door. The jailer slid open a viewing hatch, grunted, closed it again   lled a bunch of large keys from his belt. He selected one and unlocked the cell door. Stepping back, he turned to Tom with a sly grin.

'All yours. Take as long as yer like.'

Tom pushed the door open. The stench hit him in the face. He took an involuntary step back before moving into the cell. The door slammed behind him and he heard the key turn in the lock. The air was hot and fetid, the rushes on the cell floor caked with excrement and dried vomit. He felt suffocated by the oppressive stink of urine and struggled not to retch.

A single window, high in the opposite wall was barred on the outside and thick with grime. Pale light filtered through, consumed instantly by the gloom. Tom saw four figures, each sitting on the filthy rushes. He guessed at once which was the cinnamon thief, a fair-haired boy in one corner.

'You are the one who tried to steal the spice from my warehouse yesterday, are you not?'

The boy looked at him but said nothing. Isaac was right, Tom thought. He does not look frightened or angry. Simply resigned. Tom got down on his haunches, closer to the stinking rushes. He fought to push the nausea back.

144

'My name is Thomas Tallant. My family own the warehouse where you were caught. I want to know more about you, and why you took such a risk stealing from us in daylight. What is your name?'

A figure stirred on other side of the cell.

'You're wasting your time. He's hardly spoke since he came in. No name. No nothing. The only thing he did say chilled us all, didn't it, Ned?'

The man nudged a dark shape next to him. Ned started coughing. A hacking, retching eruption deep within his body. He spat loudly.

'Said he was cursed. Said he was the Devil's spawn, so he did.'

Ned crossed himself vigorously.

'If you can get him moved out of here, we'd be much obliged,' the first figure continued. 'Gives me and Ned the frights, and no mistake.'

'I mean you no harm.'

It was the boy. His voice surprised Tom. Calm, measured and, underneath, a certain gentleness.

'He speaks!' Ned said, mocking.

Tom turned to the boy. 'And I also mean you no harm. Please, tell me your name.'

Eventually the boy lifted his head, his face wet with tears. Tom reached in his pocket for a handkerchief, leaned forward and gently wiped the grime from the boy's face.

'How old are you? Sixteen years?'

The boy took a gulp of air and looked at Tom.

'I believe I am fifteen years of age, sir, and my name is Matty... Matty Morris.'

Tom was struck by the realisation that his brother Matthias would also have turned fifteen this year if he had lived. He tried to keep the memories of his brother at bay. He needed to focus on this Matty, sitting in front of him now. He encouraged the boy to continue and slowly pieced his story together. He said he was the son of a tenant farmer in Surrey. At the age of thirteen, famine fever killed half his village, including his father and mother. Matty moved to London to live with his elder sister Prudence who was married to a lay preacher and living near Coleman Street.

'I could tell Prudence did not want me there. They'd had their first baby and were living out of two rooms. She said there was no space for me but her husband Caleb said it was the Christian duty of God's children to look after the weak. I did not like all the preaching. Church twice a day and more at home. But it was a roof over my head and Caleb was kind enough to begin with.'

Matty stopped talking and stared at the cell wall. Tom could crouch no longer and raised himself stiffly to his feet. He kicked at the squalid rushes to clear some room, before sitting gingerly on the stone floor.

'So what happened, Matty, to make you feel cursed?'

The boy sighed. 'Feel it? I do not merely feel it. I know it to be true. I must be cursed. I was happy living with my parents. I worked the land with father and at night mother showed me how to cook and sew. She wanted me to attend the village school. Father said I could not be spared but agreed in the end because it meant so much to Mother. After a month the schoolmaster said I showed promise and Father was proud, I could see it in his face. I learned my letters and within six months could read—still can a little—and began to learn writing. But the fever came and everything changed. Killed my parents, and the schoolmaster. Caleb said it was God's providence and there must have been great wickedness in the village. But I did not see it. He said I must be wicked to lose both my parents, and Prudence missed the fever because she left the village to join the children of God in London, and was one of the chosen. That's what Caleb told me and he said I must join him in prayer to seek God's forgiveness.'

The flow of words ceased and Matty dropped his head again. His voice became a whisper.

'The baby was a poor sleeper at night and Pru was exhausted looking after him. They would often doze in the afternoon. Caleb would wait until they were asleep and then tell me to pray with him in the other room.'

Another pause. More tears. With a growing sense of misgiving, Tom sensed what was coming.

'We would kneel together, facing each other, and Caleb would thank the Lord for sending me to him for his protection. He said it brought joy to his heart. He would put his hands on my shoulders, then my back... and my arse. The first time I did not realise what was happening but Caleb's voice got excited and he started stroking my arse saying it was as soft as Pru's. He stopped when I shouted at him. He was terrified Prudence would wake and discover us. But a few days later, he tried it on again, begging me to do God's bidding. He said Prudence had not been interested since the baby and God had sent me instead. I told him it was not right and, if he did'nt stop, I would tell Prudence. It was the worst thing I could have done. Two days later, I came home from the market to find my sister sobbing her heart out. She screamed as I came in the room, got hold of the baby and pushed herself tight into a corner. Caleb heard the noise and rushed in from the other room. He pointed at me. I can still remember, his finger was trembling. He pointed at me and said I was the Devil incarnate, come to lead him from the path or righteousness through lust and wickedness. I tried to talk to Pru but she would not look at me. Kept her head turned towards the wall, screaming about saving her baby from eternal damnation. When I said it was Caleb who had been trying it on with me, she was like a mad woman, shrieking and moaning about how Satan must have lay with our mother to produce me. Caleb came at me, holding his Bible out in front of him like a shield. He called me Lucifer and told me I had no place in a house of God's children. If I did not leave

he would summon the brethren of Coleman Street to drive me out with stones.'

Ned turned to the man next to him. 'Told you he was no good. Devil's spawn, he said.'

Tom looked around, touched the hilt of his sword, and glared at Ned who shrank against the cell wall, silenced.

'I left that very minute,' Matty continued, 'and never went back. I ran to the river and slept rough on the wharves. My coat was stolen two days later and I was forced to start thieving so I could eat. That's when I realised Caleb was right. I was cursed. Everything had gone wrong since the fever came to the village. I lost my mother and father, and now my sister, good as. I had nowhere to sleep, nothing to eat and I had finally stooped to sinning—stealing bread.'

'But you were hungry, Matty.'

'No matter. I was raised to be God-fearing, never tell a lie and keep the law. I had turned my back on this and become no better than the thief who stole my coat.'

Tom shook his head. 'Was that why you took the spice, Matty? You had given up all hope?'

Matty looked Tom in the eye. 'I did not take no spice. I told you that.'

'But Isaac said he found you with the bag in your hand,' Tom persisted. 'Was he lying?'

Both Matty's hands were balled into tight fists, his nails digging into his grimy skin. 'No,' he muttered.

'Well, have it your own way, Matty Morris.'

Tom sighed and got to his feet. He looked around the filthy room and a growing conviction filled his heart. Yes, the boy had been trying to steal from him, but he'd been driven to it by ill treatment. The coincidence of this opportunity to help another Matty weighed heavily in his mind, burdened as it was by years of chafing guilt.

'I will arrange for you to have a clean cell and will pay for food and drink.' He leaned forward and spoke softly. 'I believe you Matty. I must go away and consider what I can do to help. In the meantime, do not lose heart. I will return.'

Chapter 19

Later that day
The garden at Bolton Hall

Lady Beatrix turned around, clay pot in hand.

'Oh, Tom, what a surprise you gave me.'

Her son was standing behind her, hand raised in apology. She smiled and showed him the plant she was carrying. It was tall, about two feet, and covered in small deep pink flowers.

'Clematis?' Tom ventured.

Lady Beatrix nodded.

'Yes. It's like a pink variation of the common blue we know as virgin's bower. Your Uncle Jonas brought it back from his last voyage to Japan. It's taken me a little while to learn how to cultivate it successfully. Look at this beauty, still flowering in September, and what colour! So pleasing. I was just thinking of your father and saying a prayer for his safe return.'

Sir Ralph was in Amsterdam for a series of meetings with Uncle Jonas and a group of new clients. Tom knew this was his best chance to talk to his mother alone and confidentially.

'Mother, I need to speak with you. I need your advice.'

Beatrix placed the plant carefully on the path and straightened her back.

'Ooof! I am getting no younger, Thomas. Too much weeding over the years has taken its toll. Come, let us sit by the glasshouse and you can tell me what is on your mind.'

They walked arm in arm. The September sun was still warm, bathing the garden in glowing, pale sunlight under a peerless blue sky. Swallows swooped and chattered, gathering insects. As he did every year, Tom wondered where they hid, sleeping, through the winter. They reached a bench and sat down. Tom paused, not wanting to break the garden's spell, but then told his mother all he had seen and heard at New Prison: Matty's story, what Caleb had done to the boy, the curious circumstances of the theft.

She shook her head and murmured, 'Men, they are worse than animals.'

When Tom had finished, Beatrix sighed and looked around the garden.

'And how old is this boy? Fifteen years?'

Tom nodded. Beatrix's eyes glistened in the sun.

'I know, Mother. Our Matthias, my brother. He would have been the same age now if I hadn't —'

Beatrix put her hand on Tom's arm. 'Please, Tom, stop. Matty's death was an accident. You weren't to know.'

The desperate images, so long buried, returned to Tom. Twelve years old, standing by a frozen pond. Two-year-old Matty with him. A voice,

148

his father's, a distant echo. 'Tom, keep off the ice.' His feeling of wanton disobedience still vivid as he stepped on to the frozen surface and walked, then ran to the centre of the pond, laughing. His father's voice, now shouting with alarm. A crack, another, then the ice giving way beneath him. Tom's feet sinking into freezing water. A smaller voice. Matthias: 'I help you, Tommy, I'm coming.' Then silence. Just pictures. Matty moving forward, stepping on a crack and suddenly disappearing beneath the surface. Tom on his knees, not daring to move. A small wet hand rising from the water, grasping for the edge of the ice. Then gone.

'Father warned me to keep off the pond, but as always headstrong Thomas took no notice. I know he still blames me for Matty's death.'

His mother squeezed his arm.

'No, Thomas. You must understand it was a dreadful shock for us all, but particularly your father who saw it all happen but couldn't save Matthias. He's never got over it, but he doesn't blame you. You were just twelve. There is not a day when I do not think of Matty and little Mary, when I do not talk to them, here in my garden, where I feel closest to them. I think of what… of who they might have become. But that cannot be, and we cannot change that.'

Beatrix took a lace handkerchief from her dress pocket. She dabbed her eyes and straightened her back.

'However, we can do something about your Matty. We cannot see another life laid to waste, can we?'

Tom reached over and hugged his mother. She had understood his need to try, in some way, to atone for that dreadful winter day when his brother was swallowed up in a second and taken from them forever. For the guilt he still felt. He had prayed this would be her response and it released a flood of hope that banished the cold, dark memories.

'First we must help him with his trial. Then I would like to apprentice him to the company. I can show him how to write and some mathematics. He can read a little, apparently, and—'

'Tom, Tom, slow down!' Beatrix smiled. 'We must take this one step at a time. You must get him out of prison before we can consider anything else. You have not long met the boy. We need to find out more about him and, Tom…' and his mother squeezed his arm tight, surveying him with her grey eyes, 'you cannot make him the younger brother you lost. That would not be fair on the boy. He has to make his own choices.'

Tom nodded.

'I know, Mother, but if you had met him… ' Tom saw the pain on his mother's face and stopped. 'At least we must help him if we can.'

His mother reached over and tucked a wisp of loose hair behind her son's ear.

'And so we shall, Thomas. So we shall.'

They walked towards the rear of the house.

'Mother, thank you for your understanding. I could not have asked Father. I seem to be a constant disappointment to him, not living up to his standards.'

Beatrix stopped and turned.

'Thomas. Your father is not trying to make you be like him. In fact, he would be the first to say people must live according to the code they choose. They cannot follow the path of another, even their father. They must follow their own star.'

'What code does father live by?'

'Oh, that is easy, Tom. Family and business guides your father. Family and business.'

Tom smiled and resumed walking. His mother's brow furrowed.

'Yes, family and business, but not necessarily in that order,' she murmured

As they approached the house, Sam Barnes was walking towards them. He bowed to Tom's mother.

'Good morning, Lady Beatrix. Good Morning, Master Thomas. I have news from Sir Ralph.'

Beatrix looked anxious. The message must have landed with a morning boat. Why the urgency to seek her out?

'Is he well?' she asked

Samuel looked bemused. 'Err, yes my lady, as far as I know, his health is excellent. No, the news is for Master Thomas. Isaac told me to ride here immediately to inform you.' Sam turned to Tom. 'Sir Ralph requires you to join him in Amsterdam for an important meeting with your Uncle Jonas and a group of Moluccas traders. They have agreed terms to provide a monopoly supply of mace to us, but will only sign the deal if they can first meet the merchant they will be dealing with in the future.'

Beatrix clapped her hands and smiled.

'Jonas and your father must have decided it will be you, Tom! Finally this is good news after the disaster of those damned tulips. No?'

Tom did not share her pleasure.

'When does father want me to travel, Sam?'

'On the first available ship, Master Thomas. We're not putting a boat out for another week but Isaac has secured you a berth on the Grey Heron from the Jackson fleet. She sails on the tide tonight, Master.'

'That will not be possible,' Tom replied. 'I have to help young—'

'Nonsense,' Beatrix interjected. 'I can sort out the matter we discussed.' She pulled Tom to one side.

'Tom, if you think your father is disappointed in you, why would he offer this opportunity? Here's your chance to prove you're finally ready to make your mark in the family business.'

She turned back to Sam.

'Let us travel to the warehouse in one of Sir Ralph's carriages so we can plan what needs to be done on the way. Sam, perhaps you could ride Meg back? Good, that's settled then. Let me get my cloak. We do not have a moment to lose!'

Sam looked anxious.

'My lady. Please have a care if you propose to come into the city. The streets are alive with news of a Scottish victory. The King has forbidden any public support for the rebels but people are cheering for the Scots, saying they do not mean fellow Protestants in London any harm. Last night the Apprentice lads gathered near Whitehall, hundreds of them shouting that the Queen's mother was gathering a Catholic army. "Filthy Papists", they shouted, and worse. People are afraid her army will be used to take over London. They say Archbishop Laud is in the plot, right up to his neck. They were all set to burn down the Queen's private chapel but providence intervened.'

'What do you mean, Sam?'

'It started to rain. Pouring down, it was. That soon sobered them up. But there will be more trouble, you can count on that. The fire is stoked.'

'Well, Sam, I thank you for your concern but I am travelling to the warehouse in daylight, and I will have my son with me in the carriage and your good self riding escort. I could not be in better hands. Come, we must leave if you are to be on that boat sailing tonight, Thomas.'

Journeying to the city, Tom was troubled. He knew better than to swim against the tide of his mother's will when in full flood, but he was not prepared for this, being away when Matty needed him and leaving the warehouse during so much unrest. However his mother reminded him of the debt he owed to Jonas and his father. In any case, Matty's trial would not be for weeks, if not months, so Tom should be back in plenty of time.

They made plans for Matty's welfare while Tom was away. Then he packed a bag and two hours later was sailing out of the Thames Estuary as darkness fell.

Chapter 20

4th October 1640
Southwold, on the Suffolk Coast

Tom and Sir Ralph walked along Southwold quay. The early morning sun was burning off the sea mist, revealing a river running from the rear of the port's harbour into the distance.

'Is that the way, Father?'

'No, that's the River Blyth. We want the Dunwich, which branches off to the left. The boat will be waiting there.'

They took a path along the left bank and spotted a small skiff moored near the mouth of the Dunwich. They settled onboard and sent for their baggage, still on the quayside. Tom was about to visit his parliamentary constituency for the second time.

'Easier to hire a boat than a pair of horses in these parts,' Sir Ralph said. 'Quicker too, like as not.'

The skiff set off and its shallow draught was soon making light work of the river's twists and turns under the owner's skilful hand. The sun was now bright in the sky and Sir Ralph stretched in his seat.

'It was inconsiderate of the King to recall Parliament while you were in Amsterdam, Tom. It will convene in less than a month, so no   have the Moluccas contract agreed, we must confirm your election ɛ   wich as soon as possible. Isaac has been in the village for the past two days making sure all is prepared. Let's get your seat secured so we can return home to London, a warm fire and a decent meal.'

Return to the city. Tom had considered little else since he had heard the King's decision. Home to Elizabeth. But first to Matty. He would go straight to New Prison on his arrival.

Sir Ralph shifted in his seat to face his son.

'It is important you attend the new Parliament as often as possible, Tom. I know I have complained about the King of late but events at home appear to have taken a serious turn for the worse. I am told the militia has refused to muster to fight the Scots in Wiltshire and Lincolnshire. The Lord Chamberlain has been forced to intervene personally. Soldiers have turned on officers they suspect are Papists. I read an account of an officer in Farringdon. His troops believed him to be Catholic and attacked him in his lodgings before leaving him for dead in a ditch, like a dog. The unfortunate man crawled to a friend's house and was being treated for his wounds when his soldiers burst in and beat him to death. They put his body in the pillory as a trophy. That is not indiscipline, Tom. That is mob rule.'

Sir Ralph surveyed the flat, featureless landscape as it slipped past. An offshore breeze stiffened the skiff's single sail. They were making good time.

'The soldiers who agree to serve are little better. Their route to Scotland was littered with broken altar rails, smashed statues and burned communion tables. No church has been safe. They see Archbishop Laud and the Catholics as one and the same, all part of a popish plot to take over England... Archbishop Laud, the head of the Protestant church!' I hear the Queen Mother's carriage has been attacked and pelted in Surrey and her guards roughed up. I fear for our country, Tom. The King must get a grip of the situation. The treaty he's signed with the Scots at Ripon is ruinous. They now sit tight on English soil until Parliament, mind you, not the King, agrees their terms for returning to Scotland. This will be nothing less than the abandonment of Laud's reforms for the Scottish Church. Pym and the Scots have the King pinned from both sides in a crab's claw, exactly where they want him. And where is the Earl of Strafford? In his sick bed, I am told.'

'What do they make of our turmoil in the United Provinces, Father?'

'Your Uncle Jonas is not surprised. He says most of Europe has been fighting religious wars for over twenty years and it is a miracle England has escaped until now. But it does not make sense, Tom. The wars in Europe pitch Protestant against Catholic. But in England it's Protestant against Protestant, the Puritans against Laud's Anglican Church. And in the middle of this, we are meant to run a business!'

Sir Ralph banged the side of the skiff in frustration. Tom did not know what to say. His father was usually more prone to anger than despair. It was unsettling to see him so troubled. They fell into a ruminative silence. Twenty minutes later, the village of Dunwich came into view.

They disembarked at a small wharf and walked to the only tavern, the Swan, where Isaac had arranged to meet them. Tom was glad to see a wood fire burning in the parlour. The early sunshine had been swallowed by a bank of cloud and the air was cold. His father stopped to talk to a group of men as Tom walked to the fire. He turned his back to the blaze to warm his legs and saw Isaac walking towards him.

'How fare you, Isaac, and what news of London?'

Sir Ralph was now sitting at a table, deep in conversation with the men.

'Master Thomas, I hardly know where to begin. So much has happened. The city is in turmoil. The Apprentices are on the march, the trained bands of militia are mustering on Moorfields and there are gangs walking the streets at night, hunting Papists and spoiling for a fight.'

'I know, Father told me. And what news of Matty Morris, Isaac? How is he faring in New Prison?'

Isaac beckoned Tom away from the fire and they sat together at a table.

'He is not in New Prison, Master Thomas.'

'He has been transferred? Not to Newgate, I hope, although that would mean his trial is close.'

'He is not in any prison, Master.'

Tom felt a lump in his throat. 'Isaac, he is not… not—'

Isaac's troubled face cleared. 'Dead? Oh no, Master. Quite the opposite. He is free. Free as a bird. But the bird has flown.'

Tom looked across the tavern and saw his father approaching. Isaac stood up.

'Here you are Isaac, good man,' said Sir Ralph. 'Was your carriage to Suffolk comfortable? Is all arranged?'

Isaac nodded and bowed stiffly.

'Excellent. Thank you. Tom, I am retiring to my room as I have correspondence to conduct. I have spoken to the mayor and he will meet us presently outside the tavern for the election. Be sure you are there—and looking respectable. Until later.'

He gave them a mock salute and headed for the stairs at the back of the parlour, bending to pass under the doorframe. Isaac sat down and Tom ordered food and ale for two, eager to hear more about Matty.

'It was about a week after you left, Master Thomas. Matty had been moved to a different cell with clean rushes, a bucket to piss in and regular food, like you ordered. Your mother, God bless her, insisted on coming with me when I delivered the neck verse. It had been carefully written by Miss Ellen on a piece of cloth, English on one side and Latin on the other, exactly as you instructed, in case the judge tried to pull a fast one. Lady Beatrix said they would have embroidered the words if there'd been time but Miss Ellen's lettering was beautiful. I told Lady Beatrix that prison was no place for her but she would not hear of it. She sat with Matty until he could read the verse on both sides. She told him to practise every day, as his life would depend on it, and not allow the cloth into the hands of anyone else, lest it be taken from him. She slipped him a piece of her game pie and asked to leave. I could see she was upset. I paid him a visit a few days later and he was in better spirits. Said he had learned the verse but would keep practicing it, and was there any more pie? Then, while we were talking, the jailer came in and told him to be ready to move. He was off to the Bailey that night!'

'But how could that be, Isaac? What about all those awaiting trial before him, if Newgate was full?'

'That's what I said to the jailer, Master Thomas, but he shrugged and said orders were orders. Matty was frightened but I told him not to worry and keep practising his verse. I went straight to your parents' house. Your mother was surprised but soon got to organising.' Isaac smiled. 'She said she would take lodgings in the city to make sure she did not miss the trial and would I ask Mr Edmund to accompany her, as you and Sir Ralph were away. Again I said the Old Bailey was not the place for a lady of her

standing but she scolded me and told me to do as she said, as there was no time to lose. Mr Edmund was wonderful, Master Thomas. As soon as I explained the situation, he visited the Bailey and was told Matty's hearing would be in two days. On the day, he arranged for Lady Beatrix to enter through a side entrance to avoid the crowd and have her own seat in the courtroom.'

Once again Tom was in Edmund's debt. He must find some way to express his gratitude. Something from India, perhaps.

'Did you give evidence at the trial, as we agreed, Isaac?'

'Yes, Master Thomas. I was at the court when Mr Edmund and your mother arrived. Matty's case was the second on. He looked awful small when he was led into the dock but he lifted his head and spoke well, with a strong voice. The judge read out the charge and called me as the only witness, as I had been the one to discover Matty in the warehouse. I told the judge what had happened.'

'Did he ask what was in the bag Matty was holding when you caught him?'

'He did, Master Thomas. I said it was five pounds of pepper. He asked would I swear to that and I said I would. He asked me how much five pounds of pepper was worth on the London Exchange. I said, "Not much... we're lucky if we can give it away since the Chancellor ruined the market." Well, that caused a right hullaballoo. The judge was not best pleased and said he had a good mind to lock me up for sedition. I was worried for a moment, Master Thomas, I can tell you, but he let it pass.'

The value of the stolen spice was a vital piece of evidence. Anything more than forty shillings and the crime would be too serious for Matty to claim benefit of the clergy. Cinnamon cost forty shillings a bag; pepper less than a quarter of that. Tom had been unhappy asking Isaac to lie in court.

'Isaac, how did you feel about saying it was pepper?'

'I was worried when you first asked, Master Thomas, but I found a passage in the New Testament where God makes it very clear we should never take oaths. It was from the Gospel of St Matthew and I took that to be a sign, being Matthew. When the judge asked me if I swore it was pepper, I said I did, because I would have swore it was apples, if I felt like it. It was God's work to disobey that pledge.'

Thank the Lord for the New Testament. Isaac's conscience, and his own, were clear.

'The judge asked Matty if he had anything to say. I was afraid he would read out the verse there and then, but he did what your mother had told him and waited to be handed the Bible. The judge asked if he wished to take the benefit of the clergy. Matty nodded.'

Isaac paused, his face flushed with excitement. Their food had been served but lay untouched on the table.

'Go on Isaac. What happened?'

'Well, Master, it was over in a moment, before you knew it. Matty was taken to the Bible and the verse pointed out to him. He looked at the page carefully before reciting it, clear as a bell, being careful to follow the words with his finger, as Lady Beatrix had told him. I could see Her Ladyship across the court as Matty spoke. She was reciting the verse herself, under her breath, and when he finished she clasped her hands together and looked fit to burst. Then, when I believed all was completed to our satisfaction,' Isaac said flatly, 'everything went to shit.'

'What do you mean?'

'The judge had listened to Matty read his verse, nodded and said it all appeared to be straightforward. The defendant Matthew Morris was caught in the act taking five pounds of pepper from Tallant's warehouse and was guilty of theft. However, because of the value of the stolen property, the defendant had been offered the benefit of the clergy which he had proved to the court's satisfaction. Then Matty started shouting, "No, I did not take anything. I took nothing." Your mother was frantic, signaling to Matty to be quiet but he was not looking at her.'

'What did the judge say?'

'Well, he looked amazed and then furious. He banged his gavel and told Matty this was the verdict of the court and if he did not like it, he could swing after all. Still Matty shouted. "I don't tell lies. I wasn't going to take nothing, I told them." Lady Beatrix and I were in a panic. Any minute now, I thought, the loon will talk his way on to the end of a rope. Your mother looked in despair over to Mr Edmund. He stood and asked permission to address the judge, and spoke most handsome. He said he was an old friend of the Tallant family who, in your absence, had taken the liberty of arranging lodgings and employment for Matthew Morris if he was released from court. He offered his personal guarantee for the boy's future good conduct should the judge see fit to overlook this outburst. It was, he was sure, because the defendant had been overwhelmed, appearing before such an… an "august", that was the word, such an "august" court of law. Well the judge liked that, and it quietened Matty down as well.'

Tom frowned. Why was Matty still insisting he hadn't meant to take anything?

'His Lordship asked for Edmund's name and the address of the lodgings,' Isaac continued, 'and passed sentence of branding on the thumb and release from court custody. Matty was taken down below and it was all over. The clerk of the court waved Mr Edmund over while the next case was being set up and I escorted your mother from the room. Ten minutes later we met outside the Bailey. The clerk had wanted more details about Mr Edmund, including his address and occupation. He found out from the clerk that branding would take place in the Bailey straight

away and then Matty would be released through a side gate. We went to the gate and waited another fifteen minutes.'

'How was my mother during all of this?'

'Edmund and I could see that Lady Beatrix was becoming fatigued, Master Thomas, so he suggested I went back inside to see what was happening. A coin in the palm of a court official got me straight to the punishment room. Horrible smell it had. Burnt flesh. A guard checked the ledger and said Matthew Morris had been marked over thirty minutes ago. At that point, another cove wearing an apron walked out of the back room and said, "A brave young'un he was too. Hardly a whimper. Like he was resigned to it. And he didn't hang around. Some of them faint and have to sit down. He was off like a rabbit out of its hole. Ran up the cellar steps he did."'

Isaac took a swig of ale. He stirred his bowl of cold pottage before pushing it away.

'And we have not seen him since, Master Thomas. None of us. Your mother was upset and this made Mr Edmund cross. Called him an ungrateful little swine. That was over a week ago. We've been checking his lodgings and I've walked around Thames Street a couple of evenings since, when I've had the time, but nothing. I think Lady Beatrix has got over it. Before I left for Dunwich, she asked me to tell you not to be too worried. Everyone has to follow their own star, she said.'

There was a noise behind them. It was Sir Ralph.

'Are you two still here? I hope you are not in drink, Tom. It's time to be elected.'

Chapter 21

20th October 1640
St Paul's Cathedral

Barty Hopkins bent down with difficulty to examine the floor. His breeches strained under the spread of his ample girth as he rummaged through the scraps of paper at his feet. Flushed with effort, he picked one up, straightened his back and read it carefully.

'Oh my, what have they done? What have they done?'

His face, usually alive with merriment, was creased in concern.

'How could they? In St Paul's!'

Tom turned to a pale young cleric standing next to them. 'When did this happen?'

'Less than an hour ago, sir. I was in the vestry when I heard a great commotion inside the cathedral. I entered the nave and was knocked off my feet by two men running past. It was madness, sir, thirty or more ruffians, running up and down the aisles, shouting insults about His Grace the Archbishop. They ransacked the bookstore and pulled out the Book of Canons, ripping them to pieces, throwing the pages in the air. They destroyed both volumes, in English and Latin.'

Barty stirred the paper at his feet with his shoe. 'Disgraceful... quite disgraceful.'

The cleric sat down wearily on the edge of a pew. His voice began to tremble.

'They set about the altar, pulling the rails out of the floor and jumping on them until they were broken. I was afraid they might set light to the cathedral, but no sooner had they arrived than they left, a swarm of angry bees, out of the main door... leaving this desecration.'

The young man wept and Barty put a consoling arm around his shoulder.

'My good fellow. My companion and I are both Members of the new Parliament. You can rest assured we will bring this appalling act to the attention of the appropriate authorities. You have my word on that!'

Barty raised one eyebrow at Tom and nodded towards the door. They stepped into a chilly breeze. Rain was coming.

'Did you mean what you said back there Barty, about raising this in Parliament?'

'Not really, Thomas. What would be the point? Churches are being attacked all over the country, and now St Paul's. Trouble is, it is entirely possible some of the Members are behind this. Each new Parliament seems to produce more rebellion and unrest.'

They strolled from the cathedral towards St Paul's Yard. Barty had suggested they meet to celebrate Tom's election in Dunwich. He too had regained his seat and both would be in the new Parliament in three weeks' time. They had been lunching on the Strand when they heard a rumour about the attack on St Paul's and came to investigate.

A group of men wearing large cloaks approached. Tom sighed. Pamphlet sellers. They would get no peace now until they reached the other side of the cathedral yard. Before he could suggest they try another route, Barty beckoned a tall figure. The man listened, nodded and reached into his cloak bag for a pamphlet. Money changed hands and the man moved off promptly. Barty did not move. He was reading the pamphlet intently. Tom approached his friend.

Barty looked thunderstruck. 'It's true. I do not believe it.'

'What's true, Barty?'

'This.'

He thrust the pamphlet into Tom's hands. He straightened the crumpled paper and read the headline. "England's Complaint to Jesus Christ against the Bishops canons". He scanned the page quickly but could not see what had upset Barty so much.

'Barty, what is it? What does it mean?'

Barty walked briskly down St Paul's Yard towards Cheapside, muttering under his breath, not waiting for Tom who hurried to keep pace.

'They have gone too far, this time, Tom. Much too far. This must be stopped.'

Barty stopped, breathing heavily.

'I was told about this pamphlet yesterday but I needed to read it with my own eyes. The writers of this... this poison are accusing His Majesty of being in league with the Devil, of... of allowing a popish plot to grow in the heart of Whitehall, of allowing Catholics everywhere in Government. I am told if you read it carefully which, by God, I will, it suggests the people now have a right to resist His Majesty because he has broken his covenant with them. This is treason! Tom, I must go and tell others. Forgive me, this is too urgent. I enjoyed dining with you very much and look forward to seeing you at the opening of Parliament, if not before.'

Barty Hopkins set off down Cheapside as fast as his short legs would carry him. Tom looked at the receding figure and recalled his chance sighting of him with Robert Petty at Lambeth Palace. Perhaps they were both working for the Government? Barty was certainly connected to Henry Jermyn. Who were the 'others' he must tell? He realised he was still holding Barty's pamphlet. Tom glanced at the page as he folded it. Something familiar caught his attention. The page started with the letter "T", printed in a large ornate design—identical to that used by the Perfumed Press.

159

Tom flushed inwardly as he studied the sheet. Stone Face was back in business. But how? And when would Jermyn realise this? God's wounds, had he missed some of the print blocks when he and Edmund raided the cellar? He searched his memory of that night but could not think beyond the sneering face of his pursuer cursing him at the entrance to Moorgate.

Tom set off down Watling Street at a brisk pace trying to put the matter out of his mind. He was back on Thames Street within ten minutes. He turned down the passage towards the warehouse and saw Andrew in the front yard brushing Meg. The horse whinnied softly and pawed the ground as Tom approached.

'Not today, Meg. I will take you out in the morning. How are you, Andrew?'

Brush in his hand, the groom said, 'I am well, thank you, Master, but same cannot be said for Isaac.'

'Is it about Arthur. Has he news?'

'He has, Master. Arthur has been released from Newgate.'

'Thank the Lord for that,' Tom exclaimed. Then he saw an expression of concern on his groom's face. 'What's wrong, Andrew?'

'He cannot walk, Master. Arthur cannot walk or use one of his arms. Can hardly sit for the pain. They racked him, Master, in Newgate. Isaac says on the first day he was locked up, they racked him and left him to rot in a cell. His legs and arm were pulled all out of place. They released him because they needed the space. Isaac is right upset about it, Master. Says they are devils.'

Andrew bent down and slowly brushed Meg's pale flanks again. Tom could feel the colour rise in his face as his anger boiled. Damn Henry Jermyn! Did he know the boy had already been tortured when he struck his deal with Tom? That they'd already got everything they could out of him? Tom would not bet against it. What was it Jermyn had said? "The boy will continue to be held in Newgate but you have my word he will not be interrogated." No need when he had already been racked, and then not given any medical attention either. Elizabeth was right. What a bastard that man was.

Tom went to the front office. Sam was hunched over his ledgers.

'Good afternoon, Master Thomas. Is Sir Bartholomew well?' Sam had recovered his cheery equilibrium since he knew the Perfumed Press was no more. He clearly had not seen Stone Face's new pamphlet.

'Fair to middling. Sam, I have heard about Arthur. Is Isaac here?'

Sam's face clouded.

'No, Master, he is with his sister and Arthur. I hope you do not mind but I said he should go. He could not think to work. It's dreadful cruel, doing that to a boy simply for banging a drum.'

'No, Sam, you did the right thing. Please tell him, from me, to take as long as he needs. We can manage until he gets back.'

'Thank you, Master Thomas, he will be glad of that.'

Tom was considering whether he should visit the Uffords when Andrew Lamkin walked in from the wharf side, his face stilled by shock.

'Andrew, what is it?' Tom asked.

'You'd better come out to the wharf, Master. Right away.' Andrew stepped out on to the wharf followed by Tom and Sam. The berth nearest the warehouse was empty and the young man was staring at the water's edge. Tom looked around the quay but could see nothing unusual.

Sam stepped forward. 'Come on Andrew, what is it? If this is one of your pranks—'

'I came out to the wharf, as you told me,' Andrew interrupted, 'to prepare for the next ship coming in. I cleared the sides and was checking the mooring posts when I saw someone had left a fishing line tied to a post. I took a look and saw the float bobbing on the water. I was thinking that could foul a rudder, that could, so I got hold of the line and hauled it in. My luck was in. We'd had a nibble. Weight on this line. Fish for tea. But it wasn't.'

Andrew looked blankly at Tom.

'Well what was it, Andrew?' Sam exclaimed impatiently.

'Best see for yourself.'

Sam pushed past and looked over the wharf's edge. He pulled in the line, water dripping from his broad freckled hands onto the quayside. The float came first. Sam briefly examined it, frowning, and then continued pulling. The line gathered by his feet in a wet pool as he got down on his hands and knees and leaned towards the water's surface.

'Jesus, Mary and Joseph,' Sam whispered. He straightened his back and, still kneeling, slowly pulled something out the water. Sam swung it onto the boards of the wharf. It was a human hand, a left hand, palm-side down and severed at the wrist.

'My God,' Tom said. 'Is this someone's idea of a hideous joke?'

Tom pushed the hand with the end of his shoe. It was grey, flaccid and marked by feeding fish.

'We will have to inform the constable, though I have no idea how they will trace the owner, poor soul.'

Tom gently flipped the hand with his boot and got down on his haunches. He studied a brown mark on the wrinkled thumb.

'Looks like it might have a birth mark. That could help.'

Sam crouched down next to him.

'Master Thomas. That's no birth mark. I have seen it on men before. It's a brand—to show you've had the benefit.'

Tom's eyes swam. The sound of his rapid heartbeat filled his head. A distant voice was shouting, 'No, no, no, no...' He felt his gorge rise and the world went black.

He awoke in his room. Sam was sitting by his bed and offered him some small beer. Tom lent on his elbow and sipped a little.

'Are you all right, Master? You took quite a turn there.'

Tom pictured the grey hand again. It must be Matty's.

'It's from someone who's had a neck verse brand,' Sam said. 'Always on the inside of the thumb. Looks like it belonged to a young man, from its size. Hard to tell what the skin is like but it's not seen hard labour. No scars or cuts.'

It could be a coincidence, but Tom knew it was a hollow hope.

'Master, there's something else. I hardly know how to tell you.' Sam leaned back and rummaged in his jerkin pocket. 'Tis the float.'

He pulled out a dirty rag and unwrapped its contents. Tom held out his hand and Sam gave him a damp piece of wood. He turned it over and found himself looking at a familiar piece of printing type—a letter "M" with an ornate pattern carved around it.

Chapter 22

21st October 1640
Shovel Alley, East London

Tom shuddered. The immense stone walls of the Tower of London bore down on him through the early morning mist.

He was near the foot of its east wall, close to St Katherine's Church. Shovel Alley was the address Edmund gave in court for Matty's lodgings. Matty had not been sighted there since he disappeared, but it was the only lead Tom had. It was a short walk from Tom's warehouse but in a district he did not know well.

The church was surrounded by a warren of grimy back alleys and gloomy courtyards with names like Pillory Lane and Dark Entry. Tom walked past a jumble of tenements and walkways before finding the address he sought. It was quiet, too early for the local whores and petty thieves to be up and about.

Stone Face's words ran through his head: "You will live to regret this. That I swear on my solemn oath." My God, the man was exacting his revenge, but at what price! Why mutilate the young boy? The severed hand had been a message, but of what? Even if Matty was not ..d, he must find his body for a Christian burial, and find answers to these questions.

He peered down Shovel Alley. It was empty with high walls stretching either side into the mist. Tom crept forward and saw wooden doors to his left and right. He gently tried the first. Locked. The second was also locked, and the third. He could now see the alley ended in a small courtyard. There was no other way out. The hairs on the back of his neck bristled.

He tried the next door on the right. The hinges creaked but the door was stuck at the bottom. Cursing the noise, Tom checked the entrance to the alley. All was clear. His breath clouded in the damp morning air as he put his shoulder and leg against the door and pushed again with all his weight.

The door scraped across the ground and opened six inches. The smell of death hit him. He closed the door, stepped back into the alley and took a deep breath. His heart pounding, he pushed it hard again, prizing it further open, enough to shuffle sideways through the gap.

A rotting corpse lay at his feet. Putting his handkerchief to his mouth, Tom looked closer. It was a mastiff, a giant of a dog, lying on its side against the inside of the door, with a wide, putrid wound running the length of its decaying right flank.

He was in a small yard, surrounded on three sides by high walls. In front was a three-storey brick tenement in poor repair. The

ground was choked with rubbish—old barrels, a broken handcart, pieces of brick and wood. The house looked empty. If so, given its position, the dog must have died after the last person left, otherwise how could they have made their exit through the door? But who would leave a dog in such a condition? Tom began to doubt this could be Matty's lodgings but, having worked so hard to get in, he was not leaving without investigating further. He pushed the door closed and turned towards the building. It was typical of the dwellings in the area, mean and run down. He picked his way through the rubbish to peer through the grime on the ground floor window. A low-ceilinged room contained rough furniture, a table, chairs and an empty fireplace, but little else. Tom tried the front door which opened. The house was silent. He waited a moment before stepping inside. He stopped again and listened. Nothing. He walked silently into the back parlour which was bare save for a wooden pail for gathering water. Light filtered into the room from the open staircase by the back wall.

Tom looked up the stairs, listening carefully. He began to climb. The first step creaked under his weight. Another step, another creak. He heard rapid movement above him. He took another step and two shapes flew at him from the top step, all teeth and thick, thrashing tails. Rats, fat and black, landed three steps in front of him. Before Tom could move, they leapt again, straight at him.

The taut, heavy body of the first hit his right leg. The second bounced off the side wall and onto his chest, squealing and scrabbling, before tumbling past him onto the pantry floor. Tom spun around to see both rats loping towards the front room. He gasped and sprinted up the remaining steps two at a time. He reached the room at the top and tumbled through the open doorway, sinking to his knees on the bare dusty floorboards.

The body of Matthew Morris was sitting on the floor in a corner of the room, his head leaning forward. His shirt was stained dark crimson across both shoulders, his black sightless eyes staring at the dusty floorboards. His right hand, clenched in a fist, was resting in his lap. His left arm was stretched in front of him, beckoning Tom to join him. Only there was no hand, just a torn sleeve, ripped and matted with blood. Fragments of bloodied cloth and flesh were scattered around the floor. His stomach heaved.

He touched Matty's cheek. It felt like dusty marble. Tom looked for the source of the blood on his shirt and noticed the blond hair behind Matty's left ear was thick with congealed gore. He had been hit from behind. Tom studied Matty's face. Awful as it was, he did not want to look away. This would be the last time he would ever see him. His mind flashed: Matty's staring eyes, a small wet hand reaching above the water, Matty's empty gaze, the hand gone. Everything lost.

He knelt and prayed over the corpse, his whispered words echoing through the silent house. Tears fell freely from his face to congeal in the

dust on the floor. Finally he moved forward to kiss Matty on the top of his head, and felt a sharp pain under his knee. He lifted his leg and saw a piece of wood, stained yellow on the floor. He turned it in his fingers and saw one side intricately carved with the letter "T". He studied the small printer's block, unable to take in what he was seeing. Then he quickly lifted Matty's right leg, where his knee had been resting, and felt underneath its length. A second block. He patted the pocket of his breeches and felt a lump. A third piece—also stained yellow.

Panic was growing in Tom's chest. Stone Face must have set a trap, to link Tom to the Dutch press, and a murder for good measure, and he had walked right into it. However, a trap only worked if you were caught. My God, had someone been watching him enter the house? Was Wilmot from the Stationers' Company in Shovel Alley at that moment? Tom pocketed the printer's blocks and feverishly surveyed the room for any more. His eyes rested on Matty's right hand curled tightly in a fist. He knelt down and held the stiff fingers. Sam had been right. They were untouched by the scars of life. Tom felt something inside the fist and gently prised the fingers open. Tears again flowed. He pulled at the threads of a piece of fabric and his sister Ellen's familiar handwriting appeared. Slowly Tom unravelled the neck verse from Matty's dead grasp.

Despair and anger coursed through him. Matty had kept his verse close until the very end. It had saved him once… the Tallants had saved him once. Faced with death again, it was his only defence. His talisman, his hope of better things. He would have grasped it with all his might. Miserere mei, Deus… O God, Have mercy upon me. But this time no one answered his call. No one came, until it was too late. Tom had failed him, just as he had failed his young brother Matty on that frozen lake. Misery enveloped him, kneeling in the room, bereft of purpose, his willpower extinguished. He stumbled to his feet and wandered back and forwards, his body wracked by deep, overwhelming sobs.

Slowly the tears ceased and Tom looked around him. He brushed a tangle of cobwebs from the window and peered outside. To his left he could see over the yard wall to Shovel Alley. To his right, a corner of the courtyard at the end of the alley. The huge body of the dead mastiff lay in the yard directly beneath him.

His body stiffened. Voices, young voices, and a man shouting. He saw two boys run along the alley away from him, towards its entrance. They ducked out of view and re-emerged in the same spot. And then again. He realised they were bending down, picking up stones to throw.

The boys turned tail and ran, laughing. Tom moved away from the window. He could not be found with Matty's body. If he did not escape the building unseen, his life could be over. A movement outside made Tom turn back to the window. An unmistakable figure appeared, in pursuit of the boys. Nathaniel Franklin, the City Magistrate. Tom flushed

with shock. Why was he here? He remembered something Elizabeth had said: 'There will be a common thread linking these seemingly chaotic events.' In his worst nightmare he had feared being discovered by Wilmot, never Franklin. Oh, Elizabeth, find me an answer!

He looked again. Franklin turned out of Shovel Alley in pursuit of his tormenters. Tom glanced for a final time at Matty, arm extended in eternal invitation, before running past his body and down the stairs, three at a time. Franklin would be back in a matter of moments. He must get out of the yard.

Tom charged through the pantry into the front room. He opened the front door carefully and listened. Nothing, so he walked into the yard. He stepped over the stinking corpse of the mastiff and peered through the small opening in the yard door. No sign of Franklin. Should he step into the alley and make a run for it? It was too dangerous. What if he reached the entrance of Shovel Alley as Franklin was returning with a constable, to find his pockets full of the printer's blocks and the neck verse?

He closed the door and desperately searched the yard. He took hold of one end of a broken fence post and wedged the other against the ribs of the mastiff and pushed. The end of the post sank into the putrid flesh before holding fast against the animal's spine. Tom held his breath and pushed hard. Slowly the dog's carcass slid across the yard floor until it was jammed, once again, against the bottom of the yard gate. The dog's ribcage was impaled by the post and, keeping it in position, he lowered his end to the floor. He then dragged a large barrel across the yard. No time for silence, as long as he wasn't seen. Tom rammed the barrel against the end of the fence post and stood back. That should slow Franklin down.

He scanned the yard again. A broken cart was leaning against the wall to his right. He jumped on it and thrust his body upwards. The cart skewed to one side under his weight and his chest hit the wall, knocking the breath from his body. He gripped the top with both arms and swung his leg over. Keeping low, he scrambled up and, without stopping to look, dropped into the yard next door. Tom tensed himself for a long fall and a hard landing. Neither came. He hit a wooden roof a few feet below and felt himself sliding. Then he was in mid-air again, twisting his body before landing in the yard on all fours. He had bounced off the sloping roof of the yard privy. It did not look strong enough to take his weight but he was glad it had, given the smell seeping under its rough wooden door.

He remained crouched, listening intently. Unlike next door, the yard was clear except for the privy and a pile of bricks in one corner. He carefully studied the windows in the house facing him. Nothing moved. Then he heard voices getting louder, out in the alley. Franklin.

'That's the door. Open it.'

'It's stuck, sir. Locked, I think.'

'Break it open.'

'Should we not try to raise someone first, before we start breaking doors down?'

'What, and let our fugitive know we are coming?'

Tom realised with relief that Franklin was still hoping to catch him by surprise. That meant he hadn't been seen climbing over the wall. Tom heard muttered grumbles and a crashing sound, and another.

'Oh my Lord, what a stench! Sir, there's something dead in the yard. I can smell it.'

Tom heard the excitement in Franklin's voice.

'Exactly as I expected. Come on lads, I need to be in that yard... NOW.'

Seconds later there was another crash, followed by the sound of creaking boards.

'It's no good, sir. It seems to be stuck fast at the bottom. I think there's a body behind the door. Ripe, an' all.'

There was a pause, then Franklin's voice.

'Very well, we will have to enter one of the yards on either side and climb over the wall. Tom cursed. What a bloody fool he had been to jam the door so well. Instead of delaying Franklin, it was sending the magistrate towards his hiding place. He pictured Franklin and the constables in the alley, choosing whether to try the door on their right or left. He willed them to go right. He heard a noise outside his yard and stiffened.

'This door's locked, but it don't look too strong,' a voice called.

'Break it, just break it,' Franklin shouted. Tom panicked. He looked around the empty yard and eyed the privy. Only one place to hide.

The door from the alley collapsed with a splintering crash and a man fell into Tom's yard, followed closely by Franklin and another constable.

'Quick. We must see inside that yard next door. One of you get on top of this privy,' Franklin ordered.

The first constable cupped his hands in front of him and his companion stepped into the cradled palms. With a push, he vaulted onto the top of the wooden hut. Franklin followed and the constable pulled him up. Tom held his breath as the privy roof creaked and groaned under their weight.

The magistrate and the constable looked over the wall.

'Told you something was dead. Look at the size of that dog.'

'Yes, but what is it doing there?' Franklin snapped. 'Lower me down, I need to take a look.'

Tom heard scrabbling as the magistrate was lowered into the yard, then silence, broken by the constable on the wall calling to his mate. 'You should see this dog, Gilbert. Big as a horse, what's left of it.'

Gilbert did not answer. Instead, Tom heard a low groan.

'What's wrong, Gilbert? You in trouble?'

'Damn those whelks. I knew they didn't smell right. I'm using this privy.'

Hidden in the gap between the privy and the yard wall, Tom spied the constable through a pinhole. He desperately looked around for some kind of weapon.

'Best be quick, Gilbert. Old fart-face Franklin will be shouting for us again in a minute.'

Gilbert groaned and the privy door stared to creak open. Tom readied himself.

'Men, men. I need you in this house. NOW.'

Franklin's voice, urgent and excited, came from inside the building next door. Tom's tension eased. He never thought he would be glad to hear Franklin's sneering tone.

'Told you, Gilbert. You'll have to hang on.'

Gilbert stood with the privy door half open. Tom silently cursed and picked up a piece of wood lying at his feet.

'Can't wait,' Gilbert gasped, and stumbled into the wooden shed.

'Well you will have to answer to Franklin. I'm off.'

Gilbert's mate dropped out of view into the yard below. Tom dared not move or breathe, standing inches from discovery as Gilbert banged the thin wall between them, feeling around for the wooden pail. He finally located it and, tearing off his breeches, lowered himself gratefully.

Tom silently inched his way from the narrow space behind the privy. He stood for a moment and exhaled slowly. Lord, that had been a tight fit. He tip-toed across the yard and stepped over the remains of the shattered door to peer into the alley beyond. It was empty so, dusting off his clothes, Tom walked calmly away, fighting the urge to run as fast as his shaking legs would carry him.

Ten minutes later he was descending Tower Hill towards Thames Street. The more he considered it, the more he was convinced that Franklin had been tipped off. The magistrate did not try the alley doors in succession. He went straight to the house containing Matty's body. Could Stone Face have done that? Perhaps he had been caught by Josiah Wilmot from the Stationers' Company and provided information in return for his freedom? But that was not possible. How did Stone Face find Matty in the first place to murder him, and then set the trap for Tom?

Tom stopped in mid-stride. Of course… the judge had asked Edmund to read out the address in open court. Anyone could have told Stone Face. One thing was certain: in their hurry to leave, Edmund and he must have missed some of the printer's blocks at Grub Street.

Tom felt exhausted and his head ached abominably. He trudged down Thames Street, lost in thought, and straight into the back of a woman, knocking her tray of pies onto the muddy street.

'Oi, Mister. Mind where you're going. You have ruined my pies. I won't be able to sell them.'

'Mistress, please excuse my clumsiness. I was not looking where—'

He stopped and stared past the woman's shoulder. There, further down Thames Street, standing near the entrance to the Tallant warehouse was the unmistakable figure of Robert Petty.

Tom picked up the broken pies, careful to keep the woman between him and Petty. He offered them to her.

'No point giving them to me. What can I do with those... oh, thank you very much, sir, most generous. A real gent.'

She walked off with a skip in her step and a crown in her hand, the first coin Tom could find in his purse to press into her palm. Enough to buy twenty trays of pies. He moved into a shop doorway and studied Petty for five minutes. He was clearly watching the entrance to the warehouse. Tom turned and headed back towards the Tower. He felt a net tightening around him. Where could he go? First he must get beyond the city walls before the guards on gate duty were given his description by Franklin. He cut up Water Lane onto Tower Street. The nearest way through the walls was Aldgate, to the east of Fenchurch Street, leading into Whitechapel. He walked briskly along Mark Lane and right into Crutched Friers. His plan, such as it existed, was to mingle with others waiting to enter the gatehouse. With luck, the tide of people would carry him through unnoticed.

Tom put his head down and walked as quickly as he could along the curving length of Poor Jewry. He could not get the picture of Matty's dead, empty eyes out of his thoughts. He shook himself and tried to think of the boy's face when alive, his determined expression as he protested his innocence: 'I didn't take nothing. I didn't take nothing.' Tom fell into repeating the phrase as he walked, to keep the image of Matty's death mask at bay. His voice kept time with his rapid footsteps. 'I did not take no-thing... I did not take no-thing.' His steps slowed. 'I... did... not... take...' Tom looked up and felt the boy was close. He stopped and, for the second time that day, prayed for Matty's forgiveness.

How could he be so stupid? The boy had tried to tell him the truth time and again, but Tom had not listened. Matty had not gone to the warehouse to take anything. No, he was sent there to leave something... pieces of printer's type that would link Tom to the Scottish Press. Someone had told Matty to break in and leave the type hidden in the warehouse, likely under the sack of cinnamon in his hand when Isaac caught him. That person would tip off Josiah Wilmot who would raid Tom's warehouse.

Tom considered the timing of this and deduced it must be Stone Face. At that time Jermyn believed the Scottish Press was finished and Tom was very much in his favour. It would have been pointless for Jermyn to implicate Tom at that moment. He remembered the printer's eyes. Black and hard as coal. Yes, he was capable of any and all of this. What else did he have in store for Tom?

Approaching the end of Poor Jewry Lane, High Street ahead looked busy. Aldgate was close, and he joined the throng shuffling towards the gatehouse. He crouched a little as the crowd streamed through the gate house entrance. The guards surveyed them as they passed. One looked straight at Tom, who steeled himself for flight. The guard lifted his hand. Tom tried not to stare. The soldier stifled a yawn before turning his gaze towards the river of people behind. Tom continued with his head down until he was twenty yards past Aldgate and into Whitechapel. He ducked into a passage and leaned against a wall to steady his nerve. Looking at the sky, he calculated it was an hour past noon. There was only one place he could go for help. He set off left along Houndsditch to put distance between himself and Aldgate before seeking food and drink; then the dangerous walk to Clerkenwell, in the open for anyone to see.

Chapter 23

Later that day
Bolton Hall

Tom sat on a milestone near the entrance to his parents' house and removed his left boot. He held it upside down, shook out a stone and rubbed his aching foot. It was late afternoon and the gathering grey cloud overhead was slowly darkening. He had walked without break from Houndsditch and was bone weary. His single thought had been to reach safe haven; but now, with sanctuary in sight, Tom was reluctant to enter. If Franklin was looking for him, he did not want to get his parents involved. Worse, he would have to give his mother the shattering news of Matty's murder.

A carriage approached. Tom quickly replaced his boot and ducked behind a bush. He doubted Franklin would stray so far beyond his City jurisdiction but he couldn't be too careful. The carriage came to a halt and a door opened. It was Elizabeth. He stepped out from his hiding place.

'Tom! I was coming to see you but you have saved me a journey into London. Are you staying at Bolton Hall?'

Sitting on the edge of the carriage seat, Elizabeth's face radiated vitality and he drew strength from her presence.

'Get inside, Tom. I have something important to tell you.'

'And I, you,' Tom answered, as he hauled himself in.

'What is wrong? You look completely worn out. But tell me later. I need to speak to you about the death of Sir Joseph Venell.'

Joseph Venell. A name from a different time given the events now overwhelming him. He shook his head. Elizabeth looked puzzled and Tom reached over and held her hand.

'Elizabeth, so much has happened since we last met. I am on my way to explain it all to my parents.'

'Yes, but let me give you my news first,' Elizabeth pressed him. 'Tom, it's important.'

Elizabeth leaned forward and lowered her voice.

'I have gone through your account of Sir Joseph's death again and again in my mind, searching for a loose thread to follow, some sort of clue. Then, the other day, I was in the garden when it struck me. Where was the hat?'

'The hat?'

'Yes, the hat, Tom. When you saw Sir Joseph in the cellar of his home he was wearing a new beekeeper's outfit. However, you did not mention his beekeeper's hat and veil. Did you see it?'

Tom sat back and tried to recall his visit to Venell's house with Petty. It was almost a year ago. He remembered the room in the cellar containing Sir Joseph's body and the dreadful injuries to his head, but that was all.

'I do not think I saw a hat, but it was dark in the cellar. It could have been in another room or upstairs in the house, but what does it matter—'

'It was not in the house, I will wager that,' Elizabeth interrupted.

'How do you know?'

'Because yesterday I visited Venell's house in Kensington and spoke to the stockman who had discovered him dying in the field. He is absolutely certain Venell was still wearing his hat when he found him. He remembers drawing its net back to help his master breathe more easily. It was still on Venell's head when he picked his body up to return to the manor house but, when he arrived at the front door, the stockman noticed the hat was missing. He had slung Sir Joseph's body over his shoulder to carry him home and believes the hat must have fallen off as he was climbing up the field. He went back to the field immediately but the hat was not there. He had not mentioned it to anyone because he did not want to get into trouble.'

'But, Elizabeth, I still do not see why this is so important. It's only a beekeeper's hat.'

She squeezed his hand and spoke softly.

'Tom, you said falcons would not attack humans. But what if they were trained to attack a mark or a certain symbol, such as a black cross, or two circles, one inside the other, or something similar? Symbols that could be embroidered onto the crown of a hat?'

The mist began to clear for Tom.

'You mean wearing the hat would make Venell, or rather the top of his head, a target for the hunting falcons?'

Tom winced, imagining the swooping birds grabbing at the hat with their talons. He had felt their lethal grip through a leather glove on many occasions.

'Falcons can be trained to hit a mark. But this is merely surmise, Elizabeth. It could equally be that the hat was plain fabric.'

'Then why did it go missing? I asked the stockman if it was windy on the day of Sir Joseph's death. He said there was a light breeze but no more. I got him to show me the field and exactly where he found his master. Tom, the meadow is large, a good half-acre, and sloping downhill. The hat would have to travel a long distance to disappear. The grass was long at the time and its netting would have snagged on the grass or a stone, and remember he had gone back immediately to look for it. No, I think someone was watching the field and removed the hat from where it fell when the stockman left with Sir Joseph's body.'

Elizabeth's eyes sparkled with excitement. 'But there's more. If there was a target on the hat, it must have been there when Sir Joseph bought

it. If it had been added later, he would have noticed. Two black circles inside each other could have looked like decoration, like the stripes around a bee's body, don't you see?'

Tom's mist was replaced by a bright light.

'So if we discover where Sir Joseph bought it and the beekeeping suit, it could provide our first link to the owner of the peregrines?'

'Yes, exactly,' Elizabeth replied. 'It's not much, but it is something to investigate further.'

Tom hugged her.

'It is the first thing I have heard in this whole affair which makes any sort of sense and I thank you for it.'

Another carriage appeared in the distance, this time on the road from London. Tom pressed himself back into his seat.

'Elizabeth, I need to get out of public view and reach the safety of my parents' house. I can explain all when we get inside.'

Ten minutes later, Tom was by a wood fire in Bolton Hall, sipping a tankard of hot grog. His father, mother, sister and Elizabeth sat in a half circle around him. Ellen was holding her mother's hand. Lady Beatrix looked devastated.

'So you think this radical printer is responsible?' his father asked, giving Tom a searching look.

'He swore revenge on me, Father, that night at Moorgate, and he had access to any blocks we left behind in our haste to escape Grub Street. He must have paid Matty to hide some in our warehouse, planning then to send an anonymous message to the Stationers' Company suggesting they search the building. That way I would be implicated in the Scottish press, diverting suspicion from him. When Matty was caught, he became a danger to the printer because of what he knew. He must have decided to… to kill him,' here he looked at the red face of his mother, stained with tears, 'and hit on the idea of implicating me, both in the murder and the ownership of the Scottish press, by laying the trap in Shovel Alley, using Matty's body and more of the type. Then he will have sent the anonymous note, but this time to the magistrate.'

Elizabeth looked troubled, but said nothing. There was a gentle knock on the hall door. Ellen answered it and talked quietly to one of the servants before leaving the room.

'And you are sure no one saw you arriving or leaving Shovel Alley,' his father continued.

Tom nodded.

'As sure as I can be. I could hear Franklin talking to the constables most of the time and he did not mention my name once.'

Tom heard voices in the hall and the door opened. Ellen stood in the doorway.

'Father, there is a man here who insists on being—'

Ellen stopped mid-sentence as a small figure pushed past her into the room. Nathaniel Franklin.

'Enough of this delay… ah, there is the man I seek, Thomas Tallant.'

Franklin pointed a bony finger at Tom who jerked upright, gripping the arms of his chair. He recoiled at the sight of this odious creature, the bane of his life, standing in his family home. The two constables from Shovel Alley followed Franklin into the room, followed by another man with billowing white hair and bushy side whiskers who turned to Tom's father.

'I regret this intrusion, Sir Ralph, but Mr Franklin does have a warrant for young Tom's arrest. The paperwork appears to be in order and, given the magnitude of the charge, as the magistrate for Clerkenwell I am duty bound to cooperate.'

Ralph Tallant nodded.

'I understand, Septimus. And what is the charge, Mr Franklin?'

The magistrate sneered at Tom.

'Why, murder of course, Sir Ralph. Your son is charged with the foul murder of one Matthew Morris. There will be other charges in due course, but I think that gives us enough to be going on with for the time being, don't you?'

Sir Ralph's anger was stirring. 'Where is your evidence, man?'

The magistrate looked around the room and Tom could see his mind working. Franklin had spent his life in the shadow of people like the Tallants. Finally he had an opportunity to wield power over them and he intended to savour it. He stalked the room, leering at the family and Elizabeth.

'Well, where do I start? Perhaps by observing that it is strangely apt you should be brought to justice in this house. I told you once before I smelled the Devil's work around you, Thomas Tallant. It was outside this very room Sir Hugh Swofford met his untimely end, overwhelmed by a vision of flying demons shown to him by Sir Ralph Tallant. Now I have in my possession a statement from Ned Smithers, signed with his mark, declaring the boy Morris described himself as the Devil's spawn when they shared a cell in New Prison prior to Morris's trial, and that Thomas Tallant did visit said Matthew Morris and consort with him in lengthy and mysterious conversations.'

Sir Ralph flashed a questioning look at Tom. Franklin was getting into his stride.

'And the day after your visit, Morris was moved to another cell where he was treated most royally, according to Smithers. Why should that be? Let me paint the picture for you, Tallant. You and Morris first consorted as the Devil's disciples. Intent on all kinds of wickedness, you joined in a pact to invoke demonic forces against Sir Joseph Venell, a God-fearing member of the City community, and a rival merchant to you. Following Venell's death, his partner Swofford confronted you at his house party

accusing you of involvement in Venell's death. Fearing he had stumbled on the truth, you arrange for him to be invited to your parents' house where again your sorcery, combined with Morris's powers, invade Swofford's body. He falls to his death seeing the demons you have conjured.'

'Oh this is ridiculous.' It was the voice of Tom's mother, her tears replaced with a look of steely resolve.

Sir Ralph placed a restraining hand on her arm. 'Let the magistrate say his piece, Bea.'

Franklin paused, sniffed and started pacing again.

'The Devil's kind are not to be trusted, even among their own. You started thinking, didn't you Tallant, that Morris knew too much? He had too much on you. So you decided to get him out of the way, accusing him of stealing from your warehouse. As soon as I heard your account I knew it was a fairy tale. Who in their right mind would walk into a busy merchants in the middle of the day and try to walk out with a valuable bag of spice under their arm? Cock and bull, the whole of it. But it would be enough to get him into court where you intended to sink him good and proper when the trial came up. You would be called as a witness. You meant to lay it on right thick, didn't you? Would have told the court Morris was stealing a bag of gold, not pepper, if necessary. There'd be no benefit of the clergy then, would there? So you visit him in New Prison. He's angry, fit to tell the world about you, so you keep him sweet by saying it's all a misunderstanding and you'll get him sorted with a cosy cell. You'll tell the judge you'd made a mistake and it wasn't Morris after all. Anything to keep him quiet until the court case. But that's when things started to go wrong, didn't they, Tallant? You got called away to Amsterdam and, blow me, when you got back, the trial was over and Morris free. You panic, but then your man Ufford tells you he knows where Morris is living because it was read out in court. The rest is simple. You drop by one night. "Hello Matthew Morris, me old cock. Didn't expect to see me again, did you?" Ten minutes later the deed is done. He didn't have a prayer... Lord forgive me for saying so of such a blasphemer.'

Franklin paused for breath, his eyes wild with excitement.

'We found a piece of printer's type under the body that puzzled us at first. So I visited my old friend Josiah Wilmot from the Stationers' Company. He said you had been busy doing Mr Henry Jermyn a favour breaking up an illegal print house, using your contacts in Amsterdam. And I could see then how clever you are Tallant. You must have retained one of the blocks and left it at the scene to shift the blame onto the radical printers. But that don't fool me. I know too much about you.'

A shocked silence hung over the room, which was soon broken by a gentle tapping on the door. Ellen hurried out again.

Sir Ralph cleared his throat. 'Magistrate Franklin, I have listened carefully to what you have to say. You clearly believe you have a case but I cannot see a single piece of solid evidence against my son. You pin this Faustian connection between my son and this boy on the word of another man in prison. What, pray, did Mr Ned Smithers get in return for his statement?' Sir Ralph held up his hand. 'No, do not tell me. I would much prefer my lawyers to find this out; and they will, by God, Mr Franklin, they will. You also say my son was undone by the speedy trial of Morris. But that's the point, is it not? The trial was brought forward by months to take place when my son was away. I wonder who might have arranged that, Mr Franklin? A magistrate's influence is extensive in the courts. But again, my lawyers will get to the bottom of that. No. I suggest you leave us this instant before I throw you out personally, if base accusations and wild fancy is all you have to offer.'

The door clicked open and Ellen stepped back into the room.

There was another silence and a smile on Franklin's face that Tom did not like.

'Constable. Pass me the bag, will you?'

Constable Gilbert, recovered from his trip to the privy, stepped forward and produced a linen sack from behind his back. Franklin opened the top, fished inside and smiled again before pulling out an object. It took Tom several seconds to realise what it was. His heart lurched.

Franklin addressed Sir Ralph. 'Before you do that, Tallant, I suggest you look at this and tell me what it is. Be careful, it is rather dirty. I retrieved it this very morning from inside the broken skull of Matthew Morris.'

Tom's mother moaned and put her hands to her face.

Sir Ralph's voice was flat. 'It's a wooden hammer.'

'Yes, but what kind of hammer?'

'It's a beetle hammer used for caulking joints in ships. There are hundreds in the London dockyards.'

'Yes, but how many have this on the shaft?'

Franklin moved his grip to reveal a carving. Sir Ralph visibly buckled. He looked at Tom and back at Franklin. He cleared his throat and spoke.

'It's a letter "T", and before you ask, Franklin, yes it does stand for Tallant. It is carved on all our tools at the warehouse. But anyone could have stolen it.'

'Oh, like young Morris "stole" the bag of pepper?' Franklin sneered. 'Enough of this.' He turned to Tom. 'Thomas Tallant, I am charging you with the murder of Matthew Morris and causing the deaths of Sir Joseph Venell and Sir Hugh Swofford through diabolical means. You will be taken to Newgate prison to await trial at the Old Bailey, and may the Lord have mercy on your soul.'

Pandemonium erupted. Lady Beatrix stood up, shouting, 'No, No, No.'
The constables stepped forward to apprehend Tom but were blocked by
Sir Ralph. In the midst of this, Ellen calmly embraced her brother.
Holding him tight, she whispered, 'Edmund at front of the house—with a
horse.'

He nodded and pressed something into her hand.

'Ellen, give this to Elizabeth. On no account let anyone else see it.' They
broke from their embrace. 'Don't worry, dear sister. I will survive this.'

Elizabeth called out, 'God keep you, Tom, and remember May still my
love descend… May still my love descend.'

Tom held her gaze before turning to see the magistrate pushing past the
constables.

He looked to Lady Beatrix. 'Sorry mother, I will build you another.'

The momentary confusion cleared on her face, then she nodded
vigorously.

'Yes, yes!'

Tom spun on his heel and sprinted out of the room, pursued by Franklin.

'Stop, Tallant. This confirms your guilt.'

Tom ran through the next room towards the back of the house, pursued
by both constables who had forced their way past Sir Ralph.

He tipped a tall wooden chair onto the floor behind him. There was a
yelp of pain and a crash, and, when he looked back, one of the constables
and Franklin lay in a tangle on the floor, but the other was still in pursuit.
He charged through the back room, past shelves of potted plants. Bending
down, Tom covered his head and crashed with all his weight through the
end of his mother's new glass house.

He rolled on the garden lawn and back onto this feet, a searing pain in
his left palm. He ran to the side of the house, blood pouring from his hand.
Without breaking stride, he carefully gripped a long shard of glass
impaled in his palm and pulled firmly. A flash of pain shot through his
hand, and he staggered as he threw the glass on the ground. Ahead lay the
low stone wall marking the front of the garden. He vaulted over it and
landed on the drive. Edmund was standing near the front of the house
holding a horse by its halter. Tom ran to him.

'My dear fellow, what on earth has happened to you? Here, wrap my
scarf around your hand.'

Raised voices could be heard in the garden.

'I was calling on your parents. Ellen has told me everything. You'd
better go,' he said, offering Tom the horse's reins.

'Shouldn't I… well, shouldn't I hit you?'

'Why? Do you want to?'

'No, no, of course not, Edmund, but you don't want to be seen as my
accomplice, do you? Better that I overpower you.'

'Well, I must say I'd prefer my good looks were not ruined with a broken nose, thank you. And the whole case against you is a farce. Franklin would make a goat seem intelligent. No, I am with you on this one, Tom. Fiddlesticks to what they think, but you really must go. You will have left a blood trail even Franklin could not miss. If I am not mistaken that is him approaching along the side of the house.'

Tom could hear the magistrate's voice getting louder. Pausing to embrace Edmund, Tom hauled himself into the saddle and took off down the driveway into the gathering dark.

Two hours later, Tom was walking Edmund's horse towards Elizabeth's house. The night was black, stars sparkling through fleeting gaps in the cloud. Since escaping from his parents' house, he had criss-crossed the countryside north of Clerkenwell either side of the Islington Road. Now it was dark, he was safe until Franklin renewed his search at first light tomorrow.

He thought again about his confrontation with Franklin. The magistrate had made his case and concocted his evidence. The City wanted a culprit and the courts would oblige. There was only one way out of this now. He must find Stone Face and bring him to justice.

He softly repeated Elizabeth's chosen verse of Donne.

'May still my love descend.'

And completed it:

'Since such love's motion natural is,

May still my love descend

and journey down the hill,

Not panting after growing beauties ; so

I shall ebb out with them who homeward go.'

Not the meaning Donne had intended in his ninth elegy but the message was clear enough to Tom, and under the cover of darkness he headed for her garden. Tom tethered Edmund's horse to a tree and, crouching, walked softly to the garden wall. His left hand was now throbbing inside Edmund's scarf which was caked with dried blood. He entered through the door in the wall. The garden looked much as it had been on his first visit. One day he might see it in daylight. He walked down the side path towards the viewing platform in front of the tall hedge. There was no sign of Elizabeth or her telescope.

Tom was exhausted. Everything ached. His head, his legs and in particular his hand. Was it only that morning he had stood next to the Tower of London, searching for Shovel Lane? He had walked and ridden for miles, not eaten since midday and been accused of causing three deaths. He could not take another step. He sat down to wait for Elizabeth but was soon shaking with cold and exhaustion. He needed shelter and rest. Could he squeeze under the platform and wrap himself in his cloak?

The prospect did not invite, but Tom felt close to collapse. He looked underneath. Hardly room for a mouse. In desperation he walked around the garden and discovered a gap at the far end of the hedge. He entered, to see a large wooden building hidden between the back of the hedge and the garden perimeter wall, thirty feet beyond.

He would break in if necessary, he was so desperate. There was no need. The door swung open to his touch and light appeared. Cautiously Tom stepped into a large, windowless room. A lantern was glowing on a table in the far corner and, next to it, two covered bowls and a letter. Tom opened the letter:

My dearest Thomas,

Welcome to my secret thinking place. It has been my refuge from the world since I was a child. I suspect most of the family have forgotten it is here, which I prefer.

I hope you are well. You left a lot of blood in the garden but your mother says the Tallants are made of oak and it will only be a scratch. I like your mother very much. I think she is a remarkable person.

You know your Donne so I expect you have found this letter. I wanted to meet you in the garden but we had a visitor this evening. The odious Franklin, asking more questions about you. He might have put someone on watch, so I stayed in the house.

You will find food on the table and covers on the bed. Try to sleep and build your strength. You will need it. I can see your father is worried about the case against you, so it must be serious.

For my part, it does not feel at all right. I look for method and probability and can find neither. But I will continue my investigations tomorrow. Ellen has given me the piece of cloth and explained what it is. I will examine it closely.

If you can, meet me here tomorrow night at nine of the clock.

Yours, in truth and light,

Elizabeth S.

Tom read the letter several times before placing it inside his shirt. He devoured the food and, not stopping to examine the room further, staggered to the truckle bed, threw himself on it and blew out the lantern.

His snoring filled the room before the last smoke from the extinguished candle reached the wooden ceiling.

Chapter 24

22nd October 1640
Cheapside

Tom could see his face grimacing in the mirror's reflection. That was the problem, he could still see his face.

'Have you anything a bit larger?'

'Larger, sir? Let me see. Ah, this, I think, will be perfect.'

And it was. The largest hat Tom had ever seen, with a brim at least nine inches wide that swept across his brow and over his shoulders like a sail.

'A true cavalier, if I may, sir. Perhaps a silk band, continuing down the back, would set it off. No, sir? No, you are right. Understatement is always best.'

His new headgear looked absurd but its size was indisputable. And that was all that mattered. He paid the shopkeeper and paused to navigate the doorway on his way out. Thank God it was not a windy day.

Tom looked to his left up Cheapside. Ahead he could see the familiar shape of the Royal Exchange and, running off to its left, Threadneedle Street. He had woken that morning determined to take the fight to Stone Face. What was the alternative? He could keep running, sleeping in ditches and barns, but that was no fit way to live. Franklin had managed to misconstrue all Tom had done. Edmund was right. The man's stupidity was boundless. The only thing that would defeat Stone Face and stop Franklin's misguided persecution would be hard, indisputable evidence.

How had he missed the hammer in the room in Shovel Alley? Likely it was under Matty's body, buried in the back of his skull. Tom remembered how the boy's head had been leaning forward and shuddered.

His destination was Threadneedle Street. He would avoid the route directly past the Royal Exchange as Tom and Meg were familiar sights in this part of London. However, he was riding Edmund's mare and, with his face now also hidden, he hoped to escape detection.

Tom had gambled on a double bluff to get into the city that morning. He chose Aldersgate, the entrance nearest to Clerkenwell, hoping Franklin would believe Tom would avoid it for that reason. In addition, Aldersgate Street would be choked with stragglers returning south from the ill-fated Scottish campaign. Again, safety might come in numbers. His gamble had paid off and now he was on Cheapside facing his next challenge. He set off along Poultry towards the Exchange, his injured hand throbbing with pain. He had cleaned the wound this morning but it was still red and angry.

The midday exodus from the Exchange to the surrounding taverns was underway. Two merchants well known to Tom approached. He pulled his hat still lower and worked his way through the side streets to avoid the

Exchange's entrance, emerging further up Threadneedle Street. He saw his destination on the left, next to an alley entrance, where he dismounted and tied the mare to an iron ring embedded in the wall. Without looking right or left he ran up the steep stone steps into an apothecary shop. A thin, balding man with aquiline features stopped pounding a wooden mortar on the counter.

'Good day, How may I be of assistance?'

'I wish to see Mr Nicholas Culpeper, if he is in.'

The man's smile of welcome faded. He nodded towards the back of the room and returned to his work. Tom walked past the counter, pushed aside a hessian screen and entered a small room. Rough wooden benches were placed around its walls. Two were occupied. A young woman was crouched in one corner, her face twisted in pain. A grey-haired man was sitting opposite her, his left eye bright red and almost closed, with green pus oozing from both corners. Tom could hear voices behind a door at the far end of the room. He sat down with the others and waited.

Ten minutes passed and Tom's impatience grew. He was safely out of sight in this small room but time was passing. He needed to track down Stone Face as soon as possible. The door opened and the familiar figure of Nicholas Culpeper emerged. A small, elderly woman limped out of the room behind him. He bade her farewell and turned to the man with the swollen eye.

'Would you come in please,' Culpeper said.

Tom stepped forward. 'Mr Culpeper, I would speak with you on a matter of the greatest importance—'

Culpeper ignored him, ushered his patient into the room and closed the door. Tom felt foolish. He glanced at the woman now rocking gently, her face contorted, before returning to his seat.

It was only when Culpeper had seen all his patients some thirty minutes later that he spoke to Tom.

'My goodness, that is a hat. You are Elizabeth Seymour's beau, Thomas Tallant, if I remember correctly? What are you doing here? In need of remedy? I see your hand is injured.'

Tom glowed inside at Culpeper's description. Is that what Elizabeth was telling her friends?

'Mr Culpeper, can we talk in private, please?'

'No one will hear us here, Mr Tallant. Please wait one moment.'

He disappeared into his room and emerged moments later with a pipe and tobacco pouch and sat on one of the benches.

'Pray continue.'

Tom knew he was taking a risk, but it was his one hope. Culpeper was the only 'friendly' radical he knew. He must convince him Stone Face had gone too far in murdering Matty and planting the printer's blocks at the scene. If discovered it would discredit the radical movement. Culpeper

might know someone who could exert a restraining influence on the printer but, to do this, Tom would have to explain his part in the Grub Street raid. Tom did not know how he would react, but he had to try.

Nicholas Culpeper listened in silence, but frowned at the mention of Henry Jermyn. He leaned forward in his chair, and puffed on his pipe. Finally he straightened and took the spent pipe from his mouth.

'Come to the Star Inn in Coleman Street at four of the clock today.'

He pointed the stem of the pipe at Tom's face.

'And you must come alone. I will meet you there. Good day to you sir.'

And before Tom could ask him to examine his wounded hand, Nicholas Culpeper was gone, back in his room with the door firmly shut.

A soft rain was falling as Tom approached the Star Inn that afternoon. His hand was now pounding with pain and he winced as he pushed through the tavern door. Inside he was surprised to see faces he knew from the Commons. He pulled his hat down and sought out Culpeper who was sitting at the back of the tavern, next to a small wooden door. He beckoned him over.

Culpeper frowned.

'Tallant, if your aim is to escape notice, I suggest you discard that ridiculous chapeau, especially here. You will be mistaken for one of the court dandies. Not a good idea in the Star Inn, I can assure you.'

Tom sat with his back to the room and slipped off his hat.

'That's better. Now, I have spoken to my contacts in the movement about what you have told me, Tallant. It has been agreed you should see one of their leaders.'

'Not Stone Face... or should I say Richard Overton?'

'I have no way of knowing if the man you describe is Richard Overton,' Culpeper countered. 'However, the person you are about to see will be able to answer that question, should he wish.'

'Is he more senior than Overton?'

'Oh yes, most certainly. Any information that can be given will come from this person. I will not add a single word afterwards. You must not even ask. Do you understand?'

Tom nodded. Culpeper's face was cold, different to his usual demeanour. He reached over and gripped Tom's right arm.

'And this meeting... it never happened. Are you clear?'

Tom nodded. Culpeper held his gaze before releasing him.

'Go through this door. The man inside will tell you what to do.' He rose from the table. 'Oh, and if that filthy rag tied around your hand is covering a wound, I would get it seen to before you come down with a fever.'

Culpeper walked out of the tavern without a backward glance.

Before he reached the door it was opened by a giant of a man, a foot taller than Tom with hands like shovels. He was led down a short corridor

which ended in a stairway on his left. The man also spoke like a giant. Deep and rumbling.

'Go up the stairs and through the door at the top.'

Tom climbed the stairs and paused on a narrow landing before knocking on the door and entering the room. The giant followed, closed the door and stood behind Tom, guarding the exit. The room spanned the whole width of the tavern. Autumn sunlight filtered though a window on the left, bathing a leather-bound Bible placed on a long table with a pale gloss of light. Three men sat behind the table, facing Tom.

'Hello, Tom. It's been too long. How is mother?'

'Peter... you?'

'Come in and sit down.'

Tom did not recognise the two men flanking his brother. There were no smiles of welcome.

'Perhaps we should get straight to business as I imagine there are pressing matters requiring your attention elsewhere.'

Tom looked at Peter in fascination. Yes, this was the same Peter Tallant who, as a boy, raced toy boats with him on their garden stream, the same Peter who stole the best apples because he could climb higher and faster than his brother, and who was now talking to Tom like a judge preparing a case.

'Nicholas Culpeper has recounted all you told him. It is deeply worrying, Tom, deeply worrying.'

The two men either side of Peter nodded in agreement. Tom relaxed. Thank goodness, they were taking Stone Face's crimes seriously.

'We are greatly concerned you are working in league with Henry Jermyn, one of the evil counsellors leading our King astray. Jermyn is an agent of Lucifer. He is known to be privado to the Catholic whore who sits on the throne with our monarch. The whore who has no shame. She has even called her newborn child "Henry"!'

The two other men shook their heads and muttered under their breath. Tom could not believe what he was hearing.

'Through your actions the righteous voice of the Scottish Covenanters was silenced for a time in London, although we thank the Lord their message is once again reaching the city's streets.'

Tom felt he was sinking, being pushed under by the hand of his own brother.

'Peter. I helped Jermyn to save Arthur, Isaac's nephew.'

'It is not for us to obstruct God's divine purpose. Arthur is a child of God, leading his brothers in their march against the Arch-Papist Laud. His sacrifice would have inspired many others.'

Tom was aghast. So Peter wanted Arthur to hang simply to fire up support for the radicals? He must break through this madness.

'And what about Matthew Morris? Crushing his skull? Was that a sacrifice worth making? So Richard Overton could get his revenge on me? Is that why Overton killed him? And at what price to the cause of your Scottish brothers? Leaving their printing type all over the murdered body to implicate me? That's not helped them, has it?'

Tom realised he was standing and shouting. His left hand, hot and bloated, was throbbing violently. He returned to his seat while the two men held a whispered consultation with Peter. They broke away again and Peter spoke.

'You assume the man you confronted was Richard Overton. You have no way of knowing that. But it is not important. Whether the man you saw was Overton or one of his assistants, their actions would be the same. They would not commit murder. The Chosen do not incur God's wrath by breaking His Commandments.'

Tom recalled Caleb the lay preacher and his mistreatment of Matty and felt his anger stir, fuelled by the hypocrisy, his brother's self-righteous certitude. He wanted to throw the story of Caleb in their face but they would never believe it of their own. He understood the hopelessness Matty had felt.

'Tom... brother.' Peter's tone softened. 'There was concern that meeting you, an associate of Henry Jermyn, would be highly dangerous. But Nicholas Culpeper told us you offered your knowledge of Jermyn without prompting or questioning. It is also noted you have not had further association with him in recent months.'

My God. How do they know that? Am I being spied upon every day? Is the bearded man one of theirs?

Peter paused. 'Is that how you intend to proceed?'

'What do you mean ?'

'Do you intend to keep your distance from Jermyn, or is it possible you might be of service to him again?

'Is that what you want?'

Another pause.

'It could have its advantages, having an ear so close to the court. The opportunity to relay misleading information from time to time.'

'And if I did that?'

'I think the brothers would feel it appropriate to recognise your support by offering what assistance they could in your current troubles.'

'And what would that be?'

'There are many ways of doing such a thing. A man like Nathaniel Franklin can be led by the nose.'

'God forgive you, Peter. You have become no better than Henry Jermyn with your plotting and persuasion. A good friend recently told me Henry Jermyn should be avoided at all costs. I intend to follow the advice. Our

parents would be ashamed of you, Peter, to hear your hypocrisy, encouraging me to have truck with that Devil.'

Peter pursed his lips. His face hardened.

'Very well. If that is your position, we have no information for you about the person you call Stone Face. There is no connection between the press operated by our brothers and the murder you have described. We can help you no further.'

Peter pushed his chair back to leave.

'Peter, for pity's sake, what about me? I am falsely accused of causing the deaths of three men. Do you think I am capable of that?'

Peter remained seated.

'No... no, Tom. I do not believe the brother I have known all his life would do such things. But God works in mysterious ways. You must search your heart, brother. You are clearly being tested. Search for the sin that has aroused God's anger and pray for his forgiveness, as I will, for you.'

Peter lowered his eyes and prayed quietly to himself, the pale sunlight catching the top of his bowed head. Eventually he looked up.

'Tom, a year ago I believed all godly folk should leave this country for a new world in the Americas, to live and worship according to God's Holy Scriptures. And our numbers are growing in Massachusetts and elsewhere. I thought then the King's support for Archbishop Laud could not be challenged. But now I see just how weak our monarch is, and corrupted by his wife's popery. I see I am being called by Almighty God to rid us of this Papist pestilence, here in England, because we will not survive in the Americas if our base here is destroyed.'

Peter stood and placed his hand on the Bible in front of him.

'We are in a war, Tom. On the streets of London, in churches across the country, soon perhaps across the fields of England. We have strapped on the Lord's armour to smite the Papists and their allies, Laud's Arminian Anglicans, from our land. We are fighting for our faith... our God. In any war there are casualties. Friendships. Family. Even the lives of innocents. I will continue to pray for you, brother.'

Chapter 25

That evening
The garden at the Manor House

Tom sat in Elizabeth's garden house. He turned a silver box in his hand, its edges shining with reflected lantern light in the growing darkness. He opened its lid, sniffed and pulled his head away, his brow creased in a frown. The pungent aroma of nutmeg with an undertone of tobacco. He pushed the remains of his meal to one side and placed the silver box in the centre of the table. Elizabeth stood to light another lantern.

Tom had returned to his refuge in the Seymour garden house preoccupied by Peter's refusal to help. Now Elizabeth was giving him more to ponder.

'Where did you get this?'

Elizabeth leaned forward.

'I had been thinking through the circumstances of Swofford's death, over and over, as I did with Venell. I asked you to tell me everything you could remember and one thing stuck in my mind. You said that, according to your father, Robert Petty examined Swofford at Bolton Hall the next morning and appeared to smell the body at one point?'

'That's what father said, but I do not know how close he was to Petty at the time. Perhaps Petty was simply examining the body closely?'

'Perhaps, but it made me think. Could there be a link between something with a strong odour and Swofford's behaviour on the stairs at your parents' house? It is my mathematical training, Tom. I examine all information for patterns or probabilities. So I looked in my books for substances which might make a person lose their senses, even to see things that are not there.'

'You mean the way Swofford was clawing at the air?'

'Yes. Clearly Venell's attack, and the manner of it, was on Swofford's mind. Then your father unfortunately showed him the Schongauer print which put a picture of demons in his head. And if he was also under the influence of a narcotic of some kind...? But how would you administer the substance at a dinner party? The wine was an option but it was under the care of your father and his servants.'

'You do not suspect him, do you?'

'My goodness no. But he is an interesting man, your father. I sense mysteries and secrets within... but no. Of course it was not him. But, if it was not the wine, how else was Swofford drugged? I considered Petty's actions again. What would make him smell a dead body? Did he smell the corpse of Venell in the cellar, or comment on its odour?'

Tom shook his head.

'Of course not,' she continued. 'No, the only thing that might make Mr Petty use his nose would be if he could already smell something and was trying to locate it, or he saw something that might have a smell, like a stain, perhaps. My mind went back to Swofford's party. I tried to picture him, staggering around the room, leering at the young girls. And it came back to me in an instant. Snuff.'

'Snuff?'

'Sir Hugh Swofford had many vices but perhaps the most unpleasant was his vast consumption of snuff. He was forever stuffing it up his nose and, when he was drunk, he would regularly spill it down his shirt, waistcoat and breeches. I returned to my list of stimulants and an interesting possibility emerged. Did you know if you imbibe large and regular quantities of ground nutmeg, it can cause delusions?'

Tom considered their nutmeg cargoes and remembered the men could find the smell overpowering when unloading at the warehouse.

'I visited your mother this morning and asked if Sir Hugh had consumed his usual quantity of snuff on the night of his death. She said he had and it had been a disgusting spectacle. Did she recall him using a snuff box? Yes, she did, but no, she did not recall seeing it on his body, or on the hall floor where he landed. She showed me exactly where Sir Hugh had lain and I noticed it was near your parents' beautiful wall hangings. I needed to ask your mother a difficult question. She could see I was hesitating and said, "Come, Bessy, ask what you must. You are a good girl and I know I can trust you. You would not ask if you did not have to." I love the way your mother acts on her instincts, Tom. She does not know me well but has decided I am worthy of her trust. I admire that. And "Bessy"! No one has called me that since I was six!'

'What was the question?'

'I wanted to know if any of the household staff might have found the snuff box and pocketed it, without telling her. She considered my question for a moment then left the room. Ten minutes later, she returned and put this box on the table. She did not tell me who had given it to her, and I did not ask. She simply said a servant found it under one of the wall hangings the morning after Swofford's death, when they were cleaning the hall.'

Tom tried to work out who might have taken it, but could not. For him it did not matter, but he knew his mother would be furious.

'So Swofford had the box in his hand as he fell and when he hit the floor it slid across the floor and under the hanging?'

He lifted the lid again and smelt the nutmeg. My God, to think Swofford inhaled this by the ounce each day. His senses must have been blunted by years of excess. He examined the silver box. It was a little over one inch square with a flat lid and a strong clasp. The image of a squatting frog was etched on the lid. It was an amusing piece, well executed. It had been

cleaned inside but Tom could still see traces of powder engrained in each corner.

'Why a frog?' he asked.

She shrugged.

A frog… a frog. There was something about this silver box that was familiar to him. What was it? He searched his memory for images of frogs but came up with nothing.

Elizabeth picked up a piece of paper on which she had drawn a broad cross and next to it a circle within a circle. She placed it next to the snuff box on the table.

'So what can we surmise from this? Well, in the cases of both Venell's and Swofford's deaths, it is likely that someone tried to delude both men into thinking they were being attacked by flying demons, one by trained falcons and the other through the consistent but unwitting self-administration of a powerful narcotic.'

'So the deaths are linked, if your reasoning is correct?'

'It would appear so'

'But why demons?'

Tom recalled Peter's accusation that Jermyn was in league with the Devil. My God, perhaps he was, and was invoking powerful magic? Tom had discounted magic and witchcraft. But perhaps he had been too hasty. Could this be possible?

'I have been so desperate to find a reason for all that has happened,' Tom continued haltingly, 'that I'm ashamed I even considered whether witchcraft was at play, or some other Devilry.'

'Ashamed? Why ashamed?' Elizabeth replied.

'I thought you would think such notions ridiculous.'

'Why should I?'

'Because you would look for more logical explanations.'

Elizabeth held Tom's eyes in her steady gaze.

'Tom, we are all of us too ignorant to discount any explanations of the wonders of our world. Yes, I am eager to discover scientific knowledge but I challenge anyone to stand beneath a night sky, swathed with a thousand stars, and not feel our world's spirit force.'

She squeezed his arm and smiled, before looking away.

'But tonight, we need to focus on a logical review of the earthly facts and, in particular, who could be the person who links these deaths? After visiting your mother this morning I travelled to Kensington and called again at Venell's former home. Would any of the servants recall who had bought Sir Joseph his beekeeping clothes? But the staff have all gone. The new family in residence brought their own servants. Venell's people, except the stockman, left months ago.'

'Oh, Elizabeth, why didn't I ask you to apply your scientific mind then? Now the trail is cold. And what of Matty's death? I am convinced the printer is behind that. If not, why would my brother be so unhelpful?'

'Tom, it is possible that two completely separate misfortunes have befallen you, but it is not likely. As I said when we first talked of this, we must look for the common thread.'

Tom's body sagged and he held his head in his hands. 'I cannot think. I am so tired.'

Elizabeth reached across and put her arms around his shoulders. She looked steadily into his eyes.

'Tom. We will win this battle. We must.'

She pulled him towards her and kissed him softly on the mouth, a lingering kiss. He pressed forwards but she gently withdrew and looked searchingly into his face.

'Thomas Tallant, what have you done to me? I have always been one who lives for each day. However, increasingly I find myself thinking of a future with you. It is most unsettling. But first we must ensure we have a future. Let us catch our killer and set you free.' She pulled away. 'As for the trail going cold, well I am not sure about that.'

She plunged her hand inside the top of her dress and withdrew a piece of fabric. It was the neck verse.

'You have given me another clue here, but I do not know what to make of it.'

Tom could smell the fragrance of Elizabeth's warm body on the cloth as she straightened the fabric on the table.

'I have studied this closely over and over and, finally, it has revealed its secret to me; but what it means, well, that's another matter.'

Tom's weary brain struggled to make sense of Elizabeth's words.

'If you look at the cloth, it has Ellen's writing on both sides,' she continued. 'The verse in Latin is on one, with the English version on the other. Now, look again. What can you see other than the writing?'

Tom picked up the fabric. It was creased and dirty but the writing was clear except on the Latin side where dark splashes obscured several letters.

'I cannot see anything, other than a few stains.'

'Consider where you found the cloth, hidden within Matty's fist. Why would it be there? Why not in his pocket or secreted under a floorboard? Let us assume for one moment it was there to send a message, and Matty is holding it both to help you find it and make you realise he wanted you to find it. If that is true, any changes, no matter how slight, to the original cloth should be examined closely. Look again at the stains which I think are blood. Note that one side only of the cloth has been marked and, more interestingly, the stains only land on letters. It looks like random splashes of blood but not a single drop lands on plain fabric, even though there is much more of that.'

Tom looked again. Elizabeth was right.

'I think this is very clever because, like any code, it means nothing unless you know what to look for. At a casual glance, this seems like an old cloth splashed on one side with blood. But to an experienced eye, it is saying, "Look deeper for the message". I looked up the verse in my Latin Bible and discovered which letters had been obscured. I have them here.'

Elizabeth stepped over to a small side table and returned with a piece of paper. Tom's heartbeat quickened. Could this be the key to unlocking the mystery? Elizabeth's next words were not encouraging.

'I can show you the letters, Tom, but they do not take our search any further. There is a meaning there, I am sure, but I cannot divine it.'

She placed the paper on the table and drew the light closer. The Latin version of the neck verse was written across the page with seven letters or groups of letters marked in red.

Miserere mei, Deus: secundum magnam
misericordiam tuam
Et secundum multitudinem miserationum tuarum,
dele iniquitatem meam.

Underneath, she had written out the obscured letters.

n o nd i ta

Tom's eyes feverishly scanned the letters. 'Nondita... nondita... what does it mean? It must be an English word because Matty didn't understand Latin. Could it be a word game? What if we re-arrange the letters. Let me see ...ond, no, and... and I... and I not ! Could that mean something? And I not?'

'Possibly, but there can be more than one message within a code. You must consider all the information. You can see that, in several cases, two letters, not one, are obscured. They are the "nd" and the "ta". Each of these letters is present singly elsewhere in the verse but they are obscured in pairs on the cloth ...nd in secundum and ta in iniquitatem, and that must be for a reason. If I'm right, Matty was telling us to keep these letters together, each in their pair, in the word we create from these clues. In addition, if Matty did this deliberately, he chose which side to stain. Ellen told me she was careful not to write the verse in the same place on both sides of the fabric, in case the ink bled through and spoiled the lettering on the other side. So not a single word of the English verse has been obscured either accidentally or deliberately. They are all in tact.

'I'm sorry, Elizabeth, but Matty choosing to obscure only the Latin words does not make any sense, because, as I say, he could not read Latin.'

'I assumed not. But, despite that, I am convinced that was his intention. The method is too deliberate to mean anything else, especially when you study the letters again… and discover what he actually said.'

Elizabeth carefully wrote the letters again, this time in a different sequence, keeping the double letters together as denoted in the message. She held the paper up.

n o ta nd I

'Notandi? Does that not mean "Take note" or "Observe"?'

'Exactly, Tom. Matty managed to choose a Latin word telling us to take note of what he is saying. I do not know how he has done that. Perhaps he learned the odd word of Latin at school. But he doesn't say any more! We do not know what to take note of! It is so frustrating. This is a message from him, I am convinced of it, but I am too stupid to see it.'

Tom threw himself back in his chair in frustration. He could see Matty's face. His pride in his schooling and the praise from his teacher, probably the only encouragement he received in his short life. For a second time he felt the young man close to him. Elizabeth had found Matty's message. He wished they could have met.

'Two conclusions remain,' she said. 'Either Matty intended to say more but was interrupted, or had said enough and we are missing something staring us in the face. But either way, Matthew Morris was a remarkable young man with a sharp mind and a natural gift for coding. I suspect he would have made a first-rate mathematician. It angers me greatly that his potential has been snuffed out like a candle.'

Tom stayed in the Seymours' garden house that night but slept poorly. Elizabeth had dressed his injury with a herbal balm as his hand was swollen and the wound red and yellow. He had tried to make her stay but she said she must go. Their time would come, but it was not now. He must rest and think. Think to save his life.

She left the clues with him: the drawing of the cross and circles, the silver snuff box and the piece of fabric with Ellen's writing. He rose twice during the night to study each again by lantern before drifting into a fitful sleep.

He awoke with the dawn chorus and, in that moment, he knew he had the answer. He lay on his bed, staring at the wooden ceiling, breathing deeply. Yes, all had become clear.

A little after seven, he unhitched the chestnut mare from the tree outside the Seymour garden and rode her slowly down the lane towards Bolton Hall. He would need his father's help for the day's work ahead. At last he knew what he must do. For the first time in weeks, he dared to hope.

The dark was receding and he could see lights in the downstairs windows of the Hall. The household was coming to life, fires stoked, breakfast prepared. He paused and checked the drive. It was unlikely Franklin would post constables on guard overnight but he must be careful. He waited a few moments before moving forward slowly, smiling at the thought of hot food.

A hand shot out of the bushes, aiming for his mare's reins. The horse veered to her left with a loud whinny and Tom instinctively continued her movement, bringing his mount around in a single turn. He felt strong fingers scrabbling to grip his right leg and then heard a grunt as the mare's heavy rump pushed his attacker to the floor. Tom dug his heels into her flanks and the horse, now facing away from the house, jumped forward towards the road. Tom glanced over his shoulder in time to see a bearded man scramble off the ground and come running after him.

'Stop, stop,' he shouted but Tom was away.

The man abandoned the chase at the front gate and slapped his thigh in frustration.

'That man again. Perhaps he's not a Puritan. I was a fool to think Franklin would not post a guard.' He patted the mare on her neck. 'Well done, lady.'

Tom maintained a brisk canter down the road to London. He did not slow to a trot until he was certain they were not being followed. His early morning optimism was fading with the last stars. He needed his father's help to catch the killer, but now he could not reach his family or go to Isaac while the warehouse was being watched.

But there was still one person he could turn to. The only one left that he could trust.

Chapter 26

23rd October 1640
London Bridge

Tom looked through the enormous window and once again marvelled at Edmund's view. The Pool of London was alive with ships and he scrutinised the Tallant warehouse for activity. He turned back to Edmund's room and eyed the fine furniture. It looked French and expensive. Edmund was out when Tom arrived but Beesley had invited him to wait. Tom wondered if the manservant knew why he did not wish to linger on the street. No matter, he was glad to be out of sight.

There was a noise below. He heard Edmund's voice rise. 'Here? He's here?' before footsteps bounded up the stairs.

The door flew open. 'Tom, thank God you are safe. Your hand, is it mended?'

'No, Edmund, it will take a little while yet.'

In truth it felt no better for Elizabeth's care, swollen and too painful to grip anything.

'Franklin's men are crawling all over the city, searching for you. There's been a watch on the warehouse.'

'I know. On my parents' house too.'

Edmund looked surprised. 'Really? Franklin is determined. What a bloody mess, Tom. I heard the detail of the charges from your father. Franklin is insane to think you could do such things.'

Edmund sat at his writing table in the centre of the room, reached over to a glass decanter and held it aloft.

'Refreshment? No?'

He poured a goblet of wine for himself and leaned back in his chair.

'So, what will you do? You are safe here but it is only a matter of time before Franklin searches my house and posts guards. Maybe you could slip out of the country for a few months until matters cool down? Go and visit your Dutch relatives?'

'It is something I have considered a number of times in the past weeks, Edmund, but thankfully it is not necessary now.'

'But Tom, I beg you to see sense. You will be caught if you remain in London. Your face is too well known. Perhaps Amsterdam is a little obvious. I could smuggle you to France in one of our boats. You could stay with good friends of mine near Paris. Live to fight another day.'

'Edmund, my old friend. As ever, that is very generous of you but there really is no need. I now know who the killer is but I need help to trap him.'

Edmund leaned forward in his chair, his face animated.

'Tom, you know who it is? Thank God! How can I assist? Simply say and it will be done.'

Tom paced from the window to study a sumptuous wall hanging in the corner of the room, a silk embroidered hunting scene rendered in exquisite detail.

'I have been putting all the pieces together for several days but none of it made sense. However, when I awoke this morning, the answer was there, clear in my head as this picture.' Tom touched the hanging.

'Gracious,' Edmund replied. 'How impressive.'

Tom smiled and turned to face Edmund.

'I say all the pieces are in place but there is still one question left unanswered... and that is "Why?"'

'Why?'

'Yes, why on earth would you do such a thing?'

Edmund looked blankly, glass in hand.

'I would do what, Tom? I have said I will help you.'

'Yes. But that's the strange thing, Edmund. Why have you constantly helped me out of these scrapes when it is you who placed me in them in the first place? You who caused the deaths of Sir Joseph Venell and Sir Hugh Swofford and murdered Matthew Morris.'

Edmund lowered his glass to the desk.

'Tom, have you lost your senses? It is your wound. You have a fever. You do not know what you are saying.'

'At first, I found it impossible to believe, but I now know it must be you, Edmund. However, I simply do not know why.'

Tom reached into his pocket and placed the silver snuff box on the table in front of him.

'This was owned by Sir Hugh Swofford. It was with him the night he died at my parents' house. It contained a powerful mixture of ground nutmeg and tobacco, sufficient, if taken in the amounts Sir Hugh enjoyed, to cause delusions. I knew I had seen the box before, it was such an unusual design, and it finally came to me. It had been in the window of the silversmith's shop below your house, here on the bridge. A coincidence perhaps? So many people shop on London Bridge, after all. But then I considered Venell's death. When I saw his wounds it looked like a falcon attack but how could that happen? Falcons do not attack humans. But maybe they weren't attacking Venell, just something he was wearing? They can be taught to fly and grip any mark. Why not embroider a target, such as a series of darks bands like the body of a bee, onto the crown of his beekeeper's hat, the same hat that couldn't be found after the attack? And why was Venell wearing such an ornate hat and costume anyway? The man was a miser. He never spent a penny on himself if he could help it? Maybe someone bought it for him, as a gift. But who would do him such a thing? Then I remembered your father's leg ulcer. He had

been so grateful for the honey cure, no doubt he wanted to thank Venell. What does he buy a man who appears to have only one interest other than making money? Why, of course, a beekeeping suit! The very best! And what an opportunity for his son to make Venell a marked man.'

Edmund poured himself another glass of wine, his face now dark with anger.

'Why have you concocted such monstrous ideas, Tom? It is outrageous to accuse me, of all people, of such things. I am the one who helped you in Grub Street and assisted your escape from Franklin. You have gone mad.'

'Ah yes, Grub Street… the Scottish press. When Matty was paid to hide the print blocks in my warehouse, I assumed it was Overton, getting his revenge. Who else had access to the blocks? Why, only me… and you, of course. But why would you do such a thing when you'd risked your neck helping me to recover them from the cellar in the first place? Then the trial was held while I was away. I believed changing the date was the work of Jermyn. Overton could not influence such a matter. But the only connection between Jermyn and Overton is mutual enmity. Why would they work in league against me? However, a generous bribe from a man of your wealth would be enough to move the date, letting you attend the court in my absence and manage proceedings. It also allowed you to tell everyone where Matty would be living, which was a brilliant idea. You could lay a trap for me for which anyone could be suspected because his address was read out in court. And it was a trap. Franklin was expecting to find me there. None of this was clear until last night, when I received the conclusive evidence that will hang you, Edmund, although it grieves me to think of such a thing. The irony is that the same words saved another neck from the rope.'

Tom put his hand into his shirt and withdrew the piece of frayed fabric containing the neck verse. He held it out in front of his old friend.

'This is the work of a genius, Edmund. Not a twisted mind like yours which has designed such a labyrinthine plot to ruin your oldest friend. No, a young, unfulfilled genius, who has left us a message to thwart you, using only his wits and life blood. Matthew Morris hid a code in this verse that spelled out a single word in Latin… yes, Latin. I lay in bed all night wrestling with this word. Where had I seen it?'

Tom reached into his cloak pocket and produced a sheet of paper. He pushed it over the table to Edmund who read it out in a flat voice.

'Notandi… hmm… notandi,' then looked past Tom to the Thames beyond. He moved back in his chair and reached into the table drawer in front of him. The next moment Tom was looking down the barrel of Edmund's pistol.

Edmund shook his head. 'Notandi sunt tibi mores. Observe the manners. The Dalloway family crest.'

'Yes, but I read enough Latin to know it can also mean "Watch the behaviour",' Tom replied. 'That was the message. Watch this man's behaviour. Matthew Morris could not know that, of course; he did not understand the meaning of the word, but he knew it was connected to you. He wanted to send a message in Latin because it would be easier to conceal, and the only Latin he knew that was linked to you—'

'Is on the family crest over the entrance to my house. But how did he know that? I never brought him here, it was too dangerous.'

'Matty Morris survived on the waterfront by living off his wits and being careful. I suspect he followed you home after your first meeting to know more about you, and read the crest then.

'So, the toerag had more sense than I gave him credit for. You know, Tom, it is such a pity you have spoiled my little arrangement. It was working perfectly. After the confounded bad luck I suffered with the two merchants, I believed I was finally on a winning streak.

'What do you mean, Edmund? And may I have that drink now?'

'Of course, my dear fellow, but you won't mind pouring it yourself, will you? Probably not a good idea to put this pistol down. Oh, and don't be fooled by all my play-acting, firing the gun in Grub Street and almost falling over. I am a crack shot and swordsman. Trained by the best in France.'

With his uninjured right hand, Tom filled a glass with wine and sat on a chair near the window. Edmund remained seated, his pistol aimed at Tom's chest.

'The wool trade has declined in recent years. To maintain a good living, one must secure licenses from the King to operate a monopoly in important markets. A lucrative contract became available last year and Father and I worked assiduously at court to ensure it would come to us. Imagine our horror when we discovered Venell and Swofford had the King's chief advisor in their pocket! I decided to weight the odds in our favour. I knew the King took a personal interest in granting licenses and was extremely fastidious in his dealings. He would tolerate Swofford's appalling vulgarity if it guaranteed a handsome return for the royal coffers. But what if something more... unsavoury came to light? Then your mother showed me her birthday present. Yes, Tom, this whole sequence of events started with that Schongauer print. I was fascinated by the picture and an idea formed in my mind. Venell was a recluse, and a godly sort, forever talking about sin, God and Satan. What if I could re-enact that scene from the print, and persuade Venell it was happening to him? It would affect him deeply, and that would not go down well at court. Who wants to deal with a man ranting that he has been attacked by flying demons? Not the simplest scheme, I know, but the theatricality appealed. And the challenge, well... it was interesting. It would be fun to try!'

Tom frowned at the memory of Venell's savaged head.

Edmund noticed his expression.

'Tom, try to understand. Killing Venell was the last thing in my mind. I only wanted to scare him and, more importantly, scare the King away from him. In France I had seen how these birds could be trained to fly to any mark and so I made contact with a falconry school near Versailles. I flattered Sir Joseph into accepting the beekeeping suit, made sure the right mark—a cross in a circle—was stitched on the hat and paid a small fortune for a hunting pair and their trainer to be shipped to London. On the day, we hid in the woods beside the field in Kensington to wait for Sir Joseph who, I knew, would follow his daily habit of checking his bees. After two hours he finally appeared and the man released the birds.'

Edmund paused to take a drink from his glass, his pistol still aimed steadily at Tom's heart.

'I had not seen falcons at such close quarters and it was terrifying. Venell did not stand a chance. I told the trainer he was only meant to scare the old man and should stop. But Sir Joseph was already on the ground. When he saw Venell was not moving, the man panicked, called back his birds and fled. Never seen him since. I did not know what to do. I had not intended to injure Venell, simply make him believe he'd received a demonic visitation. I had miscalculated the speed and strength of the birds and did not know about the rocks in the grass.'

Edmund paused again and, looking at Tom, shook his head slighty.

'I sat in those damned woods for over an hour, petrified. Venell did not move once. I feared the worst but what could I do? If I went to check Sir Joseph I could be discovered. How would I explain that? But I could not leave without knowing his fate. If he was dead I had to get the suit, or the hat at least, to remove any link to me. Eventually the stockman arrived, but then sat with Sir Joseph for another hour! I was getting desperate when he finally slung the body over his shoulder and started walking up the field. Then my luck changed. I saw the hat swinging on Venell's head before sliding to the ground. The stockman carried on walking. He had not noticed. I waited until he left the field and ran out of the woods up to the drive. Keeping to the trees, I went past the house to the rear paddock where the stockman had entered the field. This route was well trodden so I did not leave fresh tracks in the grass. I ran down, retrieved the hat and rode hard for home.'

'And then you pointed Petty in my direction?'

'I thought it would help if I showed willing, so when Petty mentioned falcons I thought of you. I had no idea you would become involved. I was simply trying to ensure that I did not.'

'Sir Hugh Swofford. What about him?'

'More damnable luck. Venell's death, even under mysterious circumstances, produced royal sympathy, not approbation. His partner Swofford benefitted and once again looked favourite to win the King's

license. I was forced to act again. I got the nutmeg idea from Isaac while at the warehouse. I asked him why the men were taking turns to unload the hold of a ship. He said it was a cargo of nutmeg which could make them feel queer if they did not take a break for air. A number of apothecaries confirmed that nutmeg, particularly when freshly ground and inhaled in large quantities, could induce light headedness and even visions. So I set about befriending Swofford, an arduous task, I can tell you. I told the old goat that, as a mark of respect to his late partner, I wished to put aside our rivalries, and so we went out on the town. I saw the prodigious quantities of snuff he consumed and one night presented him with this amusing silver box full of the stuff, heavily adulterated with fresh ground nutmeg. When he finished the contents he asked for more and I insisted he retained the box as a keepsake and let me keep him supplied with the disgusting blend. My God, Tom. I have no idea how he could have it near him, but he couldn't get enough of it.'

'But if you'd made his acquaintance,' Tom interrupted, 'why didn't Swofford recognise you at his party in Lincoln's Inn Fields?'

'He did!,' Edmund replied. 'But thankfully only from the other side of the crowded salon. I managed to slip away, then later I heard him bellowing at Ellen. I was terrified he was going to call me out of the crowd to support his accusations. That's why I intervened and marched us out of the house before he could say another word. He wasn't best pleased when he saw me next, but soon cheered up when I gave him more of his odious snuff. After several more weeks I could see it was affecting his faculties and I chose my moment to make use of Mr Schongauer again. I let it be known to your father that Swofford might wish to make peace after the altercation at the masque ball and suggested a dinner invitation. I knew your father would show off his pride and joy, the Schongauer. But I did not know it had been moved to a more prominent position, at the top of the stairs. I had last seen it in the dining room. Swofford was meant to make a fool of himself swinging at imaginary flying demons among the dinner guests, not fall down twenty steps and break his neck. When I found out the following morning, I galloped to your parents to retrieve the snuff box but good fortune had deserted me again. It was not in his pockets. I searched the hall when no one was looking. But it had gone. Where did you get it?'

Tom said nothing.

'Oh well, never mind. It does not matter because I have it back and it will go to the bottom of the Thames. That was stupid of me to buy the box from the silversmith's below. Very careless.'

Edmund lapsed into silence and refilled his glass. The pistol in his other hand never left its aim for Tom's heart.

'I could see at once I had involved your family in a second death which was not what I had intended. However it deflected attention from me,

which gave me another idea. With Swofford gone, the way was clear for father and I to claim the King's license. It was now even more important that not a whiff of suspicion should attach to the Dalloways in this matter because we were the obvious people to benefit from the deaths of Venell and Swofford. Such suspicion would not gather as long as the blame remained with you. But I had not reckoned on Franklin's lack of intelligence, or the cleverness of Petty. He was hard work. Petty was very thorough and became convinced it was not you. On the other hand, Franklin was such a lunatic he tried to accuse you of everything, and also implicate your father. The Aldermanic Court knew they could not take on Sir Ralph Tallant merely on Franklin's hearsay. So I needed to keep the pot boiling and when you told me about the Perfumed Press the opportunity was too good to miss. If I could get hold of the type I could implicate you and draw more suspicion towards the Tallants. So I removed a number of blocks from my bag before dumping it in the river. But my goodness, Tom, it was fun that night in Grub Street. Just like the old times. I recruited young Morris to place the type in the warehouse but the tiresome boy managed to get himself caught. He could reveal my plan at any moment, so I crossed the palm of the court clerk with enough silver to bring the trial date forward, while you were away. If the boy failed the neck verse, he would hang and my troubles would be over. But in case he passed, I paid a few lads to pick him up when he left the court by the front entrance, while I told your mother and Isaac he was coming out the side gate. They hid Morris, locked away, until you returned and people had got tired of searching for him. It was then a simple matter of laying the trap for you and informing Franklin, anonymously of course.'

'What about his death. The death of Matty Morris.'

'Oh, that? Well, as I say, he knew too much and I thought surely the Tallant beetle hammer was a clue not even Franklin could muck up, so I stole it from your yard. The hammer didn't kill him by the way. Too light. No I used a piece of lead pipe. It's in the yard. Under the dog. I stuck the hammer into what remained of the back of his head. I knew Franklin would be too stupid to see it was not large enough to do that much damage.'

Tom was in a daze. His head ached with hatred for Edmund's callousness.

'Matty's hand... did you—?'

'What?'

'Did you cut it off while he was—'

'While he was alive? Good God no, Tom. What do you take me for? A barbarian?'

'And the dog. Why the dog?'

'Ah. As I said, I can be guilty of a little theatricality. I was at one of our old haunts, the bear baiting in Southwark. An old bruin was in the pit, on

his last legs but full of cunning. He lowered his arms and tempted a young mastiff in closer, then ripped it down the flank from neck to tail with a fearsome swipe. They dragged the dog off, half dead. I bought the carcass from the dog master who delivered it to Shovel Alley. Said I was a medical man and wanted it for dissection. In truth I needed something to deter any street sleepers from breaking in overnight and spoiling the surprise prepared for you in the house. Also, the mutt would provide a bit of a flourish, so I dragged it into the yard and, when the time came, propped it against the door before hopping over the wall and away.

'So you killed Matty Morris, simply to stir the pot and point the finger once again at me?'

'Well, yes. But Tom, you are my oldest friend. I would never wish to see you imprisoned or worse, hung, for murder. So whenever danger approached, I helped you escape and did so again at your parents' house.'

'You knew Franklin was there?'

'Oh yes, I had been following him. Waited ten minutes after he went in before knocking on the door as if I had just arrived.'

'You are mad. You kept getting me into trouble, so you could rescue me?'

'But Tom. Don't you see. It's perfect. I don't want Franklin to catch you, just think it is you. It would have worked forever as long as no one, including you, suspected anything. The more I rescued you, the more innocent I appeared to you and the more guilty you became to everyone else.'

'But this perfect plan has made me a fugitive, running and hiding from something I did not do.'

'Well, yes, I thought of that. Hence my offer of lodgings in Paris. To me, exile is the ideal solution—you remaining the accused yet completely safe. But you have spoiled that with your cleverness, Tom. I can see Elizabeth Seymour's hand in this. You are not astute enough to work this all out yourself. And now our game must end, and this breaks my heart, Tom, it truly does. The adventures we had together... I wanted more!'

Edmund's chair scraped as he stood, pistol in his right hand. He cocked the gun. The sound echoed through the room.

'I will tell Franklin you came to see me in a deranged state, saying I knew too much, and tried to make me your next victim, but I shot you in self-defence. Goodbye, Tom. I will miss you terribly.'

The moment had arrived, suddenly. After all Edmund had done, the peremptory, almost casual nature of his impending execution still surprised Tom. He flinched and closed his eyes.

'I would not do that if I was you, Mr Dalloway.'

Edmund spun around. Robert Petty was standing in the corner of the room.

'Petty, how in God's name did you get here? But thank the heavens you have. I caught Thomas Tallant breaking in. He intended to attack me because he believed I knew—'

'You can stop that. I have heard all you have said. Edmund Dalloway, you will hang for the murder of Matthew Morris and for causing the deaths of Sir Joseph Venell and Sir Hugh Swofford.'

For once, Edmund was speechless. Tom stepped forward.

'Edmund, earlier I said I needed your help to trap the killer, and I did. I needed you to admit your deeds and provide the missing information. But I also required someone I could trust to be my witness. I couldn't get near Father or Isaac, then I realised the one man who had always judged me on the evidence, or lack of it, was Robert Petty. He was not influenced by religion, politics, rumour or superstition—rare in this city. I knew where to find him—watching my warehouse—and when I explained my suspicions, I thanked God he agreed to accompany me. We arrived on London Bridge early and watched your house until you went out. I knocked on the door alone. Beesley let me in and, once upstairs, I went through the secret passage to let Mr Petty in through the side entrance. He hid behind this wall hanging to wait for your return.'

Edmund laughed. 'So, there are two of you. Excellent, Tom! I would rather shoot this man than you. You can take your chances with the sword. Much more sporting, although I will win, of course.'

Tom moved forward a step. Edmund's pistol swivelled towards him. Petty responded with a step of his own. The muzzle switched to him.

'Gentlemen. Interesting tactics but they will not work.'

Keeping his aim, Edmund reached behind his back with his left hand and produced a long duelling dagger from his belt, which he lay on the table.

'Another foot forward from either of you and I will discharge both pistol and dagger.'

Tom slowly reached towards his belt and pulled out his leather gloves. Without comment, he placed the right glove on his hand, stretching his fingers into place. He reached across his body and withdrew his sword from its scabbard.

'Bravo, Tom. The sword. I agree. But first, let me dispatch our Mr Petty here.'

Tom stepped back and raised his sword. Edmund took aim at Petty.

'Now!' Tom shouted, and, reaching back, hit Edmund's window hard with the pommel of his blade. A pane shattered and another, then another, as Tom moved along the window, striking it again and again. Distracted, Edmund roared in anger as his prized possession was destroyed, large shards of glass crashing to the floor and out of the window into the river below. Tom swung again as Petty threw himself forward. Edmund twisted and fired his pistol and the agent slumped to the floor. With a shout of

triumph, Edmund threw his dagger at Tom who dived to his left as the blade flashed past his head. Blood gushed down his face and he felt for the wound. The knife had sliced the top of his right ear. Another half inch and his life would have been over.

Petty's lifeless form lay on the floor and Edmund had gone. If Petty was dead, Tom's only chance of proving his innocence was to capture Edmund alive. He could hear footsteps clattering down the stairs as he ran out of the room in pursuit.

He reached the open front door and pushed past Beesley standing in the entrance. His hands and right shoulder were covered in blood from his ear wound. The bridge was busy in both directions with travellers and shoppers. Sword in hand, he looked both ways and saw a commotion to his left. A woman was on the floor screaming and, beyond, the back of Edmund's head was disappearing into the crowd, heading north. He chased Edmund into the swarm of people. They were both pushing their way through the throng, leaving a trail of complaints and curses in their wake.

Occasionally Edmund turned back to check on Tom's progress and then pushed on even harder. Slowly Tom gained on him, but soon he felt a searing pain in his left hand. It had become trapped between two people and an old man had hit it with his walking stick. Tom's fingers were turning purple. Something was seriously wrong.

The press of people thinned as they approached the abandoned Sir Thomas Chapel. Tom broke away from the crowd's edge as, further ahead, Edmund stopped to open a small wooden door in the chapel wall.

He grinned, cupped his hands to his mouth and yelled, 'See, see the Papist! That man. He's a filthy Papist. Papist! That man.'

Tom looked around.

'See!' shouted Edmund, pointing at Tom. 'He has the blood of the godly on his hands. He is a killer. Save me. Save me.'

Edmund disappeared through the chapel door as people turned towards Tom—blood on his hands, arm and shoulder; sword in hand. Two heavy-set Apprentices ran at him.

'Papist scum. Kill him!'

If he didn't reach the chapel door in the next ten seconds he would be torn apart. He put his head down and sprinted. He was halfway to the door and losing the pursuing Apprentices when a young boy carrying a stave hesitantly stepped into his path. Tom was on him in a second, clubbing him to the floor with the hilt of his sword. He hurdled the boy's body in the wake of a howl of protest from the people around him.

'Stop him, the Papist devil,' a woman screamed.

A stone bounced off Tom's shoulder as he threw himself against the door, wrenched it open and dived into the darkness of the chapel. He slammed the door shut and rammed its bolt home. Was this another of

Edmund's cat and mouse games? Why had he not locked Tom out and left him to the mercy of the mob? The door was being pummelled by a dozen fists on the other side. The bolt would hold for a while but would not take the force of a ram.

The chapel was gloomy, lit by a single small window high on one wall. He could see wooden cases, rope and barrels but little else. He pushed the barrels against the door and turned to look for Edmund. He heard a loud crack and the edge of the stone column next to Tom's shoulder shattered. Edmund had brought his powder and shot with him.

Tom estimated how long it would take Edmund to reload and decided to take his chance. He stepped quietly forward and heard a door slam. He edged around a pile of barrels and saw the door, set in a stone wall in front of him. He cautiously pushed it open. Five stone steps led down into a dark room. The air was damp. Using the faint light from the chapel behind him, inside he could see the outline of a vaulted ceiling and the stone altar of a crypt. The inky black was broken by a shaft of bright light from the far end of the chamber. He briefly saw the silhouette of a figure before the light disappeared as a door was shut.

Tom tried to still his breathing as he carefully felt his way down the stairs into the crypt. His left arm was now throbbing as the burning pain spread. Behind him the hammering on the door had turned into a rhythmic banging. Ahead, it was pitch dark and silent. Was Edmund lying in wait, recharged pistol in hand? What was that light he had seen? How could it appear in an underground crypt? Behind him came the sound of splintering wood and a loud cheer. The mob would be through the outer door at any moment. He must keep moving forward. He tried to pick out and memorise the dim features of the crypt, then shut the door to the chapel behind him.

Complete and final blackness. Tom could see no shapes. Nothing. The cheering was now quieter but more constant. He edged forward and headed for where he had seen the light. Every three feet he stopped and listened for Edmund. All he could hear was a distant rumble, seeming to come from beneath his feet. What was that sound? Of course, the river. St Thomas Chapel was a church for watermen who would tether their boats under the middle of London Bridge and enter the chapel through a door at river level. So this was Edmund's escape route. Tom moved as quickly as he could. He was now certain Edmund had left the crypt. There was no danger in front. Only behind.

Tom stumbled in the dark towards the end wall. He desperately felt along its length until he found what he was seeking, an iron handle. He pulled and felt it turn stiffly. Cautiously he pushed the heavy door ajar and was stunned by bright light pouring through the gap and a deafening noise.

The River Thames was on floodtide, roaring under the bridge just yards below. The sight and sound of the pounding water were overwhelming.

He pushed on the door and peered through the gap. To his right, a stone arch support; in front, a dozen stone steps ran down to a narrow platform at the base of the arch. Beyond the platform, a torrent of brown water crashed past.

Tom opened the door and walked carefully down the steps, which were awash with river water and weed. The air was wet with flecks of foam and when he reached the platform the pummeling noise and brute force of the rushing water made him gasp. To his left, upriver, he could see Whitehall and Parliament; in front, the rushing water, and beyond that another platform carrying the next arch of the bridge. Edmund was nowhere to be seen.

Tom noticed a mooring rope attached to the stone wall. Surely Edmund had not tried to launch a boat and shoot the bridge? Tom considered the water rushing past his feet and shook his head. For no reason he could fathom he suddenly felt a pain like a red-hot iron sear through his good, right hand. He dropped to his knees and clutched it with his bandaged left hand, but could not stop the blood flowing onto his legs.

'There, you have a matching pair. Your stigmata!'

It was Edmund, shouting from the corner of the platform to Tom's right. He lowered his pistol. Tom had not even heard the discharge in the roar of the water which Edmund was now studying.

'A little faster than I am accustomed to. But our friends upstairs will be with us soon, so I must bid you goodbye, Thomas. Remember me to your family, won't you?'

He faced downriver and walked across the platform, turning around the back of the arch and disappearing from view.

Tom knelt. The pain, now in both hands, was agonising. He gritted his teeth and clambered to his feet, shouting as he took his weight on his bandaged left hand, a scream lost in the endless, roar of the churning water. He staggered around the corner to see Edmund climbing into a small wherry on the east side of the bridge. It was tethered to the platform at both ends, bobbing nervously on the edge of the water where it gathered to rush through the arches.

With a roar like a wounded bull, Tom launched himself off the platform onto Edmund's back, sending them both sprawling into the bottom of the wherry. Tom howled in pain as his left hand became trapped under Edmund's body, staggering onto his knees as Edmund threw his head back and struck Tom across the bridge of his nose. Edmund pushed himself up but fell again as a clubbing right fist from Tom caught him on the base of his neck. Tom almost passed out as the pain from his injured right hand lanced through his arm. Momentarily dazed, he remained kneeling in the bucking boat as Edmund rose and twisted around. He got hold of Thomas by his jerkin and headbutted him twice. Tom swayed in the boat, half conscious, held by Edmund's tight grip.

'Sorry, Tom, but I really must go. Au revoir, old friend.'

With a twist of his arm he threw Tom over the side of the wherry. He hit the freezing water and immediately came to as the strong current pulled him towards the torrent passing under the bridge. He reached out for the wherry's side, crying again as his crippled hands gripped the edge of the boat. Edmund ignored him and sawed through the mooring rope on the right with his sword. Tom tried to shuffle to the stern as the prow of the boat swung in an arc away from the platform towards the mouth of the water disappearing under London Bridge.

Edmund reached towards the stern mooring rope and cursed when he saw Tom clinging on. He slammed the pommel of his sword onto Tom's fingers then slashed repeatedly at the rope. The stern of the boat shuddered and jerked away from the platform as the rope snapped. Tom lunged with one hand for the rope and hung on to the stern with the other. He bellowed in pain as he took the strain as the prow of the boat was dragged towards the torrent.

The wherry was now half in the powerful current pulling the water under the bridge and half out, held to the platform by Tom's bare and battered hands, one gripping the mooring rope and the other holding the stern. The boat was starting to kick and buck as it struggled to make headway in the flow. Twice Edmund tried to stand and swing his sword at Tom but each time the boat veered violently and he was forced to sit. Tom was starting to lose consciousness as the pain in both hands went beyond measure. He noticed in a detached way that it was his shoulders where he could now feel the real agony. One thought remained. He could not let go.

He must not... but he knew that was not possible... he could feel his strength ebbing... he stared at Edmund through misty eyes. The boat was taking in water as its submerged stern was overcome by the flow. Its prow was kicking and shying from side to side like a stallion. Edmund stood and leaned forward to balance the boat and Tom knew this was his last chance. He pulled on the stern with his left hand, and, harnessing the shaft of searing pain and the desperate jolt of consciousness it provided, pushed down with all his might. The wherry's stern dipped alarmingly, throwing Edmund backwards. Tom then let go. The stern shot up as the wherry flew into the middle of the torrent. Edmund was suspended in the centre of the boat like a marionette, poised between falling forwards and backwards. A surge of water hit the wherry, tipping it to the left. With a scream he disappeared over the side. In a moment the boat had gone, and Tom was alone in the endless rush and crash of the water. He twisted and grabbed the mooring rope with both hands. Could he find the strength to pull himself out? He doubted it. His clothes were heavy with water and he could not feel his legs or arms. His hands still screamed with pain but they no longer felt connected to his body.

He became aware of movement and voices above the roar of the river. Peeping over the edge of the platform he saw a man cautiously appear from behind the arch. The Papist hunters. They had finally broken through the door and found the vault and entrance to the river. He ducked his head and remained as low in the water as possible before looking again. Three more men were on the platform but their earlier bravado had disappeared. They stood nervously next to the torrent and, after a cursory glance around the empty platform, disappeared behind the wall, back towards the stairs. Tom thanked God he had been pursued by a gang of landlubbers.

Now he faced a desperate struggle to hang on. Slowly he felt the pain receding and, ridiculously, sleep approaching. He looked again over the edge of the platform but there was no sign of the men. He made one last effort to haul himself out of the water with the rope. The pain returned and, with it, his roaring courage. He strained and felt his shoulders emerge from the water. The weight of his soaking clothes pulled him back but, shouting and screaming, he inched forward and stretched his left arm to grab the rope further up, but his grip had finally gone. His fingers would not move and he could no longer feel the rough twist of the rope's hemp. With a sigh his body slithered back into the cold water and the pain finally left him. Hanging on with his right hand, he felt warmth return and Elizabeth's face next to him… her soft lips… her milky white breast... So this is what it is like. The end. How absurd to sail the seven seas only to drown within sight of his own warehouse. He smiled and felt the Thames water fill his mouth… the old river reclaiming her own…

A rough hand grabbed Tom by the shoulder and his body left the water. The face of Elizabeth faded, replaced by a man with a thick dark beard. Tom tried to shout 'No!' but only coughed up river water. He feebly pushed his rescuer away as he landed in the bottom of a boat. The man looked at him closely and smiled.

'Goed, hij leeft.' (Good, he is alive).

Tom heard a familiar voice.

'Don't know what you are saying, matey, but if we don't move smartish, we'll be shooting the bridge. Keep still now.'

Old Jonah's deep breathing and the creaking of oars faded as Tom drifted into unconsciousness.

Chapter 27

13th November 1640
Bolton Hall

Someone was gently shaking his shoulder, dragging Tom from the edge of sleep. He opened his eyes. His father's face appeared and Tom smiled weakly. Sir Ralph sat next to his son. The wood crackled in the grate, sparks flying up the blackened chimney. The room was warm and Tom felt tired.

'Still sleeping a great deal?' Sir Ralph asked. Tom nodded. 'Your mother says it is your body drawing strength again. But you are over the worst, thank God. How are you feeling? Are you well enough to talk?'

Tom nodded again.

His father looked at him closely. 'Tom, we came very close to losing you. When Adriaan brought you home, you were not conscious. Your body was as cold as winter and your breathing very shallow. Your mother got to work, removing your soaking clothes and rubbing your body by the fire. But when she cut free the cloth on your left hand, she broke down. It had swollen to twice its size. Your fingers were purple and the wound in your palm had turned green. The smell was putrid.'

Sir Ralph frowned at the memory.

'Your fever grew each day. The servants removed your bed covers every three hours, each time soaked in sweat. Elizabeth, Ellen or your mother stayed by your bedside day and night for two weeks, Elizabeth dressing your wound every morning and evening with a fresh posset of herbs she prepared herself. Your mother is convinced that is what saved you. Seven days ago, the fever broke and you slept until yesterday morning when, praise be, you finally woke and took some broth.'

Tom felt too weak to move and his mind drifted... he recalled the voices of Elizabeth and his mother... other shadowy figures. Isaac? Yes, he was sure. Isaac had been there, by his bed. And the man with the beard. Definitely the man with the beard.

'Adriaan... the man with the beard?'

Sir Ralph smiled. 'Yes. He's one of Uncle Jonas's best men. I've had him keeping an eye on you for weeks to make sure you did not get into too much trouble.'

Tom laughed softly at the idea of not being in too much trouble and started coughing. His body lurched forward, shaken by racking convulsions. His father held Tom gently until the coughing subsided, then lowered him slowly back onto his pillows. Uncle Jonas. So he was indebted to Uncle Jonas again, lending father his best agent, Adriaan. Dutch, yes, that was what he had spoken in the boat. A memory fragment

resurfaced in Tom's tired mind. It was Adriaan again, sitting by his bed. What was he asking? About a cart? Why was he asking about a cart?

'Adriaan is upset he could not keep hold of your reins that morning outside the house. I had put him on lookout in case you came home. But he made amends, pulling you out of the river, although he gives the credit to Old Jonah. They had seen you enter Edmund's house and were skirting back and forth along the tidal edge on the east side, looking for you on the bridge, when Jonah spotted you in the water.

Adriaan says he has never seen such skill, the way Jonah dashed across the water and backed his wherry towards the arch's platform, somehow rowing against that tide. Dibdin later told Adriaan he could not afford to lose such a good tipper as Master Thomas Tallant!'

'Did he find his cart?'

'Who, Jonah?'

'No, Adriaan. He came to my bed and asked me about his cart. Did he find it?'

Sir Ralph's frowned in puzzlement.

'Adriaan does not have a cart, Tom. You must have been dreaming in your fever. You were raving at times. Anyway, he was never by your bedside. Only family and Elizabeth were allowed, although we made an exception for Isaac, he was so worried about you.'

Tom smiled weakly and raised his hand in apology at his confusion. Another memory landed, with a shock. Petty. His witness.

'Father... Robert Petty?'

'Petty survived the attack. The musket ball pierced his left shoulder but his leather jerkin took some of the impact. He is recovering and no infection, thank God. He has told the authorities all about Edmund. I had the difficult task of breaking the news to Alfred Dalloway. He is devastated and I do not think he believes his son's guilt yet. However, he was civil enough to apologise for any harm done to you and to wish you well. Tom, did you see Edmund fall into the river under the bridge?'

Tom nodded. His father looked relieved.

'His boat was found tipped over, floating upriver on the tide. There was no sign of him. I did wonder whether, if he managed to shoot the bridge, he might have abandoned the boat and gone into hiding. But no one could have survived falling into that torrent.'

Tom nodded again and closed his eyes. A picture of Edmund flopping around like a doll in the wherry returned.

'Tom, forgive me. Here I am prattling on, tiring you out. Your mother will have my neck. It's just good to have you back.'

He smiled and kissed his son on the forehead. Tom opened his eyes to see his father walk away wiping his eyes with a handkerchief.

Sleep overcame Tom again. He was woken a short time later by his mother with a bowl of broth. She fed him by hand before announcing that

he needed fresh air. Ten minutes later, he was propped up in a chair, sitting in the garden, cocooned in bed covers. It was a clear autumn day. The lawn was carpeted with bronze, gold and copper as the final leaves of the season fell from the trees. The caw-caw of a solitary rook drifted from the field opposite.

The air was clearing his head. He studied a group of men in the distance repairing his mother's glass house. A world away. Was it really him who had jumped through the glass? He looked down at his bandaged hands and realised he would bear the scars as a memory for ever. He saw a movement in the corner of his eye and turned to see a figure walking with a familiar bustling gait across the lawn towards him. Barty Hopkins.

'My dear Thomas, it is so good to see you. I have had heard such dreadful stories.'

Barty looked around and pulled up a garden bench.

'I am under strict instructions from your mother to spend no more than two minutes with you, and I would not wish to cross such a formidable woman!'

Barty's small eyes twinkled with merriment.

'However, I wanted to inform you of developments in Parliament. Do not worry, the Sergeant at Arms knows you are indisposed and all is prepared for your return, when you have recovered. However, you have already missed the most extraordinary scenes. It is still hard to believe but, yesterday, the Earl of Strafford was impeached for treason! Pym and his cronies made their move and the King did not lift a finger to stop them. I tell you, Tom, we are descending into the dark pit of chaos. The Puritans feel they have the wind behind them and the devil take the hindmost!'

Tom collapsed back into his chair and considered Peter and the 'war' he was fighting. How much had his brother known about the move against Strafford? Had it already been planned when Tom went to see him? He lifted his hand and placed it on his friend's arm.

'Barty, thank you for your news and I hope to join you in Parliament in due course, when my strength returns.'

Tom's voice was no more than a whisper and he tried to pull Barty closer.

'But there is one thing I must ask you, for it has been bothering me. Robert Petty—'

'Oh, I understand he is mending nicely, Tom. Not nearly as bad as you. I would not worry about Mr Petty.'

'Yes, I know… but I what I mean is you and Robert Petty. What is your connection? I saw you together.'

Barty studied Tom closely and moved in still closer.

'So, you did see us at Lambeth Palace. I had spotted you in the crowd and wondered if you had also noticed us. I doubted it but Robert said he would wager half a crown that you did. He said you do not miss much.'

Barty stared at the lawn, playing with a ring on his finger, then looked back at Tom.

'He also said you were a man to be trusted, so I will tell you why we were there together. However, I will deny all knowledge if you mention this to anyone else.

'Robert and I are... of the old faith, the true faith.'

'What... you are both Catholics?'

Barty looked over to the workmen with alarm, and spoke in a hoarse, urgent whisper.

'Tom, I beg of you, lower your voice. You'll put a rope around my neck! We had been attending mass in secret at a friend's house in Lambeth when we heard the commotion and went to investigate. It is the most damnable luck you were there also.'

Tom leaned back and laughed weakly. Everyone in London had secrets, even Petty and Barty Hopkins. He put his finger to his lips and winked at his friend.

'Your secret is safe with me, Barty. It shall never be mentioned again.'

Barty looked relieved and nodded. He glanced at Tom's bandaged hands.

'Well, Thomas, I cannot shake you by the hand, but I thank you from my heart and wish you joy, and a speedy recovery.'

Barty embraced Tom warmly before leaving.

Tom's thoughts meandered over the events of the past months. Strafford charged with treason. What now for the King? He was too exhausted to think about it, and too confused. He returned to his lost fortnight of fever, when he drifted in and out of consciousness.

Wilde hij de kaart?... Wilde hij de kaart? The phrase surfaced in his mind. It was Adriaan, sitting by his bed, Tom's father next to him. He was sure.

Wilde hij de kaart?... 'Did he want the kaart?'

The cart? No. Of course. In Dutch kaart means map.

'Did he want the map?'

Did who want the map? Which map? Tom's head was fogged by weakness. But of one thing he was certain. He had not imagined Adriaan's question. Tom was fluent in Dutch. But it was not the language of his dreams. The question from the bearded man had been real. He had wanted to know about a map, not a cart. But why had his father deceived him? The question stayed with him until sleep returned.

He woke to see his mother walking across the garden carrying a box. How long had he slept?

'Time for you to come in, Thomas, and warm yourself by the fire, and we will try some solid food, a little game pie perhaps? But first, I think you will want to look at this.'

She smiled, handed the container to Tom and returned to the house.

It was the tulip box, the one he had given to Elizabeth. He saw a letter pinned to its top in her familiar neat handwriting. He placed the box in his lap. It was not heavy. With trembling fingers, he pulled the letter open.

My dearest Tom – I owe you a great debt.

I have never been sure about God. What he, or she, is. But I have prayed to God every day and night for the past fortnight to save you, and my prayers have been answered, so someone must be listening, don't you think?

I have also been given something else in this terrible ordeal. A blessed friendship with a wonderful person, your mother Beatrix. I will never forget our conversations by your bedside late into the night.

So I am richer by far, but the greatest gift of all is to know you are getting better. It seems our world is descending into chaos but it is still a thing of great beauty and wonder. Shall we explore it together?

You once gave me a precious gift in this box which I now return with a gift of my own. Inside you will find another splendid invention from your clever Dutch cousins. It is called a microscope. It can show you the wonders of nature, right here in your wonderful garden. So I can explore the heavens and you the Earth! What discoveries await us.

Soon it will be time to rise Tom. I need you by my side.

Yours, in truth, light and love

Elizabeth S.

Tom folded the paper and carefully opened the lid of the box. Inside he found a brass device on a stand, mounted on a wooden plinth. A plate was fixed to the front of the plinth, and another at the back. He lifted the microscope out of the tulip box and saw the plates were inscribed. He read both.

Vita est Inventio – Life is Discovery
Inventum est invita – Discovery is Life

Tom grinned, returned the microscope and hugged the box. He was alive. Elizabeth was alive. Their future was alive. He felt strength welling in his chest. He looked across the garden to the fields beyond. A solitary figure was walking towards a thicket of trees, which disturbed a chattering of starlings that took off and rose into the pale blue sky. Another group joined them, followed by more. Their numbers increased as they gathered to roost.

Tom watched in fascination as, soon, many hundreds swooped and turned together, forming a liquid shape in the sky. He had seen this behaviour before, but not with so many. They acted as if by common will,

changing direction again and again, one moment a cloud, the next a spiraling smoke trail.

Tom was experiencing a familiar sensation. He could not say how, but he knew both Mattys were near. His heart filled as the birds came closer but then, in an instant, the starlings swooped as one, away towards the horizon.

They were gone. The sky was empty. The sun almost set.

He held the tulip box close and waited for his mother, as the call of the solitary rook echoed across the fields.

THE END

Printed in Great Britain
by Amazon

First published in 2019 by Burnaby Press.

This edition published in 2020 by Sharpe Books.

Rags of Time

MICHAEL WARD